Hangman

Library of Congress Control Number: 2006901337

To order additional copies, please contact us.
BookSurge, LLC
www.booksurge.com
1-866-308-6235
orders@booksurge.com

ROGER
MEADOWS

HANGMAN

A DEADLY GAME

Barbara,
Thank you for your
help. Janet B. Agnew
June 27, 2006

Roger Meadows
May, 06

2006

Hangman

For Wanda, for always

PROLOGUE

A small twin-engine plane lifted into the late evening darkness from a private strip on the north side of Detroit. It skirted the east side of the city, passing low over Lake St. Clair to avoid the control zone around Detroit Metro. No flight plan disclosed its intentions and it communicated with no one.

The pilot navigated southward over the flat expanse of Ohio, then Kentucky, following the glittering pattern of small towns in the darkness below. Near the West Virginia border he caught up with a March frontal system that had left rain and snow in its wake. The plane was engulfed in dark turbulence and ice began to form, overpowering the deicing equipment.

The pilot failed to consult his charts before descending to get out of the ice. By the time he reached a warmer altitude, he was over the mountains of North Carolina.

A sudden flash of lightning lit a stark expanse of smooth granite, almost parallel to the flight of the plane, but rising in its path. In an instant, there was a grinding impact, demolishing both propellers and silencing the engines. The belly of the fuselage screeched against the rock surface.

The plane skipped off the granite like a flat stone from the surface of a pond. It cleared the low growth of the bald mountaintop and plunged into the void of the valley beyond. The last seconds of flight were that of a falling leaf, spiraling aimlessly toward earth. The pilot fought the controls but the plane would not respond. It drove through the top of an enormous hemlock, shearing off the cushioning green branches. Next came a grove of poplars, tearing away the wings. The fuselage plunged into the forested mountainside in a thicket of laurel, killing both occupants instantly. There was no fire.

Rain continued throughout the night, gradually diminishing to a gentle drizzle. It mingled with the fluids from the plane, and all seeped into the soggy humus of the forest. The cargo would go undelivered.

1.
FINDERS

Morning brought the rain I expected. It was light but cold, falling from a pewter sky. I stuck my nose out, then dressed completely within the confines of the tent. I blessed the heavy Scottish wool sweater and Gore-Tex. Outside I shivered myself warm, made coffee, and finished the last bagel with Mary's jam.

I'd spent my second night out since leaving Israel Buchanan's remote cabin over on the Tennessee side of the Smoky Mountain National Park. From the boundary of his farm, I had hiked up Laurel Ridge to the Appalachian Trail, then along the spine of the mountains, spending the first night on a western slope. I rose early in the frosted heights and continued to Old Black and Mt. Guyot, to an elevation of over six thousand feet. From there, I picked a wrinkle in the mountainside and bushwhacked down to the headwaters of Big Creek and to this point. When Israel heard of my troubles and my antidote, he said, "Matthew, there ain't nothin' better to cure what ails you than a walk in the mountains." Of course, he didn't know the whole story.

I was in a small, relatively flat little valley deep in the Park, with steep slopes on either side. Tall poplars towered around me, almost limbless to the tops, where small umbrellas of foliage provided the engines for their growth. Only a few dead leaves remained up there. The rest provided a bright yellow carpet on the forest floor around my feet.

I chewed on a piece of jerked beef and drank the last of the coffee. Two gray squirrels were busy at the base of a tree, rummaging in the dead leaves for forage. They had their tails laid flat along their backs, all the way up between their ears, serving as ponchos to shield them from the cold rain.

A giant hemlock stood a short distance downstream, its crown practically destroyed, broken branches dangling. Hmmm. Exposed wood wasn't old yet. No lightning blaze down the trunk. Strange. Freakish twist of wind?

It took but a few moments to break camp, shake out the water, and bundle everything into my pack. As a matter pride, I removed all traces that I'd ever been there.

My campsite was on the west side of the creek. As I shouldered the pack and started downstream, clinging to the slope, a glint of white caught my eye from the opposite side of the creek. It flashed through an opening in the thick clump of smaller hemlock and mountain laurel. I shed the pack and crossed the creek, then crawled through the growth up the steep hillside. Before me was a twisted and mangled panel of white-painted metal, unmistakably the wing of an airplane.

It lay at the base of a large poplar, and I looked up to see a gouge about twenty feet off the ground where the bark had been peeled from the trunk. The wing was lying on its leading edge, the engine still attached.

I felt excitement and dread at the same time. Something unpleasant lay ahead of me. The scars on the trees looked like weeks or months, not some long-ago, discovered and forgotten wreckage. The companion wing lay nearby with its matching scarred poplar tree.

I pulled myself forward through the baby hemlocks and tangled laurel. The empennage of the plane came into sight, hiked into the air above my head, as I followed the path the plane must have taken in its last few seconds.

The broken fuselage had plowed into the upslope, meeting the rising flank of the mountain with enough force to collapse the nose all the way to the instrument panel. I approached from the left side, since the plane was tilted in that direction. The fuselage was buckled upward in the middle, giving it a hump-backed appearance. Since both wings had been ripped away almost simultaneously, the decelerating effect must have kept it from splattering all over the hillside.

I felt certain no one would have survived the impact and it was unlikely anyone had been here before me. Even if there were survivors, how would they have been found, or how would they have made their way out of here?

The Smokies are famous for their toll on private aircraft, their teeth raking unwary pilots out of the sky with unrelenting regularity. It seemed that most of the victims were used to flying over flat terrain and forgot about the mountains.

The windscreen and the left side window were broken, with chunks popped out as the fuselage buckled and warped. I pulled myself forward, avoiding the jagged edges of aluminum around the stub of the wing.

Leaves had blown into the interior and thorny green vines had crept over part of the wreckage. I grasped the frame of the side window and forced myself to look inside. Despite the scattering of wet leaves, I could tell there were two bodies in the front seats. The rear was more amorphous, also filled with leaves.

The left occupant embraced the control yoke, or rather seemed to be impaled upon it. Bare white vertebrae glistened above the wet fabric of a dark jacket; and the head, now virtually a skull, was jammed between the yoke and the instrument panel. Bits of black hair clung to leathery patches of skin still attached to the skull.

The jacket and its contents were deflated, leaving what appeared to be an empty suit of clothes. Judging by the vines and the condition of the bodies, they must have been here for months. Small forest denizens had done their work, scavenging from the inside in minute detail and efficiency. Apparently no larger animals had gotten inside or the corpses would have been dismantled and scattered about.

The right-seat occupant had twisted sideways during the impact, or his body had folded into the floor as it began to disintegrate. A skeletal hand and wrist reached out across the seat toward me through a too-large leather jacket sleeve. The skull peered up at me through the leaves on the floor, with a set of even white teeth and black empty eye sockets.

What was I to do? I withdrew from the grisly site and sat upon a stone to think. The tail number of the plane was clearly visible, and I committed it to memory to report to authorities.

I thought about trying to find more complete identification, but convinced myself the tail number would be enough for now. They could match it with missing aircraft reports and discover the identities of the victims. Nothing would help these guys, anyway.

I gathered myself and started back down the slope to recover my pack. Cold drizzle was still falling, but the sky was becoming lighter. I wanted to get past Walnut Bottoms before lunchtime, which could get me back to my parked Explorer before nightfall.

Before I had gone more than a few sliding steps, I thought about the rear seat of the aircraft. Did the accumulation of leaves obscure more bodies? I struggled back to the fuselage to take a look inside. Reaching through a window with a stick, I raked the leaves aside to reveal faded olive drab canvas. It appeared to be a lumpy Army duffel bag, held in place by the seat belt and shoulder harness. Thankfully, not another body. Further scratching revealed a second one occupying the other seat.

What had been at the back of my mind came to the surface. Drugs...the only logical explanation. Chastising myself for jumping to conclusions, I pried open the side window and crawled halfway in, unlatching the nearer bag. The stench of death struck me for the first time, a mixture of decay and mustiness made heavier by the dampness of the falling rain.

The bag was heavy and would not fit through the side window. I was able to tilt it forward and drag it through the pilot's window, struggling with its weight and my slippery footing on the wet wing root.

Panting from exertion, I set it upright and unfastened the snap. The bag was as heavy and lumpy as it looked. The lumps were slippery against each other, shifting inside the bag. It had no lock. The shoulder strap end terminated with a snap closure, a series of three grommets overlapping each other successively over a steel wire tongue extending from a fourth.

As I opened the bag, I was struck dumb. Expecting to see firm packets of white powder, instead I saw bundles of currency: U.S. hundred-dollar bills neatly banded and encased in ziplock plastic bags. I took out several of them and they were all alike. All hundreds, all used bills. I laid them about my feet where they contrasted with the scattering of yellow and brown leaves. The light rain beaded up on the plastic and began to trickle across and around the rectangular bundles. I stared at them in fascination. Before I stopped, I had emptied more than half the bag, and more money surrounded me than I had ever seen before. I had the foolish impulse to look around me to see if anyone was watching.

The piles of money confirmed my thoughts about drugs, but it was the other end of the transaction. They were making a pickup of the proceeds and delivering them back south. They must have hit the mountain above, since both engines had been cranking, then fallen into this valley.

Nothing could keep me from checking the other bag now. First I gathered all of the packets and put them back in the bag. With the last one, I couldn't resist opening the plastic bag and removing one of the bundles of bills. It felt good in my hand. I flipped through the stack. How many bills are in a bundle of hundreds? I couldn't remember.

The second bag proved to be just like the first. I went through the same drill, unlatching the snap and taking out the bags one at a time. This time I didn't stop until the bag was empty, the unbelievable shining packages in a pile all around my feet. The cold rain continued to fall as I stood, still awestruck and staring at them. A shiver traveled down my spine, and I felt the strange feeling of exposure that had come over me before.

I looked over my shoulder again, and at the undergrowth around me, somehow expecting to be discovered. I hurriedly replaced the packets into the bag, feeling relieved not to be looking at them, out in the open, exposed to the eyes of my imagination. What was I to do? I had temporary custody of perhaps millions of dollars in cash and two bodies.

If they were part of the drug underworld as I suspected, no official search would have been mounted, and no public notification issued. What if they were innocent charter pilots hired to pick up cargo and fly it to a destination, no questions asked? That didn't make sense, since the bags were unlocked and unsealed. No one would trust that much. They had to be part of the organization, with full knowledge of the contents, and just as sure what would happen if they tried to run.

Why would they not have brought it back by a safer method? Perhaps the risks of land transportation were greater. It is just as possible, perhaps more so, to be involved in an auto accident or be stopped in a roadblock for some other reason. Maybe a major purchase was being set up, and they needed cash quickly from the outlying regions of their market. I could only imagine the impact of the airplane's failure to arrive—the frantic nature of the search; accusations, recriminations.

I went over to the wreckage again and stared inside. My mind formed silent questions. Who are you? Are there loving families waiting for you somewhere, maddened with uncertainty and wondering where you are? Do they think you ran away from them?

I suppose even criminals have families, but it was harder to generate as much sympathy for them. In any case, it was obvious nothing immediate could be done about them. They had to be left where they were. Not only would it be repugnant to touch them, but also some authority would want to inspect the wreckage and its contents intact...except for what I had already removed. That was the other problem.

The money could not be left lying out in the middle of nowhere, trusting it would be here when authorities arrived. I'd have to find a way to hide it or take it with me until deciding on the next step. The bags must weigh more than fifty pounds each, and were not the best of shapes to carry. They had a handle mid-way down the side, but the diameter was such that the things would bang against my legs, making walking difficult.

I wrestled and dragged them down the slope to retrieve my pack. I was struck by the absurdity of having so much paper currency I could not properly carry it all. But who wouldn't trade places with me? I needed some method of carrying my pack and the two bulky bags. I needed a pack mule. At the very least, I needed a travois or a yoke.

I cut a sturdy, bowed sapling and fashioned a yoke that could be balanced across the top of my pack, with the bags suspended on either side. It took some adjustments to get the cords the right length so I could partially carry the bags with my hands. The weight nearly overwhelmed me. Even with it in a shaky balance, my legs trembled with the load and I had to stop every few hundred yards and rest.

This would not work for long, but maybe I could get them nearer to the trail that came down the mountainside along the other tributary of the creek. There was no way I could carry them all the way to the Explorer. I'd have to hide them, then lead authorities up here with some proper way to haul them down. They'd need to get the bodies out, anyway.

After what seemed hours of struggle through the undergrowth and rocks bordering the stream, I saw the other branch of the creek ahead, splashing in from the left. I had to find a hiding place away from the trail before someone would chance along and see me. Up to my left, about a hundred feet above my position, there was an out-cropping of rock. It was a jumble of Buick-sized boulders that should give a good chance for concealment. As a bonus, rhododendron grew in a tangle around the perimeter. Gratefully I unloaded and went to explore. I found what I was looking for, a crevice at waist height where a large flat rock leaned across two smaller ones. The crevice tilted away from me so objects placed at the back were virtually out of sight. Perfect. Also, the likelihood of anyone coming to this exact spot was near zero. I went back and brought up one bag at a time.

It was approaching noon. The best plan was a forced march back down to the Explorer without stopping for the night. I sat down and ate as much of my supplies as I wanted, keeping only enough for a snack and one more quick meal on the trail down. I bundled most of my gear in a tight pack in my ground cloth, tied securely with cord. I left it in the hiding place, but taking one of the plastic bags of money. I could see how much was in a bag and if anyone doubted what I had found, it would serve as a sample.

It was a relief to start out with a lighter load. It made me feel nimble and energetic compared to the pain of the load I carried before. I figured it to be about ten miles back to the parking area. Now that I was on a good trail with a light load, I figured to make good time.

After a half-mile or so, I came around a large pile of boulders and was suddenly face-to-face with a man. In my solitude and the apparent emptiness of the trail, it gave me a start. He noticed my uneasiness and a sly grin spread across his face.

"Gotcha, di'nt I?" he said.

"Yes, I have to admit it. I thought I was the only one in miles, and I didn't hear you coming."

"I heered you for some time now, your boots scratchin' gravel and such."

He was a beefy man about my height and looked out of character, if there was such a thing, for a hiker in the park. He had a red, scraggly beard and long, unkempt hair held in place by a watch cap that had been watching for a long time. There was a rim of rusty discoloration at the fold of the cap. He wore old running shoes of considerable size and age, denim overalls, and a rough flannel shirt under a duck coat. Rather than a backpack, he carried a duffel bag of sorts slung over one shoulder. His right hand gripped a twisted staff of rhododendron, with the root end at the top carved into a large, rounded knob. His voice was high-pitched and soft, and seemed shy and menacing at the same time.

"Whar ya headed?" he asked. He never looked at me when he talked, but shifted his pale gray eyes to a space just left or right of direct contact, or upward to the west where an opening in the boulders revealed the ridge of mountains in the distance. I thought about the .380 Beretta packed away in a pocket of my backpack.

"I'm heading to Walnut Bottoms to camp for the night," I lied. "Make an early night of it." The invented story rolled off my silver tongue with no effort at all. God, what would have happened if he had been a few minutes earlier?

"How about you?" I asked.

"I go wherever my feet take me. Sometimes up on the Trail and sometimes not. When it gets too cold up here sometimes I take to the roads." His eyes traveled over my clothing and pack, taking inventory.

"Travelin' light, aincha?"

The scrutiny made me uncomfortable, but I maintained my calm and said, "That's the way I like it. Well, I'd better get moving. I hope you have a good day."

"You too," he said, and walked past me, looking again at my pack as he did so. I resisted the urge to hurry down the trail or look back over my shoulder. Soon I was out of sight around another outcropping of rock, and increased my pace. Few people can out-walk me when I'm motivated and I couldn't picture his running to catch up.

If my imagination turned out to have some truth in it, his would be the stealthy approach, keeping his distance until I stopped for the night. After I had gone a fast quarter-mile, I took off my pack and fished out the Beretta. I jacked a cartridge into its chamber, and put it in my hip pocket beneath the drape of my parka.

I knew I wasn't supposed to carry firearms on the trail or anywhere in the Park system, and normally I didn't. On this expedition I knew I'd probably be completely alone and it would serve as some comfort to me at night. I'm a responsible person, I reasoned. Problems on the trail were rare but I knew a couple of stories that weren't too pleasant.

I soon came to Walnut Bottoms, a nice open area for camping that was popular with hikers and horseback riders. No one was in residence at this time, since it was mid-week and out of season. I zipped right on through it, putting as much distance as possible between the stranger and me.

The rain had stopped, so I took off my outer layer of Gore-Tex and stuffed both pieces into my pack. The wider, well-traveled track was a boulevard compared to the descent the previous afternoon. I'd spent so much time on Big Creek that most of it was familiar, although my day hikes, fishing for the small brook trout, seldom took me this far.

I humped along, rarely stopping for rest, and soon reached the halfway point from the Bottoms to the bottom. I sat on a rock and ate a snack, sipping from my canteen now that I had reached civilization. Another mile farther along was the spot where I first met Israel.

Our unlikely relationship started here more than seven years ago, on a spring afternoon. It had an Androcles-and-the-Lion quality we joked about in later years. I had spent nearly all that day fly-fishing the sparkling pools and rapids, taking and releasing several small trout, enjoying the rare solitude.

Working my way downstream, I'd skirted a room-size boulder and nearly stepped on a man lying at the edge of the water. He was lean and tanned, a two-day stubble on his face, jaws set in pain. He was wearing a gray chambray shirt and bib overalls, the legs tucked into knee-high gum boots. He was carving into the base of a two-inch sapling with a large clasp knife.

"I've kinda' got myself in a fix," he said.

"I'll do whatever I can," I replied. "My name's Matthew Cross. Now, tell me how bad you're hurt."

I knelt beside him and he shifted the knife to his left hand, reaching with his right to shake.

"Israel Buchanan," he said, his voice subdued.

"Now here's the problem," he continued, "I slipped on a rock out there, and I think I busted my ankle-bone. I felt it pop when it jammed in a crack in the rocks."

I cut off his boot and splinted the leg with the top of it; then decided I'd have to pack him out on my back to the parking area. When I picked him up he felt like a collection of jointed pipes encased in leather.

Being carried was embarrassing to him, I could tell, as he continued to ask how I was and if I needed to rest. I kept reassuring him everything was fine, despite my protesting body. After several stops, increasing in frequency with distance, we reached the vehicles.

When I saw him the morning I started on this hike, he referred to it again, as he often did. "I'll never forget what you did, you and that boy of yours, gettin' me to the hospital, then takin' me home. David stayin' with me 'til I mended—"

"You know he still talks about that," I'd replied. "He was just making the move to grow up, and that helped him along."

I wondered what Israel would think of my discovery. I wondered what *I* thought of my discovery.

A few more hours brought me within a couple of miles of my Explorer. Twilight was at hand as I stopped to eat by a large, deep pool of water surrounded by a tumble of granite boulders. It was fed by a rushing rapid, and was one my favorite spots on the creek.

One time Israel and I had been fishing the creek together, and when we approached this spot, we heard splashing sounds and shrieks of laughter. Two men and two women were swimming in the icy water, naked as they were on their original birthdays. They climbed about on the rocks, not at all self-conscious, and waved greetings before plunging back into the water.

"Lord, have mercy!" Israel exclaimed, as we walked on. I could see a reddening of color beneath his weathered skin. "When I was young, if you saw a girl's ankle it embarrassed both of you. Now look how they carry on. Times have shore changed, ain't they?"

Yes, Israel, they have. I don't feel like I fit in anymore. Personal integrity used to count for something, but now it seems only for the gullible. Maybe it will just take a while for me to live down the resentment against those guys that destroyed my company and position.

Darkness had fallen in earnest by the time I finished eating. I shouldered my pack and completed the last of my three-day walk in less than an hour. It was great to see the Explorer sitting where Israel had helped me deliver it. The dome light blasted my night vision when I unlocked the door. The Diehard had not died. Gratefully I climbed into the leather seat, cranked the engine, and headed for home, about an hour away. Lights were on in the ranger's house as I drove down the dirt road, and a dog barked. I could think only of getting home and organizing my tired and scrambled thoughts for tomorrow.

Few lights were on as I drove into my neighborhood on the east side of Mountain View. I whirled into the basement driveway, hitting the opener for the garage door and then closing it behind me. I grabbed the pack and hit the stairs to the dark rooms above. Nothing feels as empty as a house shared with no one else, especially when it holds a dozen years of happy memories. It was late enough that my timed lights were out, and the only sign of contact from the outside was the blinking light on the answering machine. It was too late and I was too tired to contend with it, even if it might hold good news. I removed the Beretta and the bag of money from my pack, and went straight to the master suite I had shared with my Caroline.

It was wonderful to shave and take a long, hot shower before settling into the comfort of the empty bed. I pushed away all thoughts about financial problems, my career, the plane in the mountains, and my schedule for my tomorrows, and fell into a deep sleep.

I had purchased an old, architecturally rich building on a steep street in a European city. The cobbled streets sloped toward a body of water like the Firth of Tay in Dundee. The building, an old theater or hotel, had been closed abruptly decades before and its contents had remained untouched.

The entry was a circular room finished in white and green marble, with spiral staircases rising toward the balcony from left and right. A crystal chandelier hung from the high domed ceiling over the center of the room, its facets and surfaces heavy with dust. Directly below the chandelier stood a circular white marble table, its top inlaid with the same green marble as the columns. A large vase with dried stems and wisps of vegetation from an ancient bouquet stood on the table. A handful of change, keys, and other undefined small objects were carelessly lying in the dust on the tabletop as if some long-ago inhabitant had cleared his pockets. I scooped them up and thrust them into my pocket to examine later. I was excited at the prospect of their value and the potential they might provide for solving the mystery of the building.

I wandered through upstairs rooms, the walls covered with heavy velvet fabric, gold framed paintings, and heavy mirrors. Furniture was ornate and carved from dark wood, with heavy comforters and spreads on the beds. Victorian lamps stood on the dressers and tables and personal articles still lay on yellowed lace runners—silver hand mirrors and brushes, powder boxes and bottles of perfumes.

The inhabitants had vanished without taking their belongings. Who lived here, and where did they go? I awoke with a sense of yearning...The mystery troubled me. Did it represent the road I was unable to take because of the changes in my life? Or was it simply the aimless meandering of the subconscious, as meaningless as less interesting dreams that occurred and were quickly forgotten?

After a period of wakefulness and regret, I drifted back into a deep sleep, not awakening again until morning. When consciousness came, I remembered what was under the bed. I pulled out the zip-lock bag to confirm that it was part of reality. I began to count. There were ten large bundles of hundreds in the bag, each bundle made up of five smaller ones. Each small pack contained twenty bills, or $2,000. That made each larger bundle an even $10,000. Therefore each bag, including the one in my hand, was worth $100,000! Wow! What about those two large bags tucked in a crevice in the rocks, up in the mountains? The thought got me out of bed and moving.

2.

WOODY

After a quick shower I headed into the kitchen to start the coffee and get out bacon and eggs. Juggling utensils, I called my neighbor. She answered on the first ring.

"Hey Mary, it's Matt. Did I interrupt anything important?"

"Well I just about had the UPS man coaxed into the bedroom, but you spoiled it all. Are you kidding? I chased Ralph off to work an hour and a half ago, and I'm workin' the crossword in the Knoxville paper. You're back, are you? How was it?"

"The high point was eating the jam you gave me, up on top of a mountain."

"Really?"

"Over six thousand feet, in fact. It was all downhill from there."

"Very funny."

"Would you like bacon and eggs? I'm fixing breakfast and the coffee's ready. Bring your mother with you, if she'll come."

"Matt, darlin', you know I can't afford to eat another breakfast. I'll see if the old gal wants to come over for coffee. If she won't, we'll just have to risk being without a chaperon. But does Mother want to come to breakfast? Is a bullfrog waterproof?" She continued without taking a breath, "Of course I'll bring your mail and papers over. That's what you're really after. You can traipse all over the mountains and can't make it next door. Don't look like you got much in the mail you'll be excited about. I didn't even steam anything open."

The doorbell rang in a few minutes, and Mary enveloped me in a well-upholstered hug. Her mother appeared right behind her and I bent down for her hug and a peck on the cheek. Mama was about half the size of her daughter, with bright eyes, wispy white hair, and dependably happy disposition.

Mary and Millicent took places at the table and I poured coffee. Due to the slope of the lot, the breakfast area appeared cradled in the top branches of a large dogwood. The fall red-purple leaves were half gone, with the morning sun streaming through.

"You can either watch me eat or you can participate."

"It's tempting, Matt, but I'll just have coffee. Well…maybe some toast and a strip of bacon," said Mary.

"I want some of your delicious bread, toasted, with some of Mary's jam, if you have any left," said Millicent.

"Just for you, Mother McClarty. How have you been keeping yourself?"

"I'm busy as I can be and I never felt better," she said, slathering butter on her toast. "You know I still have a daughter to take care of and I've been scouting around town looking after your interests."

"My interests?"

She put a bony hand on my arm. "Matthew, I'll be perfectly frank with you. I know you can handle it. We know how you loved your dear wife, and we all did too. But she has been gone for…what?…three years now. It's time you got on with your life."

"Mother! Mind your own business. We're guests."

"It's okay, Mary. Mother M, I appreciate your concern. I know you mean well."

"There's the nicest woman down at Binkle's Department Store. She's a widow now for ten years, and she's quite attractive. I'll be glad to drop a few hints and take you shopping with me." She gave me a vaudeville wink.

"Millicent, why do I have a feeling you've already 'dropped a few hints'? I know you have my best interests at heart, but I have to do things in my own time and in my own way."

Millicent sighed dramatically and turned toward the window. "That dogwood is really pretty."

"Mother, you're really something," said Mary.

"By the way, Mary, here's your tiny jam jar back for a refill. Have you ever thought of putting it up in quarts, or even gallons?"

After they left, I scanned the mail. Mary was right. There wasn't much except junk mail, a couple of magazines, and bills. There was one form postcard from a company acknowledging receipt of my resume. From a number of choices, it had a box marked, "This is to acknowledge receipt of your resume. If there is further interest on our part, you will be contacted. Please do not call this office because of the volume of resumes being evaluated." Disappointing, but on the positive side, they were the only one so far to send any reply out of a hundred letters I had mailed.

Perhaps those blinking lights on the answering machine held more promise. I'd put that off until last so I could maintain some optimism for a few more minutes. The first three were alike, containing electronic beeps and the modulated recorded voice of an operator, "If you'd like to make a call…." Probably nothing important, but frustrating. Maybe a call wanting to sign me up for another fabulous platinum card, with low interest rates and almost unlimited credit. If those people would bring their records up to date, they wouldn't be calling me so much.

The next call lifted my heart, "*Buon giorno*, Dad! I just called to tell you I'm having a wonderful time and I love you. The work is hard, but it's everything I wanted it to be. I went to Como for the day on Sunday with some of my new friends from school. I know you and Mom liked it, and I can see why. Give me a call sometime if you get a chance. I don't need anything. Giorgio and Betta send their regards. *Ciao.*"

Before my walk in the mountains, I'd delivered my daughter Catherine to Milan to begin her studies in fashion design. I couldn't afford it, but I wasn't ready to tell her…not with this chance that she'd get her life back on track.

Her voice on the recorder made me think of the night before I left her. Her eyes were shining, and she glowed with excitement at being there, with the prospect of dreams fulfilled. For me it was pain and pleasure. She had so much of her mother in her, despite the spiky cut of her dark hair, her tight clothes, and the string of earrings climbing the rim of each ear. Her mannerisms and her smile were echoes of how Caroline looked when I first saw her.

She'd smiled at me and said, "Dad, I'm going to make you so proud of me. I'm going to work so hard, and I'm going to soak up all they have to offer."

"I know you will," I'd said to her.

I hoped she would.

I sighed to myself and continued with the phone messages. Next were two more "If you'd like to make a call…" messages, then one with an instant of hope, quickly dashed, "Mr. Cross, this is Jim Dawkins of Conversion Machinery. You may recall we met at the Plastics Show in McCormick Place last year. I really like your background and I know your reputation in the industry. However, we just don't have a thing right now. We're having to scale back ourselves. If I hear of anything I'll let you know. Good day."

That was it. I sipped my coffee and stared at the phone. There was a wreck up in the mountains with two bodies in it. A large quantity of cash was stuffed in a crevice among some boulders. I remained the only soul who knew about these things. It would have been logical to call the sheriff or the highway patrol last night when I came in, but I was tired and I knew timing didn't really matter. Now I'd had my breakfast, visited with my neighbors, looked at my mail, and checked my messages. I sat there staring at the phone on the kitchen desk in front of me.

I reached for it and dialed a number. Just as I started to hang up and give it more thought, a soft voice with a touch of the mountains answered, "Hello?"

"Eileen, it's me, Matt. How are you?"

"Matt! I'm fine, but it's far too long since we've seen you. How are you and the children?"

"We're all fine."

"Do you have time to come for supper and catch us up on everything? I heard Dave and Cathy are both overseas."

"That's right, they are. I'd love to come for supper, but I don't know if I can, thanks. I have a favor to ask of Woody, so I might come by for a few minutes. Is he around?"

"He was out there under a car, last time I looked. If you'll hang on a minute, I'll carry the phone out to him."

Woody Hendrix is an entrepreneur. His main operation is a car auction every Thursday evening. In addition, he trades real estate, horses, or anything else he comes across that might make a buck. I met him when Eileen and Caroline became best friends many years ago.

"Matt, sure enough, he's where I thought he was. Here he is. Bye, Matt."

"Matt! I thought you'd died or left the country, it's been so long! What can I do you for?"

I held the phone away from my ear. It was easy to guess his vocation as an auctioneer. He spoke like a machine gun with an East Tennessee accent, and a volume that required no amplifier.

"Woody, you must be busy puttying over a cracked block in time for the auction tonight, and I'm sorry to interrupt you. I do need a favor, though."

"Matt! You hurt my feelin's. Whatta ya need, buddy? Just ask."

"I felt like taking a ride. How's your stable of horses? I'd need one for a day or two if you can spare it."

"Anytime you say, Matt. I've got a bunch of 'em, and they all need ridin', especially with the cool weather. They're all full'a piss and vinegar. When do you want one?"

"This afternoon, if that's not too soon and you're not too busy."

"Sure."

"I suppose you've got a horse trailer?"

"Yep."

"How about a pack mule or a donkey? Do you have that, too?"

"Jesus, you don't want much, do you? But how can I say no? Eileen'ud make life miserable for me if I didn't do everything you asked."

"She'd be perfectly right to do so."

"Yeah. Sure, I got just the donkey you need. Got the ornery little bastard just the other day. What ya gonna do, take a body up in the mountains and bury it?"

Close, but not exactly. "No, I don't think I'll do that this time. I haven't knocked off anybody lately, though I might have a couple of candidates."

"We prob'ly all do."

"I want to travel heavy for a change, take a regular tent and stuff like that. The horses will give me a chance to get a little farther into the mountains in less time. Is it okay if I come out after lunch? I'll gather up everything by myself so I don't interrupt your work."

"Come on out before lunch. I know Eileen'd want you to."

"Thanks a lot, Woody. I will, if you promise to ask her if it's okay, and call me back if she has other plans. I'll see you in a couple of hours, unless I hear otherwise."

I had one other call to make, then a scramble to gather what I would need. It wouldn't be much, as I would use the night for other purposes.

I let the phone ring several times because Israel's neighbor Fred wasn't the quickest person around. Finally, an answer that sounded like a drawn out pronunciation of the color: "Yelllllll-o!"

"Hi, Fred, it's Matt Cross. How are you?"

"I'm jest fine, Mr. Cross. N'you?" He insisted on calling me Mr. Cross, because he heard from Israel that I worked in an office and sometimes wore a necktie.

"Me too. I was wondering if you'd be seeing Israel in the next day or two?"

"This afternoon, as a matter of fact. What kin I do fer ya?"

"If you will, give him my regards and tell him I got back from the mountains okay, but I didn't have time to stop by. I'll drop by in a couple of days and tell him about it. But tell him to go on about his business, because I'm not sure of my schedule. I'll make sure I find him."

"Could you run that by me one more time to make sure I got it all?" I repeated it slowly for him.

"Your regards. Got back, but didn't have time. Drop by in a coupla' days. Yep, I'll be glad to, Mr. Cross. And he ain't usually too hard to find. He don't go nowhere much, jest like me."

"Much obliged, Fred." Why did I start talking like that?

As I hung up, it was already getting close to 9:30. I went through the kitchen and grabbed a bag of food for a couple of meals. Normal heavy stuff in cans this time, since Woody's donkey would carry it for me. Next a change of clothes and a poncho, and a tarp and rope from the garage to cover my donkey cargo on the way back out. I grabbed a headlamp and my jacket and hat.

What should I do about the plastic bag of money? I went to the attic and put it in the bottom of a large plastic storage container full of boating gear from my sailing days. The Beretta went with me again, a small black talisman to satisfy the paranoid feelings that people could look at me and know I had an enormous secret.

I hit the garage door opener, and headed out, stopping for gasoline at the corner Exxon on my way through town. As I impatiently waited for the numbers to turn, I scanned the newspaper vending machines, looking for a headline reading, "**LOCAL MAN FINDS MILLIONS IN MOUNTAINS.**" It wasn't there.

It took me a half-hour to get to Woody's place out in the hills. He had put together several hundred acres of hilly land by starting with his father's farm and gradually buying up adjoining parcels as they became available. He did no actual farming, and the land really wasn't suited, since it was mostly hilly and wooded. He kept it stocked with a constantly turning trade inventory of cattle and horses. Neighbors along the twisting country road were accustomed to a constant procession of horse trailers, cattle trucks, and scores of cars coming and going at all hours.

I drove into the yard about 11:00. There were a dozen cars scattered about among the trees in the non-lawn part of the yard, an open area around the circular gravel drive, and between the fenced lawn and the barn lot. He kept most of his churning inventory of cars in town on his auction lot. These were the special cases he wanted to tinker with for a while to increase their appeal. He had a corrugated metal garage, but he seemed to prefer working on them out in the open. I spotted his legs poking out from under the front bumper of a late-80s Ford pickup with its hood up.

I tapped the bottom of his shoe with the toe of my boot. "Hey, Woody, what are you doing under there? Are you asleep?"

"Nope. I'm just puttin' the last capscrew in the oil pan. Had me a bad leaker." He shuffled out, crawling on his back, and straightened up. He flashed brilliant white teeth, the front uppers gapped "too much to hold a dog tag," as he liked to phrase it during his military days. He was deeply tanned from the preceding summer in the sun, not only in his face but over the bald crown of his head, with abundant dappled freckles showing through. He had a dense fringe of curly black hair, now showing some gray around the ears. He never wore a cap or hat, except during his auctions.

He swiped at his hand with a rag and grabbed my hand in a fierce handshake. The tan emphasized the smile wrinkles radiating from his gray eyes. He was as lean and tough as his days in the Special Forces.

"Matt, how the hell are you?"

"Getting by, I guess."

"I'm surprised to see you loafin' in the middle of the week, but I reckon you must have been gone somewheres for a while. Otherwise, I'm *sure* we'd have heard from you. We've got a lot of catchin' up to do. How long can you stay?"

I sneaked a look at the smear of black grease in the palm of my hand. "Well, I know you have a big day today. How about if I borrow the horses and get out of your way for a couple of days, then visit when I bring them back?"

"Whatever suits you."

16

"Would Saturday or Sunday make sense? I'll catch you up then."

"Why don't we shoot for Saturday morning, if that fits. I don't have nuthin' planned, unless the little woman catches up with me. Speakin' of her, she wants you to stay for lunch, and I see you timed it about right, as usual. Can't say as I blame you; that's why I'm so fat. Ha, ha!

"Say, Matt, I heard a good 'un the other day down at the sheriff's office. I was thinkin' about it layin' under the pickup, and I couldn't wait for you to get here." He launched into it without pausing. "Seems this feller was feeling poorly and he went to the doctor for a checkup. After the doctor runs his tests, he comes back in and says, 'I got good news and bad news. Which do ya want to hear first?' The guy thinks about it, and says, 'I reckon you'd better hit me with the bad first.' Well the doc says, 'You got terminal cancer, just a month or two to live.'"

I saw Eileen coming around the corner of the house and heading toward us behind Woody as he continued.

"The guy just about collapses, and he says, 'Quick, doc, what's the good news?' Doc says, 'Didya see that blonde with the big boobs up in reception?' Guy begins to gets his hopes up and says, 'How could I miss!'"

Eileen drew closer and smiled at me as she approached.

"The doc says, 'The good news is, I'm f—'"

"Matt! It's really good to see you!" Eileen gave me a hug, and a kiss on the cheek. She patted Woody on the neck. "I'm sorry, Hon, I interrupted your story. I know you must have been telling Matt a joke, because he wasn't saying a thing. Now you go ahead and finish and I'll be quiet."

"We was finished, Dear. It's all right. Wasn't we Matt?"

"No, Woody, I didn't get the punch line. Could you repeat it for me?"

Woody stared at me and colored under his tan. He cleared his throat a couple of times. He wiped his hand over his bald scalp, leaving a streak of black. "She...he...he said, 'Didya see that blond in reception? Well, she's finally agreed to go out with me!'"

I couldn't help laughing, but not at the joke.

"Who was it said that, Hon, and what's funny about it? Explain it to me." Eileen took a handkerchief out of the pocket of her crisp print dress and wiped the smudge from Woody's scalp. She started to put it back in her pocket, thought better of it, and wadded it into her palm.

"It's not important, Dear," Woody said. "Let's go inside and eat, before it gets cold. I know Matt's got a lot to do today, and we don't want all your work to not be at its best. Matt, you and Eileen go on in. I'll take my coveralls off and wash up on the back porch."

We let Woody off the hook and did as he suggested. The farm house had received a complete facelift, but it retained the character of the original two-story, early 1900s farm house, with white clapboard siding and green shutters, and an open porch across the front and around one side. It was surrounded by a half-dozen large sugar maples, just now beginning to lose some of their topmost red leaves so that bare branches were beginning to show. The leaves littered the lawn around the black trunks.

Entering the house was like walking into *House Beautiful* or *Better Homes and Gardens.* It was all coordinated into a haven that always seemed relaxing and comfortable to me. I kicked off my boots in the foyer, over Eileen's protests.

"Matt, you don't have to do that. A house is to live in. Just come on in to the breakfast room."

"It's alright Eileen, I'll feel better with them off. I'll just step into the bathroom and wash up." I had to get rid of Woody's grease.

He worshipped Eileen, and was awed by what she was able to do with the house he grew up in. He made plenty of money, a fact that he concealed as best he could from his business contacts, but he spent anything for Eileen. They'd known each other since high school, and had married after Woody came home from several months in the Army. He'd enlisted right out of high school. He buzzed through basic and advanced infantry training, then Airborne and Ranger schools. After the marriage, Eileen stayed in Mountain View, while Woody trained in Special Forces, most likely without her knowledge. I doubt he ever told her he jumped out of airplanes, not to mention the other experiences he had during his tours in places unknown. I never saw the two Purple Hearts, or the Silver Star with cluster I knew he had received. Women were soft, gentle, refined creatures that didn't need to worry about such things, in Woody's world.

Among men, Woody was profane and funny. Around women, however, especially Eileen, he was polite, quiet, and careful not to say anything offensive. The double standard was out of fashion in some circles, but not in eastern Tennessee, and not in Woody's universe.

I entered the kitchen as Woody came in from the porch. He was wearing clean clothing he had worn under his coveralls, and his hands and face were scrubbed pink. We stuck our stockinged feet under the round oak table in the end of the kitchen.

"Matt, what do you want to drink? Do you want wine with lunch?"

"No, if I drink in the middle of the day, you just as well shoot me. I'll have some water, and maybe some coffee if you have it."

"Me, too," said Woody. "What'er we havin', Darlin'?"

"Matt, in your honor, we're having tortellini. I happened to have some in the freezer. Maybe it will set the stage for you to tell us about Cathy and what she's doing. No telling what poor Woody would have had if you hadn't called."

"Now, Dear, don't kid around. You feed me real good all the time, and I wouldn't want anyone to think different."

"Cathy's doing great, from what she tells me. She really seems to be enjoying Milan and the classes. She's also made a lot of friends, and I have a feeling it will be hard to get her to come home."

"When do you get to see her again?" Eileen asked.

"Not until Christmas break, I guess. I'd hoped to see her in Europe, if things had continued on an even keel, but it doesn't look possible now. At least, I think she and David can get together sometime between now and when they're planning to come home."

"What do ya mean?" asked Woody. "What's changed?"

"Well, I just as well tell you."

I gave them the short version, telling them how the company I worked for had collapsed, putting me in the job market. I didn't tell them the pension fund had been looted, leaving me in the equivalent of cyberspace.

"Couldn't you do something to save the company? I'm sure you could if they'd let you," Eileen said, her blue eyes wide with concern.

"Thanks, but they told me I was through some time back. I had the project in China to finish, and I didn't tell any of my friends because I thought the problem might go away. The last few months were a 'working severance' arrangement. I could have left immediately, or continued to work and draw my salary until the project was completed. I chose to keep working."

"So that bunch of yo-yos wrecked the company? They should have had you more involved. And I don't want to embarrass you, but if you need any ready money—"

"Thanks, Woody. My main concern is to keep the kids on path for their dreams, and not cause them to do anything foolish like coming home before their foreign studies are complete."

"Matt, again I don't mean to stick my nose in, but you've always been too nice a guy. You need to get meaner, and learn to be a little under-handed."

"Woody! How could you say such a thing?"

"Well, it's true. I mean it as a compliment, but he's Mister Nice Guy. I know the Bible says that the meek shall inherit the earth, but the strong ain't been clued in on it."

"He's right, Eileen."

"*I* don't think so," said Eileen, closing that subject. "How's David doing?"

"He's doing great. You know how serious he usually is, how he had to grow up fast because of my travels and his mother's illness. He sounds like a different person, he's so excited about being in Paris."

"I can understand that," said Eileen.

"I think you know his foreign studies grant calls for six months there, then six months in Bern. I may lose both of my children to Europe, if their excitement continues. David has a great job waiting for him at Goldman Sachs in New York, though, so I think his practical side may reel him in. And of course there's the money. He's not selfish—more like a squirrel putting away nuts for the winter."

"I know you're really proud of them," said Eileen, who had no children, but loved mine specifically, and all others in general.

"I truly am. I talked with David a few days ago, and he was all excited about a girl he'd met in one of his classes."

"David and a *girl?*" Eileen laughed.

"Not so much about the girl, I think, but because her parents lived on a houseboat moored on the Seine outside Paris. She'd invited him there for lunch on Saturday, and he was taken with the setting, and the family, too, I think. We'll see whether it's the girl, also."

Eileen laughed again, "We could never pin him down much on the girl situation, could we? They were always around, and seemed to be after him, but he kept his eyes on the future."

"As well he should, at that age."

"'Enjoy them, but don't get too serious' was his motto. He has a lot of his father in him. I don't want to pry, but you should be getting on with life, Matt." She gave me a motherly look.

"That's what people keep telling me nowadays. You know my neighbor Mary's mother, Millicent McClarty? It seems she's made a project out of me now."

"Somebody needs to."

"I don't know how to explain it to you or to her, but I just can't imagine getting into dating or anything like that—actually going out and seeking another woman. I can't say it could never happen again, but I believe it would have to be something that just happened, like a lightning strike or a car accident."

"It says something about your state of mind that you compare us women to a car accident. Thanks a lot."

"I didn't mean you, of course, Eileen. If we could figure a way to get rid of Woody without getting in trouble with the law, you know I'd do it."

"I suppose you think I ain't listenin'? Now I know what kind of friend you are, always wantin' to borrow a horse or something. Now it's Eileen!"

Woody should have stopped there, but he didn't. "I tell ya' what, there's this good lookin' gal down at the truck stop on the way into town where you cross the main highway. I eat breakfast there now and again. She's real good lookin' with a body on her that won't quit. Man! She'd be just right for..."

Woody finally started listening to himself, and glanced at Eileen. "Somebody told me about her down at the Sheriff's office. I think they was talkin' about fixin' up their brother..." His voice had grown fainter and he stole another glance at Eileen.

Eileen continued to eat her food daintily. I could hear the grandfather clock ticking in the great room. Woody buttered a roll with the concentration of Rembrandt producing another masterpiece.

"Well! Who's for dessert?" Eileen said brightly. "I have apple pie I baked yesterday. I can give it a shot in the microwave and put some ice cream on it. I'll pour you some more coffee, Matt. You want some, Hon?"

"Sure, Darlin', that 'ud be real nice." Woody said.

Eileen went into the kitchen to bring the dessert, then to the utility room freezer for ice cream.

Woody whispered hoarsely to me, "Matt, I've visited with that gal, while she was servin' me, but you know I'd never go no further or do nothin' wrong."

"I know, Woody, and so does Eileen. Wives don't like to think about or hear we notice other women. Especially when they start to think they're getting a few years on them, even when they look as good as Eileen."

"I ran my mouth too much—"

"You could have done without that 'body that won't quit' comment. But she's okay; she just wanted to watch you squirm a little, and you didn't disappoint her."

Eileen came back into our end of the kitchen and served the coffee and dessert.

I asked about her work. She was the volunteer director of the auxiliary at the county hospital, where she had made an immediate soul-bond with Caroline those many years ago.

"It's going just fine, Matt, but we always need more money. In addition to helping out with all the regular work at the hospital, we're always trying to raise funds. What bothers me most now is all of the problems we're seeing with drugs."

"Really? I guess I'm out of touch. I worried about Cathy and that crowd."

"I don't believe she did anything. She was after the appearance of rebellion. But now we're getting all kinds of cases hauled into the emergency room from the drug culture. We get the drug overdoses themselves, even among young people. Matt, you wouldn't dream what we see sometimes, especially late at night on the weekends."

I thought about the duffel bags high in the mountains and all of the pain they must represent.

21

"Matt, why don't I go on out and see about the horses. You stay here and talk to Eileen a while, and then we'll get you loaded up and on your way."

"I can't let you do that. I know you're busy today. Let me mess with the horses."

"Naw, naw. I'll make sure they're in the lot and you can do the rest. Have another cup and visit a little longer."

Woody left the table, and Eileen sat looking at me. "Matt, there's something about you that's different. Is there more to this story than losing a job? You seem to be struggling with yourself."

"Why is it you can read me like a book? Eileen, my thoughts are all in a tangle. I doubt myself, I'm angry; I'm worried about taking care of my kids. I can't get my emotions in check to carry on after Caroline, and it's been nearly three years ago. I don't want sympathy, but it's really good to be with you and Woody."

She patted my hand. "We're always here for you."

"I know. Please be patient with me while I sort things out. The new millennium is coming up, and my future is a big blank. It'll do me good to take Woody's horses out for a little ride. Speaking of Woody, you really had him on the griddle and you didn't have to say a word."

"Who, me?" she said, touching her fingertips to her breast, and fluttering her eyelids.

"I'd better go help the poor little guy. Now, don't be too hard on him. He's not guilty. Thanks for the great lunch. I'll see you when I bring the horses back." I gave her a kiss on the cheek and went out the back door.

I found Woody in the tack room in the barn, amid an assortment of riding equipment. He preferred western style equipment, rather than the English style used by a few of the elite in our area.

"Pick out what you want. I think you said you'd want a pack saddle for that little pest I told you about."

I went to a large mahogany-colored saddle with a pelican horn and a cushioned seat. "Is this okay?"

"You got a good eye. It's my favorite. You're welcome to it. I'm not ridin' anything for a few days at least."

Woody handed me a matching breast collar and bridle, and I followed him out of the barn to one of his horse trailers, a small two-horse model. While he headed for the horse lot, I hitched it to the Explorer and backed it against a bank for loading.

The horses were congregated in the far corner after seeing our activity around the tack room. I guess horses aren't fond of the sport.

"What kind of horse do you want, Matt? I got Quarter Horses, American

Saddle Bred, and a Tennessee Walker that can really pick 'em up and put 'em down."

"Well, as to the Tennessee Walker, I like to ride one, but I don't necessarily need a lot of style on this ride. Also, I don't suppose your donkey is a Tennesse Walker Donkey, and he'll be roped to whatever I'm riding."

"You got a point. See the buckskin mare over to the right, behind that sorrel gelding? She's a good ride and won't give you no trouble. She's five-gaited. Might be a little hard to catch, since I ain't rode her since mid summer, and she's smart. She's named 'Daisy'."

"Let me give her a try while you catch the donkey. I don't have any experience with those things and he's probably smarter than I am."

Daisy succumbed to the lure of a feed pan I carried, and my sleight-of-hand with a leather thong. It wasn't so easy for Woody. He took the direct approach, twirling a lariat. The donkey showed some ingenuity by keeping his nose close to the fence so the noose couldn't pass over his head as he tried to escape. The two of them raised a cloud of dust, cutting in and out of the other horses, until Woody emerged dragging the creature behind him.

"Woody, you and the donkey were mixing it up out there, and sometimes I couldn't tell who was who."

"Just remember I'm the one with the hairy ears. I'll get you a halter for the mare, and for this...this...thing here. We'll get some feed and get you on your way. Do you know how to do a diamond hitch for the stuff on the packsaddle?"

"Probably not, but I'll figure out something. Maybe I can get a roll of duct tape and just wrap him up with it. What do you call him?"

"Nuthin' so far, but he's a' ass by birth, if that gives you any ideas."

I was sorry I asked. Woody was again a hundred yards from Eileen's kitchen.

"Matt, before you go, eyeball the red 'Vette convertible over there. Man, you ought'a cruise in that thing for a while and see what happens! I'll hold it out for you and you can borrow it for awhile if you like, just 'til you can troll 'em in and set the hook."

"Thanks, Woody, but you go ahead and sell it. I'm hauling off enough of your stuff today."

I was soon on my way, after thanks to Woody and goodbye to Eileen. I headed back to the mouth of Big Creek, hoping to get on my way by mid afternoon. If the donkey would walk fast enough, I might get to the stash before late night. The ranger was in his driveway and waved as I passed. He knew me from my many visits here over the years. When I got to the parking area, there was one other rig there, a big pickup with a four-horse trailer attached.

I unloaded Daisy first and saddled her, so she could get used to the feel of it. The donkey performed as expected, puffing up his scrawny rib cage when I tightened the cinches. I'd see how long he could hold his breath while I tied the stuff on the packsaddle, covering it with a small tarp and binding it into a tidy bundle. I tightened the cinches before "Woody II" could react, then did the same for Daisy. She didn't do anything except shake her head up and down, then turn and stare at me. Now I'd find out how much trouble this was going to be.

I mounted without getting the lead rope wound around me, and we were off. Daisy pranced about and the donkey tried to resist the pull of the rope, but he soon saw it would do him no good.

Daisy settled into a fast walk with an easy, swinging gate. She kept her head low, picking her footfalls with a minimum clashing of hooves on stone. Her ears would flick forward to the trail in front of her, then back to check on the donkey and me. Then one forward and one back, continuously monitoring the world around her. The donkey kept at a trot most of the time so the lead rope didn't jerk his neck.

Now that I had all of the busy arrangements out of the way and a few hours in the saddle ahead of me, it was difficult to continue hiding my thoughts from myself. I have been satisfied with my character, for the most part, throughout my life.

Honesty about money has never been an issue. If a clerk ever made a mistake in my favor, I always corrected it—then silently congratulated myself on what an upstanding citizen I turned out to be. Straight Arrow, that's me. My father was always honest to a fault and just assumed his children would be.

I have seen plenty of the reverse, people who cut corners on everything and try to take advantage of every situation to grab for more and pad their own pockets. I don't have much respect for people like that and have always considered them lower forms of life. The three who ran our company into the ground fit nicely into that category.

The primary question for me now was: What are my intentions? Secondary questions tumbled out now that I'd admitted I had to think about my situation.

I'd had several opportunities to pick up a phone and call somebody and tell them what I'd found. Why had I not done so?

I told myself I just wanted to get the money safely out of the mountains before I turned it in.

I wondered who had jurisdiction. Probably the county sheriff. Is it in Haywood? I could have talked to Woody. He's an auxiliary deputy and would know what to do.

He might have asked why I hadn't reported it already.

The money was lost. It was in possession of crooks. What claim did they have to it? There may be laws allowing finders-keepers on found property.

The thoughts tumbled over each other in conflict. I knew the current phase would continue. I would go to the stash, get the money and haul it out, then decide what to do about both plane and money. No one at this time would be the wiser. Only I knew about it, and I could keep it that way indefinitely. No point in making any tough decisions now. Just go ahead and get it out, then decide. Woody would know what to do. I know what he'd say if I asked him. But could he know what it feels like to open those bags out in the forest, alone?

3.
KEEPERS

As Daisy carried me up the trail, the evening shadows lengthened, climbing the wall to my left until it was completely shaded from the setting sun. We were in Big Creek's valley with mountain ridges growing in height on both sides as we climbed. The sun had long before been obscured by the forested mass on my right and the chill of the autumn day was making me appreciate the warmth of my jacket. Daisy and the donkey were getting all the exercise. The donkey hustled along, only occasionally letting some tension develop in the lead rope.

As the trail dipped nearer to the creek bed, I stopped to give Daisy and Woody II a breather and a drink. Dismounting, I led her to the edge of the pool of clear water and gave her some slack in the reins. The donkey, apparently with more thirst than discretion, tried to dash past her to the water. Daisy laid her ears back and bit him on the neck, sending him in a scramble through the rocks and brush. He lost his footing and fell, tumbling on his back and rolling almost under Daisy's hooves. She started a fit of her own, whirling sideways so quickly I barely managed to avoid getting stepped on.

I finally managed to get them sorted out. I had to take the packsaddle off and remount everything. Daisy was unhappy and glared at the donkey, showing the whites of her eyes, but we resumed our journey.

After another hour's ride, we neared Walnut Bottoms. It had grown darker. Occasionally I saw the flash of a spark struck by one of Daisy's shoes. I wondered if the other riders were camped here, of if they had gone farther up the trail. They would have come today, because I was here only yesterday myself. As I wondered how close we were, Daisy answered my question by stopping suddenly and emitting a thunderous whinny. The effort tightened her rib cage, giving me a start. There was an immediate answer a few hundred yards ahead. Now I knew we would be meeting the other party, perhaps a small complication to overcome.

Three horses were scattered in the clearing, their front legs in hobbles. Daisy chuffed another soft whinny, and the others answered. Despite the dusky light, I could see two were saddle horses, and one was a medium-size pony, a deluxe version of my donkey. A dome tent was erected on the far side of the clearing, with two people in the brighter light of a campfire. They stood and looked expectantly in my direction, no doubt wondering about their late visitor.

"Hi! Get off your horse and have a cup of coffee."

I returned their greeting as I drew the mare to a halt. The donkey wasn't paying attention and collided with her hindquarters. I realized I knew the campers, casual acquaintances from Mountain View. He worked for the city, something to do with the water department. His wife was a real estate agent I knew from her occasional picture in the paper as salesperson of the week. It would be much simpler if they had been complete strangers. The list kept growing of people who knew I was stirring around the area.

"Hi, Carol. Hi, Tom. I'm surprised to find anyone I know way up here."

"Mr. Cross, is it?" said Carol.

"Yes, Matt." I dismounted, let Daisy's reins drop to the ground, and shook hands with both of them. Was it my imagination, or did she hold on a fraction of a second too long? Their faces were in shadow from the campfire at their backs. "Let me tie up the mare and her side-kick, and I'll take you up on the coffee."

"We haven't seen you for a while," Tom said. "You must have been traveling."

"I've been out of the country for awhile."

"My customers seem to own me," said Carol. "We decided to come out for a long weekend."

I tied Daisy and the donkey away from each other and the hobbled horses.

Tom gave me a cup of coffee when I returned to fireside. "Are you camping here for the night?"

"No, I think I'll go farther up the trail and camp in the woods. I have some oats for the horses, and there's not much grazing here anyway. I'll leave it for your horses."

As we seated ourselves on logs, Carol asked, "Didn't I hear something about your company having problems? I've been getting some listings out of some guys who were part of management."

"Bad news travels fast. I may want to list my house. My kids are out and around, so I may get a smaller place. Perhaps I'll give you a call."

"I'd be glad to have it. You have a nice house. Call me anytime and I'll come by and make some recommendations. I have to warn you things have started to slow a little."

Then she gazed directly at me to emphasize what came next. "Call me. I'll make myself available."

Tom added, "Things may get tough for a while for such a small town. Do you have any idea what happens next?"

"No, I don't. Sometimes the banks take over and put in their own team, then keep the company going just as it was before. From what I understand in this case, however, there isn't much left to operate. They might just decide to write it off."

"That'd sure be a shame," Tom said. "The scuttlebutt around town is you were the glue that held the company together. They say you really got shafted on the leveraged buy-out. Is there a chance the bankers might get you back to run it?"

"No. Thanks for your kind words, whether they're yours or someone else's. Starting way behind with a big handicap is never much fun and I doubt it would be successful."

Carol turned and leaned toward me. "You strike me as being the kind of man who could handle it."

"Thank you," I replied, uncomfortable with her appraisal. Better to change the subject. "Also, thanks for the coffee. I really must be on my way. It's getting darker by the minute."

"What's your hurry?" Carol said, looking me over again. "You just as well camp here, then move on in the morning. Where are you off to, anyway?"

"Carol, don't pester the man," said Tom.

"I'm just meandering, but I think I'll stick with the original plan. I like camping alone, in the depth of the woods." I'd been studying the clearing and its surroundings to plan the return trip later. I'd have to wait until Tom and Carol were asleep and their horses quiet, then hope I could slip by without being seen or identified. In Carol's frame of mind, it might take a while for her to settle down.

I rose and shook hands, noting again a lingering grasp on Carol's part. Was I beginning to imagine things? I went back to my charges, finding both resting a lifted leg, signs of fatigue. I tightened Daisy's cinch, gathered the donkey, and mounted, waving at the Fentons as I left the clearing. Tom turned back to the fire, but Carol stood with her hands on her hips and watched me disappear into the darkened woods.

The trail was pitch dark, and staring into the campfire had ruined my night vision. I depended on Daisy to pick her way. I could tell she was growing tired. At the same time, the darkness seemed to make her more tense and nervous. She held her head higher and shifted her ears more quickly in all directions, monitoring the darkness around us. Gradually my night vision returned and I could make out the dim shapes of the undergrowth, and the rocks bordering Big Creek. We crossed the stream after a short distance and I let them drink, not dismounting this time to repeat our earlier performance.

We moved on, gradually distancing ourselves from Walnut Bottoms and drawing closer to my destination. A wind had started to rise, moaning in the tops of the tall trees. The upper branches moved across the night sky, arcing in random patterns with the gusts of the wind. It remained relatively calm at ground level as we plodded on. Suddenly Daisy stopped, seeming to jump inside her skin, bracing all four feet. Her move startled me, and the donkey hit the end of his lead rope, cutting into my thigh. The night was spooky, but perhaps there was something out there. Daisy trembled, but consented to continue, taking smaller steps with her head high, listening.

At last we came to the confluence of the trails, near where I had left the stash. I dismounted, weary to the bone. It was hard to imagine it was only that morning I'd awakened at home and had breakfast with Mary and Millicent.

I unsaddled and watered the animals in turn, and tied them to trees with ropes, replacing Daisy's bridle with a halter to get the bit out of her mouth. They were both acting strangely. I arranged all the equipment on the tarp, which I had spread in a level spot. I measured out oats into feedbags and left them both munching while I thought about my mission. I'd have to carry the stash down to my makeshift camp, then rest until the time was right to make my run past the Fentons. If the wind held, its background noise would help mask my return past Walnut Bottoms.

I got my headlamp out, in case I had to have it. I preferred working in the dark to avoid killing my night vision. I crawled up the slope through the brush toward the outcropping of rocks. It was in a Y formed by the main part of the stream and a tributary cascading down the mountain on the west bank.

The boulders were where they were supposed to be and I recognized the largest one that fronted the jumble. My hiding place was around the right side. I squeezed between the rock and its neighbor and entered an opening surrounded by boulders, although their presence was more in my memory than in my sight. As I felt my way toward the crevice that held my stash, there was a loud, snorting grunt, and a black shape with a strong odor barreled past me, knocking me to the ground.

My heart hammered in my chest and I gasped for breath as I assessed the damage. My right shoulder was bruised and my head had banged against the boulder, but nothing seemed to be broken. I heard a high-pitched whinny from Daisy and several brays from the donkey. It was the strange whistle-grunt donkeys do, and was the first sound I had heard from him since we were introduced. This was probably their first scent of a bear.

I slid back down the slope, feeling my way through the brush. The strong halters and lead ropes had held, but the donkey had managed to wrap his around the tree several times until his nose was against the bark, his feedbag awry. I patted his scrawny neck and untied the rope, getting him calm again and settling his feedbag back in place. My own pounding pulse had subsided, though no one was there to pat my neck.

Daisy was in better shape. She shied away from me, disdaining my leadership. I rubbed her neck also and talked to her until she was calm again. I groped back up the slope to the rocks, a path now growing more familiar. This time as I approached the cache, I turned on my headlamp. I skirted the sentinel boulder again and entered the crevice that led to the encirclement of jumbled rocks.

The scene that greeted me was not a surprise except for the extent of the devastation. The bear had been after some remnants of hiking food, which had been wrapped so carefully in my ground cloth, along with my camping gear. I should have had more presence of mind. It must have been the shock of finding the money, and the strain of indecision over what I should do about it.

The bear had torn everything to shreds, including my down sleeping bag. Goose down was everywhere, as though a captive snowstorm had fallen among the rocks. My small stove, my kit of pots, my tent and its frame, were all mangled and trampled into the brush. Food packets and cans had been chewed open, their contents licked clean.

The money! I checked the crevice and found to my relief that he had not reached it. I could only imagine the scene if I had given him more time. Now instead of resting with the horses for a couple of hours, I'd spend all my time cleaning up after the bear. The ground cloth was still reasonably intact, so I started with clearing a space and spreading it on the ground. I tediously gathered all the remnants of my belongings and made a mixed heap of them in the center, gathering the edges into a large hobo bundle. It took most of an hour, working in the shadows cast by my headlamp. At least it would not be littered with man-made objects, and anyone stumbling upon the spot would think a flock of geese had met some inglorious end.

I made two trips getting the two heavy bags and the debris down to the pile on the tarp. I was through with this spot for all time. My watch told me it was midnight, too late to sleep, but time to sit under a tree until late enough to go. I realized I had not eaten since lunch with Eileen and Woody, so I fished out some granola bars and a small can of cashews, along with two cans of warm beer.

Seated against a tree, I turned off the headlamp, plunging the woods into total darkness. The wind still tossed the tops of the trees with its sighing sounds, and I could hear Daisy munching away on her oats. The food and the chance to relax made me aware of how tired I was, and the aftermath of the rush of adrenaline in my system now brought a relaxed weakness to me. Considering my surroundings and the unusual nature of my mission, I reached a measure of contentment. My mind began wandering through its deepest recesses, moving aimlessly through memories both recent and from long ago until my awareness faded.

I awoke with a start, disoriented by the darkness. Daisy must have snorted, perhaps impatient with me for leaving her feedbag in place. I arose, stiff and cramped, my shoulder sore. It was two o'clock in the morning, with no time to waste. Working with the headlamp would be faster, so I turned it on. I soon had them saddled, but it took another half hour making up a pack for the donkey. One bag of money balanced nicely on each side, with the remainder of the gear and bag of refuse tied on top. The donkey looked wide and bulky, but the weight was nominal. I roped it all together and covered it with the tarp. It lacked the professional look, but I hoped no one would see it.

We set off down the trail, now more familiar with each passage. My night vision was destroyed again, but Daisy knew we were headed home and set off at a brisk pace. The donkey, now familiar with his role, trotted meekly behind. He was unaware he was laden with the most valuable cargo on a donkey since Bethlehem.

When I knew we were within a half-mile of the campsite, I stopped and cut four squares of canvas from the tarp to bundle Daisy's hooves. Each hoof resembled a large Hershey kiss. The donkey wasn't heavy enough to make much noise and he wasn't shod. I mounted and chanced another quarter mile, before dismounting again and leading the mare and Woody II. We walked steadily, crossing the stream where the animals drank. We padded on.

A sharp bend in the trail signaled our approached to the clearing, and we began to skirt the left side. One of their horses sensed our presence and nickered a greeting. I stifled Daisy's answer by closing her nostrils, the way the Indians do it in Hollywood. We were halfway around when the nicker was repeated by two of their horses. Again, the trick worked with Daisy, but the donkey, silent for almost the entire trip, felt someone should answer and he brayed in reply. I walked swiftly on but looked at the tent, silent in the darkness. A dark head thrust through the front opening.

Within seconds we plunged into the velvet darkness of the trail to begin the long descent to the parking area. Dull with fatigue, stiff and sore, I mounted and we were on our way. Whose head was thrust from the tent, and what did they see? They heard the damn donkey and it wouldn't take a genius to figure out who had been stirring at such a strange hour. I was more uncomfortable with Carol than with Tom. I read him as rather steady and dull. Carol, on the other hand, appeared to have a quick mind and a suggestion of cleverness that was unsettling. There was nothing to be done about it now.

The ride back was long and tiring for me and for the animals. At times, my consciousness would fade and I would jerk upright, grasping the horn to keep from falling. Daisy would jump each time, then resume her weary march. In spite of the chill air, she was lathered with sweat around the breast collar.

Dawn brightened the sky when at last we approached the parking lot.

The Explorer and trailer were undisturbed but covered with frost. I pulled gratefully to a halt and dismounted. I patted the mare's neck.

"Good girl, Daisy. You're a good horse." I couldn't summon the same feelings for the donkey, although I suppose he did the best he could with the intelligence he possessed.

Daisy lifted one leg to rest and let her head hang. I untied and unloaded everything from the packsaddle into the Explorer, placing the two bags of money on the back floor then heaping everything else around and on top, covering it all with the tarp.

Eyeing the wretched little creature, I felt a flicker of compassion. "I'm sorry, donkey, I guess you did okay," I said, as I removed his packsaddle and put it in the front of the trailer. I wiped him down with a burlap bag, then clothed him in the smallest horse cover Woody could find. It still swallowed him so only his feet and head emerged. Daisy got the same treatment. I spent a lot of time rubbing her down, somewhat guilty at the length and speed of the expedition, with her out of condition. She'd be okay, but probably sore-muscled for a few days. With them both in their stalls, I broke open a fragrant bale of late summer hay and filled their racks in the front of the stalls.

I scraped off the frost, cranked the engine, and headed down the road, gliding by the ranger's house with as little stir as possible. I'd thought about my next step, and the only thing that made sense was to impose upon Israel again. He had asked me to report back to him after my hike, and there was a lot to report. I would present a modified version and would have to create a white lie or two to explain the horse trailer and its occupants. I couldn't go directly back to Woody's. I hadn't been gone long enough to make any sense. Obviously I couldn't take the horse and donkey home with me.

The whole episode had become complicated. To Woody, I'd suddenly developed an urge to ride and I needed a pack animal. "To bury a body?" He'd joked. To Israel, I'd have to invent some explanation that probably wouldn't make a lot of sense. To the Fentons, I'd gone zipping through Walnut Bottoms in the middle of the night in two different directions. What kind of blundering trail would I leave next? Did I really plan to keep the money? How, and for how long? Perhaps all would be answered in time. I couldn't come up with anything in my present state of exhaustion.

4.
ISRAEL

I drove into Israel's yard in the early morning light. How long since I was here? I'd lost track of time. I counted on my fingers: one night up on the mountaintops, one in the valley before the discovery, a night at home, then this one on the trail. That would make this Friday morning. The next day was when I'd made plans to take the horses back and visit again with Woody and Eileen.

The log house was set back from Hanson Creek far enough to be on high ground, nestled against the mountainside, but still within hearing distance of the water's music as it rushed over its bed of boulders. I saw a thread of smoke rising from the chimney. Breakfast preparations had begun.

As I drove up, Israel's big redbone hound, Toby, catapulted through the rhododendrons that grew along both sides of the porch. He bayed a loud warning, and bounded across the yard to meet me as I stepped down from the Explorer. He stopped in mid-voice when he recognized me, but charged forward, leaping up and slapping a wet tongue against my cheek and into my ear.

"Toby! Get away! Now git!" Israel yelled from the open front door. "Good mornin' to you, Matthew."

Toby turned and slunk toward the porch, looking back at me with an abject apology I knew was insincere. I wiped his affection from my face and ear.

"Israel, if you ever greet me like that, I'm not coming back."

He grinned. "I ain't that hard up yet."

As I stepped up on the porch, he gripped my hand, hard calluses pressed against my soft palm. "Matthew, it surely does amaze me how you can tell when breakfast is about ready. Fred told me you was comin' in the next day or two, but I didn't expect this rig. Are you comin' or goin'?"

"I'm coming, I guess, Israel. Good morning to you. I've come to impose on your hospitality again, and I've brought friends."

"You know you ain't imposin'. I'm anxious to hear about your trip." He looked me up and down. "You look like you've been drug through a knot-hole backwards."

"That good, huh?"

"It ain't my business, but I've never seen you lookin' like this. You could use some breakfast and some rest, I'll bet."

"I sure could. Do you have a place I could let a horse and donkey out for a few hours?"

"Is that what you got in there? I couldn't see but one real animal."

"When you get right down to facts, that's all there is."

He chuckled. "Sure, put 'em in the barn lot. There's nothin' else in there. The water tank stays full from the spring. I'll bring you a mug of coffee while you get this here rig out there."

Israel hurried into the house, while I drove alongside the fence to the barn lot. The old barn was built of logs, now covered with weathered oak siding.

By the time Israel arrived with a steaming mug of coffee in each hand, I had the tailgate of the trailer open.

I eagerly slurped a large drink and burned my tongue.

"Israel, this really hits the spot. I'm sleepy, tired, hungry, and just about everything short of dead. What would I do without you?"

"I don't know, Son. Without you, I wouldn't have much comp'ny, either, is another way of lookin' at it."

With Israel's help, I got the mare and donkey unloaded, uncovered, and brushed down with a stiff brush, keeping my coffee cup sitting upwind from flying horsehair. I set them up with fresh hay and oats, far enough apart to allow the donkey to have a chance. The mare got on the ground and rolled, wriggling her skin against the rough soil and getting the kinks out of her muscles. For his part the donkey went straight to the water and then the oats.

Back in the house at my usual spot at the kitchen table, I had trouble keeping my mind from fading and my chin from hitting the table while Israel fixed breakfast. There was a painful knot of fatigue between my shoulder blades, and my head and shoulder complained from the brush with the bear. Israel could see my condition, and did not try to engage in small talk while he busied at the stove.

As he brought the food, I said, "I'd sure appreciate it if I could lie down and take a nap for a while. I've been up about all night. Maybe we can visit a bit after I rest. Were you planning anything I'm interrupting?"

"Nope. You take a rest, and help yourself to a hot bath if you want. I'm just goin' up to the hill pasture to see the cattle and I'll be back about noon. Do you want me to wake you up then, if you're asleep?"

"Sure. And thank you for everything."

The hot shower and the bed in the quiet cove instantly took away my consciousness. I knew nothing until I heard a tap at the door, and Israel stuck his head in.

"I came back here to wake you up 'bout noon, but I could hear you snorin' so loud I didn't have the heart to do it. I thought you'd get more good out of the sleep."

"What time is it now?"

"'Bout three, or so."

"Goodness! I slept all that time and I still feel groggy. I'll be in there in a minute."

Israel closed the door and left, and I splashed myself awake in the bathroom. I had to go in there and talk with him, and I didn't know what to say. How could I explain anything to him, when I couldn't explain it to myself?

I found him in the kitchen, pouring fresh coffee. "Would you like for me to heat you up some food?" he asked.

"No, just some coffee and maybe a snack. If that ham is still left over from breakfast, I'll put a cold slab of it in some bread."

He prepared it for me and nodded toward the living room. "Let's take it in there and sit by the fire." I knew he would not push me, but would expect to hear some explanation of the last few days.

Sitting comfortably in front of the fireplace, rocking on the oval hand-braided rug, I told him about the walk on the Appalachian Trail and down the valley of Big Creek, leaving out any reference to the wreck in the mountain laurel, the bodies, and the money. We both looked into the dancing flames as I talked, and he listened without interrupting, except to replenish the coffee and the fire, or to add a comment to show his interest.

"What do you suppose that fellar was up to? The way you described him, he seemed outa' place up there."

"I agree. He gave me the creeps, and I was glad to get away from him. Maybe he was just taking a hike, or maybe he was looking for a victim."

"Was there anybody in Walnut Bottoms?"

"Not a soul when I walked through there. Only when I went back later."

"I'm surprised you went back so quick, without taking time off to rest up."

"Well, I called Woody Hendrix to see how he and Eileen were doing. You remember him? You know Caroline and Eileen were close friends."

"Yeah, I remember meetin' them at the funeral..."

"Well, I got to talking to him about horses and decided to go for a ride while I was in a camping frame of mind. He hadn't ridden any of his horses for a while and they needed the exercise."

Israel looked into the fire without commenting, and my excuse for riding sounded weak to me.

"I always enjoyed horses, and haven't had a chance to ride for a while."

Silence.

"When I got up to Walnut Bottoms, there were too many people there to suit me, so I turned around and came back without camping."

"Too bad you went to all that trouble."

"It made a long ride, but I enjoyed it anyway, and Woody's horse got plenty of exercise."

Two was too many people. "I never did like to camp among other people. Anyway, here I am. Would it be too much trouble to put me up for the night? Then I can take the horses directly back in the morning."

"Of course it's no trouble. I didn't figger you'd take them to your place. I might even put you to work for a few minutes this evening."

"I'd be happy to."

"I've got a couple of metal gates to hang, and it works better for two people. I've got the posts set, just need to mount the gates and level them. Fred was comin' over tomorrow, but he ain't much good anymore on things like that."

"You don't often give me much chance to earn my keep."

We worked together for a couple of hours and hung the gates, replacing some old board gates that had warped and sagged. I checked the horse and donkey, and helped Israel see about his livestock. As we came back to the house, I eyed the Explorer, sitting innocently in the drive, containing more liquid assets than most banks. I had the feeling it should glow in the dusky light, but it did not.

Israel fed me again and we washed up together, soon taking our places again before the fire. Single malt scotch on ice would have been good, but I settled for another cup of coffee in deference to Israel's beliefs.

"Israel, I'm struggling with myself over the future," I began, with the feeling of a rehearsed speech. "You know all that stuff I told you—about being out of a job. Now something different has come up and I can't say, even to myself, what I'll do. I probably know what I should do, but the longer I ponder the questions in my mind, the cloudier they become."

"You'll do okay. You've always done the right thing, no matter what."

"I'm not sure that got me anywhere."

"Sure it did. The right way is always the best way."

"Sometimes I wonder."

"You've had a rough go of it the last few years, losing your dear wife, and now this company thing.

"When I lost my Sarah," Israel continued, "I near lost all my faith, and any reason to go on livin'."

He stared out the window in the direction of the tumbling creek. I saw his expression change as his mind sorted through his memories, oblivious of my presence. We sat in silence for some time before he returned to the present.

"Our minds are strange," he said. "We can never know for sure what'll come out of our own senses. I know, in time, we can come to terms with 'most anythin'...even what we don't understand. It was so in my case. It just took a long time."

"Israel, I wish I could be more like you."

"Me? I can't figure why you'd say that, me just an uneducated old mountain farmer."

"You're 'grounded,' if that's the right word. You have faith; you have strength. No matter what comes along, you set your mind to take care of it."

"Well, I reckon I do, but I've never made much difference in the world, like you have. I admit I'm stubborn. My Scotch ancestors had to be, to make it, when they come over here. But you'll be okay."

"I wish I could be so sure. Right now, it doesn't feel that way."

"I'm truly sorry," Israel repeated. "But you've got a lot goin' for you. You'll land on your feet."

"Thanks, Israel. It's been a comfort to me just to be here with you."

"Matthew, you know I'm here to listen if it'll help. Also, you know I won't pry into your business. Tell me nothing, or talk to me about what troubles you. Sometimes it jest helps to speak your mind, even it the listener don't know a thing."

"I guess the main issue is how we perceive ourselves. It's hard to put it into words, and I've never tried to before, but sometimes I feel like there are two people living inside my skin."

He looked at me and nodded without comment.

"There's the 'me' that walks and talks and goes through life, doing whatever I do. My actions are sometimes thought through pretty well ahead of time, but sometimes they're spontaneous, reacting to whatever takes place. The other 'me' hovers in the background and grades my actions, most of the time saying, 'You're okay. You did a good job.' Other times this second 'me' is pretty disgusted, such as times I've lost my temper and then regretted it later."

He squinted at me and nodded again, a rare listener who would listen.

I continued. "I'm not talking about the kind of people I'm sure you've known that are artificial, that put up a false front and never let you know what they're thinking. I think you've probably known the kind that never expose their inner soul and the other kind that couldn't tell you the truth if their lives depended on it."

"Yep, I've seen both kinds."

"What I'm trying to put into words is what I think must be in all of us as we talk to ourselves. Maybe the cartoonists who show the little angel and devil figures are onto something. They illustrate quite well how we monitor our actions against whatever standards have been instilled in us. Am I making any sense at all?"

"Sure. I know what you're gettin' at. You must be thinkin' of doing something you're not sure is proper. That's hard for me to believe about you, and I reckon whatever it is, it's hard for you to believe, too."

"Israel, as you just said, we can't be sure of our own minds when we're confronted with situations we haven't encountered before. I'm not talking about something clearly dishonest, like robbing a bank or killing someone. Just something that's a bit different and certainly overwhelming."

"Matthew, I have faith that in the long run you'll sort it out properly, whatever it is. You've been what you are too long for any real change in your makeup."

I wasn't so sure.

He rubbed the stubble on his chin and thought for a moment. "We all start out about the same way, you know. We come into this world thinking only about ourselves...where our next meal is comin' from, and demandin' with our loud squallin' that somebody takes care of us. My church teaches that we are born as sinners, meanin' that we're really no different from animals—"

"I've seen a few that never got beyond that."

"You got that right. But anyway, as I was sayin', we believe there's a wick inside that has to be lit by the Holy Spirit before we get to be better than the animals."

He waited for my nod before continuing.

"Who knows what really lights the flame? Maybe different things in different folks. In some folks it never happens. In some, it grows to such a force that everybody around them is affected by it. They can almost see a glow from it. I think, too, that in some people it begins, then flickers out for whatever reason...maybe lack of workin' at it."

"I understand."

"To carry it a step farther, I have this opinion, after studyin' folks for a long time, that a lot of problems are caused by people not likin' themselves enough. I've seen people that went out of their way to cause people to marvel at how bad they were. I think the person mis-behavin' is sayin', 'I'm no good, nobody cares, I'll show you just what bad is. If bein' bad is the best thing I got goin' for me, then I'm really gonna to be good at it!'"

I laughed aloud. "You know, that's the best insight into bad behavior I've ever heard."

"Yeah, well, I don't claim to be anything special or smart, but I'm old, which helps, I reckon. I think family is still the most important part, if they don't foul it up. One's folks can either make them feel worth somethin', or the other way around. If they keep tellin' their kid they're no-account, then the kid either starts to believe it, or they go the other way and make somethin' special out of theirselves. I've never been able to figure the one that goes opposite to the usual."

"Me either. I've seen kids turn out poorly with loving parents, and the other way around."

"Matthew, I have no doubts about you, even if you question yourself. It'll turn out all right. All of us have doubts sometimes."

"I hope you're right. In this case, I really don't know yet what I'll do, or whether it's a good idea."

"You'll have to think it through and decide. We seek forgiveness from others," Israel said, "but if it don't come, those of us who are believers have the church to help us through bad times. I'm sorry, I don't mean to start preachin'."

"No, no, it's fine. I learn a lot from you."

"Well, I happen to believe what my church teaches, but I'd be the first to admit it's a long shot anything good will come out of a person that ain't learned somethin' at his mama's knee. Or sometimes *across* his mama's knee."

The fire in the fireplace popped, sending a shower of sparks. I waited for him to continue.

"I do know what you were talkin' about; that sometimes a body goes off in the wrong direction and is disgusted at himself. Some things still cause me to be ashamed from when I was just a little kid."

"It's hard for me to picture you ever doing anything you were ashamed of."

"Oh, I've done a few things. I'm not about to tell anybody what they *all* are. I could tell you one where I didn't do what I said I would. And I don't regret it one bit."

"Israel! I'm surprised to hear this."

"I ain't a saint, but a sinner. You'll enjoy this'n. When I was a young man, there was this fella I knew, but didn't like much. He was a few years older than me, and a kind of braggart and sort of a bully. Never did anything terrible I knew of, but liked to make someone else look bad if he could. Stuck on himself. He was good lookin' and thought all of the girls should be privileged to make his acquaintance."

He took another sip of coffee. I kept quiet.

"He'd seen this girl over to Little Cove he liked the looks of, but hadn't had the chance to give her the bounty of his charm, him bein' in a hurry at the time. He heard I was goin' over there because I had cousins that lived there, and it was a long ride, probably thirty miles or so. He told me who she was and where she lived, and told me to see if he could come and see her on a certain date, so's he wouldn't waste the ride. I told him I'd do it, since at the time he asked me it didn't make any difference. To make a long story short, I went and found her, and when I set eyes on her, there was no way that guy would have a chance gettin' me to speak for him."

Israel glanced at me and I saw the shine of a tear in his eye. He swallowed and looked into the fire.

"It was my Sarah, the first time I beheld her."

"Oh, Israel. You never told me how you met."

He glanced at me, then back into the fire. "She was the most beautiful thing I'd ever laid eyes on...there I was, bashful as I could be around girls anyway. Somehow, I got out a few words to get things started, since my intentions was to just deliver a message, you understand. She had long, shining black hair, standing there in the sunlight, and big brown eyes. I can see her like it was yesterday. She was wearin' a long, everyday dress and she was barefoot, but somehow she couldn't have looked better if she'd been dressed for a fancy ball at the governor's mansion."

He looked down at his callused hands. "But I'm gettin' side-tracked, just like I did that day. Naturally, I didn't say a word about that other fella, so I pretended to have lost my way and asked for my cousin's place. The point of the story is I felt guilty about not doin' what I said I'd do. But not *too* guilty."

"Did he cause you any trouble about it?"

"Naw. When I was young, people didn't mess with me much. Also, he didn't want to let on any particular female meant anything, since there was so many in the world oughta' be swoonin' over him."

A log shifted in the fireplace, breaking into coals on the hearth. Israel got up, shifted the screen, and built the fire back to his satisfaction. I thought about this man, dredging up an incident from his memories that didn't measure up to his own standards. From what I knew of him, he would have to struggle to come up with anything worth calling dishonest.

I said, "As the world gets more complicated, we know more ways to get into trouble, don't we?"

"That's for sure. But people think these mountains are peaceful, that all the crime's in the big cities. It's pretty quiet now, but in my daddy's and grandaddy's time, when there was more people and less law, they used to pretty well settle things theirselves. Not always in the best way. There was people who cheated others in money, in livestock, and in women. There was feuds and killin' sometimes in the worst of it. Overall, though, most folks tried to do the right thing."

We mused by the fire until sleep beckoned. We were both early risers, and I looked forward to a full night of rest and sleep, comfortable and safe in the mountain setting. We rose together, and Israel turned to me and gripped my hand.

"Good night Matthew," he said. "I have faith in you. Whatever it is that troubles you, I'm sure in the end you'll make the right decisions."

"Good night to you, also, Israel. And thank you for all you do for me. I don't know what I would do without you."

Another crisp fall day greeted us in the morning. We had our usual breakfast before I rounded up my charges and loaded the trailer. Although it was always in the back of my mind, I was able to ignore the contents of the Explorer at times and assume a feeling of normalcy, as though the events of the last few days had not taken place. I said goodbye to Israel, and left him standing in front of his log house waving to me as I drove away. I felt I was seeing through a window into the past, that a turning had been reached that would not allow me to go back to the way things used to be.

5.

CAROL

After leaving Israel, I decided to stop at Woody's favorite truck stop and give him a call. I threaded through the ranks of eighteen-wheelers to a spot I could observe through the windows of the restaurant. The horse trailer bore watching, but I had several pretty good reasons in the Explorer as well. Many of the rigs were clattering at idle, like the rasping breaths of prehistoric beasts. By contrast, however, most were objects of considerable beauty. Gleaming clear-coat colors ranged from red to chartreuse to purple, with gold pin-striping accents.

Banks of phones inside were occupied with a murmur of negotiations going on by denim-clad, bearded, stereotype truckers in cowboy boots. I fit perfectly with my riding clothes of the day before. Snatches of conversation around me revealed a potential cuckolding in progress on one side, and threats on the other to let a load of produce rot if the damn load wasn't paid for on delivery. Eileen's soft voice answered on the first ring.

"Hi, Eileen. I have a couple of animals to deliver. Is the master of the house around?"

"Speaking."

"I knew that. How about Woody? If you'll be there for a while, I'll bring these creatures back and turn them loose."

"Sure, come on. Woody's going to be here all day, and we'll be glad to see you. I'll make you stay to lunch."

I said goodbye and moved in to the restaurant, sitting at the counter. I spotted her immediately, Woody's idea of the future Mrs. Cross. She wore a deep pink uniform and a tired expression. When she approached a customer, in this instance, me, she turned it into a smile. It was genuine, but failed to cover the weariness beneath. The place stayed open all night, and she would probably go home after the breakfast rush. To a teenage family she was raising alone, if statistics held.

"Coffee, sir?"

"Yes, thank you. Black. And I won't need a menu, just the coffee."

I sipped my coffee, turning sideways on the stool to watch the Explorer and the trailer. I'd give Eileen ample time to get organized, even though she probably never needed it. I don't know if I came for any other reason. Perhaps to confirm the truth of what I told Eileen and Millicent.

A young deputy sheriff entered my vision, headed for the Explorer and trailer. I watched as he circled the Explorer, peering in the windows. I felt a twitch in my gut. What could he be doing there? Had I made a mistake? He moved to the trailer and looked inside. Best to face it straight on. I left five dollars on the counter and went outside.

He heard me coming and turned to face me. He was big, young, and muscular, with red-blonde hair and freckles.

I spoke first. "Can I help you with something, deputy?"

He gave me a boyish smile, "I just thought that might be Woody's trailer. Ya never know what kinda' car he's gonna be drivin', but that looked like his trailer."

"You have a good eye, which I guess you get from police work. It is his trailer, and his horse and donkey. I'm a friend of his, Matt Cross." I extended my hand and he took it, giving me a grin and a blush from the compliment. "I'm on my way right now to take them back home. Do you ride?"

"Deputy Pearson, sir. I shore do. If we have a manhunt or somethin' where we use horses, I usually go. Lot'sa times we use Woody's horses. I've seen that trailer before, so it really wasn't all that special, me recognizin' it, and all." He crushed my hand in an eager handshake and said, "Say 'hey' to Woody for me, will ya'?"

I promised I would, and was grateful when he walked away. I checked the animals and headed for Woody and Eileen's.

The maples around the house had continued to molt. The garland of red-gold on the grass had increased. Woody was tinkering with a car as usual. I waved as I went by and drove directly to the low bank to unload. By the time I'd made the maneuver, he was there to shake my hand.

"Well, how was the ride, Partner? The horses act okay for you?"

"They were great. I had a little donkey trouble here and there, but can't complain."

Woody gave a great laugh, showing his white teeth and the crinkles around his eyes. "I shouldna' done it to you! That little rascal has been nothin' but trouble since he got here. Always into something. I figured you was tough enough, though, and he needed a workout."

"You're right, and it's okay. I think the trip did him some good. Daisy didn't care much for him to start with, but once he learned his place, she was satisfied."

"I figger by now, you'd like to keep him."

"I couldn't do that to you, Woody. In fact, I named him after you."

Woody laughed again.

We got them unloaded, and all the tack put away. The mare was a little stiff, but seemed in fine shape. She immediately distanced herself from the donkey. We unhitched the trailer in its parking spot and headed to the house to see Eileen.

This time we went in through the back porch. Eileen was in her bright kitchen, and came forward to hug me. I kissed her cheek. "Hi, darling girl. What are you up to, this morning?"

"Just the usual. The bigger question is, what are you up to, Matt?"

"What do you mean?"

"Don't be innocent with me, Matt. All of this hiking and riding, all scrunched up together, like you're in some kind of hurry. And you look tired and worried. Want to tell Eileen about it?"

"I do? Look tired and worried? Are you sure you know what a forty-eight-year old man is supposed to look like?"

"Look at Woody," she replied.

Woody posed for us, wearing a vacant grin.

"I see what you mean. But, honest, Eileen, I'm just fine. Of course I'm a little tired right now, and I still don't have a job. But otherwise, I'm okay. Woody is so happy because he has you, and he has two or three jobs to keep him busy."

"He's right, Darlin'. If I didn't have you, I'd look just as miserable as he does."

"You two are impossible. If you don't want to talk to me, you don't have to. What can I fix for lunch? I have a couple of pies in one oven, and bread in the other one."

"We got some chicken noodle soup left from last night, ain't we Hon? That stuff was great, Matt."

"Woody, I don't want to serve leftovers."

"Please, I insist," I said.

We sat together in the sunny kitchen and talked until lunchtime. Not about anything in particular. Woody's work, her work with the hospital, my children. I caught her looking at me a few times as though reading my inner thoughts. I told them about my ride in the mountains, censoring to suit myself. I elaborated on the donkey's antics at the watering place, to Woody's delight and Eileen's amusement.

Nearing the end of our lunch, Eileen asked me straight away, "What are you going to do with yourself now, Matt?"

"Honey! Now you ain't his mother!" Woody scolded.

"It's okay. I'll get back and push the telephone lines again for a few days. I'm thinking I might travel around a bit and talk to some of my business contacts. Maybe see if I can network into something."

She patted my hand. "We're just concerned. We want some good things to happen to you for a change. I'd like to see you more settled and happy."

I could interpret the meaning there. "Settled and happy" meant married and a job. It was okay coming from her. I said my goodbyes and repeated my thanks for her care and the use of his horses, and headed back home.

It was a relief to pull into the basement garage and close the door, out of sight and out of contact with the outside world. I'd stopped at a county collection site on the way home and disposed of the trashed equipment from the bear encounter. The remainder of the equipment had to be cleaned and put away, so I made that my first priority, even before checking messages. The two duffel bags were still in the Explorer. They posed a dilemma both in the short and in the long run, a problem not easily solved. I couldn't walk into the bank and deposit the money.

In the middle of my cleaning and repacking the gear, the front doorbell rang. I turned off the lights in the basement and made my way up the stairs. I could see the shadow of someone at the door as I approached in the slate entry hall. I peered through the peephole. Carol Fenton. I didn't want to talk to her yet about the house, but I couldn't hide and ignore the doorbell. She may have seen me come through town. I assumed a neutral expression and opened the door.

"Hey, you've been a bad boy. You haven't answered my phone messages." She gave me a coy look with the same hint of challenge I had picked up when we met in the mountains. This time, however, she was on my doorstep.

"I just now arrived and haven't checked the machine. I thought you'd still be in the mountains. Please come in." I stepped aside, and indicated the sitting room, but she brushed past me toward the back part of the house, the family room and kitchen. She trailed the fresh scent of a recent shower and expensive cologne. She headed straight through the family room to the refrigerator, as though the kitchen belonged to her, and produced a bottle of Asti Spumante from a bag she carried. She placed it in the refrigerator and turned to face me.

"I thought we could have a glass of wine and get better acquainted," she said. She was dressed in a tailored tan suit, with a bottle green silk blouse. It was open at the neck for the first several buttons, revealing an ancient gold coin suspended between the swell of her breasts. She tossed her blond hair, just like in the Herbal Essence ads, and settled her gaze on me. I probably looked as surprised as I felt.

"You do tend to move right in. I don't know how you knew I just got back to the house, but I haven't had time to think about the listing. So your visit is a little pre—"

"Oh, I don't want to talk about a listing."

"Then what on earth...?"

"Where do you keep your glasses?" As she spoke, she went into the dining room and answered her own question. "Here we are."

She came back to where I stood in the middle of the family room, still gaping at her. She came up to me and put one hand on my chest, dangling the ringing crystal flutes in the other. "I want to talk about what you were doing up in the mountains." She started pushing me firmly toward the couch. Still dazed, I sat.

"What do you mean?" I replied. "I was out riding, just as you and your *husband* were."

She smiled at me as she started back to the kitchen. "You don't have to remind me about my husband. I *do* remember about him. What I want to know is the real reason for your escapade. Nobody rides all the way up there to turn around and ride back in the middle of the night. I've been wracking my brain ever since I saw you sneaking back, and it's driving me crazy." She returned with the bottle. "Here, open this. Whatever you're up to, it sounds exciting. I like excitement." She sat beside me on the couch and leaned toward me.

I didn't know how to react, except to open the bottle, have a drink, then get rid of her as reasonably as I could. The only other choice appeared to be rudeness and a scene, tossing her out on her shapely behind. "You came to the wrong place for excitement. I lead a pretty dull life, and I think your imagination is working overtime."

She clinked her glass against mine. "I don't believe a word of it. Here's to excitement!"

The doorbell rang. Thank God. Potential rescue.

"Get rid of them," She hissed.

I rose, shrugging off her hand on my forearm, and went into the foyer. She remained on the couch. I opened the door to find Mary on my doorstep, with a handful of mail in her hand. What a beautiful sight.

"I wasn't sure when you were coming back, so I picked this up for you. I saw you come home a few minutes ago. I won't bother you, since I see you have company."

"Not at all, Mary, thank you. Please come in. Mrs. Fenton is here to discuss the possibility of listing the house. We were just having a glass of wine. Why don't you join us?"

She started to demur, "Oh, I won't intrude..."

I urgently mouthed the word "please" and tugged at her sleeve, pulling her into the house.

"...Well, maybe I will, if you're sure it's okay," she continued.

We went into the family room and Mary drank in the situation in a single glance. She smiled sweetly at Carol. "Hi, there, I'm Mary from next door. I think we've met before. It's so nice to see you again."

"Yes, yes, hello," Carol replied. "How nice to see you." She gave me a fleeting look that would melt lead.

I retrieved another flute from the dining room and poured Mary a glass of Carol's Spumante. Mary settled comfortably into a leather chair, with all the appearance of spending the evening. Bless her. "You two go right ahead and finish your discussion. Matt and I are old friends, so I'm sure it's okay. I'll just enjoy the drink. Matt, you wouldn't have some chips or nuts, would you? Drinking makes me hungry. In fact, most things make me hungry, right?"

"Well, I'm not sure about that, but I'll get us some." I went into the kitchen and opened a can of cashews and served them into bowls. Carol watched without comment.

Rising, she said, "Well, Mr. Cross, remember what I said. I have to be on my way, but you can be sure I'll get back to you on the subject. I'm a very determined person, as you will see. I'll let myself out. I'm glad I got to see you again, Martha."

"Mary. Me too. Have a very pleasant evening."

As soon as the front door closed, Mary turned to me with eyebrows lifted, eyes in the round. "What was *she* after? Well, I *know* what she was after, I could see that, but what was she *after*? Didn't look like a house listing to me. Not by a long stretch. And of course, you don't have to tell me anything. However, you will admit I saved you from whatever it was. If you really wanted to be rescued, that is." She stopped for a breath.

"I wish I knew. That was the strangest thing I ever saw. Just barged right in. It's a mystery to me."

She drew back and gave me a look. "Mr. Innocent, huh? Like I said, you don't have to tell me anything. But that female had TROUBLE written all over her manicured, perfumed, made-up, well-dressed, tight little bod. Are you gonna' open up, or would you like to talk about the weather?"

"How's Ralph? I haven't seen him for ages."

She snorted. "So that's how it's going to be. I take such good care of you, and when something juicy comes along, you clam up. Oh well, I'm glad you're back." She pinched my cheek as she got up. "I'd better be getting back, or Mother will come looking for me. You're just lucky it was me, who minds my own business, instead of my mother. She wouldn't have let you off the hook." She downed the Spumante and gathered another handful of nuts before heading out of the house.

"Bye, dear," She said in parting.

Now I could worry about Carol Fenton on my own. She had been the one summoned to the tent flap by the donkey that night. She correctly sensed something strange was going on. Adding some sexual aggression—if that's what it was—to the mixture, was something I could do without. It added to the increasingly complex fabric I had started to weave for myself.

My first priority was the money. I could now admit after all of the dancing about with myself that I intended to keep it under my control for the time being. It had insinuated itself into my sense of judgment, tilting my control by its sheer magnitude. I kept reassuring myself I was not making a permanent decision, that I could always change my mind later. I had to do something with it. I could just see the scene if I walked into the bank, heaved the bags up on the counter, made out a deposit slip with lots of zeros, and said, "Please put this in my account, will you?"

I began to think about hiding places. As long as no one knew anything, it didn't matter much—just a safe place out of sight. But if someone became suspicious about anything, and started observing me, then it had to be more secure. Anywhere in this house would be a bad idea. On the other hand, any location outside my direct control posed a different set of problems. It would need to be secure for only a short while until I could decide on a more permanent solution...perhaps turn it over to the proper authorities. Right.

I rose and cleared the glasses and snack dishes. I poured the rest of the Spumante down the sink. Not to my taste...neither the wine nor the woman.

What if I took the bags of money back to my roots in Eastern Ohio? No one connected me with that location anymore, since my parents had been gone for years. There used to be an old barn on the farm my father owned. It stood in a part of the property remote from the rest of the buildings. My elderly uncle owned the farm now, and didn't work the place anymore. I don't think he did anything with his regular farm buildings, much less that old barn. I'd have to think about it.

I finally got to the answering machine, winking its red eye at me from the kitchen counter. Sure enough, Ms. Fenton had left me three cute little messages to call her as soon as I got in. They were mixed in with several hang-ups, a couple of "got-your-resume-but" messages, and one from David. It was too late to call him in Paris until morning. I'd been neglecting him during this past eventful week. I hoped he hadn't heard about the situation at the company, but he did have some friends here in town that might have said something.

There wasn't anything in the mail, either. I decided to finish the cleanup of equipment. Carol Fenton was still a disturbing turn of events, and I had no solution as long as she had a chance to return and find me here. If I decided on the location in Ohio, I'd be disappearing for a couple of days. Fine thing, being a fugitive in your own house.

I went to the basement and finished washing the camping equipment that had escaped the bear, draping it about to dry. All that remained were the two bags of money in the back of the Explorer. I dragged them out one at a time and carried them to a back corner room in the basement, where a long-unused pool table sat, protected with a vinyl cover. There were no windows, as this room was all on the underground side of the basement.

It was time to find out exactly what I had on my hands. I closed the door and turned on the bright light hanging over the center of the table. The strange feeling of being watched came over me again, which was ridiculous considering my surroundings. I went back out of the room and canvassed the rest of the house, turning out all the lights and checking the door locks. Returning to the basement room, I took a deep breath and opened the first bag, dumping its contents in the center of the pool table. The bag gave off a musty odor that took me back to the scene in the mountains.

The pile of plastic bags filled the center of the table. They looked uniform in size and I had already determined how much was in the one bag, now hidden elsewhere in the house. I began to count them and stack them at one end of the table. There were thirty-five of them. My mathematics gave me the stunning answer: *three and a half million dollars!* Could that be right? Yes, it had to be. And I'd opened only one bag. If the other contained the same amount, I was in a room with *seven million in cash!*

My hands were trembling as I hoisted the other bag and fumbled the snap out of the wire tongue. The pile of bags looked just like the other one. I counted them out to the other end of the table. Only thirty-four. Did I miscount? I went through them again. Same answer. Suddenly I remembered the bag I had removed. Things were all symmetrical after all. *Seven million dollars!*

What turn was my life taking? Would Caroline approve? Of course not, but she wasn't here anymore, and how could I know what effect it would have on anyone? I didn't yet know what to do about it myself. It was dragging me inexorably along an uncertain path.

The next morning I felt exhausted, but I forced myself to get up and go in the kitchen to start the coffee maker. Mary and Ralph were heading out to early church, with Millicent in the back seat of the Buick. A steady rain was falling, beading up on the car's waxed finish. As he turned into the street, the drops gathered into rivulets that gushed from the fenders and sent a spray from the tires. Wet leaves were plastered to the sidewalks, driveways, and streets.

Sundays always used to mean church for our family. The children had grown up active in Sunday school and various music programs and youth activities. Much of the time I was absent on some project elsewhere in the world, but I was always grateful they were so well connected to the community. Now it was my responsibility to provide family stability, and I had become the least stable of the three of us. I hadn't been to church since the funeral.

Not from a sense of anger or rebellion. It was just another facet of normal life disappearing.

The night before, I had carefully stacked the plastic bags in a closet in the basement poolroom and thrown the duffels into the washing machine. I couldn't stand the olfactory reminder of where they had come from.

I breakfasted on toasted French bread, a chunk of Romano cheese, and some grapefruit. It was time to see if I could reach David in Paris. He answered after the first ring.

"Hi Dave, it's Dad, finally."

"Hi, Dad! It's great to hear from you. Is everything okay? I talked to Cathy and she said she hadn't spoken to you for several days, although she left a message or two."

"I'm sorry I didn't call sooner, but I've been out and about. I took a hike in the mountains, which took most of last week, so I was out of touch. How are you? Are you having a good time?"

"You were hiking during the week? Did you take some vacation? You probably need to, but you never used to do that."

"David, I don't want you to worry, but the company has collapsed due to poor management. I hesitated to tell you, but we've always been honest with each other, and I didn't want you to hear it from somewhere else." At least until now I've been honest with you.

"What does that mean, Dad? Are you out of work? Do you want me to come home and skip the rest of the course? I don't mind, and—"

"No, not at all. That's precisely the reason I hated to tell you. I think you should go ahead with your plans. Don't worry about me. How are your studies? Tell me about your visit on the Seine. What was the main attraction, the houseboat or the girl?"

He laughed. "Come on, Dad! Actually I like them both. Her brother is in my classes, and that's how it came about. The students are great ones to gather for coffee and talk about how to fix the world. I'm getting pretty good with my French, and I really enjoy these sessions."

"Sounds good to me."

"It's funny to hear how the Europeans are trying to make the common market work, but you get the idea they don't like each other much under the surface. As you've told me, the Parisians are probably the worst for looking down on other societies. They're funny when they talk about the British and try to imitate them. They're jealous of the Americans, but they treat me okay."

"How could they help it, Dave? You're getting more than a financial education, I believe."

"For sure. On the financial subject, I don't know how they'll ever carry it off. In my opinion, monetary value is so entwined with government, taxes, and work ethic and efficiency of the country involved, it seems difficult to have a common currency. But it seems to be working. They have no idea what to do with Italy, for example."

"I haven't kept up, but I'm with you. I always felt the same as you do about common currency, but I admit I don't know everything. When you come back, you can explain it to me."

"Now, Dad, what are your plans? Are you sure you don't want me to come home?"

"I've got some feelers out in several places. No, you hang in there, and I'll stay in touch."

After some small talk, we said goodbye.

Next I dialed the Molinari's number in Milan. He was a business associate from years ago, and we had become personal friends. When they heard Cathy was coming to Italy, they insisted she stay in their vacant servant's quarters.

"*Pronto?*" Giorgio answered with his usual inflection.

"Giorgio, how are you? It's been a while since we spoke. And how is your wonderful wife?"

"Matt-yew! We are both doing famously. Much better these days, now that we have a daughter. Such a lovely girl, your Cathy. She is such a pleasure to us. Betta will wish her to stay forever."

"I'm happy to hear all is well. I'm proud of her also. I think her mother did well with her. She's not giving you any trouble, I take it?"

"Ah! You joke! She has brought laughter and light into our home. We were happy before, but now we are young again. You are a very lucky man, Matt-yew. Unfortunately, she isn't home right now for you to speak with her. She's at the studio this afternoon, even though it is a Sunday. She has a big presentation in her class tomorrow, she says. Each student, in turn, must show what they have learned so far by presenting a design of their own. The theory is that it will not be so good, and they can learn by mistakes. Our Cathy will show them! They will learn from her. You wait and see."

Wasn't too hard to conclude my daughter had some support in her corner. "Thank you so much for caring for her, Giorgio. It's such a comfort for me. May I ask you to give her a message?"

"Of course."

"Just tell her for me I love her, and not to worry about anything. I may be gone for a day or two, so there's no need for her to call back. Give my best to Betta." We rang off, and I felt alone in my empty house. The rain and wind outside continued.

I spent the rest of the day cleaning house. I scrubbed all of the bathrooms, vacuumed the floors, and dusted everything in sight. I mopped the kitchen floor tiles and the entryway. Part of me expected a reappearance of Carol Fenton but it did not happen. Performing these chores gave me the time to let my subconscious reach the decision I had not wanted to face directly. Tomorrow I would drive up into Ohio and hide the money. After that, I would take one step at a time toward my ultimate goal, whatever it turned out to be.

6.
HIDE

I timed my departure the following day to put me at my destination after darkness. It would take most of the day, so I left shortly before noon, my Explorer packed with various options: food, camping gear, warm changes of clothing, tools, lights, and the two duffels. I took Interstate 75 north out of Knoxville to Lexington, where I picked up I-64 east to Charleston, West Virginia. I stayed strictly on the speed limits, risking the occasional ire of truckers and other drivers who found me an impediment. I paid cash from my dwindling supply for my gasoline and kept a low profile, stopping only at impersonal fast food restaurants.

It appeared my timing was right. The sun was setting as I exited I-77 halfway between Marietta, Ohio, and Cambridge. I headed into the setting sun. A heavy dusk soon cloaked the countryside in darkness, and lights were on as I entered the small town of McAdden where I had gone to high school. I skirted the back streets and found the familiar state highway, winding its way toward the rural community where I was born. I had not been back for years now, but the road unwound in the same way it always had, taking me back to a time when my parents were living. I turned off on the gravel road that would take me to my parents' farm, which now belonged to my Uncle Oscar and Aunt Bertha. There was no traffic. The moon was shining brightly now on the rolling wooded hills and meadows. The countryside looked just as it did when I lived here.

After I passed their nearest neighbor, a quarter mile from the farmhouse, I doused the headlights and followed the gravel road with the beam from my parking lights and the illumination of the moon. Just before reaching their farmstead, my former home, I turned down a wooded lane that bordered the farm. It used to lead to two other farms where families lived decades ago, before they left and my father bought the land, adding it to his farm. My destination was an old hay barn on one of these properties, the only building still standing from the early days. My father had rebuilt and enlarged it to hold the hay crop from that end of the farm. I hoped it was still standing and in reasonable repair. It was remote, and now unused, perfect for my objective.

I turned down the lane and memories came flooding back. The sides were overgrown with the summer's weeds, and years of neglect threatened to choke out the lane altogether. The growth brushed both sides of the Explorer as I followed the twin tracks through the woods. Trees and patchy woods lined both sides, and decades of phototropism had tangled the treetops into a canopy over my path so I seemed to be traveling through a narrow moonlit tunnel.

When I was a boy, my father sent me down this dark lane to recover an axe we had left behind when we had finished work for the day. It was a black night and my imagination was over-active as I hurried down the lane, holding my breath to listen for sounds of wild beasts. These same trees were moving in the wind then, looking to me like black claws hanging over my path. I alternately ran, then walked softly, fearing the noise of my running feet would obscure sounds I did not want to hear. At last I had recovered the axe, and feeling comforted by its heft, had made my way back to the house. I remember the gratitude I felt on seeing the bright pool of light from the pole light behind the house. Finally, I reached the porch, then the inside of the house where I assumed a careful nonchalance. "Did you find it?" He'd asked. "No problem," I said.

I bounced down the rutted track, the moonlight flickering on the hood of the Explorer. After nearly a half mile, I stopped and opened a wire gate to enter the barn lot. The barn presented a dark looming shadow, its corrugated roof silvered by the full moon. I drove through the chest high growth of weeds and parked on the side of the barn away from the entrance. The weeds and neglect confirmed my hope that the location was in disuse and likely to remain so. I got out of the vehicle in the chill silence in the moon-shadow of the old structure. Making my way to the entrance, I used a penlight to find the latch to the slatted board gate that served as an entrance.

The barn was a pole-barn, originally open all the way around beneath the eaves, but my father had enclosed the north and west sides to protect from the prevailing weather. Brushing aside cobwebs, I shone my light into the central section where hay was stored. It was half-filled from a harvest of many years before. It looked perfect for my plan, but I decided to wait until morning light for a better chance to conceal the duffel bags.

It took only a few moments to unload the things I would need for the night. I spread a ground cloth on top of the baled hay at the corner farthest from the entrance, away from the moonlight, and unrolled my sleeping bag. It was cold, way below freezing, but the down protected me and I was soon asleep.

I awoke in the pearl gray light of pre-dawn, surprised at first by my surroundings. A heavy coating of frost covered the dried vegetation outside and my breathing produced clouds of condensate in the still air. By the time I could get the duffels inside, the light would be sufficient for my purposes.

I found a rusty pitchfork and carefully peeled the loose hay back from the corner of the barn where I'd slept, revealing the bales underneath. I levered four of them out of the top layer, one row in from the outside wall, and set them aside to be fitted back in place. With difficulty, I pried two more from the layer underneath. The bales were almost identical in size and shape to the duffels that would take their place. I put in the money, then replaced the top bales. There seemed to be no mouse damage. The hay appeared to be all grass, with no seeds to attract them. As a precaution, I had emptied a box of mothballs into each duffel. The top layer of loose hay went back in place, as close as possible to its original position to keep from revealing the brighter inner hay. By then, light seeped into the loft enough for me to put the finishing touches on the arrangement. There were two bales left over, of course, so I loaded them into the Explorer and covered them with a tarp. They would be disposed of on the return trip.

With time to kill before I could show up at Oscar and Bertha's, I got out a little spirit stove and made coffee. With two hours to go, I sipped coffee, munched on breakfast bars and fruit, and read a novel that seemed tame compared to other books I'd read by this same author. Thoughts of the money nearby intruded into the plot, overshadowing any drama from the printed page.

Nine o'clock finally arrived. I made a last inspection of the area, then crept back up the narrow track in the Explorer. When I looked back at it, The Second National Bank of McAdden looked about like it did when I arrived; an old run-down, disused hay barn. The lane looked different in the daylight, but still overgrown and untraveled. It entered the gravel road just out of sight of the house, allowing me to appear without arousing suspicion. I wheeled into their ample yard, a yard I used to mow as one of my regular chores. Their old black shepherd dog roused from the porch to announce my arrival. He came galloping out to meet me with a geriatric gait, having long since retired from active duty just like his master.

Bertha peered through the picture window of the family room with a quizzical expression, then it changed suddenly and she disappeared from view. She came charging out the back door too fast for her eighty years, and rushed up to embrace me as I alighted

"Matthew! It's really you! Land sakes, why didn't you let us know? Why, I look a mess and I haven't got my place all picked up." She brushed back her unruly hair, and smoothed her apron. "My, it's good to see you. I was just tellin' Pap the other day I wondered how you were. How are your kids?"

"We're all very well, thank you, Aunt Bertha. And how are you and Oscar?"

"We do okay. When you get to be our ages, you wake up in the morning and say to yourself, 'how about that? I'm still alive.'"

Oscar was by now making his way out of the house, having taken the time to put on a coat and hat. He moved slowly out the walk, bothered by stiffness and rheumatism from years of work. He was very thin, with sunken abdomen and slightly bowed posture, giving him the profile of an elongated C. Undemonstrative in the old days, he surprised me by giving me a hug.

"It's good to see you, my boy. We don't get out much anymore, and people are usually too busy to come around."

"Well, I'm glad to be here."

"Our kids are scattered all over the world now and we don't see 'em as often as we'd like to. But we can't complain. We got good neighbors...although they have a way of dyin' off," he added.

"Come inside, you two," said Bertha, leading Oscar by the hand.

She plied me with coffee and cookies, and I caught them up on the children. I didn't burden them with my personal trials. They seemed hungry for social contact as much as anything else, and I felt guilty for not having come sooner and more often. Oscar had lost some of his hearing, so most of our speech was at a high volume and spoken slowly. Oscar had always been a listener, and Bertha a talker, and she kept the conversation going for both of them.

"I'm really glad you're here, Matthew, but what brings you back home?

"I had some time off, so I thought it was time I came back to see how you're doing," I lied.

"You must have stopped on the way. If you'd got here a little sooner yesterday evenin', you coulda' stayed. You know you're always welcome here for as long as you like."

"I didn't get an early enough start, so I stopped on the way."

"You will stay tonight, won't you? You can have your old room. In fact, you can have any room you want, including ours, can't he, Oscar?"

Oscar beamed at us without answering, not having caught the inflection of the question.

"I'll stay if you let me take you out to supper tonight. We can go into McAdden and see what's happening there."

"It's a deal," exclaimed Bertha. "We almost never go anywhere so it'll be fun."

I brought my things in from the truck, and we spent the day visiting, much of it reminiscing about the old days of my childhood, and my late parents, who were close to Oscar and Bertha. At the close of the day, Bertha started bustling about and prodding Oscar to get himself ready to go out, stopping just short of dressing him.

I thought about the musty bales. "Do you mind if we take your car? I have a lot of junk in mine."

"Not at all, but you drive," Bertha said.

Oscar climbed into the front seat next to me, the place of honor for the man of the family if he was forced to ride while some other man drove. Bertha sat behind him as we drove into McAdden and we continued a diagonal conversation. Oscar concentrated on the signs along the road leading into town, reading them aloud.

"You won't see much of a change in the town since you left," said Bertha. "Oh, the names change here and there. If a son doesn't come back home and run the family business, then it's sold and changes its name, or it goes broke and stays vacant for a while. There just isn't much to generate business around here. The window plant closed and moved out, and some plastics outfit came in, so it's about equal there."

"Psychic Reader. Palms read. Know your future," said Oscar.

"They've tried to copy the bigger places," she continued. "We have a little shopping center with a Walmart on the outside of town now."

"McAdden Automotive, The Parts Professionals, 121 Hickory Street," said Oscar.

"I suggest we go to Charlene's. It's the only place still around you might recognize, and they're still good and clean. There's lots of fast food places, but the old way is best."

"To reject God is to accept Hell," said Oscar.

I found my way through the familiar streets, little changed, as Bertha had said. A classmate of mine, Christy, Charlene's daughter, now the proprietor, welcomed us inside. She shyly gave me a hug and expressed surprise at seeing me back. We were led to a table, Oscar moving as regally as he could muster, drawing a chair for Bertha. She looked surprised and pleased.

They had considerable affection for each other, but I knew enough to stay out of it when their communications broke down.

He said, "This is genuine French bread!"

"I intend to before I leave," she replied.

"What?" he asked.

Now looking him in the eye, "I said, I *intend to* before I leave!"

"INTEND TO *WHAT*?" he said, now face to face and coloring slightly.

"WHAT DID YOU *SAY*?" also growing exasperated.

"When?"

"Just a *moment* ago. You said, 'Have some French bread'."

"No, I didn't. I said no such thing. I said, 'this is genuine French bread.' But do have some, it's really good and you'll like it," He concluded.

They settled back to finishing their dinner, lost in their own thoughts again, enjoying each other's company. Nearby diners had paused for a moment. Now they also went back to their meals and the buzz of conversation resumed.

Oscar dozed on the ride home, and Bertha was quiet for the most part after thanking me several times for the night out. I settled into my room, looking up at the same ceiling of my youth. It was unchanged, with the same cracks in the plaster, and a small stain in one corner from a leak of decades ago.

Mid-morning found me on I-77 headed south. Without the burden of the money directly in my vehicle, I should have been able to breathe easier. However, I had brushed the lives of more people who were important to me. Whatever came of this, I must keep innocent people from being harmed by it. I could not become a modern-day Typhoid Mary, infecting those I contacted with the dangerous disease that had started to take control of me.

What did I know about depositing large sums of money? Why not call it by its proper name—money laundering? It was constantly in the news the last few years, due to the rise in drug trafficking. I'd paid little attention to it. A few incidents stuck in my mind.

One had occurred several years ago in Puerto Rico. Residents of a small coastal town suddenly went on a spending spree, buying houses, boats, cars, and electronic equipment, paying with wads of cash. Federal investigators, quick to catch on, suspected something unusual, unless fishing had picked up considerably. The FBI found a steel drum containing over a million dollars in cash, and several empty drums nearby. Using clever deduction, they figured where the cash might have come from. They pleaded with the populace to bring in the money, but I couldn't recall the rest of the story—whether the FBI recovered it or not.

I needed to know what the international rules were for making bank deposits…which countries had the least stringent reporting requirements. I believed a way could be found, with some risks, to get cash into a country. I'd have to discover which country and what banks or institutions. The days of the numbered Swiss accounts with no questions asked were over, as far as I knew. Long-term passage of the money through a business operation did not appeal to me. Either I got it over with quickly, or I would do the original right thing—get it to the proper authorities.

As soon as I got home, I would do a quick search on the Internet as a starting point. After that, there were libraries full of information. I would really like to talk to someone familiar with international banking, but that would carry the risk of spreading contact and suspicion even farther. What motivation could I claim for asking such questions? Writing a book? Starting a business? At least I had extensive international business experience, which could lend some credibility.

I arrived home late in the evening, checked my messages, and went to bed. No worthwhile messages. Two disturbing, teasing messages from Carol Fenton were along the lines of her first contacts. What did she know, or think she knew? Why wouldn't she go away?

7.

SEEK

The next morning, after a fitful sleep, I put the coffee on to perk and flipped on the computer power bar. While it went through its beeps and squawks, checking and awakening its electronic brains, I did the same for my organic one with my coffee and breakfast.

A key entry "money laundering" hit on a site called "Alert Global Media, the home page for money laundering information." Could it be this easy? I soon found the answer was no. Their seminars and publications weren't designed to teach me how to launder money. Their focus was more on catching people who did, and safeguarding businesses from running afoul of the burgeoning regulations.

I browsed through the references, then printed out the lists of government agencies around the world having laundering responsibility. There were also lists of pamphlets, forms, bank examiner handbooks, indictments and court documents. Ordering them was out of the question.

I took the time to read through one sample article from *Money Laundering Alert.* It concerned a retired international bank vice-president who had gone into business laundering money for a ten percent commission. Naturally his customers were drug traffickers. There was little detail in the article about how the transactions were made, except for one scheme involving purchase of luxury cars in the United States and selling them overseas, depositing the proceeds into foreign accounts set up in the client's name. An informant gave him away and he was stung setting up a deal for U.S. undercover agents. The amount of the deal was $100,000. Other amounts mentioned were in the $500,000 to $1,000,000 range. Not much that would help me.

I decided to make a trip to the University of Tennessee campus and spend a few hours in their periodical files. I arrived on campus by mid-morning and began an almost endless search for a parking spot, finally successful over near the old World's Fair site.

Wearing a tweed sport coat over jeans and a turtleneck, I walked uphill to the campus in the brisk, clear morning. I had been back through the campus with some frequency for UT sports events and other activities, but had never been a joiner of alumni events, and hadn't entered the functioning school buildings.

The UT library was built some time in the '80s, long after my graduation. As I approached, its cubic architecture gave the impression that a large child had left his building blocks in a jumble when his mother called him for his nap. Before entering, I glanced up The Hill, remembering the traverses up and down long flights of steps to classes.

Inside, the architecture really worked. Large open areas provided views to the open spaces above, full of air and light. The book stacks were more conventional in design, but away from the walls, providing secluded cubicles off to the side for study or whatever.

I attempted to avoid looking lost while I searched out the periodical section. I approached the desk, where a bright-looking Asian girl smiled at me. She tucked her long hair behind her left ear in a practiced motion, and asked, "May I help you?"

"Yes, thanks. I'd like to search back issues of *Business Week*, and perhaps *Wall Street Journal*." I smiled down at her in return.

"Is there any particular subject I can help you with? How far back do you wish to go?"

Just money laundering, my dear. "No, I'm just doing some general research. Why don't we start with *Business Week* the last two or three years."

"Okey-dokey," she said, soon returning with the microfiche books and leading me to a reader station. Activity was light in this area of the library.

The tedium began. Searching for key words in the indices about banking and laundering, eventually I scored a few hits. The first article was not encouraging or informative. The U.S. Customs Service had gone after a Luxembourg bank, BCCI. The new bank was a new fast-growing bank owned by wealthy Persian Gulf investors. Agents charged the bank and nine of its officials with planning to launder $32 million they had traced to cocaine sales by the Usual Suspects. U.S. agents, in cooperation with France and Britain, netted forty suspects and were on the trail of forty more.

The bank, not surprisingly, was growing rapidly and had assets of $20 billion in seventy-three countries. The laundering ring was accused of collecting cash from U.S. drug traffickers and depositing it in the bank's Tampa branch. From there it was transferred to Panama, then presumably back to enrich the original "entrepreneurs." Eventually BCCI had opened other offices in Latin America, the Bahamas, Europe, and the U.S.

I read further, "The money was passed through dummy companies and eventually was converted into certificates of deposit against which loans were made to put the laundered cash back into circulation." The bank had denied the charges of course.

What could I learn from this? Was it necessary to plug into an international conspiracy of some kind? What about dummy companies, considering the stifling regulations and bureaucracy now present in every facet of today's business climate? I could visualize the specter of visits from OSHA, EPA, IRS, EEOC, and other bowls of alphabet soup.

I stood and stretched, then found the next *Business Week* article.

This one was about DEA agents exposing another money-laundering scheme. It began when a banker noticed that a Los Angeles jewelry broker had made cash deposits of $25 million in only three months—a lot of jewelry. In this scheme, jewelry stores took armored car deliveries of drug money from the streets and deposited it in a bank. The bank then wire-transferred it to several other banks. Typically it would go to a New York bank, to the account of a supposed "refining company," thence to banks in Uruguay and the accounts of the drug kingpins. To make it look legitimate, the refining company appeared to sell gold bullion to the jewelry broker and its chain of stores. Not only did they make up invoices to cover all of the flowing cash, but actually painted bars of lead with gold paint and shipped them west to the stores.

The justice department went after the accounts of the fake businesses of course, but also the accounts of the foreign banks, even if they were unknowing of the scheme. The banks had routinely filed currency reports required for $10,000 or more, but the gold business is cash-based. Wire transfers need not be reported, a fact of interest to me.

I couldn't see how this applied to what I wanted. It was set up as a sustaining network intended to function continuously. It was elaborate and complex, and required a large organization.

The next article was entitled "The New, Improved Money Launderers." Scanning this one, I got the impression the underworld had the Feds outnumbered. Many were variations of the previous article. One successful one (until it got caught) was a Miami-based precious metals dealer. It should have caught someone's eye sooner than it did. Many were even by-passing banks, since there are so many shadow systems such as check-cashing outlets, currency-exchange shops (*casas de cambio*), and even Western Union and the U.S. Post Office. One Panamanian-linked ring bought $200 million in money orders in 18 months from scores of New York State post offices, all for amounts of $10,000 or less. Good grief! That's at least 20,000 transactions…but, hey, it's a living.

One of the "importers" brought in cut emeralds from Panama at $975 a carat, twenty times normal price. Another stretched credibility a little farther by bringing in cane sugar from Britain for $1,407 a kilogram, versus the normal price of fifty cents.

As usual, the government's reporting system actually seemed to be helping the launderers. The number of reports filed had started to choke the computers designed to monitor them.

Well, none of this was for me. There had to be a simpler way, a way I couldn't read about because those doing it hadn't been caught. My back ached between the shoulder blades. I was tired of this exercise, though it was interesting.

I decided to go for lunch and sort out my thoughts. I took the microfiche books back to the young lady at the desk. She looked up and smiled, with the same toss of the long hair and the tuck behind the ear. She needed either a change in hairstyles, or a bigger ear on that side.

"Did you find what you wanted, sir?" she asked brightly.

"Some, yes. I'd like to have some lunch, then resume later. Thanks for your help."

"That's what I'm here for." Another head toss, another ear tuck.

I found a student hangout with plank booths, encouraging the carving of initials and slogans of various orientations. Neon beer signs and Tennessee Vols paraphernalia covered the walls, along with the incongruity of '50s memorabilia. I managed to convey my order for a hamburger and a Pete's Wicked Ale, over the din of music.

While the waiter went to turn in the order, my dilemma returned. What was I doing here? Was I like the Gadarine swine, infected with demons, and preparing to plunge myself off a cliff into the sea? I couldn't seem to reach the point of handing the money to the authorities. Not yet. I wanted to find a simple way to turn it into one piece of paper...a bank statement recording a deposit somewhere. That way I could postpone a decision on what to do. I was already in trouble with the authorities for removing it from the crash site. The only way to undo what I had done would be to borrow the stupid donkey again and take it back where it came from, "discover" it anew, reporting it properly this time. That is what I *should* do, then go back to facing my uncertain future. That option did not appeal to me. Not yet.

I finished the burger and beer, occasionally getting glances from the student clientele that said, "What's the old man doing here? Is he a professor? What else could he be?"

Back at the workstation in the library, I delved into the *Wall Street Journal*. There were more articles similar to the ones I had already seen in BW. The Feds wanted everyone to know when they caught someone.

I started searching for foreign bank articles and found an interesting one about an old-line Swiss bank. The bank fired one of their senior officers and accused him of theft; making improper loans that had since failed; receiving kickbacks. They were suing him for his alleged improprieties, claiming damages of over $150 million. He reacted with indignation and started doing something unexpected in a Swiss banker. He started talking. He gave interviews to the press from Switzerland, Italy, and Germany, also the *Wall Street Journal*, of course. He claimed many others knew and approved, and had a lot of action going on their own. He reached the lowest point in his career, he said, when he paid off killers of a famous businessman by handing them a suitcase stuffed with $5 million cash.

The article was tough reading, and I read through it several times trying to decipher the part most interesting to me. I took a short break and asked the young lady to make me a copy for further study.

The interesting part discussed how the bank officials, including the chairman and the fired official, so he alleged, set up front companies to help wealthy people hide assets. Italians were mentioned several times.

Apparently the "client" would transfer assets to a trustee close to the bank, but retain the option to buy them back at a fixed price. Then the assets would be placed in an offshore holding company specifically set up for the purpose, with the trustee raking off a big commission for the service. The accused said the chairman, among others, did this, and would illegally certify he was the true owner of the assets, if asked about the ownership by authorities.

I could see how it would work to hide ownership of the assets, but the scheme didn't tell how they got the assets out of their own countries or businesses to start with. Also, it didn't explain how the so-called assets could be repatriated and used.

I decided I'd had enough for the day, so I took the materials back to the young lady at the desk and left the library. I levered the Explorer into the street and made my way back to the Interstate.

What had I learned from all of this? In the first place, it didn't look possible without some help and cooperation from someone in the banking industry, someone on the inside who could advise and help me. It could take a lifetime to learn enough about a system so complex. In simple terms, if one big deposit could be made in an offshore bank to the account of some nebulous company, then it appeared that wire transfers could move it several times to accounts set up in the various places. In the end, the idea of a trust setup in the final step had some appeal. I seemed to recall reading an article in a foreign airline magazine extolling such arrangements in the isle of Jersey. The gist of the article seemed to be a pitch to treat Jersey as Switzerland used to be treated for offshore banking. I have forgotten most of what it said, but maybe something could be dredged up about it.

I had some contacts in the international banking community because of all the foreign contracts we used to fulfill in Thermoflo. It was our normal practice to work from bank letters of credit to guarantee collection of payments. I'd go through my business card files and think about the possibilities.

Within the hour, I was back in Mountain View. It was undergoing a metamorphosis from its agricultural and lumbering roots to an arts and crafts center for tourists. I drove a narrow, winding path up Main Street, bordered by brick sidewalks and chrysanthemums in half barrels. The barrels used to contain Tennessee whiskey, and the street used to be wide and straight. At least there was enough life in the town to give me hopes about selling my house.

I passed by Binkle's Department Store, the only business standing against the exodus to malls and outlets. The lights were on, and somewhere in there was another potential Mrs. Cross, if Millie had her way.

I stopped at a combination gift and flower shop with a decal on the door of a naked running guy in a winged helmet. I picked out a fresh arrangement of flowers in a wicker basket and a few moments later, I rang Mary's doorbell. I could hear her coming down the hall, then the grate of a key in the lock. Mary flung open the door and gave me a big smile.

"Matt! Come in! Supper'll be ready in an hour or so. You're just in time."

She held out her arms and gave me a quick hug. She had the pleasant aroma of cooking in progress. She had a wooden spoon in one hand, and was wearing a ruffled red-checked apron and had a spot of flour on her nose.

"I can't tonight, Mary, but I thank you. I brought something for the ladies in residence."

As though on cue, Millie appeared in the hall, her gait being slower than Mary's. Both professed their thanks, and regrets I could not stay.

Millie gave me a sly grin, "Been shopping at the department store yet, Matthew?"

"Not yet, Millie. I'll be sure and let you know."

As I left, she turned to make her way back toward the kitchen, shaking her head at my failure. I was headed for a lonesome, miserable old age, for sure.

I decided to go for a run to pump some blood through the recesses of my brain. I'd had plenty of physical exertion in recent days but not enough cardiovascular work. I donned my running togs and set off through the neighborhood. It was hilly, but low in traffic and loose dogs. There were several loops I'd measured. This time I chose two miles to be easy on myself, but I found it hard. Sometimes the body just doesn't want to do it.

Back in the house, I paced the rooms a bit as I cooled down. I really did start to feel better. Running isn't much fun, but the result is worth it. My newly nourished brain began to lay out a list of things to do tomorrow.

I'm sure Mary's dinner would have been several cuts above what I prepared, but I wanted to think, or more properly, scheme, about the future.

I stabbed an unsuspecting potato a few times with a fork and put it in the oven to bake. At the appropriate time, I added a prefabricated Butterball chicken breast. Separately, I microwaved some mixed frozen vegetables.

Downing a couple of Newcastle Brown Ales, I enhanced and reinforced my plans as I ate dinner and drifted into the evening.

Morning came, as it always does, but this time I had slept through the night without awakening. Caroline came to me in a dream, as she has done a few fleeting times since she died. This time she appeared to me out of a grove of trees that lined a park where I sat on a bench. She did not speak to me; she appeared out of a haze that partially obscured the woods. She stood before me in the appearance she had when the children were in their late pre-teens—full of vigor, and the beauty of a woman who has matured to the peak that comes beyond youth and lasts through middle age. She was there only a moment, but she looked into my eyes with a question in her own. She did not voice the question, but I could guess what it was: "Matthew, do you know what you are doing?"

Probably I do not.

8.

CANDY

After breakfast, I attempted the first task on my mental list. I placed a call to Rudi Holenstein in Switzerland. At my nine o'clock, it was three p.m. in St. Gallen where he now lived. He'd spent his career in international banking in Bern, but had retired to the city of his birth. He had been a principal in one of our largest contracts—a multi plant installation in central U.S.S.R. We had discovered common interests, particularly sailing and skiing. He kept a boat on Lake de Neuchatel, and I had crewed for him in a couple of regattas. Caroline and I had also skied with him and his wife Veronika in the Alps for a wonderful week, in times that now seemed of a different age.

It was her voice that answered.

"Veronika, it's Matthew Cross. Do you remember me?"

"Of course, Matthew. Of course. How are you? Much time has passed."

"Pretty well, I suppose—"

"How clumsy of me! In the surprise of your call, I had for a moment forgotten the tragedy of your loss. I hope you are well. And also your children. How are they?"

"They're fine. I'm very proud of them. In fact, they're temporarily Europeans. Cathy is in Milan studying fashion design, and David is in Paris taking a few months' course of study in finance. Maybe he will follow in Rudi's footsteps."

"Good for them! Speaking of Himself, he is not here right now, and I assume you wanted to speak with him."

"Yes, nothing urgent, but I'd like to consult with him on a matter," I replied. To me it was urgent, but I didn't want to alarm him.

"He will be gone through tonight, but will be back at mid-day tomorrow. May I suggest he call you this time tomorrow? Will that be convenient?"

"That would be wonderful, but I can place the call."

She brushed off my suggestion with firm kindness.

Real estate was next on the list. I called John McMillen, an acquaintance in the business who seemed to be successful, judging by the number of listings he advertised. He wasn't in, but they gave me his cell number.

He answered on the first ring.

"John, this is Matthew Cross. Hope I'm not interrupting anything."

"No, no, not at all. How are you?"

"Fine, thanks. I'd like to talk with you about listing the place."

"Sure Matt. I just dropped off some clients and I'm in the car already. Shall I swing by, or would it be rushing you? I can be there in ten minutes."

He soon appeared in a big metallic silver Cadillac. He was dressed in a navy blue suit, crisp white shirt, and yellow tie, and his carefully styled hair matched the color of his car.

I let him in, and we spent the next half-hour agreeing on the terms of a listing. In conclusion I said, "Let me mention one other thing you should know. I bumped into Carol and Tom Fenton and selling came up, but I made no further attempts to engage her in the sale, so she will have no claim I did. I just thought you should know."

He smiled at me with a hint of smugness. "I'm sure that won't be a problem. In a community this size, we're often competing for the same business. I bet she told you things are a bit slow right now, didn't she?"

"How did you know?"

"She always does. It's a little device to get you to place it on the market at a low price. That way, she has a chance to turn it over quickly with less effort. It makes little difference on her commission, but can mean quite a bit to you. Actually, the market for places like yours is good right now. Not the best time of year, of course, but retirees are coming in here in some numbers. I don't think we'll have a problem moving it."

We set up a date for the next contact in three days, and he departed.

My next call went to Jack Regis, my long-term mentor at Thermoflo, who now resided in a condominium in Islamorada, Florida. Jack managed to escape the business world with his retirement and personal wealth intact, since he retired before the split of Thermoflo from Ohio Tool Company. He was loaded with stock options in the parent company, thanks to his success in building the company to its preeminence before the fall. He bought the boat of his dreams, a classic Grand Banks motor yacht, and he kept it in a slip at his condo complex, directly in sight of his patio. He and his wife Alice enjoyed the retirement they had targeted all their lives, visiting their scattered family, playing golf and bridge, and occasionally taking the boat out.

He had always treated me with class and honesty, and had done his best for me. I could tell he felt some guilt over his current status and what had now happened to me. He had offered his boat and his condo to me any time he wasn't using them, and often urged me to visit. So far, circumstances had prevented me from doing so, but now the time had come.

Alice answered the telephone.

"Hi, Alice, my love. It's Matthew. How are you?"

"Matthew! Just wonderful. And how about you and the children?"

"The same. We're doing fine. Sorry we don't talk with you and Jack more often."

"I'd love to talk with you more and catch up on everything in Mountain View, but I know you want Jack. He's on the boat, and has the cordless. I'll beep him. You must get down here if only for a few days, so's we can chat. Hold on and I'll get Jack."

In moments, Jack was on the line. "Matt, my son! How good to hear from you. It seems ages. I hope this means you can come for a visit."

"Actually, I would like to come down, but it might be a few weeks. I have a couple of things to arrange first."

"It would be great to have you. I have to say the timing might be a little unfortunate, since we plan to spend a couple of months in Palm Springs. We're leaving the first of November and staying through Christmas. Can you come before then?"

"I'm not sure, Jack. Maybe I could. As soon as I know, I'll get in touch. Don't change any schedules because of me, because everything is a bit 'iffy' right now."

Perhaps the schedule would be perfect for what I had in mind.

"Matt...I don't want to dredge up bad thoughts, but I want to say again how sorry I am about the company. Those slimy bastards! And to think I actually hired them! Oh, if only I could—"

"Jack, thank you. But please don't torture yourself about it. There's no way you could have known. It will all work out."

"I did hear from a couple of agencies seeking reference information on you. Of course I could sincerely give them a sterling endorsement of anything you have ever done, or will do."

Oh, Jack, if you only knew. "Thank you for that. Nothing much has happened along the job front yet, but I have hopes. The main reason I called...I had another thought. I've put my house up for sale and I'll be traveling a little for the next couple of weeks after I get it ready for showing. I've considered coming down and giving your boat a little exercise some time if the offer is still open."

"Of course! That's a great idea. Why don't you come down and stay as long as you want in our condo while we're gone."

"Are you sure Alice won't mind?"

"Are you kidding? She'd love it. She worries about the place being empty. We'd planned to have a friend come by and check on it once in a while to water the plants, feed the fish, and so on. It would be much better if someone like you actually stayed here; at least part of the time."

"Well, I'll probably take you up on it."

"Great! And you could take the boat out anytime you wanted."

"That's good of you."

"Think nothing of it. Go to the Islands for a few days. Go fishing. Anything you want. I have a young man here who can crew or skipper for you, if you like. He knows the boat, and all about local fishing. I can line him up, once you know your plans." He was growing more enthusiastic by the minute.

"Well, I'd like it much better if we could do it together. It's very kind of you. Let me get my act together and call you."

"Then it's all settled. We'd both hope to see you before then if possible, of course."

We rang off with tentative plans made. My future course of action was starting to shape up, if I could get the most delicate parts of it put together.

I fixed an early sandwich of bacon, lettuce, and tomato, and poured a glass of milk. The weather was holding cool and clear. A squirrel was working the dogwood tree just outside the windows of the breakfast area. With the precision of a machine gun, he would pop a red berry in his mouth and eject the outer hull, eating the seeds. He moved from limb to limb, stripping them clean as he went. It was nice to have company for lunch.

My next call would be more difficult. Perhaps a face-to-face discussion would be better. I handled personal stuff better that way. I got her answering machine, which informed me I had reached Drummond Software. As soon as I identified myself, Candace Drummond picked up the receiver. "I wondered when I would hear from you. I've asked about town; casually, of course. I've been concerned, after what those creeps did."

"They are creeps, all right, as you found out before I did."

"I appreciate what you did for me. It was best I left when I did. I feel regret, however, I didn't get the kind of vengeance I wanted. It's hard to go up against ownership unless you want to invest your whole soul and a lot of money. Instead, I sold out."

"You did change things, Candy. I think you made it a little easier for the women who stayed and continued to work there. At least some of the more obvious harassment, the boys' club atmosphere, went underground."

"I hope so."

"You were worshipped by the rest of the women for bringing McGowan down a bit from his arrogance. While they tried to keep it all under wraps, everyone eventually knew the basics of what happened. Now for the reason I called. Could I come by and see you for a few minutes? There's something I want to discuss with you, and I'd rather not do it over the phone."

"Sure, Matt, I'd be happy to see you. Does timing matter? I mean, could we meet later in the day? I just have some stuff to get out. First thing tomorrow morning's okay, too."

"Why don't we meet for a drink? Casey's at six-thirty okay?"

"That'll be great. Maybe we can give all the gossips something to talk about, right?"

I spent a good part of the afternoon raking leaves, getting them out to the curb for the city vacuum truck to suck them up. Large oak trees dominated the yard in front, with dogwoods in the back. I filled the bird feeders, then went inside and started calling all of the search firms with whom I'd had contact. My return to my other life was not encouraging. We had some pleasant conversations, but the results were all the same. No one wanted me.

I got cleaned up and dressed in sweater and slacks for my rendezvous with Candy. I made it a point to get there ten minutes early. Casey's was the nearest Mountain View had to a pub. They stocked a wide range of imported and domestic beer, served decent food. Dart games were in progress, along with noisy conversation from the clientele, who were yuppies up through middle-age. The bar was off to the left of the entrance, and it served as a gathering place to watch sports events. It had overhead TV monitors in every corner so a game could be followed from anywhere in the room. The dining areas were to the right. I found a booth in a corner away from the door, and watched for her to arrive.

Conversation paused as it always did when she came into the room. It was impossible not to notice her. I knew she was close to five-ten, because when she was in heels, as she was now, we were about the same height. She was a natural blonde-blonde, and her figure was stunning. Women seemed to feel inadequate around her, and most men were reduced to their baser element, with rampant fantasies and foolish behavior. It had been a problem for her all of her life, and here I was, seeking to take advantage of it. She knew I was different, so I thought she might go along with it.

I met her half way across the room and took her hands, aiming a kiss at her cheek. Somehow it wound up on her lips, but it was a chaste kiss of greeting, nevertheless.

"Hi, Candy. Thanks for coming. It's good to see you again." I took her by the hand and led her to the booth.

"Matt, I have to admit to some surprise. I'm 'curiouser and curiouser', as they say. Surely you're not in need of some special computer programs?"

We ordered a Newcastle Brown Ale for me, and a glass of pinot noir for her.

"No, not exactly." I didn't know how to begin. Better to start with what it was not, then lead into what it was. I was aware of all of the glances in our direction, and I knew they were not looking at me. She was dressed in tailored black slacks, a cream-colored turtleneck, and a camel hair jacket. Her most prominent features thrust aside the jacket, and it required some effort not to glance at them. She was perfect for what I had in mind. She had a wide smile, with perfect white teeth, and a sprinkling of freckles across the bridge of her nose. It gave her a fresh and innocent look, to go with an out-going personality men mistook as encouragement, although it wasn't how she was. Doris Day meets Marilyn Monroe.

The wait-person brought our drinks, giving me time to stall. Candy picked up her wine and clinked my glass. "Here's to the good days ahead, whatever they may bring."

Her hands were graceful and long, her nails carefully manicured, with a deep red color enhanced by clear coats of lacquer. Her lip gloss was a matching shade. Tonight she was in her usual form, wearing several rings at the same time, matching them in a coordinated look. She wore a large diamond solitaire on her right hand, flanked by a square gold ring set with diamonds and garnets on her middle finger. On the left hand, she had a large garnet on the middle finger and a pavé diamond ring on her ring finger.

I drank from my glass. "It's business, but a different kind of business. You know we've always been friends and we both want to stay that way. Correct?"

"No. I've always had the hots for you. I thought finally my big chance had come." She looked at me with a deadpan expression, gazing into my eyes. I must have looked startled. She smiled and patted my hand.

"Matt, sweet man, I've always known somehow we would always stay as we are. You were always different. You knew I had a brain as well as, you know, the rest of it. I want to keep you the way you are, because you're such a rarity." A pause. "*However*, if you change your mind..." Then she flashed that smile again.

We ordered another round of drinks, and selected a pizza we could share, a real test of compatibility for any two people.

The noise level rose in the bar, as the television volumes were turned up, and a crowd, mostly men, gathered to follow a game.

I took a deep breath and laid it all out in one shot. "Candy, I expect to go on an expedition in a few weeks to a pretty neat location, and appearances call for me to have a traveling companion. All you'd need to do is just go along, enjoy yourself, and use it as a vacation. You'd have separate quarters, of course, and we could adjust timing to suit your schedule."

"Coming from anyone besides you, this would sound like the most transparent proposition I've ever gotten, and believe me, I'm an expert."

"Upon my honor, you can trust me...you've probably heard that line also. What I have in mind is ensuring certain people are looking mostly at you instead of me. So, yes, I'd be taking advantage of the way you look."

"And how is that?" She asked.

I blushed. Why was I like that around her?

She'd become an expert in all types of lines and approaches men could come up with, but acquiring her wisdom had been long and difficult. She'd told me about herself when she sought my advice that time. Her mother had doted on her beautiful little girl, always dressing her in lavish feminine outfits and placing so much emphasis on appearance that it became a pressure point throughout her adolescence. It conditioned her to seek approval and fall for any line that told her how beautiful she was. The result was a series of three failed marriages, each one lasting a little shorter than the one before. At least the last husband had money, and left a considerable amount of it behind when he started running around and she got rid of him. She had now started her own business, and seemed to be satisfied with herself, but wary of men. The settlement she got from my former company must have helped also. A strategic tape recorder, at my suggestion, had brought that disgusting episode to a satisfactory closure for her.

I enjoyed her company, and liked having her for a friend. At the close of our informal dinner, she told me she trusted me and would help in whatever way she could. As long as it wasn't dangerous or immoral. She didn't say anything about illegal.

The noise level in the bar rose to a crescendo, and one strong voice could be heard above the rest, "Go, baby. Go, go, GO! Oh, yes, yes, yes, YES!"

Candy raised her brows and said, "Well, it's been awhile since I've heard *that*!"

I could think of no reply.

We parted after dinner and drove away in our separate cars in opposite directions, disappointing those who were watching. Except perhaps for those who liked intrigue and conspiracy. They thought we were actually circling about town and would wind up in each other's arms. Well, let them have their fun.

I drove back to my darkened house and went to bed in my silent room. Why was I so different from what I perceived in other men? I couldn't let go of the past and Caroline. Perhaps more time would release me from my memories of her and my conditioned determination to be faithful to her, even though she was gone. When I thought of Candy, or any other woman who knew and respected me as a friend, I felt that I would do injustice to our past relationship if I became just another man in the hunt for what he could get. Maybe I needed counseling. I couldn't see myself doing anything but waiting until it worked itself out. But sometimes I felt terribly lonely.

I awoke to the sound of the wind sighing through the trees. I lay there for a few moments until I heard the patter of rain hitting the guttering. Looking through the top sash, I could see the upper branches of the trees next door swaying. Leaves stripped from the heights made swirls of color past the window, muted by the gray light of early dawn.

I put on the coffee, but decided I needed something more to get me out of the funk I was in since last evening. In spite of the cold, light rain falling, I put on my running gear, with a pair of tights to warm my legs and my Gore-Tex parka hooded over a cap to shed the rain. After I made my coffee last as long as I could, I dragged myself out into the rain and carefully stretched my leg muscles, pushing against the side of the house.

The run worked. I came back with my brain flushed with fresh oxygen and the cobwebs of night eliminated.

I finished my shower and my breakfast toast in time for Rudi's call. The telephone rang at precisely nine o'clock, as I would expect from him. His voice was warm and cordial. It reflected his strength of character and self-confidence.

I could picture his broad, square face, with piercing blue eyes and wide smile showing strong white teeth. He wore round, steel-rimmed glasses, giving him the suggestion of Theodore Roosevelt. The last time I saw him, which was five years ago, his heavy thatch of blond hair, parted on the right side, was laced with gray, giving it the appearance of a metal alloy.

"Rudi. Thanks for your call. I trust you are enjoying your retirement?"

"You are probably teasing me. Like so many who retire, I seem busier now. The old bank wants me to consult again. There are other offers all the time, also. I don't want to seem self-important, but it is nice to be still wanted."

"I'm sure." He didn't know, of course.

"Before, also, I had a secretary who could keep me organized, and I could lay out my plans. Now, is so unstructured, I feel I accomplish little. How is your company? I have not been in touch."

I filled him in on the basics, while he made appropriate noises of disgust. I told him briefly of my search for employment, making it sound better than it was.

"I must apologize for my talk of being needed"

"No problem. What I really need, Rudi, is a lesson in international movement of funds. I'm thinking of doing some consulting, and may need a bit of general advice about which countries are the easiest to deal with."

There was a pause at the other end of the line, while he considered the vague nature of my statement. "I am not sure exactly what you wish, Matthew, but I will be happy to talk with you about the subject. What do you have in mind? Is there some place you would like to meet? Can you come here? You are most welcome to share our home on your visit, if you can do so."

I expressed my desire not to intrude, but considering the state of my current finances, I agreed to do so. We set an approximate date for the following week, with my arrival on Thursday if I could get reservations.

The airlines cooperated when I called the Frequent Flyer reservations number, so I called Rudi back to confirm our date.

I waited until Cathy's speculated bedtime before calling Milan, and I was rewarded to find her there. Elizabetta called her to the phone, after greeting me with her usual kindness.

"Dad, it's so good to finally hear from you. I've been worried about how you're doing, since talking to David. Are you okay?"

"Yes I am, Sweetheart. So, your brother's been talking too much. I told him not to worry you while you're studying. But, I guess it's the natural thing to do."

"You know we share."

"I know. Yes, I'm okay, and I want to see you. I'm going to see an old friend in Switzerland who may help me. Do you think you could stand a visitor in a week or so?"

"Could I! I've been lonesome for you and a little homesick in spite of myself. When would it be? I'll do whatever I must to have some time, and I can't wait to show you what I'm doing. I just love the school."

"It looks like a week from Friday I would drive down from St. Gallen. It's about five hours, so I could get there in the evening."

"Great!"

"I assumed the weekend would be best for you, and I went ahead and booked the flight. I'll leave Linate early on that Monday. I took the chance you'd have a little time. You know I won't interfere with your other plans."

"Interfere! Dad, there is nothing more important than seeing you. Well... there is this one guy I met. Just kidding! I do want to show off what a great Dad I have to some of my friends."

We chatted a bit more, and I could feel her energy over the distance. Because of what I faced in the immediate future, I had to see her again. Being with her always brought a little of Caroline back to me. I needed the comfort and reassurance of that for myself as much as I wanted to support her, living and working so far from home.

I concluded with a short conversation with Georgio, in which he predictably insisted I would stay with them rather than booking a hotel. With the breaking of the connection, I was back in Tennessee, facing the unknown future.

9.

RUDI

I arranged a free business class ticket to Zurich on a combination of U.S. Airways and British Air, using a small fraction of my huge frequent flyer account. My route was from Knoxville to Philadelphia, then to London and Zurich.

Mary drove me to the airport in my Explorer, with Mother settled in the back seat, humming happily to herself and occasionally interjecting a comment totally unrelated to our conversation in the front. As we left my driveway earlier, Millicent asked if we could drop by the Binkle's on the way and get some hand lotion for her.

"I'd like for Matthew to get it for me, if he will. He just might enjoy visiting the department where they sell it," she said.

"Mother, now you behave yourself. We'll get it for you on the way back," Mary scolded.

"But my hands are dry," Millicent whined.

"I'll give you some of mine," Mary replied, ending the subject.

Mary spent most of the trip advising me on getting my rest, not drinking too much, and eating a balanced diet. Millicent held out hope I would be swept away by some exotic foreign lass of style and substance, having given up for the time being on the clerk at Binkle's.

So I wouldn't be leading an entourage through the airport, I managed to get them to drop me at the curb. I made my way to the ticket counter, entering the space reserved for frequent travelers of my standing, and First Class.

As I went through the check-in process at the airline counter, a man and a little boy walked up to the adjacent agent. The man was purchasing a ticket for a flight another day. The boy, about five years old, looked me up and down and returned my smile. He watched with consuming curiosity as the conveyor took away various pieces of luggage. He tugged at his father's trousers, and asked, "What is it doing with those?" His father grunted that they were loading them on the airplanes.

I told him he could watch as it took my suitcase away. He stood by it, watching every move.

"What will happen if it goes to the wrong place?" he asked me. Good question, always in the mind of every traveler, but particularly in mine as I considered options of transporting valuables.

"Then I'll have to wear these same clothes for ten days," I replied.

He looked thoughtful. "What's wrong with that?"

"Well, I'd get all smelly and dirty in that length of time."

"You could wash them."

"But I would have nothing to wear while they were being washed. Even my jammies are in there."

He thought about that. "You could go naked."

"I couldn't do that! People don't want to see you naked in a public place. The police would come and get me and put me in jail. Then I couldn't come home, and my clothes would be stuck in the washing machine."

I pointed out a larger problem. "If you stand too close, the agent might put a tag on you and put you on the plane."

He stepped back a step, then awarded me a big smile to acknowledge the joke. He watched my bag go down the belt, then waved goodbye, and followed his father out of the terminal.

I went through security and directly to the boarding gate, joining my fellow passengers. As usual in modern times, they were in all states of outlandish dress and undress. I boarded first and settled in with a drink and a book, then endured the flight to Philly and a four-hour wait in the *Club Europe* lounge there.

In time, I was over the Atlantic, seated in my favorite spot in the upper deck of the British Airways 747. It has always been my favorite aircraft, with more style and class than any other, with a majesty about it that the other wide-bodies lack.

If I chose this method of transporting a valuable cargo, with it in the hold below, I'd have no trouble playing a businessman off to a conference, or an upper-middle-class man on holiday. That's what I look like. My main concern would be the one expressed by the little boy. In all my years of travel, the only time I had been searched was a time I brought some pearls back from Japan and declared them. The guy thought I got too much of a bargain, and searched me thoroughly before giving up and believing me. Russia in the Iron Curtain days was an exception. Unlikely I'd choose Russia, of course. Still, I felt less in control in the public arena of an airport.

Everyone was eventually settled in, and our private flight attendant handed out menus to begin cabin service. I began with a couple of Fuller's Ales. Then the food started coming: Shrimp salad, filet stuffed with mushrooms, chocolate mousse, Stilton cheese. For wine, I chose a Margaux. I finished with Cointreau and coffee.

A card handed out with the menu urged me to "raid the larder" during the night if I felt peckish. Up until then, I was unaware I had ever felt peckish. Perhaps it was a feeling that would creep over me during the night. I hoped I would recognize it for what it was.

The hours ground on. It was a typical international flight for me. I got up frequently for water, and to stretch. I was restless, unable to sleep since there was no way to stretch out on my side. Sometimes I would reach a dazed state unlike true sleep. More like a state of delirium, with short periods of waking dreams, where my mind would wander out of control. When awake, I would read for a while, then turn off the light and gaze out at the blackness of the North Atlantic. From the cozy pod rushing through the night sky, it was difficult to imagine the enormous tube stretched out below, full of hundreds of people.

All waiting must end, and eventually the sounds of slats and flaps, then landing gear, welcomed us to our approach into Heathrow. I joined the herds of people streaming through the maze of corridors, dividing into smaller streams as signs directed us to our destinations. I took a shuttle bus to another terminal, found the *Club Europe*, and settled for another four-hour wait.

At last, I was able to take the last leg to Zurich, arriving about 3:00 in the afternoon. I walked through customs without pause, then changed a hundred dollars to Euros. After some gawking about, I located the Avis counter and picked up my car. It turned out to be a Fiat out of Italy, so I could avoid the drop charge when I left it in Milan. The hardest part was getting out of the parking garage, but Swiss roads are excellent and the car proved to be nimble in keeping with its modest size. In about an hour, I pulled off the autobahn and into St. Gallen.

The city was arranged along the banks of a river, in a valley hemmed in by steep hillsides. Not exactly mountains, but rugged changes in terrain that gave rise to steep streets around the boundaries away from the city center. The exit from the autobahn passed through a winding tunnel through one of the steep ridges, to enter the city. The Irish Monk, Gallus, must have had to climb over the ridge instead, since he arrived a bit earlier. Or maybe he came floating down the river.

As soon as I could get my bearings, I spotted the ridge and approximate location of Rudi's place on the south hillside, with its overlook of the city and the signature monastery. I managed to get lost briefly in the twisting streets a few times before solving the puzzle and climbing the steep streets to Rudi's house. Getting lost had its advantages, as I found a florist on the way and ordered flowers to be sent to Veronika.

The house was an impressive four-story structure of light tan stucco. Red brick formed the outside of the lower story on the side away from the street, and ran up the corners in decoration. The roof was steeply pitched tile in the custom of Europe. A tall, octagonal tower dominated the northwest corner, overlooking the city. A black, onion-shaped dome terminating in a tall spire topped the tower. The spire pierced a bright gold sphere that reflected the late afternoon rays of the sun. It was skewered up there like a miniature version of the sun it reflected, or like an orange caught on a spit.

I drove my insignificant car through the front gates of the stucco wall and into the cobblestone courtyard. A white-haired man in a black suit rushed out to greet me. I recognized him from my prior visit as half of a couple Rudi and his wife hired to take care of their house and social life. He spoke no English, but bobbed his head in greeting, smiling broadly. He snatched the keys from my hand, and before I could react, he had my suitcase out of the trunk and headed for the front door with me in pursuit.

He rang the doorbell, then opened the massive oak door to reveal the other half of the team bustling toward me down the entry hall. She was also clad in black, with a white apron. She trotted to greet me, clasping her hands in front of her.

"Mr. Cross, so happy to see you again." Then she paused to compose her wrinkled face in a sorrowful expression. "But I'm so sorry to hear about your lovely wife. She was so precious."

I replied with some difficulty. It always affected me to hear sincere expressions from almost-strangers who could not have known her as I did, but still discerned her nature.

"Thank you, Gerta. You are kind to remember her so well."

"Madame and Monsieur said I'm to show you to your room for some rest. They said that if they greet you, you vood insist on wisiting rather than resting, and they vant you to feel well after your long trip." Without pause, she continued her recitation. "Ve vill have dinner at nineteen hundred, and Stefan vill come to show you the way." She trotted down the hall toward a broad flight of stairs that abutted the end of the hall and led to the upper stories.

The entry hall was floored in polished red granite squares. We walked along a rich carpet runner of dark green, featuring a geometric pattern of interlocking vines and leaves. A suit of seventeenth century armor stood guard inside the front door, with gauntlets resting on the pommel of a great two-handed sword with point down, much like a golfer might pose with a Big Bertha driver. Large, dark paintings of medieval battles lined the walls above our heads as we padded silently down the long hall.

I lost track of Stefan while talking with Gerta, and by the time she had shown me to my suite on the floor above, my suitcase was unfolded on a stand at the foot of a large bed. The bed was folded down, a robe and slippers were laid out, and Stefan was nowhere to be seen. For his age, he was pretty fast.

"Madame, will it disturb anyone if I go for some exercise outside before resting?"

"No, of course not. Please do as you wish. Here is a key for the front entrance, so you can come and go while you are here. And I almost forgot, dress for dinner shall be casual, as ve vill serve in the hunting lodge room. I vill go now, and please to ring the bell if you require anything."

Although weary from travel, I decided exercise and fresh air would do me more good than the logy feeling after an inadequate nap. I changed into a warm-up suit and running shoes and made my way downstairs again and out the front door. My car had disappeared into a lower level garage.

I headed down the steep street, aimlessly taking one turn after another until I was temporarily lost in the old section of the city. It was charming and clean and it appeared the shops catered to tourism. The grand old monastery was the major draw. After a short while I headed back upgrade, past a rushing waterfall that disappeared into a narrow sluice under the road. Getting back to Rudi's mansion was tough, and I alternated walking and running up the steep streets until I puffed into the courtyard again.

I had time to cool down and take a leisurely hot shower in the exquisite marble bath. The window in my bedroom had a plush velvet seat below it, and I chose to sit there and gaze out over the city as the sun began to slide below the horizon in the west, lengthening the shadows, plunging the north-south streets into dark relief.

How much should I disclose to Rudi? There was no question in my mind about trusting him. He had built his illustrious career on trust, and I had known him for a long time. My hesitation hinged on my own self-image. Because of my regard for others, I must hope they have the same for me. During this episode, I'd struggled with my opinion of myself and it was not at its highest level. The person I used to know would not have contemplated what possessed me now. Had my positive self-image just been waiting for the right temptation to come along? If I told any of this to Rudi, would he be disappointed in me? Would he refuse to help?

There was a knock at my door at exactly 6:58 p.m. I opened it to find a smiling Stefan, who bowed slightly, and swept his hand across his waist to indicate a direction down the hall. We walked down the wide staircase to the first landing, then down the hall toward the rear of the house to take a second flight to the floor below. Stefan motioned me to the right, and led the way into a warm room with a log fire blazing in a stone fireplace.

Veronika and Rudi were standing before the fireplace, awaiting my arrival. Veronika rushed to greet me. I took her hand and kissed it, bumping my nose on a diamond the size of an acorn, before she clasped me to her velour-covered bosom. We gave each other the traditional European kiss on each cheek. Her smile was tempered with sadness, her emotions linked to our last time together some years before, with Caroline so much a part of me.

"Matthew, we are so glad you are here. Welcome to our home. I hope you are not too tired from your travel."

"Not at all."

"We won't keep you up late, but I want to hear about your family tonight when we can talk of such things. I made Rudi promise to avoid business for tonight. Unless, of course, you wish otherwise."

"No, tonight for old times' sake. Tomorrow, other matters. Thank you for having me, Veronika."

· By now, Rudi had come forward, giving his wife the first chance to speak. He crushed my hand in his firm grip.

"Matthew! Welcome! We are at your disposal. Let me get you a drink. Make yourself comfortable." He motioned to the green leather couch and matching chairs circled in front of the fireplace. He went behind a bar to one side of the fireplace, and ice cubes clinked into glasses. "Single malt, isn't it? Good! Veronika and I will join you. We'll have dinner in a haff-hour, und I think I've found a good Bordeaux in the cellar."

He poured a generous measure into each glass from a bottle of twenty-five-year-old Glenfarclas, then handed a cut crystal glass to Veronika and me.

"Salute! And again, welcome!" He bashed the glass against mine and Veronika's with a ringing crash and we drank to our shared memories of the last time we were together. The smooth amber fluid warmed a path through my breast, and hastened a momentary feeling of contentment against the concerns that clouded my mind earlier.

Veronika and I sat on the couch, with Rudi taking a chair facing us. Gerta bustled in with a bowl of large, perfect cashews and a tray of canapés. Veronika was clad in a green sweater and tweed skirt, Rudi in woolen hunting pants and green turtleneck, fitting the room where we were. It was designed to appear exactly as the inside of a hunting lodge, with sanded plank floor and pine-paneled walls. Trophy heads were mounted on the walls, victims of Rudi's earlier interest in hunting throughout the world. They were arranged by continent, Africa along one wall, Europe another, and my fellow denizens of North America on a third. I wasn't particularly fond of animal head trophies, but they gave the room the right touch. As they stared balefully into the room, they gave the appearance of having charged through the wall. I had the urge to go to the next room and see if their posteriors projected into the other side.

Rudi motioned to me when Stefan brought in wine, "Let our honored guest do the tasting for us."

Stefan removed the foil with a penknife, then inserted the corkscrew, a beautiful antique with the handle made from the polished tusk of a wild boar. I went through the ritual to Rudi's satisfaction, although I could tell the excellence of the wine from its aroma as Stefan decanted it.

As we settled with our drinks, Veronika began as old friends usually do nowadays, especially if I had not seen them for a time. "Tell us about your children. Or maybe they are not really children anymore?"

It was the best way for them to ask about changes in our lives since Caroline's passing, and to express the interest they had in our well-being. They were excellent listeners, and I found myself doing most of the talking. As I neared the bottom of my second glass, Stefan wheeled a cart into the room and Veronika rose to lead us to a round table already set for the three of us.

"Rudi had just gotten in some elk steaks from Montana, and I didn't know if you ate that kind of thing, so we fixed several choices, all with the same theme. We have grilled game hen, and sausage from wild boar, and the elk is also grilled. I hope at least some of it will be suitable."

"Yes, of course," I replied. "I never do anything very exotic anymore."

We managed to avoid all reference to my reason for coming and the downfall of my company, saving those topics for the morning.

They insisted on hearing about David and Cathy through the rest of the meal, only occasionally letting me hear about their lives. When I asked about retirement, they both laughed.

"Yes, ask Rudi about his retirement hobbies." Veronika laughed. "He saves da world from financial disaster, even today." She said it without sarcasm, but with her usual good humor, although I knew she was postponing her plans for travel and relaxation.

Rudi laughed. "Yes, now I go play chess in the park with the other pensioners. And sometimes I go fishing, or we go for long walks in de woods." They both looked at each other and laughed again.

After dessert and cheese, we shared cognac in front of the fireplace, before my drooping eyes caused them to usher me off to my room.

"Matthew, I see you in the morning. Stefan will bring you breakfast at 7:00 in your room. We do not want to be imperfect hosts, but Veronika must leave early on an excursion she had planned. I will be in my office early, which you recall is in the tower at the corner of the house. You only must turn right out of your room, then go to the end of the hall and climb the staircase. I will be there early, and we can continue with more coffee."

"So, Veronika, I will say goodbye to you now. Thank you so much for having me here. It was good to see you and be with you."

She wrapped her arms around me and gave me a kiss on the cheek. "Take care of yourself, Matthew. I am so proud of you and your children. And I thank you for taking Rudi away from his schedule, if only for a little while. Don't be away so long next time."

I was soon in my room, trying to sleep, in some turmoil as to how I would approach the next morning. I reached some peace of mind by deciding I would tell Rudi the whole story and take whatever came of it. In the other parts of my unsettled thoughts about the loss of Caroline, there was some closure added to by seeing more of our mutual friends from the past. It helped facing it with them that she was gone forever, but knowing she was treasured in the hearts of those who remembered her. At last I slept.

Morning came early for me, since I was out of sync with the time zone. I crept down the stairs in my running gear and went for a pre-dawn run down into the town, as I had the day before. It was cold, but refreshing to get my blood up. I finished by stretching again in the courtyard from which my car had disappeared yesterday. Then, back upstairs and into the hot shower. I seated myself on the window seat to watch the pink light of early morning touch the tops of the buildings and begin to work its way downward. As the first touch of gold from the rising sun began to light the twin spires of the cathedral, Stefan knocked at the door with my tray.

"Gude mor-a-ning, sir," he said carefully, with a smile.

"Good morning to you, also, Stefan. Thank you very much." After he had placed the tray, I shook his hand, and he bowed and left me to my breakfast.

A short while later, I walked to the end of the hall and ascended a spiral staircase leading to the upper floor. Rudi had propped open the door to his office, and I walked inside to find him peering at a computer screen covered with a financial spreadsheet. He turned in his massive leather office chair and rose to greet me. "Matthew, good morning. I trust you slept well? And was your breakfast okay?"

"It was great. And I slept well, thank you, considering it was my first night over. What a fantastic office! This looks more like a control room for launching a missile, or something."

The room was finished with white plaster walls above bright wood wainscoting, for the part of the room not taken up by the built-in desk that consumed half of the octagonal room. On the desk were three different computers, and in shelves below, at least two printers. Also there were two facsimile machines, three telephones, and a couple of other gadgets I couldn't immediately identify. Three more sections of the octagon anchored a built-in leather sofa facing a low table and two chairs. The eighth wall contained the door through which I had entered. A silver tray and coffee service sat on the table, waiting for us. Plate glass windows overlooked the city from five of the walls, above the desk and one end of the sofa. The overall feeling was of an eagle's nest, surveying the world from great height. It was wonderful.

"So this is where you relax in retirement. I can see there is not much going on in your life."

Rudi raised his eyebrows, looking over his glasses at me. "You know about the Euro, of course? I can't say I've ever believed common currency would come to reality, but here we are. So. And here I am, and they want my advice. Not only people in banks and businesses, but some in government as well. You know I am not the only one they talk to, but they wish to seek the best path for the future, of course. Who can tell? Certainly no one knows. So far it seems to be working. If it doesn't, the only power in economics in the future is the United States. If they can keep this together, then Europe is on more equal footing."

A FAX machine chirped and whined, spitting paper into a tray. "All I can tell the government people is that we know a currency must be backed with an authority which can guarantee its value, and take steps necessary to adjust to conditions. In the case of a common currency, they all must agree to giving up certain freedoms in the financial area, or it doesn't work. Maybe the guy in the Netherlands who wants to buy a house will have his interest rate affected by financial people from Germany or France. It's a giving up of some sovereignty. Now, they have a fight over who gets to oversee the Central Bank, mostly a fight between France and everyone else. So what is new?" He smiled and shrugged. "They don't have someone who compares to your Mr. Greenspan."

He paused for a moment. "But I'm sure that is not what you came for. It must be something more personal, or perhaps in the realm of business?"

He poured coffee for us, giving me a chance to begin.

"Rudi, I want to tell you I don't know the rules for this sort of thing. I mean, I don't know what limitations are placed on you concerning what you can listen to, or what you can say that is outside the bounds of the legal system—"

He held up his hand, "This sounds serious. But I am a private citizen, not a bank officer, which makes some difference. Of course, anyone can be an accessory if something illegal takes place. I hope that is not the case, but I must say I am intrigued. How about this: No one can say what I heard here except you. The same goes for what I say. If anything gets to a point either is uncomfortable, then we simply stop, and we talk about old times, and part as friends, just as before."

"Thank you, Rudi. I accept those conditions. I only hope you will not think less of me after you hear what I have to say. Not a soul knows what I am about to tell you."

He pursed his lips and stared at me in silence, waiting for my next words.

"I have in my possession a very large amount of unmarked cash. I found it. It is seven million dollars, if I counted correctly. I don't know what to do with it."

Rudi's jaw dropped. *"If you counted correctly?* My word! Are you serious? One doesn't just *find* that much money...did you? Whose is it, or was it? Where does one *find* seven million in cash?"

My words spilled out in a flood. "I certainly did find it. No one can possibly know I found it. I am certain it must belong to the drug world. My first impulse was to turn it in, of course, but the longer I thought about it, the more I began to convince myself I could do that later, or perhaps I could do more good with it than whatever would happen with the authorities. This may sound crazy, but when I try to explain it to myself, it seemed to take possession of me."

Rudi slowly shook his head. "Even I, a banker all my life, can have some appreciation for that. All of my working life I have dealt with large sums of money—huge sums of money sometimes—but always as numbers on paper or on a computer screen. But few of us see actual cash in large amounts."

He stared at me for a moment, turning it over in his mind. *"However,* I can give you advice right at this point. Turn it in. You have already jeopardized your chances of coming out of this in a clean fashion. It even becomes difficult at this point to devise a plan to give it up. Also, what do you think happens to you if *they* find out who took it?"

I had no answer for him, or for myself.

He paused again, still staring at me, "But first, tell me where it came from."

10.

SCHEMES

As I told him the story, it took me back to the cold rain in the mountains, and I thought of the bodies of the two men. A chill went through me, and I vowed to do something when I got back to the States.

I told Rudi about the dilemma of transporting the money, about the antics of the donkey, and about the bear.

"Most people don't realize money is so heavy in large amounts. It is amusing to think of you struggling to carry it all. Money is really inconvenient. As you know, it is anonymous, and can be lost. Also, it is impractical for most transactions of any size. It is why We are all using plastic and electronics. Where, if I may ask, is it now?"

"I stashed it in an old barn on the property of my aunt and uncle in Ohio. It's the farm I grew up on, before my father passed away and it was sold to my uncle. It's in the hay. You're now the only one who knows, in case I don't make it back to the States in one piece."

"Forgive me if I do not recommend the same system to my former bank."

"I didn't know what else to do with it. I didn't want it in my house, and I couldn't think of a better place. It's remote, and the building is no longer used for anything."

"Matthew, my next question: who saw you during all of these maneuvers? Did anyone comment on strange behavior; all this traveling about in the mountains and into Ohio? You know, people are curious; they want to know all of your business if anything strikes them as strange."

I had to admit to a couple of connections that made me uncomfortable. There was Carol, who openly expressed her suspicions. There was the strange man on the trail, although I could see no connection. Of course my friends, Woody, Israel, and Mary knew I was unsettled. There was a pretty good explanation for it, I thought—my company's failure.

He stood up and stretched, and I did the same. I looked out over the city, now bathed in cold sunlight under a clear blue sky.

"There is a bathroom just outside the door on the right, if you like to take a short break before we continue," he offered.

I took the opportunity to collect myself before the next discussion, while

Rudi checked his electronic messages, sending a terse sentence or two in reply via e-mail.

We settled back on the couch, and he began with his usual expression. "So. What do you want to know? I assume your question is the same as what everyone wants. How do I launder money? How do I get it out of the clutches of my government without being taxed to death, and without going to jail? Does that sum it up pretty well?"

"I'd not put it in such clear language to myself, but I suppose you're pretty accurate. I do think I can get it out of the country."

"The problem is not to get it out, but to get it back in so you can spend it how you wish. Getting it out is easy, as I'm sure you can understand. Oh, perhaps you would have some questions. When you think about the subject, governments are interested in two things: controlling crime, and collecting taxes—not necessarily in that order. The overwhelming interest governments have is to collect taxes. They obscure it in other language, and they focus on the drug problem, perhaps with some sincerity, but the main interest is taxes."

He struck the coffee table with his fist. "Money! The lifeblood of all politicians."

I nodded. "It's the same everywhere."

He sipped from his cup. "For a long time, you know, Switzerland was known as the place to hide money from governments, especially those with oppressive taxes. A good example was Italy, where those with wealth would squirrel it away anonymously here or elsewhere, then use it in the future to live a high life without giving a large portion of it to the government. Now, of course, all of those things become more difficult as countries make treaties with each other to prevent this loss of revenue, and of course, hamper the efforts of the drug people."

The telephone rang, but he glared at it, letting the answering machine pick up. He continued. "There are still tax shelter locations around the world, as you probably know. The Channel Islands, The Bahamas, The Cayman Islands, and so forth. There is increasing pressure on them from the big countries, and it might work on the Channel Islands. Or perhaps the Cayman Islands, since they are still a dependent territory of Great Britain. However, there will be a big fight over this, because it is almost the entire economy of some of these places."

He sipped his coffee. I waited for him to continue.

"They openly cooperate where it comes to the source of the funds. You see, it's not money laundering itself that is the crime so much as where the money comes from. The Caymans, for example, make every effort to determine if the funds came from the drug trade, because they don't want to support that industry. But if the money came from business dealings, and the reason it comes to their banks is protection from taxes, then they could not care less. The big countries want the tax havens to start withholding taxes for them from depositors. So. I don't think it will happen."

I pondered my next question. "You mean, then, I can walk into a bank in Nassau and deposit a large amount of cash, as long as I can convince them I did not get it from dealing drugs?" I hoped he would say yes, because it was basically what I had in mind.

"Yes. You can. However, if you think about it, it would not be so easy, eh? What will be your story to this banker?"

"I could think of only two possible explanations. My first choice would be to tell him I won the large sum gambling, and didn't want to declare it and pay taxes on it. My second choice, which is not so good, I think, is to say I sold my company to a foreign investor from the Middle East, who had large sums of currency to dispose of."

"Well, Matthew, both sound a little thin. Perhaps this is where I can help you if you insist on going forward with this insane business. I don't want to insult you, but if I seem severe, it is because I am concerned about you, and what will happen to you. It is hard to keep a secret—how shall we say it—a secret so valuable to someone."

"I know it, and I agree it may be insane. I tell myself I'm at a low point in my life. I have this enormous pile of money and have it under my control. A current has gone through me that might make me irrational. Maybe things will change, but I want to put off any final decision for a while...keep the money under my control. I've not spent any of it."

"I will not lecture you. If you must go on in this way, then I will help you this much, and I will pray for your safety. I know a banker in Nassau, a former associate of mine. I will tell him you wish to make a large cash deposit. Also, you did not acquire it from dealing in drugs, which is the truth. From there you are on your own. I will call him; the rest is up to you."

Rudi got up from the leather couch and went to the built-in desk. He extracted a long card file, picked out a business card from the back, then wrote on a small pad.

"Here is his telephone number, and his FAX number. His name is Gerhard Wurtz. He is with *Suisse Providential*, an affiliate of my former bank. I will call him within the week. Is this suitable?"

"Rudi, of course it is. And I can't thank you enough—helping me although you don't approve. You will be the first to know, I promise, if my sanity returns."

"Well, I just hope nothing happens to you."

"Thanks for caring. I have a minor question. Assuming I take this money to Mr. Wurtz, and he makes the deposit. What do I get as proof I have it?"

"You will get a deposit slip with an account number, just like your bank at home. You can have a company name, whatever you like, for the owner of the account, or you don't even have to do that."

The FAX machine chirped again and began to eject documents. Rudi looked up, momentarily distracted.

"Matthew, the next part. What will you do with the money? After all, it is only useful if spent on something."

"I truly haven't thought that far ahead. If it is in a bank account in my control, what *can* I do with it? Can it be transferred, bit-by-bit, to a U.S. account?

"Not without calling attention to it. It's just like the original question. If you have too much coming in, then it must be explained and taxed. There was a famous family a while back who decided they wanted to spend their foreign accounts without taxation and harassment from the U.S. government, so they simply denounced their U.S. citizenship and went to live in the Islands. Well, this opened up a whole new idea, so others began doing it. Why not? They could be citizens of the world. Just ship out the money, as you are thinking of doing, then become a world citizen, escape U.S. taxes."

He wagged his finger. "Now your government has enacted legislation to take this away. If you denounce citizenship, you must declare foreign assets and pay a one-time tax, like an inheritance tax. If you don't do it, or do not tell the truth, then you can't go home again. Ever."

"Maybe that wouldn't be so bad. Home doesn't hold much for me now."

"Ah. But think of your children. Think of your own future. It is true money isn't everything. You are still a young man. Positive things will happen in time. Once more...you can give up this plan."

"For now, I can't. However, I promise to think about your advice. Now I must let you get to your work, and I must leave for Milan."

"You will stay for lunch?"

"No. Thank you very much, but I want to get there in late afternoon to avoid the darkness."

"Then let me have Gerta pack you some things for the car—some coffee, fruit, cheese, or whatever." He seized the telephone, punched an intercom button, and spoke softly, giving his instructions.

"So. We are finished? Yes?" Not waiting for an answer, he removed his glasses, whisked open a drawer, and sprayed them with cleaner. He polished them with his handkerchief, and smiled at me.

"Yes, you've been a great help to me. Shall we go? I'll go by my room and get my things."

"I'll walk with you to the front. I'm sure your car will be ready."

Everything was gone from the room I'd stayed in. There was no way to tell I'd ever been there. When we reached the front door, Gerta was waiting to open it. She did a semi-curtsey and wished me well.

Stefan was waiting in front with my little car, his face beaming. He had the trunk open so I could be reassured my suitcase was inside, then he closed it with a little bow, and dashed around to open the driver's door. The little guy had beaten me again with the heavy work. On the passenger's seat were a carton and a thermos, thanks to Gerta.

Rudi clasped my hand again and grabbed my shoulder with his left hand. "Godspeed to you, Matthew, and good luck. I will be thinking of you."

"Please remember me to Veronika again, with my thanks." With that, we parted.

I took the autobahn east toward St.Margrethen for a few miles until I could curve southward to follow a route along the east side of Switzerland toward Lugano, near the Italian border. After less than an hour, I could see the heights of the Alps beginning in the distance. The road was dry and the air cold and clear.

I targeted the town of Chur, then St. Bernardino, as Chur was overtaken and began to recede behind me. The highway was four-lane in the beginning, only occasionally narrowing to a stretch of two lanes. The little car acquitted itself well, demanding only that I keep the revolutions high by shifting through the range of gears.

Mountains grew more intense and the highway was reduced to a series of tunnels and partial tunnels, two lanes in width and about as much inside the granite depths as outside. The partial tunnels were carved out of the mountain flanks with one side open, but with an enclosing roof to shed the heavy snow soon to fall.

I passed through multiple tunnels around San Bernardino Pass, which used to require a tortuous passage over the mountain heights. The highway designations and the place names began to show the influence of the language of Italy. *"Ausfahrt"* at the highway exits was replaced by *"Uschita"*.

In due time, the highway went through a long series of valleys that funneled past Lugano and to the Italian border. Como, in Italy, began to show up on the destination signs, followed by Milano as I got nearer the border. I stopped and filled the tank.

The border came up suddenly, with traffic stopped and funneling into only one lane. I braked hard and got into line, crawling forward as directed. The Italian inspectors were stopping a few cars, their trunks open and luggage searched. In my experience in Europe, this was relatively rare, but important to my thinking. I couldn't discern a pattern, as I rolled through without being stopped. I had an Italian car; I could have passed for German, Swiss, American,

British, or a few other nationalities. As usual, when I came into Switzerland on the previous day, nothing was searched. My luggage, or this car, could have been stuffed with contraband, or any amount of money.

I flanked the town of Como, rounding a curve and charging into the tollgates of the *Autostrada*. It was a smooth and rapid drive to Milan.

If you threw a baseball really hard against the windshield of a car, you might get a city map of Milan. Like most centuries-old cities of the European Continent, it grew from humble beginnings; the streets of today followed the goat trails of yesterday.

The major arteries, like the radial threads of a spider web, directed me to the center-city. When I got that far, it was easy for me to circle the magnificent Duomo and make my way nearby to the Molinari's apartment house on *via Senato*.

They lived in an elegant old apartment building only a few blocks from the Duomo, close by the Golden Zone of designer shops. It had an imposing stone fence fronting the street, with ornate wrought iron spikes protecting the top of the fence. The only way in was by entering a complex code at the gate, or calling the residents inside. They had a maid's quarters at the front of their apartment, but no maid since their son married and moved into his own apartment. It was perfect for Cathy and they had insisted she use it, with a persistence that was genuine and without recourse.

I parked across the sidewalk at the entrance to the high masonry wall. When I pressed the buzzer for their apartment and identified myself, I heard an excited, "Dad!" The buzzer sounded and the gate began to open. I drove through the gate and was startled to see the image of Caroline sprint across the courtyard. Cathy was changed from the girl I'd left here.

I barely got the door open and on my feet before she rushed into my arms.

"Oh, Dad, it's so good to see you," she cried, as we held each other. Now I knew why I had come.

"You, too, Sweetheart. I've really missed you. And wow! You look really good!"

"Thanks. You like the changes?"

"Yes, yes!" She'd let her hair grow long and was down to only a couple of earrings in each ear.

'Thought you might. More like Mom, huh?"

"I thought I was seeing her again."

"I hope it's okay?

"Of course it is."

"Elizabetta is inside waiting to see you, and Signor Molinari will be home soon. What about the car?"

"Let's go turn it in at the downtown office, as soon as we get my bag inside."

Elizabetta gave me a warm hug and a kiss on both cheeks. "Matthew, so happy to see you! Georgio comes anytime. I make for you a dinner at home, nothing fancy."

"I look forward to it, as usual."

"Just what you like. I warn you now, you stay as long as you like, but you must leave your daughter here. We may let you have her sometime, but not now."

I chuckled, and Cathy and Betta beamed at each other.

Georgio was there when Cathy and I returned from dropping the car. She navigated the streets for me like she had grown up there. With a mix of feelings, I realized my little girl was not spending *all* of her time in the studio.

Georgio gave me a bear hug when we came in, and welcomed me with his usual enthusiasm. We settled in the living room to talk, while Cathy helped Betta prepare dinner.

We enjoyed glasses of sparkling white wine, and munched on salted nuts, proscuitto spiraled around grissini, and curled shavings of Parmesan.

"Maybe I shouldn't bring up the subject," he said, "but what of your work? Any chance of the company coming back?"

"I don't think so. At least not for some time. Because of the embezzlement of money from the pension fund, the whole mess will be tied up in court for a long time with no benefit, I'm afraid. It's a shame, because it could come back with the right management."

"That is what I thought, Matthew. I, of course, know many people, and it is not beyond reason that investors could be lined up for it. But you are right, I am sure. What a *casino* some fools create."

"I agree. Georgio, while we are alone, may I bring up another subject?"

"Of course, of course."

"This is awkward for me to ask, but there are some business situations I am considering, in which certain parties could be unhappy with me. If there are reverses...what I am trying to say is...is Cathy reasonably safe as she goes about the city?"

He stopped a grissini mid-way to his mouth, and lowered it in slow motion as the wheels turned in his mind. "Are you saying there may be danger created by these business dealings? That is the province of our brothers here to the south."

"I would hope not. Still, I worry about my children when they're so far from me."

"My friend, I will not ask what this is about, but you must only say the word, if you want more protection for her. She need not know anything about it, and she will not, if it is the way you want it."

"I hope I don't need to call on you, but it's a comfort to know I can."

Elizabetta appeared at the door. "Gentlemen, dinner is served. Is it not the way they say in English? *Sì?*"

"Exactly right. And welcome it is, too."

"You two look very serious. Is big business discussion?"

"Right, again."

We moved into the dining room, where Georgio promptly decanted a Barbaresco before we were seated. The "nothing fancy" turned out to be a first course of risotto with Gorgonzola, followed by asparagus with Parmesan, and grilled swordfish. Cathy had prepared the rice and proudly served it to the three of us, then to herself.

The rice was perfect and creamy, with just the right amount of bite. "Look at you," I said. "I never could get it to come out this way. Will you consider giving up the rest of your career and coming to cook for me?"

She smiled at Elizabetta. "I have a very good teacher."

The meal made me wish for more time in Milan, without the tension I'd constructed in my life.

Most of the dinner was devoted to Cathy and her classes, with Georgio and Betta acting like a second set of loving parents. We made plans for her to take me to her classroom the next day, which was Saturday. She had worked hard to have some time off. Her usual schedule included work on the weekends.

After a tray of cheeses, another of fruit, and some coffee, we settled for a short evening before retiring. Georgio urged us to go to Venice on Sunday. He insisted his driver would take us there, to spare us the trouble of parking and traffic.

I'm not sure what I expected to see in Cathy's design studio, but it proved to be entertaining. Classrooms were not much in evidence, the whole studio being one large, labyrinthine working laboratory. Each student had his own cramped working space cluttered with fabric samples, sketches of all degree of detail, and the stuffed animals, cartoons, and objects essential to define personality. Many of the students were there, working, talking, arguing in raucous Italian, and generally having a great time.

Three young men stopped their discussion when they saw us and started chanting, "Cath-ee! Cath-ee! Cath-ee!"

It achieved the desired effect, causing a smile and a healthy blush. She shook her finger at them.

Cath was in her element, and obviously popular with the group, receiving her fair share of teasing, and requests to take sides in the debates. They reserved a polite respect for me as I was introduced around. Cathy showed me her sketches, and led me to a sewing room where some of her creations were on display as works-in-progress on dress forms. Swirls and swatches of bright fabrics were everywhere, as were dramatic student sketches.

Another room had a practice runway where students could model their creations or have them modeled. Cathy confessed she was in demand for that role for many of the other students.

We spent the rest of the day walking about the city, renewing my senses to its familiar old dignity. The weather was misty and gray, typical of the onset of the winter season. We walked all the way around and through the Duomo, with its cavernous majesty. Hushed conversation of tourists and visitors merged with the sound of muffled footfalls to create an echoing hum. Cathy held my hand as we walked.

"I love it here," she whispered. "It is so peaceful, and feels so much like we are in God's presence...somehow connected with the past. I know it doesn't quite fit with the teachings of our church back home, but I come here to think about Mom when I feel lonely, and I light a candle to her memory. Is it okay?"

"Of course it is, Sweetheart. I'm sure she is somewhere watching out for you, and she's proud of you just like I am." I put my arm around her shoulders and held her to me for a brief moment. What did I believe for myself?

We walked the shops of the beautiful old Galleria, ordering lunch at a bar with outside tables. They really weren't outside since they were under the glass roof high overhead.

She must have noticed my long silences.

"Don't be sad," she said, reading my thoughts. "Mom loved you, and she enjoyed your time together. She told me many entire lives are lived without having as much as she had, and she asked me to remind you of that if you started feeling down."

I touched her hand, not speaking. I thought again of Caroline, and found myself staring into space.

We stood together on the ramparts at the top of La Morra, in the cold January air, our arms around each other and our breaths ghosting in the darkness. The night was still and clear, and the valley of vineyards and villages spread in a vast panorama beneath us. Snow covered the ground, reflecting the moonlight, but the valley sparkled with thousands of points of light. They were brighter than the canopy of stars above and gave the illusion of an inversion of the heavens, with the brightness of the universe below and its paler reflection above. We were told that more than a hundred villages were visible from this vantage in northwestern Italy. It was believable.

The brighter glow of Alba lay to the north, and we could pick out the handful of jewels named Barolo almost at our feet to the southeast. Our second course of wine, served with the veal that night, had come from there. The white wine, which Caroline loved, was from the Roero region. I enjoyed playing the guide and pointing it out to her to the north of Alba.

After a time, the cold began to bite through our heavy winter coats. We nestled into the BMW and navigated the narrow, twisting streets down to our small hotel. The magic of the night followed us through our time of love and into the depths of our dreams.

"Dad? Are you okay?"

"Sure, Honey. My mind wandered for a moment. What were we saying?'

"I was reminding you that Mom felt she wasn't short-changed in life."

"I know. I'm a little sad sometimes because she can't be here to see you and Dave, and see you grow into adults. She would have been proud of you, just as I am. You look so much like she did when she was your age that it takes me back to those times. Also this place carries memories that are sad and happy for me at the same time."

She squeezed my hand. "I understand."

"Dad, I don't know how to explain how her sickness affected me. At first, I tried to be brave, and it seemed to work when she was alive. Afterward, I was angry at the whole world. I just didn't care about anything."

"I know. I had many of the same thoughts."

"But you didn't do anything stupid."

I smiled. "At least not anything you knew about. I had to keep up appearances at work, and for you and David."

"David's the one who handled it best. I guess I gave him a hard time, too."

"He's okay. In any event, life moves on and we must also.

"When I zoned out a few moments ago, I was thinking of being with your mother in a special place west of here. It's a steep little mountain topped with a village called *La Morra*. It rises alone in a valley rich in vineyards, and the view from the top is simply beautiful. There's an old castle or villa at the rim of the village that's now a restaurant."

"I think she had a picture of it," Cathy said.

"I believe so. Anyway, there is a legend that speaks about it. They say when God created the earth of water and soil, he had a small ball of dirt left in his hand and didn't know what to do with it. He cast it at the newly created Earth, and it stuck at *La Morra*, creating the mountain. In their minds, it was the last place directly touched by God."

"Dad! Such a beautiful little story."

"There will be many more, if you can get the elders started talking to you about such things. Your mother loved it, too."

After lunch, we drifted along the streets past the Castle, then to the *Piazza Santa Maria delle Grazie* nearby. We were lucky to find the chapel open to display the progress on restoring "The Last Supper."

It was a joy to walk the chilly autumn streets with her by my side and soak up the exuberance of her youth. All the world lay before her and she did not question that the future was bright. In her eyes, the worst had already happened in our lives.

I passed most of the day, playing tourist and enjoying the company of my daughter, before I began to talk of matters more serious.

"Cathy, we talked about my situation with the company."

"Yes, Dad. I didn't want to bring it up, because I didn't want to spoil the visit if things aren't going well. I knew you'd tell me what I need to know."

"Well, things aren't going well in the conventional sense. The old company is not likely to revive in the near term, anyway. I haven't been getting any action from the rest of industry so far, either. It just takes time."

"You know, Dad, I'll do anything, including coming home and getting a job, until things get better."

"I know, Sweet, but that won't be necessary. We'll be okay. I wanted to tell you I'm looking at something else on my own that will occupy my energies for awhile."

"Consulting, or what?"

"Sort of. I may be out of touch for some short periods of time. I've already talked to Georgio and explained it to him. I'm sure you will be safe with them, if I'm out of touch."

"Safe? Do you mean anything dangerous?"

"No, no," I lied. "Nothing like that."

I continued my gradual slide down the slippery slope toward an unknown ending.

As we neared the City Center again, I asked Cathy to leave me behind and go on to the apartment. I needed a few minutes alone for some shopping, since this was my last opportunity before airport duty-free shops. Tomorrow was Sunday, with only tourist shops open, even in Venice.

I walked directly to Fendi's, a short distance from the Molinari's apartment. Making it easy on myself, and making a serious dent in my remaining funds, I picked out five silk scarves for five women, marking the gift wrap to identify my personalized selections for Cathy, Elizabetta, Mary, Millicent, and Candy. The last one was something of an afterthought, but she had agreed to help. I didn't think it would be misinterpreted by anyone. The bill gave my Visa a Euro jolt that was roughly six hundred twenty-five dollars.

I was able to win the battle and take the Molinaris to dinner, a hard-fought endeavor, given their unfailing hospitality and kindness. We went to a nearby favorite, *Bice,* on Borgospesso. It was a short walking distance from their apartment, and the proprietor was an old friend of theirs. For me, dining in any Italian restaurant is more like visiting with family. When there is a long-term connection such as this, it is even more so, a feeling of welcome unmatched anywhere I have been. I had my suspicions that the bill would somehow disappear, and I would be unable to treat my guests, but this time Georgio allowed me to have my way.

Over the years, I've been blessed by the unfailing kindness of my Italian friends. I soon learned to be careful of comments I might make about the life and culture that intrigued me. The smallest admiration for some type of wine or food would result in a case of it being airfreighted to my home the next day. In the old days, when Caroline and I would visit, bearing a house gift, they would also give *us* a gift for coming.

Cathy and Elizabetta were decked out this night in their new scarves. We plotted together Sunday's adventure in Venice. Cathy had not made the trip yet because of her schedule, and we agreed a first visit in the autumn would be good to be able to walk about. In the height of summer it's packed with tourists.

After a warm and wonderful evening, we walked back to apartment in the cool autumn air, and I slept a deep sleep. Cathy had moved out of her room for the two nights of my visit, giving the Old Man some privacy in her "servant's quarters."

A return to Venice was another wrenching memory that tugged at my heart. Caroline loved this spot above all others. Venice had worked its magic for centuries, each visitor connecting their memories and the setting with their emotions at the time.

This time, I saw it again through the enchanted eyes of my daughter. I took her on a gondola ride I could not afford, and I thought about my last visit years ago with her mother. It was the same kind of weather, cold and gray in the autumn. We had huddled under a blanket, swept gracefully along the canals, caressed by the words of an Italian love song sung by the gondolier. With my daughter it was different, the gondolier singing from his own heart in admiration for her beauty.

Perhaps it was here in Venice it happened. With something so gradual, one can never be sure. I know grieving takes different forms in different people, so it must follow getting over it can be different or unexpected. Visiting old haunts again, and sifting through old memories may have made me realize they were truly memories, that they were in the past, impossible to be anything else.

I saw the sparkle in Cathy's eyes and it echoed the same in Caroline's, so many years before, in this same setting. Her attentions were only for me; Cathy's a teasing smile to acknowledge the admiration of the gondolier.

Watching this interplay, I was able to smile to myself and say goodbye. I realized I had been soldiering on, unwilling to admit her absence was not a temporary situation. I faced perhaps decades of future life to live, now complicated by uncertainty.

Too soon, I found myself checking in to a flight out of Milan's Linate airport. Georgio's driver had delivered us for my early morning flight. I had said good-bye to the Molinaris at their apartment. Cathy lingered with me up to the passport check, where we held each other and said our good-byes.

"Dad, you will take care of yourself, won't you?" she said. "I'm concerned about what you said about being out of touch. You will be okay, won't you?"

"Of course, Sweetheart. I won't do anything rash. I'll remember our time together and get everything settled soon. Please don't worry. I hope I haven't disrupted your studies too much."

"No. I'm okay, Dad. Don't you worry about me."

I believed her. She would make her way much better than I.

"Cathy, I've been thinking some since yesterday, and there's something I need to ask you. I'm sorry to wait until the last minute, but I need to know. Is there anything else of your mother's that you want?"

"Well, no, Dad, as far as I know. Why do you ask? I thought we took care of everything a long time ago. You know, the jewelry, clothes and stuff."

"We did, I think. But after you made your choices of keepsakes and things, and her sisters and mother did the same, there's still this closet and some drawers with her things left in them. I've left them like they were without the drive or the inclination to dispose of them. I had no illusions it would change anything, but I just didn't want to do it."

"Oh, Dad," she said, embracing me. "It'll be okay if you give it all to Good Will, or clean it out. We have our memories and our pictures and our keepsakes. Go ahead and do it, or let me, when I come home."

"No, Sweetheart, that won't be necessary. I'll do it now. Bye, Babe."

A last quick hug, and I was through the gate and gone.

I made a short connecting flight over the Alps into Zurich, then boarded the long daylight flight back into Philly and on to Knoxville. I called Mary from Philadelphia, and confirmed that she was able to meet me at the airport. "Mother's all eager to hear about your trip. She gets all worked up about the endless possibilities for you out there in the world. Keep in mind she hasn't given up on the local department store."

"I should be flattered she thinks I'm such a good catch for someone. I'm really not, you know."

"I'm inclined to think more like my mother,   Matt. I'm just not as pushy as she is."

She picked me up on schedule, hovering outside the baggage claim area so she didn't have to park. I gave her the two little tissue packages, pointing out the marking on the back.

She delivered me to my house in the late afternoon. Awaiting me were grocery sacks of newspapers and mail. A quick check revealed mostly junk mail from those who didn't know I was an out-of-work prospect who had little interest in a time-share, the latest platinum credit card, or a new car. There was a letter from my aunt Bertha, an infrequent event, but it could wait for morning.

I ignored the blinking lights on the answering machine and dragged my luggage and myself straight to the bedroom. Unpacking could come tomorrow. A stinging hot shower revived me enough for hunger to drive me back to the other end of the house for a can of tomato soup. Then my next primary urge, sleep, sent me to bed. For the past several years, it seemed, those were the two urges that kept me going, eating and sleeping. If I continued on my present path, perhaps I could add Fear to the mix.

11.
FAREWELL

My sleep was deep and troubled. I awoke in the middle of the night from the depths, my mind confused and my mouth open and dry. My head felt hollow and swollen. I padded to the kitchen in the darkness and gulped deeply from a glass of tap water.

My mind cleared enough to contemplate the blinking light on the answering machine. I pushed the button and the electronic reproductions spewed forth, sounding eerie in the darkness.

"Hi, Matthew Cross. I'm really pissed at you. First you play games that might be fun for me, then you double-cross me with the house listing. What's going on? And where are you hiding now? I heard you were out of the country. More of your games? Hmm? Call me when you get back. I'll find you one way or another."

It wasn't hard to figure out who it was. I decided to continue ignoring Ms. Fenton.

...hang-up.

...another hang-up.

"Hello, Mr. Cross. Mr. McMillen asked me to call and see if you can phone him about the house. He says to tell you he may have a potential buyer." That call had come in on Wednesday, and it was now Monday night.

...a pause of background noise, then, "Crap!" and a slamming receiver. She hadn't decided ahead of time whether to leave a message.

"Hey, Matthew, it's Eileen. How about a call when you have a chance? Catch us up on what's happening?" Always true, Woody and Eileen. The machine said their call had come in on Friday.

Then on Saturday, "Hi, Matt, it's Candy. I don't want to be a bother, but I would like to do a little calendar planning with you, if possible. It's November sixth. You know...about the expedition?"

...another hang-up.

That was all for the present. No looming job offers, no courtesy calls from headhunters or companies I had contacted. It stirred my thoughts enough to make sleeping difficult, after my return from another time zone. The clock on the microwave said 3:23 a.m.

I would have to make some decisions soon and get organized, if my mad schemes were to continue. Plans for tomorrow began to swirl in my head. I went back to bed, tossing and turning until fatigued sleep came again.

When I awakened, a chill wind was blowing, with ragged gray clouds racing across the sky toward the mountains to the east. I donned my sweats and ran my three-mile route before the gathering clouds reached a quorum. It's tough to untangle the muscles and wake up the respiratory system after an ocean crossing. The run was bitter medicine, but the best antidote for the way I felt inside. The gathering storm tried to follow me inside, slamming the storm door behind me with a sudden cold blast.

When I returned, the coffee was made, and I decided my metabolism could handle a big breakfast. I started bacon frying, loaded four eggs into the poacher, and toast into the toaster oven. I gave myself a good grade on everything being done at the same instant. I devoured it hungrily, while wading into the papers Mary had saved.

I skimmed only the headlines, occasionally reading a paragraph or two. Spin and lies out of Washington. Re-vitalization of beautiful downtown Knoxville. Sports scores. Murders, drugs, rapes, and robberies.

In the third issue, I turned to the business page of the Knoxville paper and there was Eileen smiling at me. The caption read, "Mountain View resident Eileen Hendrix accepts post as fund-raising Chairperson for Knoxville Regional Hospital system."

The accompanying article praised her for her years of volunteer service in the Mountain View system. It listed her qualifications. She had a degree in nursing, followed by a Master's in Psychology, all from UT. I vaguely remembered that. No wonder she handled Woody so well. The Little Guy even got mentioned as a pillar of the community and an auxiliary deputy.

The hospital system hoped to hold down medical care costs for patients, the article said, by soliciting assistance from industry and various foundations. Eileen was to establish and coordinate the effort and supervise the paid staff and volunteers. I'd make sure to call and congratulate her.

I cleaned up after breakfast, feeling satisfied and well. Starting on the mail began a slide in the opposite direction. Paying the household bills and the children's credit card statements showed me the precarious state of my finances. When the bills came in from my trip, I would be unable to pay them. I thought again about all of the money hidden away. I couldn't convince myself to make the first incursion into money that wasn't really mine. If the house sold for the right price, it would give me enough perhaps to keep the children where they were for another month or two. After that, something would have to happen—a legitimate job, or something else.

The house was listed at $239,900. The way these things usually went, an interested party might offer around $220,000, and I'd try to settle for over half the difference toward my price. I really needed to get at least two-thirty. Re-financing had raised the pay-off to just under $215,000, and with closing costs and commission, I stood the chance of breaking even. I didn't have anything left in savings or retirement.

Well, I'd have to face the future when I knew what it was. Still working on the coffee, I slit open the letter from Aunt Bertha. She had used a note card with a religious passage. Rather than tuck in an extra sheet, she had covered every surface with her message. Her handwriting, once given to the circles and flourishes of the lost art of penmanship, now revealed her advanced age. You could see her tedious efforts in steering the dull, drooling ballpoint around the twists and turns to create each letter.

Dear Matthew,

I guess youll be surprised seeing you dont get a letter from me to often. I told Oscar you might throw it away not knowing who it was writing. Ha ha. Nobody writes much anymore now that telephones have come along and they dont ring as often as we like.

We were sure glad to see you when you came and we would be happy to see you again soon if you can come. I know your busy. I didnt want to say what was on our minds when you were here because we hadnt decided yet ourselves and we didnt want to go off half cocked. Our kids dont know for sure either.

What it is we sold the farm and we are moving to a small house in town. It just got to be to much to take care of here for two old people. It is operated by the Methodist Church and has regular small houses and apartments and even a hospital if you make it that far. Ha ha. We will take the money from the farm and buy a house which they call a cottage. Most of what you pay you dont get back but then you dont need to. We will still have plenty to do some things and live on and even leave some to the kids we hope.

I wanted to make sure you knew because you grew up here and if you want to take a last walk over the place or anything while we are here you come ahead. You are welcome anytime. I hope you dont feel bad we sold it, not keeping it in the family. The fellow that bought it has lots of money I guess because he never tried to beat us down on the price much and he is going to build a fine house up where the old house place is. You know where the old haybarn is your dad fixed up. You know what a pretty knoll that is with the big maples and all. He may just tear this one down. He seems to be in a hurry so we gave him the O.K. to start on the road back there which we need fixed anyways.

Well I hope you are fine. We are O.K. considering we are old.

Love,
Aunt Bertha

My God! I looked quickly at the date of the letter. It was dated a week before, and probably arrived in the middle of the week I was gone. Trying to remain calm, I reached for the phone. I could picture the old barn crumbling before the blade of a bulldozer, or worse, being set ablaze.

Considering their age and mobility, I let the phone ring about eight times before they picked up. It was Bertha.

"Hello?" She said, softly.

"Hi, Aunt Bertha. It's me, Matt."

"Oh, how are you? I'm talkin' quiet, because Oscar is asleep right here. Probably don't need to. He's out pretty deep. He gets up early just like I do, but then he goes asleep just about anyplace after breakfast."

"I hope we don't disturb him, but I got your letter. For what it's worth, I think your plan is just fine. It really makes a lot of sense for you to get rid of the headaches of keeping up with the farm."

"Thank you. What you think means a lot to us."

"I assure you I have no bad feelings about the farm being sold. Of course it's yours to do as you please, but beyond that, it's part of my past, not my future. I would like to come up again, if it's not a bother during your busy moving time."

"We'd just be tickled to death to have you. We have to get out by the fifteenth. What's today? Tuesday or Wednesday? Wednesday. No, Tuesday. That would make it Friday-week we have to be gone."

"I thought maybe later this week. Would Thursday morning be okay? By the way, how's the new owner coming on the road?"

"He's really tearin' out the bone. You won't recognize the place. Yes, that'd be fine. It doesn't matter much. We're sortin' through things so's we can have a sale after the kids get what they want. We're sortin' out what we want, which is really hard, since we don't have much space. Then they can settle for themselves how they pick out the rest, and we'll sell the left-overs."

"Did you say he was building up there?"

"Yes. Since the deal's all done, he's goin' to start anytime now."

"He hasn't started yet?"

"Like I said, he's building a road."

I still wasn't reassured. "I'll let you go for now, and I'll see you about ten o'clock Thursday morning. I won't be able to stay the night this time, just a short visit, but I promise to come and see you when you're re-settled."

"Thanks for coming up, Matthew. I'll have some coffee ready and some Toll-house cookies you used to like so well when you was a kid."

I'd get up there as soon as I could, stay in a cheap hotel, and make a clandestine trip to the old barn again. Nothing else could be done before then, except keep the fingers crossed. With the travel and tension, the knot between my shoulders never went away. And it was imperative I plan for more travel with more tension. If I picked up the money successfully, I'd need to deliver it to its next destination as soon as it could be arranged.

My immediate "to do" list included calling the real estate company, arranging the contact in Nassau, scheduling the boat with Jack Regis, getting Candy on board, dodging Carol, and congratulating Eileen. I'd have to talk to a travel agent without leaving a trail. It would be best to deal with an agent in Knoxville. Perhaps I could get Candy to do that. And finally, I had to find a way to stabilize my feelings about Caroline; the thoughts that had begun to form in Venice. Would it be possible to reach closure, to turn loose of the past enough to look to the future?

I got out my leather pocket-sized Daytimer. If I could get my Ohio schedule to come off reasonably well, then I could go to Florida the middle of next week, leaving on the thirteenth of November. It would take me at least two days driving. Maybe I should leave on Tuesday. I could have Candy come down on Friday, travel by boat over the weekend, and make the deposit on "Monday-week," as Bertha would say. I had calls to make, and it was important to make them in the proper order.

I put through the call to the Bahamas. An actual person answered the telephone. With some of the Islands in her voice, she asked how she might help me.

"This is Matthew Cross. Will you connect me with Mr. Wurtz?"

"Will he know the nature of your call, Mr. Cross?"

"Yes, I believe so. Please mention Mr. Hohlenstein will have called about me."

"Yes, sir. Just a moment."

My palms were sweating as I waited.

"Hello, this is Wurtz. Mr. Cross?

"Yes, it is. How are you? I hope Mr. Hohlenstein has called?"

"He did, last Friday, I believe. I must say it was a rather unusual call. If it had come from anyone else, I do not think we vould be talking at this moment. One cannot be too careful in these times."

"Fair enough."

"I must be blunt. While I haff my own concerns, I owe Mr. Hohlenstein a great deal, and I vill discuss whatever it is you wish to do. Not for you, but for Mr. Hohlenstein. If your plans conform to the description passed along to me, then we can proceed."

"I wish to make a deposit, and would like to do so in a little over a week from today. Is that possible?"

"Under the conditions discussed, yes. What specific day did you have in mind? And how vill you arrive?"

"I would like to plan on the seventeenth of November. And I'll be arriving by boat."

There was a pause at the other end of the line. "Yes. I vill be here. And why am I not surprised by the method of transportation? Call me when you arrive, or if your plans change. You have my office number, but here is my mobile phone number." He read the number to me and I copied it in my Daytimer. "Good day." He rang off without waiting for my reply.

It was not a friendly exchange, but it was behind me. Now, the rest of the scheduling could be done.

Jack Regis was next. I was fortunate to find him in the condo, having a late breakfast.

"Jack, I'm ready to take you up on your offer to use the boat for a few days. Is it still open?"

"Of course it is, Matt. I only regret we're leaving this Friday. Can you get here before then?"

"Gee, I'm afraid I can't. I'd love to, but I just can't make it before about a week after that."

"Well, it's okay this time. But the price of using the boat is you have to promise to come for a visit when we return in the spring."

"It's a deal. If it won't put too many hours on the engines, I thought of running over to Nassau, maybe fishing in the Stream a little on the way over and back. Did you say you had someone I could hire to skipper for me?"

"It sounds like a great plan. Maybe I'll send Alice on her way and go with you. We could hit the gambling spots on Paradise Island and have a great time....Just kidding! I know my duty."

The "just kidding" took my heart out of my throat and put it back where it belonged.

"Yes, I have a great young man who looks after the boat, and he'd love to take care of it for you. He's an expert at fishing, also. Tell you what, I'll mail you a key to the condo, along with directions on how to get here, plus contact information on the young man. His name is Stephen Connelly. I'll call him and have him on the lookout for your call. Do you have any idea about your schedule yet? I suppose you do, if I remember your propensity for planning."

"Yes. I'm thinking of arriving about a week from Thursday, and departing for Nassau on Saturday morning, if it fits with his plans. I'd guess we'd spend the best part of two days going over, a couple of days there, then a couple coming back. And Jack, I really appreciate it. It's very kind of you."

"Glad to do it. Glad to do it. Remember the deal, now. A real visit here in the spring."

"I promise. And Jack, will you include suggested compensation for Stephen in your note? And give my best to Alice, will you? I hope you two have a great winter. Of course, I'll call about the voyage."

We rang off. Everything so far was falling into place, unless I found the barn either a pile of ashes, or gone completely.

"Candy, it's Matthew. Mind if I come by for a few moments in a little bit. I got your message."

"Sure, Matt. I'll be here all day."

By now, the sound of the wind had abated to a lower key, and a cold rain was falling. I walked into the living room to look out the front windows at the weather. This type formal room was going out of style, yielding to Great Rooms for informal entertaining. It was Caroline's pride and joy, a room that reflected her good taste. My contribution was a large oil portrait of her I had commissioned on a visit we'd made to New York. I sat on the couch and looked across at it. She gazed back from the picture, her clear blue eyes sparkling, a serene smile on her face. In the portrait, she was wearing a blue silk gown with narrow straps, displaying the pearls I had given her.

I thought of the day I first saw her in the alumni office at the University of Tennessee. I had graduated from UT with a degree in mechanical engineering. It was natural for me to look for employment in this part of the country when my Army tour was over.

There were plenty of possibilities available through the alumni placement office, once I got the network going. The best possibility turned out to be the dark-haired girl assigned to help me with computer searches of the listings, and the preparation of my resume.

We began to see a lot of each other while I worked the telephone and waited for responses. Her co-workers began teasing her in my presence about her "devotion to duty" and "going the extra mile to help a poor jobless soul." Caroline and I discussed all of the career choices and every other thought that touched us. We settled on each other and a job for me at the same time.

Now I looked at her portrait and spoke aloud. "Caroline, I will never forget you. And I will never have another life like we had together. I'm doing something now you would not approve of. I don't approve of it either, but I don't care as much anymore. Something has changed. I have to go ahead, wherever the future takes me. I'll try my best for Cathy and David, to protect them from harm. But I must try to leave the past in the past."

I drove through the light rain to a section of town with large, older homes, the streets lined with stately trees. This was the neighborhood that housed the wealthier elements when it was constructed, and had been re-vitalized now to do the same thing. The doctors, lawyers, and business owners who were doing reasonably well had migrated back here.

Candy lived in a three-story Victorian, painted yellow with white trim. A porch enclosed the front and one side. She had acquired it in the last divorce settlement, and had established her software business in her home. She said there were complaints about it, but she chose to ignore them. It wasn't a business that had drop-by customers. I suspected any complaints had more to do with how she looked and how she came to be there.

She answered my ring, with a smile. "Hi, Matt. Come in out of the weather. What a dreary-looking day out there!"

I gave her my coat, standing on the entry rug to drip while she hung it in the hall closet. She was wearing a bulky yellow turtleneck, the color of her house, and black slacks. She was beautifully groomed, as usual.

"Come into the kitchen and I'll serve us some coffee."

I perched on a stool at a counter topped with blue ceramic tiles, and set with place mats and cloth napkins. Two places were set with bone china cups decorated with tiny flowers and rimmed in gold, and sterling which looked much more elegant than the stainless I used.

She poured coffee for us, and joined me on the other stool, flashing her smile. "Well, you're back from your journey. Did you get to see your children?"

"Just one of them. I went to Milan to see Cathy on my way back. Which reminds me." I reached to the inside pocket of my jacket, and brought out the slender parcel. "Here's a little something for you."

"Oh, a present! I love presents. Can I open it now?"

"Of course." She was like a little girl for a moment, as she removed the tissue.

"Fendi's! Hey, I'm impressed. You really are a man of the world. Thank you Matt. I'm touched. People don't give me presents anymore."

"Don't mention it. Now to the schedule you mentioned on the phone. I think it's beginning to take shape. Can you fly to Miami a week from Friday? I'm thinking we'd need to be gone until about the following Wednesday, but we could make it a week if you wanted."

"Don't you think it's time you told me something about where we're going?"

"Oh, yes. I'm sorry, but I wasn't sure myself until after the trip I took. Now, it's set up. I don't want to make too much of this, but you can't talk about this to anyone."

"I can keep a secret. And better than that, who would I tell?"

"We're going to Nassau. I'll pick you up at the Miami airport, then we'll drive to Islamorada and stay at Jack Regis's place. I've borrowed his boat, and we'll cruise over in it. How does that sound?"

"Well, okay, I guess. More than a little mysterious, but it should be fun. Is Jack going?"

"No, he and Alice are heading out to California for a couple of months. It will just be the two of us, plus the guy Jack recommended to skipper the boat."

She fixed me with her big, blue-eyed gaze. "And whatever it is you're taking with you, or bringing back. I don't think I want to know…"

She looked away, then continued. "What do I need to take with me? I mean, what's the plan? I've been to Nassau a couple of times. The last time was a few years ago, with my second husband. What a jerk! But that's something I'd rather not think about." She looked into space, obviously thinking about it.

"I'll arrange hotel rooms. I'd think whatever people usually do there. Do a little sight-seeing? Hit the casinos and restaurants? Whatever you'd like. I'll cover the expenses, of course."

"Will you be with me, or will I be alone and unescorted?"

"I'll be available most of the time. Just a little business that I hope to wrap up on the first morning. Then we can stay a couple more days and head back, if all goes well."

"You said you wanted people to look at me. You know they already do quite a bit. But when, specifically, do you want them to?"

"It may not even happen, I mean, need to happen for me. But if we get inspected by the Coast Guard, or Customs when we dock, then the more distracted they are, the better I like it."

She wrinkled her nose and punched me on the shoulder. "You're sneaky. And a chauvinist, I might add. This is sounding like fun."

"Uh…Candy? Do you have anything sort of…well, sort of…"

"Sexy? Revealing? Matt, you're blushing again. Honey, you don't have to tell this girl what to wear. Why, you ought to see what I have stashed away. Your blush is getting r-e-e-d-d-e-r!"

"I wish you wouldn't do that, Candy."

"Just calm down, Sweetie. We'll quit talking like this…But I can't wait to see your reaction with the real thing!"

I, too, wondered what my reaction would be. And she was right. I planned to be devious.

"We have to settle on your travel arrangements, also. Is it okay if I set it up for you? Can you leave early in the morning a week from Friday?"

"You bet your ass I can! Oh, excuse me; you bet I can!"

"I'll have them mail you the tickets." I decided to handle it myself to preclude the issue of handling the payment.

I left for the real estate office. They did, indeed, have a prospect and had shown the house once. I made a date to show it again the following Saturday afternoon, after my return from Ohio. John McMillan told me an offer could be possible.

The cemetery covered the top of a small hill near the center of town. It had been there since the town was founded, so it was dominated by beautiful old maples, now bare of leaves. I entered through the impressive stone gate, which connected on each side to the wrought iron fence. Narrow paved lanes circled the slopes like contour lines on a relief map, connected occasionally by spokes.

The older markers in the center, on top of the hill, were elaborate testimonials to the wealth and power of those buried beneath them, when their wealth and power could be measured by temporal standards. Citizens of lower standing, in the old section, lay under more modest markers, some homemade of local stone. Nevertheless, wealthy or poor, dramatic stories of a harsher time were etched in the dates and epitaphs.

The newer graves were in the outer rings, farther down the slopes. I made my way around to the eastern slope, down to the third ring, and parked the Explorer. I had not been here for some months. In my current quest for closure, it seemed the thing to do. The weather was still as it had been since breakfast; blowing rain, cold, gray, and disagreeable.

I sat in the car, thinking about that day, much like this one, when the hillside was covered with family and mourners, some crowded under the canopy, others under umbrellas, or hats and coats. Her mother and her sisters wanted her buried back "home" in Kentucky, where she would be close to her extended family, but Caroline had left definite written instructions. Mountain View was her home. She had written that she loved her original family dearly, and appreciated her childhood, but saying her life began when we were married and raised our family here.

Wet leaves had blown into the shelter along the lee side of the red granite stone. I got out of the car and rummaged in the rear compartment for a plastic bag. I tidied up the leaves and the debris from faded flowers. They, too, would never come back to glow with the life and beauty they once had.

Her call reached me late at night in my hotel room in Birmingham, England.

"Hi, I hope I didn't wake you, love," she'd said.

"It's okay. I'm happy to hear your voice. Are you all right? Are the kids—?"

"They're fine. I'm the one who needs you. I hate to jump right into this, but there's no one else for me to talk to about it, and I'm scared."

My brain cleared immediately from its fog of sleep. I remembered her annual physical had been scheduled. A cold knot developed in my inner being. "What is it, Sweetheart?"

Her voice had changed from its brave beginning, and there was a tremor. "They found a lump I had missed, and on the X-ray, a spot. They'll do a biopsy tomorrow. Matt, maybe I shouldn't be, but I'm scared to death!"

I'd tried to reassure her, trying to calm my own fear. I took the first plane home, and over the next few months we all struggled on until the sad conclusion.

I stood before the headstone and read the words I had read so many times. The polished surfaces glistened with the rain, bringing out the inscriptions in sharp contrast. She was forty-five years, ten months, and three days old when she died. Shorter by decades compared to what her life should have been. The epitaph said simply, "Our Beloved."

She was, but she is gone forever.

12.

WITHDRAWAL

I returned to the house before lunch and called Eileen at her office, where I knew she usually worked half-days. Her new assignment might create changes.

Her pleasant voice answered.

"Eileen? It's Matt. I just got back from a trip and saw your picture in the paper. Congratulations."

"Thanks, Matt. Some say sympathy is in order, because it'll be a lot of work. I don't want to neglect poor Woody too much. He does great away from home, but he needs me to take care of him when he comes in. He urged me to take it, though, because of the need. He thinks I'll be good at it."

"I know you will."

"I'm not so sure. I haven't done much in high places, and they're expecting a lot of presentations and contacts with big companies, and so forth."

"You can do it. I take it you'll have some staff and an office in Knoxville?"

"Right. I can kind of set my own hours, but I expect it to be pretty much full time and more. You know it's a paying position, so I won't want to slight it."

"Well, maybe I'll come and see you when you get established."

"Please do. You can give me some pointers on how to handle top-level executives."

"Yeah, right. Just don't pattern it after my last episode and you'll do fine."

My visit to the cemetery reminded me of the two decaying bodies in the plane, still unburied. It was my responsibility to report them and get it taken care of, but I kept putting it off. Someone out there probably cared about them or at least wondered where they were, and had endured months of uncertainty. I decided to procrastinate until the mission to Nassau was behind me. Then there would be less chance of exposure, I thought, since the evidence would all be gone. I would still need to think of a way to do it anonymously.

I spent most of the afternoon boxing up Caroline's remaining possessions. I kept her wedding dress, carefully preserved at the time. Cathy might wear it some day. Also the blue silk dress from the portrait and the slender linen dress she wore on our going-away after the wedding ceremony. I don't know why we do these things; I just couldn't throw them away yet. A few pieces of her better jewelry I had saved for Cathy were already in a safe-deposit box. The remaining costume jewelry and the cases for all of it also went into the boxes. After removing the last remaining coats out of the hall closet, I took the lot to the Good Will outlet. I tried not to think of the symbolism of turning my back on her memory. My memories were as alive as before, and not all of the pain had departed.

I was able to get a good rate out of the travel agent for Candy's flight to Miami. She would travel on Delta, leaving Knoxville at 8:02 a.m., change planes in Atlanta, and arrive before noon. Since it was over a Saturday, the pain to my credit card was not too great. The return was a week later, leaving shortly after noon, so I would have time to deliver her to the airport from Islamorada. Either we would be successful by then, or my life would have taken a decidedly different turn. The tickets would be mailed directly to Candy, and I called to let her know to watch for them. The travel agent also read off a list of hotels in Nassau. I booked two singles for the Sunday through Wednesday. I assumed Stephen would stay with the boat.

I spent the rest of the afternoon going through the house, straightening closets and cleaning, to get ready for a good impression on Saturday. The yard also needed work. The oak trees in front clung to some of their leaves all winter, dribbling them in a constant stream. Even though it was still raining, I managed to get the soggy leaves bagged and put beside the curb for pickup. Afterward, it was time to prepare for my expedition back to the barn in Ohio to make a withdrawal.

I started stowing things in the Explorer as I thought of them. Considering what the Weather Channel had to say, I put in my foul weather gear and boots from my sailing days, a tarp, and a toolbox, shovel, and mattock. A front had come roaring in to the area and stalled, spreading out over the Eastern States, parallel to the Appalachians. It left a thinning wedge of cold air in place, with warm, moist air continuing to slide in over the top. It looked like rain for the next several days.

Considering what life would be like for the foreseeable future, I cancelled my newspaper subscription. I also went by the post office and rented a post office box, discontinuing delivery to my house. I'd buy papers when I wanted them. I called Mary to tell her I had taken away that chore.

"Well, how'm I supposed to keep track of you and spy on your business if I don't get the mail?" She demanded.

"Maybe a phone tap? It won't excite you much, either, I'm afraid."

"We'll just have to make do with gossip, I guess. You will call when you're in, won't you? Mother wants to be the first to know when you get involved with someone, you know. I think she may be losing hope where her candidate's concerned. I still keep my papers for re-cycling, so you can always read them if you want to. Just let me know. I hope you're okay, and something falls your way."

"Thanks, Mary. And I'll keep in touch. Give my best to Millicent and Ralph."

I awoke at my usual time the next morning, six a.m. It was still raining steadily. Although I couldn't work up much enthusiasm for it, I put on my rainproof running clothes and ran my usual neighborhood route in the semi-darkness. As I ran, I thought about the state of my affairs. I couldn't see how I could finance my trip to Nassau, meet my coming credit card bills, and keep up routine expenses. No matter how much I hoped, I had to face the fact that the house deal, if it went through, would not be anything but a wash. The decision was an obvious one. I still had a hundred thousand in cash upstairs. It belonged to me...now. I'd use it as I saw fit until the rest was stashed safely in a bank, with my future further clarified. I would have to be careful; try to keep it low-key and inconspicuous. I rationalized it as "expense money" to protect the principle sum.

The telephone was ringing when I came in.

"Hello. Remember me? Poor me, the one you've been dodging for so long?"

"Look, I haven't been dodging anyone. I've been busy, as you might appreciate, since the company folded. Just what is it you want from me?"

"We don't want to name them all over the telephone. First, it was business, the house listing, but I am ready to concede and let bygones be you-know-what. But you're still holding out on me."

"No, you're wrong."

"You have to appreciate it isn't easy to live in a small, nothing town like this one for someone who has the dreams I have. I think you have the power to change all that. I like your heavy breathing."

"I've been running. No, I do not have the power to change your life. Further, I'm not inclined to want to do anything, even if I could. Now, please don't bother me anymore. I'm not interested."

"Well, screw you! Wait until I discover what you were up to. Then you'll do as I say. You'll be sorry!" She slammed down the phone.

My hands were shaking as I replaced the receiver. What did she suspect? I know my nocturnal movements were a bit strange, but what was she thinking? She was dangerous.

I was showered and on the road by 7:30, picking up a McDonald's steak biscuit and a large coffee on the way out of town. As I drove through the steady rain, I stewed over what to do with the money, if it was still there, after I got it to the boat. I saw two options: Take his boat apart somewhere and try to really hide it, or put it someplace obvious, covered up, of course. The more I thought, the more it made sense to just go for the gold—put it on the boat and let what happened, happen. The way quality yachts were put together, it would take some time and a really professional job to conceal dismantling some of the insulation or the joinery. And time and prying eyes would be a disadvantage at his condo complex. I'd just have to wait and see, look the boat over when I got there.

I'd reached the juncture of I-81 and I-40, and got squeezed between a speeding 18-wheeler in the left lane, and one coming in from I-40 East. Both of them showered me with spray, and gave no quarter. I talked to myself about the importance of calming down and completing my mission.

I pulled into McAdden in the late afternoon, still in unceasing rain, and started looking for a cheap motel. On the outskirts, if a town this size can have outskirts, I spotted the "Sleep-Inn." It had a neon sign that said "VACANCY," preceded by a neon "NO," which I suspected had seen little use. It was a one-story white frame structure. I pulled into the overhang next to the office and went inside.

There was no one behind the desk, but a bell to summon a desk clerk. I heard a television set, tuned to a game show, making noise in a room behind the desk. I dinged the bell. A young girl, either Pakistani or Indian, came out of the back room.

She smiled, "Yes?"

"Do you have a room available?" An unnecessary question.

"Yes, of course. For how many nights, Sir?" she asked.

"Only one. What are your rates?"

"For only one person? Thirty-eight dollars, plus tax."

"Okay. I'll take it." I pulled out a hundred-dollar bill, the first of sixty-nine thousand, nine hundred ninety-nine others awaiting my disposition. She took it and made change without realizing the significance to me of that small piece of green paper.

The room was just what I expected: park in front and walk in, window unit heating, sagging bed. The towels were small and thin, one per customer. The room had a chemical odor from disinfectant spray and was reasonably clean. It was what I needed for this night, nothing fancy, but a place to stay anonymously in my hometown.

I walked across the street to a quick shop and bought potato chips and a six-pack of beer. I had decided on the way up to make my visit to the old barn after eleven o'clock at night, after most farm families were no longer stirring. I had about three hours to kill. I went back to the room, cracked a beer, and ordered pizza to be delivered, then turned on the television set. No cable, so no continuous news programs. I turned it back off, and got out my book to read.

After the pizza, and the slow roll of numbers on the digital clock, eleven arrived and I prepared for my expedition. It was still raining continuously, so I donned my foul weather suit, bibs and jacket, over my flannel shirt and jeans. Adding rubber boots, I was ready to go. I bore little resemblance to a cat burglar. The foulies were bright yellow with navy trim, and had Scotchlight tape in several places to make me highly visible in case I went overboard, which I didn't expect to happen on this voyage. What the hell…who'd be out there shining a light on me?

Twenty minutes later, I turned off the highway onto the road leading to the farm. In a few minutes more, I arrived at what used to be a familiar entrance to the lane. I had to use headlights because of the blackness of the night, and they revealed a new, wide entrance to a straight road now denuded of the overhanging trees that had choked out the moonlight on my last expedition. I dropped the lights to park, and contemplated the glistening mud. No choice but to go for it. I put the Explorer in low range and four-wheel drive, and turned into the fresh earthwork. Too bad he had not yet finished with gravel or paving, whatever the plan. I could immediately feel the Explorer crawling, the tires turning faster than my progress, and mud began to rattle into the wheel wells.

In the dim glow of the parking lights, I could follow the middle of the muddy track, but could not see far ahead. I increased my speed and momentum to decrease my chances of becoming bogged down in the clinging mud. I knew the road had one low spot in about a quarter mile, and I was now going downhill toward it. Flowing water loomed ahead, and I just had time to come to a skidding stop. What to do? I could try to find a way around it on foot, but it left a considerable distance to carry the money…if it was still there. Also, I could not turn the Explorer around in this spot and would have to back all the way out on this slimy surface.

I eased into reverse and crawled backward up the ruts I had made, the backup lights providing dim illumination. After about fifty yards, I put it in forward gear again, and built speed all the way to the water, hitting it at about fifteen miles per hour. Mud and water came over the top of the hood and completely obscured the windshield, but I stayed with it, reduced to a spinning crawl, the engine racing. Gradually, the wipers cleared the worst of it, and traction increased. I made it through to the other side and up the track to relatively firm ground with the increased elevation near the barn.

The barn was still standing. However, the weeds and surroundings had been scraped clean of weeds and brush. A bulldozer and a lowboy trailer were parked nearby. Had anyone disturbed my deposit? With my heart in my throat, I parked the Explorer. I would soon know whether I had financed the purchase of the farm by the "fellow with lots of money." I struggled back into my foul weather jacket, got my light, and went in through the board gate. The hay was still there. Climbing up on top of the stack, I could see everything looked as it had when I left.

I found the rusty fork, peeled back the top layer of loose hay, and levered out the four bales. The duffels were still there, undisturbed. I wasted no time in getting them out and examining them. With trembling hands, I unlatched the snaps, and peered inside with the flashlight. All looked in order and smelled of mothballs. No mouse damage. The money might need airing out before I could take it on the boat. I put the bales back in place as best I could, but two were missing. Maybe no one would notice.

The Explorer was a ball of mud, completely covered and dripping, the wheel wells full. I managed to get the back window open and stowed the duffels under the tarp, then closed up and left. Going back up the road was a replay. It actually seemed to work better, following the previous ruts. Hitting the water again, and wondering whether I'd get through, was a tense moment, but I made it. Having to explain getting stuck down here was something I didn't want to think about.

Increased speed on the gravel road, then the blacktop, created a din of slinging mud. By now it was midnight, but I'd have to do something about the muddy vehicle. I'd spotted a do-it-yourself car wash on the way through town before, and pulled into one of the stalls on the way back. As I was fishing money out of my jeans, inside the bibs, a police car pulled into the lot and parked across the stall.

Two cops got out, the driver remaining on the other side of the car. The one on my side made a production out of sticking a big nightstick in a loop on his belt.

"Kinda late to be washing a car, ain't it, neighbor?"

I decided on a good old boy routine. "You got that right, buddy! Man, you don't even want to hear about it! Just look at this thang! I got lost on this detour and thought I'd never find my way out. Jesus Christ! This rain! Took me two extra hours to get here."

"Well, we just wanted to make sure everything's okay. All right?"

"Yeah. It's okay now. Have a good night."

He nodded at his partner, pulled the big, black stick out of his belt, and got back in the car. "Take it easy."

They couldn't see it was an out-of-state plate. They'd just been curious and bored. I spent four dollars on pressure washing, and finally got all the mud out from under the chassis and off the rest of the vehicle.

I slept soundly for what was left of the night. In the morning, it was still raining. I shaved and showered, drying myself on the cheesecloth towel. It took but a few moments to throw my gear into an athletic bag and stow my three pieces of luggage in the back of the Explorer. The room now had an odor of mothballs blending with the cleaning disinfectant odor. I collected the Beretta from the nightstand and put it back in the little side pocket in the driver's door.

When I stopped at the office, the same television was going in the back room. It sounded like the same program. I left the key on the desk and departed, heading for Charlene's. I took a stool at the counter, and was gratified to see no one I knew. Christy apparently emphasized the midday and evening, and was not in. I bought a *USA Today*, and killed an hour over my bacon and eggs, reading their spun and condensed version of the news.

The drive to Oscar and Bertha's was for the last time, another farewell to a past life. I met a new, four-wheel-drive Dodge pickup about half way along the gravel road to their place. Since it was raining, Bertha did not come charging out the door, but I could see her waiting just inside the picture window.

She rushed forward and reached up to give me a hug, as usual, and I could see tears in her eyes.

"You know, Matthew, seeing you brings back memories even more than seeing my own children. I think about you here as a little boy, with your parents still alive and well, and everything seeming so settled and simple then."

"I guess it was."

"Now we're all stirred up about the move, and it seems like we're just having to leave the past behind, like we're breaking a connection."

"I know what you mean, Aunt Bertha. I'm trying to do the same thing myself."

Oscar appeared and shook my hand. "I got somethin' funny to tell you, soon as you get settled! Come on over here to the kitchen table and let Bertha pour you some coffee first."

I did as he suggested. She set out a plate of fresh cookies.

Oscar was obviously amused, and more animated than usual, speaking loudly over his hearing deficiency.

"The fella' that bought the place was just here. You may 'a met him on the road. Big shiny red pickup. Well, anyways, he come out to check on his new road, with all the rain. It seems somebody was here and drove all the way down it, leavin' big ruts all the way. He was afraid to try to go down there in his own truck, and walked all the way in the rain and mud. But here's the good part. You know what was missin'?"

He leaned forward, wanting me to guess.

"I don't have the slightest idea, I'm afraid"

He dragged out the suspense as long as he could. "Some dang fool drives all the way in there in the rain and mud, and steals two bales of old hay! Can you beat it? Can you imagine havin' a coupla' cows that hungry?" He slapped his thigh, and laughed loudly.

I obliged him by doing the same.

"He's had more fun out of this than anything's happened in a long time," said Bertha.

"How did he know? Had he counted the bales?"

Oscar cackled again. "That's exactly what I asked him! Naw, he said he'd been in there lookin' around, and it looked different. He could see a couple was missin'."

"That's really a good one, somebody going to all that trouble. He can count himself lucky if it's all he ever loses. I hope his road isn't too damaged."

"No," Oscar replied. "He learned something from this rain. He'll have to put a culvert, or at least a tin whistle, down at the bottom of the hill. I told him so, but people have to see for theirselves. Then he has to bring in a grader and do the whole thing before he gravels and black-tops it. In fact, the county says they'll black-top our whole road...or his, I should say. He must have more pull than we had, which weren't much."

We visited the rest of the morning, and I could tell they had come to terms with the move. They seemed to be excited with it. Their family had helped them pare down their belongings, and were supporting their decision. It made me feel better. I simply must not forget them.

Aunt Bertha fixed chicken noodle soup for lunch. When we were finished, I said good-bye to both of them. Oscar gave me a hug, and Aunt Bertha shed a few tears again, as did I. Then I left behind my past life in this house.

The rain eased and finally quit somewhere between Johnson City and Morristown, Tennessee, just in time for the gathering darkness. I'd been eating cookies most of the afternoon, so I drove without stopping until I pulled into my driveway near bedtime. Mission accomplished.

The next morning, I went by the post office to check my new box for mail. Jack Regis had mailed me a key and map to the condo, and suggestions on compensation for Stephen. The rest was junk mail. I drove on to Candy's, without calling first.

She answered the doorbell clad in black leotards over leopard-patterned tights. Her creamy skin was glowing with little beads of sweat on her upper lip and forehead. Her hair was pulled back, with damp tendrils framing her face. "Hey, do you know it's not fair to show up at a girl's door without calling first? You caught me on the Stairmaster, Master."

"You couldn't look any better than you do right now. I did you a favor… and me."

"What a silver tongue. Come in. You saved me from the mechanical monster. Are the plans still cookin'? I got my tickets."

We drifted back into the kitchen. "Yep. All okay so far. I have to show the house tomorrow, then I'm heading down on Monday or Tuesday. It'll take a couple of days to get there, driving."

"Why don't you fly down, too? It's a long way to drive."

"Uh…I have some stuff to deliver for Jack," I mumbled. "I wanted to drop by and give you some information, and this."

I handed her an envelope. "Here's some walking-around money for after you get there. I thought I should give it to you now, so you could handle it however you wanted. You know, put it in the bank…use your credit cards…or whatever. I told you I'd cover the expenses. You may want to gamble a little, or something. If you need more after we're there, just let me know."

I had dipped into the hundred grand, and put three thousand into the envelope. I didn't know what a lady's needs would be. I'd have to play it by ear.

"Well, Matt, thanks. I'm sure you're taking good care of me. It's the way you are." She had donned a warm-up suit by now, and mopped her brow with a towel.

I laid out the rest of the information. Jack's condo telephone number, the name and number of the hotel in Nassau, and even Stephen's telephone number.

"I'll call you each night on the way, to see if everything's still on schedule for you, and I'll pick you up at the airport on Friday, a week from today. At your arrival gate if I get there in time, or at the carousel where you pick up your luggage. Okay?"

She flashed her beautiful smile. "This is going to be fun! You know, I haven't had a real get-away-from-it-all for a long time. And I'm looking forward to getting to know you better, too. I used to see you as this serious, big-time manager at work, but I know you're also a really nice man."

I'm not really as nice as I should be. "Thanks, Candy. I'm expecting to have a good time, too."

After leaving Candy's, I drove to the main post office in Knoxville and bought a $5,000 money order, made out to me. The clerk treated it like the sale of a postage stamp. On the way back through Mountain View, I deposited it in my bank account, in anticipation of the bills coming after I returned from next week's trip. No questions there, either.

My next stop was Wal-Mart's, where I selected two large athletic duffel bags, measuring by eye.

When I got home, I placed a call to Stephen Connelly's number, but got his machine. I introduced myself and told him of my plans, asking him to call if he had any problems with it. I promised to call again over the weekend to go over more details of the trip.

There wasn't much left to be done before the voyage. I had the appointment to show the house tomorrow, so more attention to detail was needed to make it show its best side. It had been our home for a long time, and memories bounced off everything in it. Depending on how the showing went, I could leave earlier than planned for Florida. No point in hanging around here. Jack's condo was already empty.

I repacked the money into new zip-lock plastic bags, then the athletic bags, and it fit perfectly, with room to put something on top. I put the foul weather suit, now dry, into one of them. In the other, I put in a large beach towel, with mask, snorkel, and flippers on top. All of the old plastic bags, and the weathered army duffels, went into the back of the Explorer for disposal in a dumpster somewhere on the way south.

Next, I prepared for the trip to Nassau by laying out everything I'd need on the bed in the guestroom. Most resort areas are casual, but I laid out a summer weight navy blazer, with slacks, dress shirts, and silk ties. I thought the bank might be more formal, and Candy would deserve a night out if all went well. The rest was easy.

I had also been stewing over another question. Would I take weapons along? I finally came to the conclusion I'd take the Beretta in the car on the way down, and have it around for protection around the condo and boat before departure. Not that I thought anything could possibly be suspected...I just didn't want some hoodlum or mugger to have a fortunate accidental acquisition at my expense. On the boat, however, or against any authorities, there was no way I would risk any confrontation.

I got up early on Saturday morning and mixed a batch of French bread, so it could be rising while I went running and made breakfast. The "lookers" were coming at ten, and they say a house that smells good, sells.

John McMillan drove them up in his silver Caddy right on schedule. Bread was baking, and coffee was perking. They looked to be in their upper thirties, good looking and well dressed in casual clothes. Yuppies.

John introduced them as Brad and Missy something. They flashed perfect smiles.

"What's that wonderful aroma?" said Missy.

"I have bread in the oven," I replied.

"Oh, do you have a machine?"

"No," I replied. "I do it the old fashioned way."

She looked puzzled, but didn't pursue the matter further.

"I'll wait in the kitchen, unless you'd prefer otherwise. Let me know if I can help with anything. Please have some coffee, if you'd like, either before or after."

"That'll be great. We'll look at the house first." Brad replied.

An hour or so later, they came into the kitchen, and I served them coffee and fresh, crusty bread. I set out butter and strawberry jam.

"We like the house," Brad began. "What's the least you'd take for it?"

I would never go first in a negotiation. It's the number one principle. "I put quite a bit of thought into it, and think I have it priced fairly. Of course, different buyers have different needs, and I've just started to show the house. I'll wait and see if buyers agree with me."

Brad blinked. "It seems to me it would save a lot of time if you would just tell us what your least agreeable price is, then we could see if it's okay with us."

John McMillan decided to advise them. "Let me suggest you and Missy talk it over. Then perhaps we can put together an offer to Mr. Cross."

I said, "John, I don't want to put any time pressure on this. You may take all the time you wish. But I plan to be out of town for a couple of weeks starting either tomorrow or Monday."

"Okay. We'll talk it over this afternoon, and at least let you know about the anticipated schedule, so you can make your plans."

They expressed their thanks and left. I took a loaf of bread next door for Mary, then sliced and froze the rest.

McMillan called me later in the day. They would have an offer in my hands at nine o'clock Monday morning, if I could wait that long. I told him it would work. I'd consider it on my trip, and get back to him.

13.
KEYS

By nine o'clock Monday morning, the Explorer was parked outbound in the lower drive, loaded and locked. I'd talked to Stephen Connelley on Sunday, and he was expecting me.

John McMillen called right on time "They really liked the place. They're offering two-fifteen, and I have an earnest money check for five thousand to back up the offer."

For almost seven million reasons, I was beginning to feel less pressured to negotiate. "John, I appreciate your efforts, but I don't consider it a serious enough offer to bother with a counter. Let's allow them to reconsider while I'm out of town. I'll call you when I return."

"Well, maybe I can talk with them again today."

"I really can't hang around any longer. Thanks again, but I really have to be going. Good day."

I was free to hit the road. I made a quick call to Candy, and told her I was leaving, promising to see her on Friday.

The computer planner gave me two choices; down through Chattanooga, Atlanta, and the west side of Florida; or through Asheville, the Carolinas, and the east side, by Jacksonville, Florida. I chose the latter, picking up Interstate 40 through the Smokies toward Asheville. Skies were clear after the stalled front had finally moved out of the area.

My route east on Interstate 40 began in the rolling hills, but soon plunged into the mountains. Some fall color remained, with gold and red, and dark evergreen, as counterpoints to the darkening approach to winter. This colorful scene lay before the backdrop of a towering, dark mountain with a lace coating of frost on its peak. Stands of tall poplar displayed light gray parallel trunks, pin-striping the lower reaches of the mountain flanks. The route took me past Waterville, on the North Carolina line at the mouth of Big Creek where it entered the Pigeon River. Up at the headwaters of that mountain creek lay the wreckage of the plane, where this whole thing began.

I-40 was chiseled directly through the mountains, clinging to the walls of the Pigeon River Gorge, passing through tunnels in some of them. It was subject to rockslides in the winter, and had been closed on some occasions. This time all was clear, with the only hazards being the other drivers.

At Asheville, I picked up Interstate 26 toward South Carolina. I followed it all the way to the Low Country near Charleston, before picking up I-95 to Miami.

I drove carefully, obeying all speed limits and watching out for other traffic. In this circumstance, a traffic accident, even of small magnitude, could be a major problem. Caribbean weather represented another major gamble. It was still in late hurricane season, and a major tropical storm had swept through the islands only a week before. I hoped a window of good weather would continue long enough for my purposes.

I began to think of a stopping point for the night. Somewhere in the vicinity of Jacksonville, Florida, seemed workable. No point in over-doing it the first day, since only a moderate distance would remain after Jacksonville.

I went cruising past all of the exits to Savannah, grinding on into the evening as signs began to indicate Jacksonville was coming up. Jacksonville soon appeared on my left, the lights of the city beginning to come on. In a few more minutes, I traversed the Trout River Bridge and the Fuller-Warren Bridge and left Jacksonville behind. I had never visited that city, but always thought it looked interesting, with all of the access to water. I'd landed at Navy Jacksonville during my Army days, making an approach in from the Atlantic, and found the view attractive. Lots of homes were on the miles of waterways, with luxury pools and landscaping.

About twenty miles farther south, I picked an exit with a Hampton Inn for my stop. I wanted the perceived security of staying on an upper floor, rather than one of those drive-up-to-the-door types. I got my key, then drove to a McDonald's for drive-through service, so I wouldn't have to leave the Explorer parked in the gathering darkness with what it contained.

Back at the hotel, I found a luggage cart and took everything up in one trip, while the Explorer sat under the drive-up canopy. I'd leave the room unattended long enough to re-park it.

Before going to sleep, I gave Candy a quick call to let her know where I was, in case anything came up with her plans. Then oblivion took over until I awoke at my usual six o'clock. Reversing the order of the night before, I was packed and driving through McDonalds for a breakfast biscuit by six forty-five.

Florida's East Coast attractions were gradually reeled in by my steady progress southward. Some of them triggered memories of my past business and family life. Caroline and I had brought the children here in various stages of their growing up—St. Augustine, Orlando and Disney World, The Kennedy Space Center. How long ago, and of a different era, some of those visits seemed now. In business, I managed to attend several sales meetings and conferences at some of the nicer resorts: The Boca Country Club, Mission Inn, The Breakers.

If all worked out, and I decided to use some of the money for myself, I could do anything I wanted. Retrace all of the good times. Buy a sailboat, and visit the coastal attractions by sea. Why not?

Early afternoon brought me to the end of I-95. I cruised through Miami's heavy traffic and picked up US-1 for the final forty or fifty miles to Islamorada. The signs to Key Largo triggered another memory of better times. Caroline and I had spent our first real vacation away from the children there, when David and Cathy were old enough to be left in someone else's care. We'd had a wonderful time sailing and snorkeling the marine sanctuary.

I arrived in Islamorada about four o'clock and had no trouble finding the condo complex on the east side of the Island. It was a gated facility, and the guard had my name on his list, with a parking pass prepared for my stay. He pointed me in the right direction and I soon pulled into the driveway belonging to Jack and Alice. The condo was two-story white stucco with red tile roof, in a Spanish style popular in Florida's resort areas. The complex was professionally landscaped, with razor cut St. Augustine grass, and pine-needled islands of tropical shrubs. Palm trees towered over the layout in strategic locations.

Balmy summer-like air greeted me. The sun was halfway down the palm trunks on the other side of the street. I was weary from the trip, eager to relax inside the condo, eager to reconnoiter the boat and dock area.

The front door was painted bright red-orange, and opened onto a Spanish tile entryway. I headed straight for the security panel and deactivated the alarm system, punching in the code Jack had sent me.

The condo was spacious and well decorated, as expected. Walls and carpeting were white, as far as I could see from the entrance. Alice had added vivid fabrics on the furniture and large abstract paintings on the walls. In the kitchen dining area, she'd placed a large round glass table on a bamboo base, with colorfully upholstered bamboo chairs. There was a note lying on the table addressed to me, along with a ring of keys with float attached.

Matthew,

Welcome to Islamorada! Treat the house as your own, and consume anything you want from the pantry, the bar, or whatever. The guestroom is the first one on the left at the head of the stairs, but you don't even have to use that one. Sleep in a different one every night! Live it up! We hope you have a good time, and remember your promise to come back when we're home.

Love,
Alice

Her note reminded me of the kindness and graciousness she always displayed, first as "The Boss's Wife," later as a friend.

Passage through the utility room led to the triple garage. The bays housed "his" and "hers" cars, a white baby Lincoln and Ford pickup, and a woodworking shop. The shop might come in handy if I decided to do anything to conceal my loot on the boat. Sliding doors from the family room opened onto a redwood deck, with steps leading to a concrete walk along the waterfront.

A broad channel led in from the bay, and it was lined on both sides with condominiums and boat docks. I saw boats of all sizes and types— sportfishermen, sailboats, and motoryachts. I would unload first, then find *Alicia Rose.*

My downstairs exploration complete, I carried all my belongings in from the Explorer, and up to my room. It had a king-sized bed, and was decorated in "resort" decor. Sea-green carpeting covering the floor, paintings of beaches with dunes and sagging drift fencing, tropical fish, seashells, and the like. The lamps were ship's lanterns, the clock set in a brass porthole. After I thought about it, I'd stay here three nights, then wash sheets and make it up for Candy for Friday night. I might conceal my cargo on the boat that night and sleep with it for security.

I found *Alicia Rose* only thirty yards from the back steps of the condo. She was moored stern-to in a slip directly in line with the back deck. Jack must enjoy sitting there sipping a drink and seeing his dream riding to the tides. She was a fifty-foot Grand Banks, a beautiful boat. The name and port, Islamorada, were lettered in elegant gold leaf on the mahogany transom. The flying bridge deck extended out over the cockpit area, which was a bit unusual. It made a nice cozy protected area in back, and gave more space up top.

Jack had it well moored, with whips to keep it off the dock. I pulled on the aft spring line and tugged the rail close enough to step over the bulwark. He'd equipped the yacht with outriggers, and a fighting chair was installed, now covered with royal blue Sunbrella. A collection of fishing rods was arrayed on the overhead of the cockpit area. I used the keys to open the cockpit lazerettes, one at a time. The duffels would certainly fit in them, and the usual mooring lines, fenders, and canvas covers could go on top. Still, I'd feel better with them concealed below.

I let myself into the saloon. The interior was finished in teak joinery, with the settees upholstered in a light brown ultra-suede fabric. There was quite a bit of storage space here, also, but the galley equipment, cushions, spare clothing, and navigation gear took up most of it. The internal navigation station repeated all of the engine and nav instruments, and was fitted with a teak and brass wheel.

The aft engine compartment housed twin Caterpillar diesels and the generator set. I had contemplated taking out insulation and concealing the money here, but when I saw how neatly it was installed, I gave it up. Despite being handy with tools, I could not make it look like it did now.

I retraced my steps back through the saloon and down a few steps into the forward cabin. A queen-sized island berth stood in the middle of the room, which was also equipped with a hanging locker and bureau. I would put Candy in this room. After opening a few lockers, I made my decision. The storage under the queen bed would serve perfectly, especially because the Queen could be taking a strategic nap at convenient times. Spare bedding was stored in these lockers, and could be used for added concealment.

Even though I had decided, I checked out the chain locker in the bow. I would bunk in a guestroom to port; or Stephen and I could use it alternately, when standing watch. He would probably assume Candy and I were together, so I would have to cover that news item with him.

Satisfied, I locked up and climbed back onto the dock. A pelican had alighted on a piling by the transom, and he stared at me suspiciously with orange-rimmed, beady eyes. He was indecisive about his safety, so I gave him as much room as I could as I walked back toward the condo. He clamped his beak to his breast and partially unfolded his wings, but stayed in place. A flight of his brethren went skimming by, low over the waterway, as the shadows of late afternoon began to gather.

After fixing myself some canned soup from their pantry, I called Candy to let her know I had made it, and reminded her one more time about her passport. Then I was able to get Stephen, and made a date for lunch the next day at a waterfront restaurant he recommended, the *Pieces of Eight*. I had barely hung up, when he called back and suggested we go by boat, so I could get a feel for *Alicia Rose* before our trip. I readily agreed. I set the security system, then showered and went to bed.

It was a nice change to go running in shorts and singlet when I awoke after a sound sleep. The rising sun, just clearing the horizon out over the ocean, lit a sky devoid of clouds. The sea birds were beginning their day's work, calling in plaintive cries.

I finished my run dripping with sweat, feeling relaxed and alive. After a shower, I drove to a small diner out on the main highway for bacon and eggs, and a morning paper. Afterward, I picked up a few groceries to last until departure. I'd have to get with Stephen about supplying the boat for the trip.

He drove in at 11:30, in a junior-sized pickup truck, and came around to the back deck to knock on the glass door. He looked to be in his late twenties, clean-cut, slender, and well tanned. His short blond hair was bleached platinum from constant sun exposure. His handshake was firm and his smile broad, as he looked me directly in the eyes.

"Hi, Mr. Cross, I'm Steve. Welcome to the Keys."

"Nice to meet you in person, Steve. Please call me Matt. I was really happy to hear you were available, after the recommendation Mr. Regis gave you."

"Well, he's a really good man to work for. I think he's pleased with what I do." He nodded toward the dock. "Shall we take her out for a little spin?"

"Absolutely. I can't wait. I've done a little sailing, but not for a long time. And I have no experience with a motor yacht, so you'll have to show me."

The same pelican, or his double, sat on the same piling, but took flight as the two of us approached. Steve stepped lightly aboard and unlocked the door to the main cabin.

"I'll check the oil, then we'll light 'em up." He disappeared below, then returned and went to the outside helm station and started the big diesels, one at a time. They made a pleasing soft rumble with no vibration. While they warmed up, we readied for departure and our landing at the restaurant. The mooring lines would stay on the dock, so I got out a couple of spares, plus some big, fat fenders. Stephen turned on all of the electronics and proceeded to run through various checks to make sure they were ready.

I detached the mooring whips, and the stern and aft mooring lines, then the bow spring line, tossing them all on the dock. As he engaged the forward gear, I walked the aft spring line forward and placed it on the piling as we eased by it. I had a boat hook in hand, but didn't need to fend off, given his precise control of the big boat.

We idled down the waterway, minimizing wake until we cleared the built-up area of condos and docks. Stephen then eased the twin throttles forward, and she rose and leveled onto her cruising attitude. It was a thrilling experience, feeling the surge of power, and the soft wind in my face. I gave him a broad grin of happiness.

"You like it?"

"You bet I do!"

"Why don't you go up on the flying bridge and take the helm? As soon as you have it, I'll come up and join you, and show you where we're going."

I happily complied, mounting the flight of stairs adjacent to the cockpit. Up top, I wiggled the wheel, then took over the steering. The view up there seemed higher than it was, and gave a feeling of flying over the water.

Stephen joined me, then pointed to a peninsula to starboard, a mile or so away. "We'll round that point, then come back into the channel between the islands. You'll need to give it a few hundred yards of clearance. You can see the depth sounder has a repeater up here." He tapped the instrument with his finger.

"You go ahead and enjoy it, and I'll just kick back and relax." He seated himself on the L-shaped settee, and I did as he suggested. I stood at the wheel and enjoyed it. He hadn't wanted to hover over me.

After we cleared the point, we were in a channel between islands amounting to a broad river whose current was determined by the tides. A bridge carrying US-1 was about two miles ahead of us, with the clutter of boat docks and businesses lining the channel on both sides. US-1 strung the Keys together like beads on a chain.

When we were within a mile of the bridge, Stephen stood beside me again to point out our destination. "Here, it's all yours," I said. "I'll go below and get the fenders out."

"Great," he replied. "At this time of day, the current will be flowing west-to-east, and it's pretty strong. I'll bring it in heading the way we are now. That'll put the dock on the starboard side."

I put out the fenders, got the lines ready, and held the boat hook, but again I had no need of it. He eased the big boat expertly into the dock so I was able to step across a six-inch gap and secure the lines.

The *Pieces of Eight* was all glass on the channel side, with trim of weathered gray wood, and a shake roof. We were seated at a plank table next to a window, looking directly down at the *Alicia Rose*. We both ordered a draft beer and the special of the day, grilled red snapper.

Stephen grinned broadly. "How do you like it?"

"It's just wonderful. I'm already trying to think of a way to avoid going back home."

"I don't mean to pry, but Jack told me you weren't at your former company now. Maybe you could retire early, or find something to do around here, if you're serious."

"It's tempting."

"I don't make a lot of money, but I really enjoy what I'm doing. I don't own the boats, but I sure go fishing a lot, and get to operate some of the neatest things on the water."

Our beer arrived and we clashed the mugs together before we drank.

"My folks want me to go back to college, and I guess I should some day. They live up in New Jersey. Can you imagine living up there, compared to here? Getting my license was sorta' like college for me. It 'ud really be hard to break away from a place like this."

"I can see why. Still, they may be right. You may want to do something else later on. Do you have marriage plans, or anything serious there?"

He grinned again, and took a sip of beer before answering. "I guess I'm kinda' playing the field there, too." He paused, then said quietly, "You'd be amazed."

I couldn't help laughing. "I probably would be, but not because it's you. I just grew up in a different age, and was married for a long time. I don't know if Jack told you, but my wife passed away about three years ago, and I've avoided any involvement since then."

"Hey, I'm really sorry. No, he didn't tell me. It must have been tough."

"It was. Terribly tough. I kept putting off winding things up in my mind, but I feel maybe I'm finally getting there." There was a pause in our conversation. I had surprised myself getting on the subject, but I liked him and felt comfortable talking with him. My own children were far away, and it made me feel good to talk to one of their generation.

"While we're talking about women, I need to tell you about a friend who is coming with us on this expedition. She's a woman friend, but really just a friend. We're not dating or anything like that. I think you'll like her, just as I do. Her name is Candace Drummond. Candy. She has her own software business, and we used to work together at the company. I didn't mention to Jack she was going, because people automatically get the wrong idea. Anyway, we should all have a great time together."

"Sure, I understand," Stephen said. He could have been being polite, or if he did believe, his belief would probably be tested when he saw her for the first time. He'd probably think I had something wrong with me. Or from his youthful perspective, maybe he'd chalk it up to age, and hope he never got that way.

We enjoyed a leisurely lunch, and talked of boats and fishing. At length, we discussed provisioning for the trip on Saturday. He said purchasing the supplies was part of his duties, and I was willing to let him do so. I handed him some cash from the "expense money." I had to do a little guessing about what Candy would prefer, but together we worked up a list. We also discussed pay for him. I told him what Jack had suggested, which was agreeable. I had counted the days, starting today, and put the amount together in an envelope, adding a thousand-dollar bonus, and gave it to him.

He didn't count it. "Gee, you didn't have to pay in advance. But thanks very much."

"I thought you'd like to get it taken care of, and I didn't want to have to worry about it later. I started it today, and counted to a week from Friday. If something comes up with the weather, or other delay, of course I'll take care of it."

"Well, thanks again. It'll be a pleasure working for you." He reached over the table and shook my hand.

"As far as sleeping arrangements, I thought it would be best to put Ms. Drummond in the main cabin in the bow. I'll put my stuff in the other one, but I guess we'll be standing watches through the night. Should we alternate in the bed?"

"No, no point in that. I'll sleep on the settee when I'm off watch. And there are plenty of places to store my gear. When we're in port, I assume you'll be staying ashore, so I might move in there then."

"I was going to ask you about it. I booked hotel rooms for us, but didn't for you. Do you want one?"

"No, thanks. I always stay with the boat if possible. I actually like it best."

"I'll want to stay on the boat the first night also, but will move out after that. She'll go ashore, I think. We can figure it out after we get there."

"Good enough. Ready to head out?"

We made a short stop at a fuel dock, then headed back into the waterway at our home port. Stephen took over the controls again for the docking procedure, and it was fascinating to watch him swing the boat around, then jockey the twin throttles and back into the slip. He made it look easy. We worked together to secure the lines and whips. Stephen finished the shutdown and we went ashore.

"Thanks for lunch. I'll get the supplies aboard over the next couple of days. If you think of anything else, just give me a call. Otherwise, I'll be here ready to go about ten o'clock on Saturday." We shook hands again, and he departed.

Thursday was a free day. I had allowed for some time working on concealing the evidence on the boat, then decided not to. It had been so many years since I'd been here, I decided to drive out to Key West and back. Just do nothing for a change. It was an easy decision to leave the money stowed in the upstairs closet, behind the security system, rather than take it with me and risk a traffic accident. Still, I left the unoccupied house with some sense of reluctance. I thought constantly about the staggering value of the money, and how anonymous it was.

I followed the chain of islands at a leisurely pace, marveling at the buildup of practically everything—resort hotels, condominiums, businesses, tourist traps, marinas. Long Key and Grassy Key were followed by more populous Marathon. Then a long bridge over to Bahia Honda was followed by Big Pine. The names themselves were magic to my ears. I had not heard them since Caroline and I last took this drive fifteen years ago.

I passed through Little Torch Key and the connecting islands, and into Key West about lunchtime. On this drive I felt again the loneliness that had been following me for the past three years. Most of the time I'd been able to stifle it with work and self-delusion. Being in a place like this with no one to share brought it into sharp focus. I wanted to get on with my life, and wanted this day and the next to pass. I wanted to commit whatever crime I would be committing by taking the money out of the country, then decide what my next steps would be. I still could not think beyond the obsession of getting it in a safe place, under my control.

The changes on the west end of the island were amazing. It was now a major cruise-ship stop, and a first-class marina wrapped around the tip. Upscale restaurants overlooked the fortune in yachts in their slips. I did the right thing, however, and walked to Sloppy Joe's for a beer and a sandwich. I wandered about, then into the museum housing the loot recovered from the *Atocha*.

It was astounding. I thought of the misery its beauty represented. The gold was extracted from the rugged mountains with primitive methods by native laborers in ancient times, then taken from them without conscience by the Spanish conquerors. It was lost in a shipwreck, with loss of lives.

The parallels to my own find were troubling. Legitimate treasure hunters found the *Atocha* through years of painstaking work. I stumbled across my smaller find and was anything but legitimate in keeping it.

On Friday morning, I stewed over whether to put the money on the boat first, relatively unguarded, or leave it in the security system and risk Candy's seeing me hauling the bags out there. I worried about her flight, or missing her at the airport. I worried about making the stash without Stephen seeing me. If you want to worry, you can always find plenty of subjects. I'd had enough of them in recent months, and had created a great deal more for myself by finding the money. Practically anyone asked would probably say without equivocation they would have turned it in. But would they?

In the end, I decided to move it to the boat. After all, who would know it was there? And, how many boats are broken into in broad daylight in a gated housing area? I got it concealed under the island bed without a hitch, then locked up the boat as usual.

Pickup of Candy went smoothly, also, no doubt because I worried about it. I made it to the gate before the plane got there. She came up the jetway near the front of the planeload. Two or three guys were trying to keep up with her and get her attention, offering to carry her small case. It was comical seeing them try to squeeze through the jetway door at the same time, like a Three Stooges sketch.

They looked uniformly crestfallen when she waved at me and I went to meet her. She gave me a hug and a quick little kiss. "Hi, Matt," she said. "I'm as excited as a little girl, it's been so long since I've been anywhere for the fun of it."

"Hi, Candy. Glad you made it okay." She didn't look like a little girl. She was wearing a black sundress sprinkled with flowers, and a light little cardigan of white lacy knit. A prodigious amount of beautiful cleavage was exposed.

"Do you have more luggage, or is this it?" I nodded at the little bag she had given me.

"Very funny." She raised an eyebrow. "Unless you'd like me to go naked all the time? Would you like that?"

I should have kept my mouth shut. "I think it might attract too much attention. I take that to mean we'd better go the baggage claim area."

We grabbed her luggage off the carousel. She had two large bags, stopping just short of the cliché about women and packing. I carried them to the parking garage while she trotted along beside me, chattering about the palm trees, the weather, and the approaching trip. She really was excited about going. I was glad I had selfishly asked her to, and hoped nothing ugly would mar the experience.

Her excitement continued as we headed south. "Oh! Key Largo! I just love the sound of it. I've seen that Bogie movie I-don't-know-how-many times. Have you seen it? Did you like it?"

"Yeah, I liked it."

"It's so-o-o romantic!"

"Unh-huh. As a tribute to the movie, then, let's have lunch here. I know a place you may like. I hope it doesn't spoil the image you have from Bogie and the movie."

She gave me a little smile and a poke in the ribs. "You know, you could be more romantic if you'd try a little harder. Maybe being here will change you. Bogart was usually a serious guy, but lovable. Now all you have to work on is 'lovable,' and I think you're getting close."

I gave her a look, but no reply.

We had a nice lunch together, but I came no closer to becoming Bogart... as far as I could tell. We drove into the driveway in mid-afternoon, and I let us in through the security system. She exclaimed over the condominium, just as she had everything else.

"You'll be staying in the guest room, Madame. I'll show you to your room." I lugged her luggage up the stairs and into the resort room.

"Hey, this is neat. Where's your room?"

"I'm staying on the boat tonight. I stayed here first, then washed everything up for you."

"You're staying on the boat?" She looked puzzled. "But don't they have another room you could use?"

"They do, but I thought it best to go ahead and get my stuff on the boat."

She gently grasped my shirtfront. "It's a big bed," she said.

"I think it best I keep an eye on the boat. We've got all the stuff aboard for the trip."

She looked directly at me, and said softly, "It involves what this trip is all about. You have something of value on the boat, and you're guarding it." She raised her hand and looked away. "Don't answer. I'm talking to myself."

She smiled at me. "How about showing me the boat? It's something I've never done. Nothing bigger than a canoe. Just give me a few moments and I'll see you downstairs."

An hour later she appeared on the back deck, all showered and changed. She was wearing white shorts and a blue-and-white striped boat-neck tee shirt. All makeup was in place. I'd had the foresight to bring myself a beer, already replenished once, for the "few moments" wait. It was pleasant sitting out here, watching an occasional boat come in, or go out. I could get used to it.

"Candy, do you want to go out somewhere for dinner, or shall I cook something?"

"Doesn't matter to me. This place is really nice. If you don't mind cooking tonight, it'll be fun. I'll do breakfast."

"It's a deal. We'll have to go get a few things after I show you the boat. It's really a yacht, I guess, but that's too high-sounding. 'Let's view the yacht, shall we, my Deah?'"

She thought it was wonderful, and examined all the nooks and corners. She rubbed her hands approvingly over the fabrics and gleaming wood. "I'll feel like royalty, having this nice cabin. Are you sure you don't want it? I can sleep anywhere."

"Of course it's for you. Stephen and I will be taking turns through the night, so we'll be cat-napping anyway." My eyes lingered on the island bed, with its stored treasure. "We'll move you in tomorrow morning. We won't be leaving until near noon, to put us in Nassau the middle of the next day."

We bought our groceries, then had a couple of hours on the back deck. It was relaxing, viewing the activity on the waterway, and talking of times past. If I lived someplace like this, I couldn't imagine going somewhere else for vacation. That's the way it seemed to work, however. We all want to be somewhere we're not.

After an hour of small talk and comfortable silence, she took a different tack. "Matt, it's none of my business, but where are you going with the rest of your life? You don't have to tell me, but I'm curious. I saw you first as the busy executive, then knew you on a more personal level when you helped me. Now I know you've lost that particular position, not to mention your wife of so many years. It must be quite a load to handle."

"It is, Candy. I don't know where I'm going, or I could be more forthcoming. Life used to be good, and I would go back to it if I could. But I've had no success so far in getting a reasonable position again, and, of course the personal side is missing. What about you?"

"Well, you know how screwed up my life has been, as far as matrimony is concerned. I've reached an understanding with myself. I like my work, and my lifestyle is okay, too. At least, I thought it was. But when you get out and see how the other half lives, you know...?"

"Yes, it's easy to see how nice it would be to have the wealth and the leisure time to enjoy it. You know the old saying about money and happiness. It's true, I think. Happiness comes from the relationships you have with others and yourself. You do have to like yourself to be happy. But to me, money can lift a lot of worries if you have the right amount. Perhaps having too much, or perhaps how it was acquired can create problems."

She laughed. "How I got mine sure came from a lot of problems. But that's all gone. I'm okay now. Again, I don't want you to say anything, but I think this trip will somehow determine your future. Madame Candy has spoken, but clouds obscure the future. And speaking of money, there's one more thing I must say. You gave me far too much money for my expenses, and I'm giving it back to you after I use it as seed money in the casinos."

"Don't worry about it," I replied.

I'd forgotten how much fun it is to cook for someone, while they sit in the kitchen and keep you company. We started on Chianti, because we both like red, even though the meal probably called for white. Who cares? I peeled some jumbo shrimp, then put together a dish for the oven, using white wine, olive oil, lemon juice, garlic, parsley, chopped green onions, and seasoning. For a first course, I made risotto with mushrooms. Mine wasn't as good as Cathy's, but it was damn close. Candy liked it. We got the shrimp right out of the oven for the second course, and had a crisp salad and French bread. We finished it off with some mixed fruit and brandy. I cleaned up the kitchen with Candy's help.

It was a change from my recent two years, being with someone else like this. We began to lapse into longer silences, with glances at each other to try interpreting the mood that had begun to settle over us. It was time for me to clear out, or risk doing something I had determined would not happen.

"Candy, it's time for me to get settled on the boat. I'll wait until I see you on the deck in the morning, before I come over. I really appreciate your coming, and the dinner was a great pleasure for me."

"I liked it, too," she said softly. "And thank you for everything." She reached over and squeezed my hand.

I showed her how to program the security system, wishing her a goodnight with a little kiss on the cheek.

I did my morning rituals, then checked out the back deck. Candy was there, sipping coffee under the protection of a striped umbrella. The deck was bathed in the pink light of early dawn. She glanced toward the boat, looking for signs of life. I obliged her by coming out into the cockpit, then stepping onto the dock. She gave me a little wave of her fingers, and I could see a smile light up her face, even from this distance. Maybe bringing her on this expedition was not such a good idea after all. My concentration had been on the objective of moving the money to a safe place, and now I risked complications I didn't want. I had no right to expose her to danger, and I had no right to take advantage of a friendship, or damage it beyond repair. We were here, however, and I could see no reasonable way to change plans at this point in time.

She rose as I approached, broadening her smile. For the first time, I saw her with no makeup, her blond hair tousled by sleep. She was wearing a thigh length white robe, and I tried to avoid thinking about what I could not see, concentrating on looking at her face.

"Good morning, Matt. Are you ready for your breakfast?"

"Yeah. After I have some of your coffee. Did you sleep okay?"

"To be truthful, no. My mind was digging into the past too much, and I was thinking about the future. Immediate and long term. Taking yourself out of a routine dredges a few things up, don't you think?"

"Yes. I agree. I've had quite a bit of that lately. In fact, routine is a condition slipping farther into the past. I yearn to have a routine again." I regretted saying it as soon as it slipped out, because it could be interpreted in a way I did not mean.

It was my turn to perch at the table with coffee while she bustled about the kitchen preparing breakfast. There was no question her bustle was more entertaining to watch then mine had been, and I fought to focus on just about anything else.

14.
VOYAGE

Stephen arrived at nine o'clock, and went directly to *Alicia Rose*. By then, I had stowed everything in my space, and Candy had transformed herself into "boating casual," with her usual perfection in grooming. She was wearing white duck pants and navy polo shirt with an anchor embroidered on the breast. I gathered her luggage and led the way to the dock.

Stephen's face lit up when I introduced her. "I'm pleased to meet you, Ma'm," he said as he offered his hand, a handshake combined with an assist over the bulwark.

"Thanks, Stephen. And please call me Candy. It'll make me feel younger." She gave him a radiant smile. He stole a glance in my direction. I don't know what he expected, but it wasn't Candy.

I got her settled, then helped Stephen with getting the boat ready. He spent some time over the chart table showing me our route, and explaining how he calculated the course. The Gulf Stream exerted a strong northeasterly component that had to be taken into account. He had made the trip several times, and had worked out all of the waypoints. He turned on the Loran and called up the proper program for the trip, already entered on a previous voyage. I was intrigued by the simplicity of it until he told me how primitive it was compared to the latest.

"That's just our back-up system. Wait 'til you see this."

He pulled the cover off of another instrument, and I watched as the screen came to life. It was a Global Positioning Receiver with cartographic display. He punched a few buttons on the panel, and a view of Islamorada came up, with a blinking cursor on the inlet where we were moored.

"Now look at this." He punched more buttons on the GPS, and a smaller-scale display showed our entire route from the Keys to New Providence.

"Wow! That's amazing. I knew some of this was available, but hadn't seen it."

"It's a lot easier than a sextant and a compass, for sure. But I try to keep in shape on the old methods, too. You never know when you might lose these gadgets."

We took our time removing protective covers, and stowing everything for the voyage. Our food was aboard and refrigerated. Candy was all set, and told me she had her motion sickness patch in place behind her ear. Good news. It's not much fun holding someone's ankles while they heave over the rail.

We had our early lunch in the condo, then cleaned up and set the security system before departing. By now, Stephen and Candy were chatting away like old friends. With the generation difference, it was an interesting mix of male-female, aunt-nephew. There was open admiration in his eyes, and warmth in hers; appreciation for his polite manner and enthusiasm. It was going to be a good crew. I had feelings of guilt again. I could not let any harm come to them, no matter what.

When the three of us were gathered in the cockpit, I said to Stephen, "Steve, neither of us know the business of operating a boat like this, so I think Candy will agree. Don't hesitate to tell us what needs to be done and we'll do it. What I'm saying is, you're the skipper and we're the crew. Okay?"

"Okay. Thanks. There's not a lot I'll need. You and I already discussed watches tonight. Other than that, we'll just enjoy the cruise. Ready to cast off?"

We had soon cleared the inlet, headed for the open ocean. It was a beautiful clear day, with the sea birds flying, and not a cloud to mar the blue of the sky. I urged Candy to join me on the flying bridge. As we ascended the stairs from the cockpit, Stephen called from the helm. "Would you like to take it up there?"

"If it's okay."

"Sure it is. I was about to put it on autopilot, but you can keep about the heading we have as long as you want. If you get tired of it, let me know and I'll re-set it."

I soon relinquished the wheel up top to Candy. She stood there, the wind in her hair, looking like the kid I became when I felt the forces of the waves in my hands. A school of flying fish burst from the green water off the starboard bow and went skittering through the wave tops ahead of us. Candy giggled with delight.

We soon approached the edge of the continental shelf, where the flow of the Gulf Stream reached its greatest strength. As the ocean bottom fell away, the color of the water changed to a deep indigo blue. "It's beautiful!" she said in wonder.

After about an hour, she announced, "With all this sun, I'm going to work on a tan. Do you want the wheel?"

"Not up here. I think I'll go down in the cockpit for a while. I'll take it down there, or in the saloon."

"The saloon? I thought that's where cowboys hang out."

"That's correct if they're in a cow town for a gunfight, or they're having a drink on their yacht. Some folks call it a "salon" on a boat, but a salon is where

HANGMAN

you have your hair done. Let me know if you see a dance hall girl in there, though, because it might mean we've strayed into the Bermuda Triangle."

Stephen set the autopilot and went into the saloon to check on something. I retrieved a book from my cabin. I had just relaxed on a settee in the cockpit when Candy appeared, towel and suntan lotion in hand. She was wearing a short cover-up. She came straight to me and handed me the lotion. "Will you do my back for me? I wouldn't ask, but I don't want to burn."

What could I say? "Sure. I'll be glad to."

She turned her back to me and removed the cover-up. All I saw were strings. Three black strings. She had put up her hair, and there were little bows tied at the nap of her neck, in the middle of her back, and some kind of crossing lower down. I dutifully spread the lotion on the creamy skin, willing my mind elsewhere. When I was finished, she thanked me and headed up top. Her ascent of the companionway ladder was something to behold. I looked away to calm myself.

Stephen came out later to check the boat's instruments. "If you want to fish awhile, let me know, and I'll rig us up. I have some fresh ballyhoo on board. We can try it, or something artificial. We ought to catch something for supper, at least. I'm a good cook, when fish are involved."

"Sounds good to me. It'll slow us down a little, but we aren't on a schedule. Why not?"

Stephen started to hurry about, setting up a bait tray with "rocket launcher" rod holders. As he started to remove a rod from the overhead rack, he paused and looked astern. I turned to look also, and saw a large vessel gaining on us in the distance. Stephen frowned, then brought out a pair of binoculars and trained them on it.

"Looks like the Coast Guard," he said. "They patrol for drugs out here. Sometimes they hail you, sometimes they board. You never know."

A tremor went through my guts. This might be it. I was the only one who had to do any acting, because I was the only one who knew. Candy and Stephen would appear perfectly innocent because they were.

We held our course until the cutter overtook us, pulling parallel to our course about a hundred yards to port. It was gray in color, powerful and menacing. The bow had a forward rake, as sharp as a dagger. We could see some of the crew on deck, and the presence of deck guns did not escape my attention.

"*Alicia Rose, please heave-to,*" came the amplified electronic voice.

Stephen did as he was instructed, easing back the twin throttles. *Alicia Rose* settled slowly into the water, beginning to rock gently to the swell.

"*Alicia Rose, we'd like to come aboard,*" said the voice again, polite, but not asking permission.

147

We watched as a *Zodiak* was lowered into the water from davits on the stern. Crewmen scrambled into it, started the powerful outboard, and headed in our direction.

As we waited and watched, *Alicia Rose* was riding to the three-foot swell, the diesels gently rumbling at idle. Momentarily, I wondered about Candy. She must have fallen asleep on the upper deck, and was missing the activity.

The *Zodiak* arrived, bumping gently against the stern. A lieutenant, j.g., and two of his men came aboard over the rear platform, the other two remaining in their boat. The cutter held its station about a hundred yards away.

"Sir, we'd like to ask you some questions," the officer said to me. He was tall and handsome, wearing a starched uniform, a recruiter's poster of officer material. He was a muscular black man and looked young to me, as servicemen seemed to nowadays. He flashed a brief smile, displaying perfect white teeth. "It's just routine, Sir."

Routine, perhaps, but he was wearing a sidearm and his men were equipped with automatic rifles. They took positions to either side of the afterdeck, in a port-arms pose, feet spread for balance against the motion of the yacht.

After taking care of the controls, Stephen approached with the ship's log and papers, having undoubtedly been through this drill before. "Sir, perhaps I can answer any questions. I'm employed by the owner, Mr. Jackson Regis, and this is a friend of his, Mr. Cross."

"I'm Lieutenant Everly, Gentlemen," he said, and shook hands with both of us, in a tableau of the coin toss before a game.

He took the log and papers from Stephen and began to examine them as he continued.

"First, is your departure port the same as the boat's home port?"

"Yes, it is," Stephen replied. "We left there about two hours ago."

"And your destination?"

"We're headed to Nassau for a short vacation, and plan to do a little fishing on the way and back." I replied, nodding at the gear Stephen had begun to lay out.

"Where do you live, Sir? And what business are you in?"

"Right now I'm between jobs, but I'm an engineer. I live near Knoxville, and worked for Mr. Regis before he retired."

Stephen and I were generally facing aft, with the three of them facing forward, toward the main saloon. Lt. Everly pursed his lips, and I could see he was evaluating how our stories all fit together. At that moment, he looked up over my shoulder, and his eyes widened. All four of the sailors looked up as well.

I heard Candy's voice. "What's going on, guys?"

She was descending the companionway ladder from the upper deck, wearing only the thong bottom of the scanty suit she'd appeared in a half-hour ago. She trailed a towel behind her, and clutched the flimsy strings of the top in her hand as she held the rail for the descent. Her magnificent breasts bobbed to the motion of her steps.

Her mouth formed a luscious red O. "Oh, I'm sorry," she said innocently. She made a gesture to hold the little string top over the front of her bosom.

"I forgot," she giggled.

As I turned to look, I managed to trip over the footrest of the Murray fighting chair on the afterdeck. With the pitch of the deck, I went staggering toward the rail. One of the sailors sprang forward and caught me by the arm to keep me from going overboard.

In the midst of this maneuver, Candy disappeared forward into the saloon toward her stateroom in the bow. All of the men laughed, including Stephen, and he blushed a crimson color.

As I straightened myself and regained my balance, I could see a decision had been made. We were not prototype drug smugglers, and the lieutenant could not have suspected what we had on board.

"Sir, we're the ones that should be falling overboard, not you." He said.

I winked at him. "I never get used to it!"

"Don't. Have a good vacation. Sorry to have bothered you."

"No trouble at all. I'm glad there are men like you out here protecting the rest of us. Have a good day."

We got underway again on our former heading. We could see the cutter recover its tender and make a slicing turn across our wake in the distance. The knots in my stomach began to unravel, and my pulse returned to normal.

Stephen had said nothing since their departure until he saw them make the turn. "Gosh, I thought you might be going for a swim," he said.

"Yeah, it was clumsy of me. I hope you would have fished me out."

"We'd have thought about it. You ready to catch some fish?"

"Let's do it."

He set up a couple of rods in the rocket launcher, then got out a small ice chest and started wiring some ballyhoo onto hooks with stainless leaders attached.

"We'll put a couple of teasers well back in the wake. I'll put these two lines on the outriggers, then I might put another out the back, down deep to see what happens. It would be nice to snag a dolphin for supper."

Candy had arrived just as he made the last statement. "A dolphin? Are you serious? We won't eat a dolphin! They're too cute!"

"Not the kind you're thinking of. It's actually a dorado, the fish type of dolphin. Have you ever had mahi-mahi in a restaurant?"

"Of course."

"Same thing. You'll see when we catch one."

"No kidding?" She didn't sound convinced.

She had not looked at me since coming on deck. Now, when Stephen's back was turned, she gave me a secret smile. She was a cat who'd just caught a mouse, and wanted me to acknowledge it. Perhaps later we would talk.

Stephen reduced to trolling speed, and we droned on for a half-hour before the first strike. He had been watching and maneuvering the baits, and scanning the wake from the flying bridge. He shouted just before the strike.

"Watch the port outrigger!"

The line snapped out of the clip and Stephen dropped the speed. I picked up the rod and lowered the tip until the slack was pulled out. Then I set the hook, sweeping the tip up and feeling the surge of a fish on. Candy had declined to be anything more than a spectator, so I kept the rod and maneuvered into the chair. Just as I got set to enjoy the fight, the other line snapped out. Stephen came charging down to control the boat from the cockpit.

"Candy!" I shouted. "Come here and take over! I'll get the other one!"

To her credit, she did so, after hopping about in a little dance of indecision. Stephen laughed at the awkward choreography as I ducked under one rod and grabbed the other. Candy hung on with grim determination, then her face lit up when she decided how much fun it was.

They were nice fish, but not too large, maybe fifteen or twenty pounds. I pumped mine in pretty fast, and she exclaimed when she saw it flash in defeat at the side of the boat.

"It's beautiful!" The brilliant colors of silver, gold, green, and blue were at their brightest as Stephen expertly heaved the fish into the cold box.

With the confusion over and the boat stationary, Stephen patiently coached Candy until she had the fish alongside, a female twin of the first one.

"Congratulations." He shook her hand. "You did just great." Then he looked in my direction. "Supper's taken care of. Want to keep fishing?"

"Maybe we should be on our way. Okay with you, Candy?"

Her face was glowing. "Sure. It was great fun, but we have more than enough fish. Maybe we can do it again on the way back." It didn't turn out that way, but we resumed our course for New Providence.

The GPS showed us our position, slightly off the original course, but the computer promptly gave us a new one to our next waypoint. Stephen and I cleaned and iced the fish while the autopilot held us on our course. Candy went below for a nap, promising to return in time to assist with the evening meal.

The sun was flirting with its descent into the watery horizon when our crew gathered on deck for our grilled dorado. Candy and Stephen made me stay away while they got the dinner together, and they presented it with pride for us to enjoy. I cleared up and cleaned the galley.

By the time I joined them in the cockpit, the sun was making its departure, changing to gold, then orange. It bulged into an enlarged, flattened pumpkin shape from the refraction of its dying rays bending through the atmosphere. The waves changed to a fleeting mix of indigo and deep purple, with gold highlighting the crests. It was a peaceful time, and we sat in silence, lost in our private thoughts.

Stephen gave me the four-hour watch from ten at night to two in the morning, and he took the more difficult one in the early morning hours. I was alone with my thoughts, listening to the steady beat of the engines, keeping an eye out for traffic, scanning the radar screen from time to time.

The door to the saloon opened and Candy came out on deck, dressed in the robe I had seen at breakfast. She came and sat beside me on the settee. It was sheltered, but cool, so I offered her an afghan I'd brought out with me.

"Hi. How're you doing, Matt?"

"Great, Candy. You couldn't sleep?"

"It's been a good day, hasn't it? I just didn't want to go to sleep too soon, and end it."

"You did a great job on your 'assignment' this afternoon."

She laughed. "You think so? Did you see the way those guys looked at me? I knocked 'em out, didn't I?"

"You certainly did. Your timing was superb. When it all started, I thought maybe you were asleep or something. Not our Candy."

"You weren't too shabby, either. Dick Van Dyke couldn't have done that fall over the chair as well as you did. You did it on purpose, didn't you?" She poked her finger in my ribs for emphasis.

"Hey, I couldn't let you have all the attention, could I?"

She looked down at her hands. "Today focused on the problem I've had all my life. It's the real reason I couldn't sleep."

"What do you mean?"

"That look in the eyes of all you men. It's what I've lived for. I try to suppress it, but today brought it back again. It's made me screw up most of my life. It's caused me to make a lot of bad decisions. It doesn't make me feel like I'm worth much."

"Hey, don't be so hard on yourself. You're beautiful, and you don't need to prove it to anyone. You're also smart and successful. Concentrate on that side of things, and let the rest take its course."

"You think I'm beautiful?"

"Of course. How could there be any doubt?"

"I just need constant reassurance that I'm not losing it, I guess. It's like a drug..."

I put my arm around her and gave her a brotherly hug. "You'll be okay. Why don't you get some sleep?"

"Thanks, Matt. I'll try again." She rose, then kissed me on the cheek. "Most of all, I wanted you to see me," she whispered.

Stephen came on deck with a cup of coffee in hand precisely at two o'clock. I had seen him through the glass, groping about in the galley.

"Hi Chief. How's the bridge deck?"

"Fine. Very little action. We haven't come within two miles of anything. Looks like we'll be coming to a change in course pretty soon, if I'm reading the GPS correctly."

He gave it a glance. "Yeah, in a little while. As you can see, we have to thread our way into the Bahamas. New Providence is about in the middle."

"Do you need anything, before I turn in?"

"Nope. Have a good sleep. I'll wake you if anything interesting comes up."

There was nothing like Candy's last comment to keep my mind turning over. I'd had nearly four hours alone in the dark to second-guess everything I had done over the past few weeks. I didn't come out of the self-evaluation with a very good opinion of myself either. Getting away from her everyday routines had dredged up Candy's insecurities, but compared to my scheme, she was an innocent. I could see our relationship was gradually becoming more complicated, and neither she nor I needed that.

Oblivion finally overcame me, and I knew nothing until I heard sounds coming from the galley. I pulled on my clothes and put a baseball cap over my tangled hair. When I emerged into the saloon, I could see daylight outside, and the interior brightly lit. Candy was working away, preparing breakfast.

"Good morning," she said, cheerily.

"Same to you, kid," I replied. "How's Steve?"

"He's doin' good. I took him some coffee. Here's yours."

Steve was checking a chart when I came into the cockpit. "I think I overslept my watch."

He smiled. "No problem. You'll have to holystone the deck later, but it was worth it, wasn't it?"

He traced the route with his finger. "You can see New Providence is surrounded by reefs and islands. With shallow draft, you can cut across, or follow other minor channels, but the simplest is to go in through the major passages. See this? That's the Northwest Providence Channel, the way we're going in. In fact, we're getting close enough you should be able to see Grand Bahama pretty soon from the flying bridge."

As casually as I could, I raised the question foremost in my mind. "What's customs clearance like, when you come in like this on a boat? I've never done it before."

"It doesn't amount to much, usually. It's a random thing, all the way from pretty easy to a complete search of the boat. Here, it's pretty straightforward, since they do it a lot. We can even check in on Sunday, although I think the landing fee is a little higher, for overtime. I've already filled out the Certificate of Pratique, and I have all of the boat information, but I need for you and Ms. Drummond to write down some personal data for me. Usually, I can just carry all the passports and papers to the immigration office and take care of it. The port captain is also there, and it should be smooth sailin'. We'll dock at a temporary dock nearby, and if they want to look us over, I'll let you know."

"That doesn't sound too bad."

"It isn't. I'll also apply for clearing out at the same time. Speaking of leaving, they're talking a little dirty weather toward the end of the week, so we'd better keep an eye out. At least we'll be going in the right direction to stay ahead of it, if we leave in time."

Candy appeared with our breakfast, and we enjoyed it in the golden beams of sunrise peeking in over the starboard quarter.

We all were up on the flying bridge to see the smudge of Grand Bahama appear on the bow. As we drew closer, Stephen waited for the magic invisible point indicated by the GPS, then altered course to pass between Berry Island and Great Abaco. When we were in the waters of the Northwest Providence Channel, Stephen hoisted the Bahamian flag on the right outrigger, as a courtesy. Later in the morning, another course change to almost due south headed us directly into Nassau.

As we approached the city, Candy was a little girl again, excited at the prospect of adventure. We fell in behind an enormous white cruise ship to enter the harbor, past a lighthouse on the tip of Paradise Island. The water was deep, but transparent pale green, so bottom features could be made out in the depths. Stephen hoisted the yellow "Q" flag to indicate we desired clearance, and called port control for instructions.

We were directed to a customs dock, where he had tied up on previous visits. Soon we were going through the ritual of making fast, fenders in place, then engine shutdown. In the unfamiliar lack of motion and sound, I could feel my heart hammering in my chest. The tension of actually being here for the next momentous step caused my hands to tremble as I tended to my tasks.

Candy was occupied with scanning the tropical beauty of the town, from the busy streets that began right at the docks, to the heights above, populated with whitewash-and-tile buildings. We were in the older section of the city. High rise hotels and casinos were clustered to the east on the far tip of Paradise

Island, and in the other direction around a crescent of beach to the west called Cable Beach.

"Well, here I go," said Stephen, as he swung onto the dock. "You guys will have to wait here until I get back."

I needed to make my telephone call, but I decided to play it straight and wait until I could use a pay phone on shore. Candy and I made sandwiches for lunch. I found small talk difficult in my state of mind.

"Is something wrong?" She asked. "You seem tense and far away. I feel like I'm looking at a screen-saver."

"I'm sorry. I'm always distracted until I get this stuff out of the way."

"This stuff? It isn't something I have done or said, is it?"

"Oh, no, no, of course not. It's just me." I gave her what I hoped was a reassuring smile. All the while I thought about the money, and getting it in a safe place. I had read one startling little comment in some of the customs papers Stephen had. Failure to make proper declarations could result in forfeiture of the vessel. It was not a pleasant little tableau to play in the mind. "Sorry, Jack, but I lied and they took your boat. I hope we're still friends."

In a half-hour or so, Stephen came walking back down the dock, a smile on his face. He gave a thumbs-up sign when he drew near. It was no big thing to him, but to me it was the last difficult hurdle before getting the money to a safe place. What happened after that was not yet in my plans.

"We're all set," he said, as he swung aboard. "We have to move to a marina where I've booked a slip. Then what's next?"

"I'd like to find a pay phone. I plan to stay with the boat until I can complete some business in town tomorrow." Then to Candy, "I won't be able to see you to the hotel, or have dinner tonight. Will you be okay?"

She looked disappointed, but smiled and agreed. "I'll be fine. I may just hang in and get room service for tonight. I'm pretty tired."

"Steve, would you mind seeing her to the hotel? Also, if you have any plans, I'm not going anywhere tonight, so I can watch the boat."

"Not at all." He gave a confirming smile to Candy. "After that, sure. I have a buddy in town who used to work with me in the Keys. We planned to get together, if you don't mind."

We cast off and headed east up the channel. Steve threaded through the boats swinging on moorings, past the tall piers of the twin bridges to Paradise Island. We tied up, stern-to, in a slip in Bayshore Marina, plugging into shore power and water.

I walked to the end of the dock, paid for the slip, then found a pay phone. I called Wurtz's cell phone number.

On the second ring, a single word. "Wurtz."

"Hello. This is Matthew Cross. I'm in Nassau for our appointment tomorrow."

"Very well. Be at the bank at ten o'clock in the morning. Do you need transportation or directions?"

"No, thank you. I'll use a taxi. I'll see you then."

Talking with Gerhard Wurtz never took long.

I made a second call to a taxi company, and scheduled a car for a half-hour later. I thought about a currency exchange, then remembered they were pegged to the U.S. dollar at one-to-one, so we could use what we had. We got Candy and her luggage into the taxi, and I handed Stephen money for the fare. I hated leaving her to fend for herself, but I had to see this through until tomorrow.

While he was gone, I made up Candy's room for Stephen, since he was staying on board for several days. He'd be coming in sometime in the night. I moved the money into my cabin and stowed it out of sight in some lockers.

The marina's slips were pretty much filled, with a mixture of sailing and power craft. Few people were about; only an occasional boater passing on the planked dock. There were three giant cruise ships at the docks a mile away, disgorging tourists into the town. I settled in the stern cockpit with my book, a bottle of gin, a six-pack of tonic, and an ice bucket. There would be no leaving my post until I left tomorrow in a taxi. The air was balmy, the sun warm, the day a delight. The music of the marina created a peaceful background sound— the creaking of lines and dock, waves splashing against hull and piling, halyards ringing against aluminum masts, gulls crying. It was close to heaven.

Stephen appeared in late afternoon, accompanied by a tall blonde young woman—apparently the "buddy" he mentioned. She was tanned, lithe, and beautiful. I could tell by the sly grin on his face that he was getting even for my springing Candy on him. He left us to chat while he went below to change. Turned out she captained charter sailboats, when vacationers wanted a qualified skipper for their island cruising. She was a sweet girl, a good match for Stephen. When they left, headed for her red Miata, I called out after them, assuming the role of their distant parents, "You kids have a good time, but don't stay out too late."

Evening came after another dramatic sunset. The darkened sky began to glow with the neon lights of the concentration of resorts to east and west. Imagining all of the activity and companionship of the players, I felt lonely. I wondered what Candy was doing, and hoped she was safe. I wondered what she was thinking about all of this. Unable to go beyond turning over these thoughts in my mind, I made myself a late meal, locked up, and went to bed.

Sometime in the unknown hours of the night, I heard Stephen unlock the door and slip into his cabin. My next awareness came as gray morning light stole into the saloon. I crept into the companionway and eased Stephen's door shut, before lighting up the galley and making coffee. The sun had not yet risen, and not a soul was about as I sipped my coffee on the afterdeck. The security guard in his booth at the head of the dock was the only human in sight.

I tried to imagine what the day would be like. How would they count the money? What if they suddenly demanded proof of the money's origin, despite Rudy's connection? Would I have to haul it back? What would the deposit slip look like?

Stephen appeared, coffee mug in hand. His hair was tousled, and a foolish grin graced his face. Where did it come from? It must be something to do with having a buddy.

"You look happy for this early in the morning. Your night on the town must not have been too discouraging."

"It was okay. How was yours?"

"Nothing like what evidently happened to you. I stayed here and contemplated the universe, then went to bed early. Do you think Candy's doing okay?"

"I'm sure she is. Maybe we can call and check on her after while."

"I'll do it. I'm leaving a little before ten for a meeting downtown. I'll call her when I order my taxi."

We breakfasted together, then I walked to the end of the dock, ordering a taxi for nine-forty-five. I rang up our hotel and asked for Ms. Drummond.

Her sleepy voice answered after five rings.

"I woke you, didn't I?"

"That's all right. Look at the time. I never sleep this late."

"Well, it's okay. Remember this is a vacation...sort of. How are you doing?"

"Yeah. I'm fine. I tried the casino for a little while, but my heart wasn't in it. I won only about a thousand before coming to bed early. Are you coming over?"

"As soon as I finish in town. I don't know how long it will take, but I'd expect it to be after lunch."

"Well, I'll either be in my room, or by the pool. Find me when you get checked in."

I went back to the boat, shaved and showered, and dressed in the blazer with white shirt and tie. When the time came, I retrieved the duffel bags. Stephen looked curiously at my burdens and me when I came out into the saloon. I allowed him to help me carry them to the end of the dock, and I felt reassured by his presence while we waited for the taxi. *"This is it."* I kept saying to myself. I trembled with adrenaline.

15.
PARADISE

We loaded my bags in the trunk, and the driver gave me a strange look when I gave him my destination. Either he guessed the nature of my baggage, or the bank was close by. I assumed the latter. "I know it's not far, but I'll take care of you," I said.

He seemed reassured, and drove off. Indeed it was close by, a short distance up East Bay Street. We rounded a corner onto a generally shabby street, arriving at a carefully maintained older building fronting the street. It was white traditional stucco, but modernization showed in the ornate entrance, graced with heavy plate glass doors. The name of the bank was discreetly carved in the pink granite facing above the entrance.

I paid the driver and lugged the heavy bags to the door. It was opened for me by a security guard in fake British colonial uniform of white military jacket with gold braid, red trousers, and white shoes. His ebony skin glistened in sharp contrast to his white "Bobby" helmet. A Sam Browne belt supported his holstered sidearm. Another guard inside was equipped with a compact machine gun. The interior of the bank was put together with polished marble, plate glass, and gold-tone metal.

I carried my heavy parcels to a grouping of leather furniture arranged on a Persian rug. A receptionist behind a mahogany desk was stationed at one side of the rectangle, guarding a row of plate glass, curtained offices. She raised her plucked eyebrows at the sight of me. For some reason, if you enter a bank with large bags, people are curious.

"May I help you?" She asked. She made two syllables out of "help." Hell-up.

"I have an appointment with Mr. Wurtz. My name is Cross. He's expecting me."

She looked at my bags again, then spoke softly into the telephone. A man came out of the office right behind her and crossed in quick strides to where I stood. As expected, he was not smiling. He reached to shake hands. "Mr. Cross? I'm Wurtz." He, too, looked at the bags by the chair behind me.

He was at least six-five, skeletal in build, and dressed in a black suit. His face was lined and his skin dry and flaking. Despite the eternal good weather, he was untanned, appearing to be a creature of the indoors. His hair was black and thinning, with flying strands crossing the bald crown of his head. His lack of hair on the scalp was compensated by ample growth from his ears, and long eyebrows were combed fan-like above his eyes. The long bony hand felt long enough to wrap more than once around mine.

He fixed me with his dark, piercing stare. "Shall ve get right to it?"

Before I could speak, he continued. "Very well. Let us proceed to the back."

He beckoned to the guard who had previously ushered me in. The guard went past us to a corner behind the offices, and returned with a small cart. He loaded my duffel bags, and preceded us past island desks and a marble-and-glass row of tellers' stations. Employees in the midst of their duties glanced without a great deal of interest in our direction as we clicked past on the marble.

The guard opened a door in the mahogany-paneled hall, and led the way into a small room. A table stood in the middle, and there were two workstations along one wall. A third workstation held a computer terminal.

"This ve call a counting room. I presume you may wish to stay, while the girls count the money? It is done by machine, of course. First ve take down basic information, and I set up the account. You have brought identification, yes?" He moved to the computer terminal. The guard had left.

I handed him my passport. "I have a question or two. What type of account is this? What I mean is, is it similar to a normal savings account, bearing interest? That sort of thing?"

He looked at me with a puzzled expression, the butterfly-wing eyebrows dancing upward. "Interest? Oh, no, no. This type of account, you see, benefits the client in other ways. Ve can assist you in certain investments, you see. Ve can discuss these matters if you wish. But, no, the basic account does not provide income...to you."

"Okay. I just wondered. Let's proceed." He sat at the terminal and began entering data from the passport, then followed with questions about contacts in case of emergency. I had to think. I decided to give him the lawyer in Mountain View who had written my will. I would have to contemplate the events following my untimely death, and find some way to instruct him. I wondered to myself what a timely death might be.

Wurtz spoke into the telephone again, to summon the "girls." They appeared soon after, in the form of two middle-aged women of mixed island heritage. He did not introduce them, but launched into his instructions.

"Ve ha'f a fair amount of cash to count, band, and tally. After this chentleman certifies your count, ve vill enter the amount into his account and transport the cash to the vault. Call me if you ha'f questions. Understood?"

They both nodded in unison, glancing quickly in my direction. I sensed they were afraid of him.

The time had come for "show me the money." I lifted the first of the duffels to the table, and opened the slide fastener. My audience of three stared in silence as I removed the plastic bags, one by one, and started stacking them on the table. After I finished with the first duffel, the motionless group dissolved. Wurtz left the room. The two women went to the two counting machines, and turned them on, zeroing the digital displays. They retrieved cardboard file boxes from the corner of the room, and still wordless, each carried some of the bags to their stations.

We began a routine. I opened the bags and handed them the stacks of bills. They took off the old bands and inserted the stacks into the machines. The money had been banded in small packs. They inserted five of the small packs in each time, then pressed a button. The machine whirred quickly through the stack, the digital display a blur before stopping on 10,000. Apparently they had pre-set the denomination. With the pressing of another button, the thick stack was spit out into a tray, with a tight paper band complete with imprinted serial number.

The "girl" would record the serial number on a lined form, place the money in the box at her feet, and then repeat the process. I kept busy supplying them with stacks of cash.

"Sir!" One of them said. She tapped the display, which read 9,900. "This one is not right. I do it again."

She proceeded to run it through again with the same result. She cast about her chair, and waved her palms outward, displaying a quizzical look.

"That's okay," I said. I took a hundred-dollar bill out of my wallet and handed it to her. She smiled, placed it with the stack and ran it through the machine for the correct count.

There was tap at the door and a young woman in a white uniform came in with a silver coffee service on a cart. She bowed quickly out of the room. I assumed it was for me, but I poured each of them a cup.

When we were finished, Mr. Wurtz was summoned into the room. They displayed the log sheets to him. One of them had three hundred thirty-one bundles, the other three hundred fifty-nine.

"Is this correct, Mr. Cross? Six million, nine hundred thousand?"

I had to think a moment. The one bag at home had been broken up for expenses, but had contained $100,000. The count was correct.

"Yes, it is."

"Then you may go." He nodded to the two women. Then to me, "Please sign each log sheet."

"Thank you, ladies," I said.

"You're very welcome, Sir," one said, as they retreated.

I signed the forms, then Wurtz went to the computer station and tapped in the figures. The guard came in, accompanied by a young man dressed in a suit. They loaded the boxes on the hand truck and left.

"Let us go to my office," he said.

It was as simple as Rudi had told me. Wurtz had me sign additional forms for the account, then he completed all of the computer entries and called for a printout.

The forms were indeed uncomplicated. The account was numbered, without listing my name, as I had requested. He gave me a separate identification card with my name and address, with the account number on it. He notarized the card and two copies of the account statement, then presented them to me in a manila envelope.

"You h'af questions, Mr. Cross?"

"No, nothing I can think of for now. I will be in town for a few days, so I will call if something occurs to me." We rose, and I shook his hand. "Thank you for your help."

Back on the sunlit sidewalk, I felt a flood of relief. For better or worse, the money was in a safe place, hidden from discovery. What would happen in the future, I could not imagine at this point. Would I go on pretending it was mine? Would I search for some way to bring it back?

Finding a post office was the next item of importance. I purchased a map at a news kiosk up the street, and proceeded to walk the four or five blocks. I purchased mailers and postage to send one copy of the form to myself by registered mail, and the other copy to myself by regular mail. There would be no way I would want to carry documents with such numbers on my person. It was bad enough to have the card in my possession. I tucked it into the back recesses of my wallet.

I found her where she said she would be, but it wasn't easy. The coral-colored hotel on Paradise Island was a huge, sprawling layout, with multiple towers. Without the bellhop, I doubt I could have found my room for the first time. I was assured it was next to Ms. Drummond, with a connecting door.

I searched through a labyrinth of tropical foliage, fake streams, and waterfalls to find the two different pools. There she was at the second one, tucked in a corner away from the other activity, reading a book. She sat under a striped umbrella, wearing a modest swimsuit, sunglasses, and cocoa-palm straw hat.

"You look like you're enjoying life."

She looked up. "Life just got better. I'm glad you're here. Everything go okay?"

"Surprisingly well. No complications. And I'm done with it, so we can do what we want with the time left."

"I thought it must have. I shouldn't tell you this, but it's easy to see you're floating about a foot above the ground. I can read that, just as I could read your worry yesterday. Maybe you'd better not play poker tonight."

"I'm that easy, huh?"

She smiled in reply. "I'm curious as a cat. I've been trying to think what you'd be doing here, but I guess if I need to know, you'll tell me. I'll put it out of my mind."

I changed into beachwear, then the two of us spent a pleasant two hours walking on the beach, watching the other adults walking and the children playing. A parasail provided a spot of color out to sea. A stick of brown pelicans flew by, drafting beak to tail, like Olympic bicycle racers. One tiny little girl in a pink bikini raced back and forth with the incoming waves as they broke on the beach. She giggled in delight as the foaming edge of the ocean chased her up and back. Her fast little feet and slender legs reminded me of the sandpipers on the Carolina coast. Watching her took me back to days long gone, to happy times I would never recover.

Candy sensed my thoughts, and walked beside me in silence back to the hotel. Perhaps she was right, and it was easy to read my face and my actions. I would have to work on it, since I'd now become a multi-millionaire, if it were possible to ignore where the money came from. Somehow, it didn't feel that way after the adrenaline of the morning had departed. I'd have to work on that, too.

"How about a really nice dress-up dinner tonight? And the casinos afterward?"

She smiled, welcoming me back to the present. "It's a date. Whenever you say."

"I'll knock on your door at seven-thirty, if it's agreeable. Now, I'm going to lie down and rest for a couple of hours. The last few days have taken a lot out of me."

By the end of our conversation, we stood at her door. "We'll want you rested," she said, as she turned to enter her room.

I called the concierge and asked for the name of a first class restaurant, one appropriate for a celebration. He suggested one in an old manor house he claimed was world-class. At the same time, he warned me reservations might be impossible.

"How about giving it a try. For two at eight o'clock. Also, I need to find a men's shop with nice clothes. I'll be down in ten minutes to see how you're doing."

I threw on some khakis and a fresh sport shirt. I'd started thinking about the blazer I'd brought, how it had become shiny in places, and how old it was.

I couldn't go out looking like that. I speculated about how Candy would look. After all, I could afford it.

The concierge shook his head when I told him my name. "I'm sorry, sir, they don't have a thing for tonight."

"If it's the place we should go, would you mind trying again? Do you know someone there who might help us?" I extended a folded U.S. hundred between my fingertips.

"I'll certainly try, sir. Maybe they will have a cancellation, or will be able to work you in. Here are the names of a couple of menswear shops. There are always taxis standing outside. Good luck, sir. I'm sure we can work something out."

The men's shop went about the same way. I can wear a suit right off the rack, except for cuffs, of course. I bought a fine Italian tropical-weight wool suit, black with thin stripes. Nine hundred bucks. A couple of Egyptian cotton shirts, woven in Switzerland of fine 100s two-ply yarn, and two silk ties completed what I'd need. Except for shoes. The ones I'd brought wouldn't work with this outfit, so I bought new ones. The ties were nice—*Ermenegildo Zegna*— a label made more famous by the president's girlfriend. Cuffing trousers would normally have taken a day, but it's amazing what money will do.

"I'll have all of this delivered to your hotel in an hour, sir, including pressing the suit and shirts," the clerk said, bowing. "And thank you very much, sir. I hope you enjoy the evening."

I'd kept the taxi standing outside, and was whisked back to the hotel. The concierge gave me a smile and a thumbs-up. I told him I'd be back down at seven-thirty.

This whole operation had taken less than an hour. Now, I could rest until my clothes arrived. What a day this had been...and more was yet to come. After the pressures of the past few weeks, I felt I was floating slightly out-of-body. The old "me" looked at the current "me" from a distance, not able to comprehend. My mind started roaming over the recent past, and so much had happened it was difficult to focus on the sequence of events. Images began to overlap and blur.

I awoke with a start, to the sound of knocking at the door. As I swam upward to semi-consciousness, seconds went by before I could fathom which door, and where I was. Nassau. Hotel. The clothes. I sprang off the bed, and allowed a bellman to hang the new clothing in my closet.

I presented my newly elegant self at her door at precisely seven-thirty, all showered, shaved, and smelling of *Havana*. She was wearing a low-cut black cocktail dress, with diamond necklace and earrings. Her hair was swept back into a French roll. I was glad I'd made the First-Class upgrade.

She looked me up and down. "Wow, look at you. Did you bring that on the boat?"

"Wow, yourself. I confess I went shopping. Are you ready for dinner?"

"You bet I am. This Tennessee girl is all rested and ready to go."

The taxi dropped us off right on time. I should have ordered a limo. You can't think of everything.

In spite of my new suit, no one looked at me as we entered the restaurant and were shown to our table. Our waiter swooped in immediately and took our drink orders, focusing all of his attention on my glamorous companion.

"We'll be ordering wine later, but I'd like a drink first. Candy, do you want something now, or shall I order wine?"

"I'll have what you're having, then wine later."

"Bring us Tanqueray martinis. Make mine double. I have a greater body mass."

Candy wagged her finger at me, after the waiter had turned away. "Bad boy. I'm going to have to keep an eye on you tonight."

"Hey, why should I be different? If you look up right now, you're being caressed in ways you can't imagine by the eyes in this place. Does it ever bother you?"

She cast a quick glance around the room. Several pairs of eyes went back to plates of food, menus, dinner companions, and other mundane subjects. "Well, we talked about this, you know. Unfortunately, most of my life I've liked it. Even tried to encourage it by what I wore. The main thing that gets to me, is when some creep won't look me in the eyes at all when he's talking to me—can't tear his eyes off my boobs."

"You mean like this?" I stared at her breasts, never an unpleasant task, and crossed my eyes.

"Yes, like that, you Cretin!" She slapped my hand. "Now stop it. If you really want to see them, I can arrange it. But not in here."

The waiter brought our drinks, placed our napkins for us, and handed us our menus. I stopped him when he started on the specials for the evening.

"I'll forget them anyway, before time to order. We're in no hurry, but we'll get some wine on order. I'll be having another drink before we order, after I finish this one. I pointed to a 1988 *Chateau Mouton Rothschild* on the wine list."

He raised his eyebrows. "Very good sir. I'll send the wine steward. And I'll keep an eye on the drinks."

I hoisted my glass and clinked it against hers. I clenched my teeth and lisped, "Here's lookin' at you, Kid."

"Bogie! You finally arrived!"

The drinks went down smoothly, the first one, then another. The waiter hovered, unsure when to approach us for our dinner orders. I half-listened as Candy told me about her business successes, and her lack of success in fulfillment in her personal life. I couldn't figure out what she wanted. Here was this woman, beautiful and smart, yet unable to plot a path for the future. She was probably more screwed up than I was. What did she want from me? By the time this thought struck me, I was on my third double, and she was keeping pace with her singles. I finally got rid of the waiter by ordering dinner.

I realized she had asked me a question. "You had someone you really loved, who loved you. What was it like?"

"I didn't think much about it at the time. We weren't happy all the time, but I look back on it, and it was pretty special, I guess. I've been able to let it go now, I think. How about you? You must have been happy some of the time."

"I don't think there was a time when I was really appreciated as a person. I made the wrong choices."

I didn't like the way this conversation was going. "Hey, let's not get too heavy. We're supposed to be celebrating, having a good time."

She smiled ruefully. "Okay. I'll quit. Here's to the present—no past, and no future." She clinked her glass to mine, and drained the last of it.

We started on the wine, delicious and deep in color and bouquet.

Dinner arrived in a steady stream—appetizers, salads, main course. The bottle of wine disappeared. I ordered another. I couldn't keep my eyes off of her—the curves of her body, her gestures, the way the tip of her tongue touched her white teeth. I told her funny stories, just to watch her laugh. And everything I said was funny. Thoughts began to build, then possess me, of the way she might feel next to me. I wanted to release her hair from its confinement. I wanted to breathe on the curve of her neck, and hear her whisper in my ear.

"Candy, let's not go to the casinos tonight. Let's pay the check, and get the hell out of here. Suddenly, I want to be in a more private place."

She looked levelly at me. "Are you sure you know what you're doing? Have you had too much to drink?"

"Yes, and yes. Or, no and yes. Or, yes and no. Whatever. How about you? What do you want?"

She paused, looking serious. "I'll have what you're having."

I felt uncomfortable being here, after my promise to Candy of a business-like relationship. What was I doing, shedding my clothes and sliding into her bed, while she changed in the bathroom? The buzz in my head from the wine, and my exultant feeling after the session at the bank, convinced me I deserved to be here. Wasn't it a natural ending to a magic day and a beautiful evening?

She came into the room wearing a short satin gown of deep rose, with a cream-colored sheer lace bodice. As she moved, the V of the bikini panties peeked from beneath the lace trim. Her perfect skin and beautiful curves presented a vision that caused a lump in my throat; not to mention other locations.

"Hey, do you have room in there for me?"

"I think it can be arranged. The person who lives here said it was okay. Maybe I can make room for one more."

"She must be a wise person, and very lucky, to have a guest like you."

She moved into the bed, and lay full length against me. I could feel the warmth and softness of her body, awakening feelings long suppressed until this night. Her sweet fragrance enveloped me.

"Ever since you proposed this trip, I've been thinking about being like this with you," she whispered in my ear. "Because of what you said, I didn't think it would happen."

I kissed the curve of her neck, just below her ear. "It was not my intention. Somehow, the evening, the circumstances..."

She pressed her finger to my lips. "Not another word about that. I know you well, I think. Your intentions were honorable in the beginning, perhaps too honorable to suit me. But tonight was different for both of us, and here we are. I want it to be like this."

Her hand began to move beneath the light covering, her fingertips sliding down my stomach and tugging the waistband of my briefs downward. "Mmm. What have I found?" she whispered. I helped her move them off and out of the bed.

She slid gracefully away from me and arose. "I don't think I will be needing these, either, do you?" She stood by the bed, facing me, and slowly lifted the top over her head, then trailed it on the carpet. She kept her eyes on me, to see my reaction, which was one of wonderment. Next, she wriggled out of the tiny bikini panties, moving her shoulders and wiggling her breasts.

She arched her back and displayed herself to me in a feigned yawn and stretch, then looked down at me and smiled. "What fantasies do you have, Matthew Cross? I can arrange just about anything you can imagine. Hm-m-m?"

"I've suppressed all of my fantasies for a long time, Candy."

"Now's not the time for suppression."

"If I allowed a fantasy to exist, what could I do to top this?"

She moved into the bed beside me again, lying full length, touching skin to skin. She spoke in a soft murmur. "It works for me. But whatever you want, I will do for you. Just move me in the direction you wish, Baby." She breathed in my ear, nibbling my earlobe. "Or, just leave it to my imagination, and you won't be disappointed."

"Candy, you know it's been a long time for me."

"Believe it or not, but it's probably been longer for me. It's because I'm particular. At least, I am now. Maybe I've been waiting for someone like you. But you don't have to worry. I'm sure you haven't forgotten. It's like riding a bicycle. You don't forget."

"It's like riding a bicycle?

"Yes, sweet man."

"Can I be the bicycle?"

"You!" She giggled, and pounced on top of me. She soon relaxed against me and snuggled at my side, and our hands began to caress.

My hand moved softly over her body. She breathed heavily and began an exploration of her own.

We touched each other gently in all the right places, and she began to move and moan softly. What began as the unhurried love of the experienced, ended with the frantic merging of two souls long-denied this sweetest passion. I was transported to the place no one can adequately describe, and cried out in a voice I didn't recognize as my own. Candy's response came on top of mine, and she exclaimed in a way that reminded me of the sports fan in Casey's bar.

Morning came, and my headache was intense. I was exhausted. My mouth tasted terrible from my deep sleep.

The night had been a confusion of sleep and dreams, of merging souls, and revival of long dormant passion. I would forget in my slumber, then awake to the unfamiliar feeling of a soft, warm body next to mine, with hands and mouth searching. A homecoming of the soul and spirit; then feelings of guilt would creep into my thoughts. The twists and turns in my mind created paranoid questions about her motives. Was she planning this all along? Was she trying to complicate my life? How could I restore things to the way they were in Mountain View? Did I want to?

Without saying a word, she bounced out of bed clad only in perspiration, and I heard the shower begin.

What should I do? I could rescue my rumpled clothes, now hanging in piles on the floor, and go back to my room. It would be a cowardly act. I chose instead to enter the bathroom and borrow some of her toothpaste, using my finger to do a bad brush job on my teeth. I'd just wait here for my turn in the shower. No way I'd go in there now.

There was no reaction from me when I saw her step out of the steam. "Good morning, Matthew. Did you sleep okay?"

"For the thirty-six minutes I was allowed, yes."

A little smile. She continued toweling herself. I could summon no interest in helping her. Instead, I moved past her into the shower.

When I returned to the room, all of the clothing was on hangers and the bed was made. She was sitting against the headboard, the sheet drawn up to her shoulders. There was sadness in her expression.

"I've ordered room service, so you may wish to put something on. You might shock them."

We sat on the bed and ate our breakfast in near silence, bacon and eggs for me, yogurt and toast for her. Coffee helped to restore some measure of function to my brain. She had dressed in a satin robe for the formality of dining.

I knew we would have to talk about this change in direction. She was first.

"You did it because you were drunk, didn't you? The Matthew I know would never allow himself to stray from the path, right?"

"Candy, I don't know what causes things to happen as they do. And I'm not Mister Clean. There are things about me you don't know. Are you sorry it happened?"

"Oh, God, no. But, I'd rather you wanted me when you were sober. Then I'd know it meant something. In many ways it was wonderful, but when I faced the morning, then I began to feel as I have so many times before. Men have always wanted my body, but they never really wanted *me*."

What could I say to make her feel better, when I couldn't figure it out for myself? I'd made a big mistake, going back on my word to her. Now, things were complicated. Tears were coursing down her cheeks.

"You've answered my question. You waited too long to answer. I'm sorry, Matthew. It's my fault more than yours. I practically threw myself at you. It's just a habit of mine."

"No it isn't. Don't beat yourself up. We don't know what the future holds. This hasn't changed the way I feel about you as my friend. I do care about you. I always have. I'm not ready to commit to anything, and I didn't think you were, either."

Her face began to collapse, and she started to rise and run away. I went around the bed and held her close, waiting for her sobs to subside. I didn't know what to do.

"Hey, Candy, please hang on. I'm sorry to cause you pain. Can't we continue to be friends?"

"I'll try, Matt. I really like you and I let my feelings go in the wrong direction."

"Things have changed with last night," I said, "I didn't intend for it to get that far. I meant what I said to you back in Casey's bar. I wanted you to come along and enjoy yourself, nothing more. Well, I did intend for men to go blind and do foolish things. I just didn't intend for them to be me."

She gave a little snort of a laugh, and wiped her eyes with her hand. She looked up at me, and spoke in a whisper. "Now, clear off the bed, and make love to me tenderly, as though I mean everything to you. Then, when we walk out the door and into the world again, we'll be like we were last week. I don't want to lose you for a friend, either."

She tiptoed and brought her lips to mine. The body I thought could never respond again after the events of the night, did.

16.
EXPOSURE

*A*licia Rose shouldered her way through the building turmoil of gray-green waves. The leading edge of the tropical storm had struck the area surrounding Nassau in the early dawn, producing a morning far different from the usual balmy paradise. The light of dawn was gray rather than golden, the wind gusty and confused.

I hadn't slept much. That made two nights in a row, but it was far different from the previous one with Candy. This time I tossed and turned, berating myself for becoming the kind of person I did not like—taking advantage of someone else. I knew she had forgiven me, but it would take me a little while longer to forgive myself.

The previous day when I returned to my own room, my message light was blinking. The hotel had a voice mail system, so I was able to get Stephen's message in his own voice. "The weather isn't looking too good, Boss. There's a tropical storm out in the Atlantic working its way toward us. Shouldn't be a problem, but we really ought to get out of here sooner than Thursday. Do you think we ought to plan on tomorrow? You must be at breakfast. I'll try you again around ten."

I guess you could call it breakfast. In fact, it had included breakfast.

Stephen called back on schedule and we agreed to depart the next morning around nine. I didn't think Candy would mind, based on our last conversation. I left her alone until after lunch. I needed a couple of hours anyway, to sleep off the previous night's activities. When we did talk, she agreed on the earlier departure. I sensed a lack of enthusiasm on her part to stay longer than necessary, thanks to me.

We managed to start over with dinner, subdued but agreeable. Then I watched her in action in the casino. We played some blackjack together at one of the five-dollar tables. I lost, she won. She moved on to higher stakes in a poker game and methodically won again, cashing in more than ten thousand dollars. Her only reference to the night before was a reversal of an old line. "Unlucky in love, lucky at cards," she said.

Candy remained below while Stephen and I rode the pitching motion, alternating at the wheel.

"It should get better, the farther we go," he reassured me. "It's not headed the same way we are and it really won't amount to much, they say. Just enough to make the ride a little rougher."

He sensed something had changed. I could tell by the way he looked at us. He and Candy picked up where they had left off, however. They greeted each other warmly as we prepared to depart. I saw them later comparing notes on the trip, laughing together as Candy told him of her experiences at the poker table. I was confident Candy would leave my activities out of her narrative.

I was the odd man out, turning my various secrets over in my mind. For Stephen's part, he was his usual cheerful self, perhaps more so. He whistled and hummed to himself during our preparations for the departure. Evidently he'd enjoyed seeing his buddy again.

In late morning, he reached into the ice chest and held up a large live lobster. "Did you remember tomorrow is Thanksgiving?" He asked.

"I never gave it a thought. Hey, am I causing you to miss any family gatherings? If so, I'm sorry—"

"Not to worry. We'll just steam three of these turkeys and have our feast on board since tomorrow's a travel day. I think the sea will settle a bit, later in the afternoon."

Except for a brief interlude with our Thanksgiving meal, the trip back to the Keys seemed much longer than our outbound journey. The northerly component of the Gulf Stream retarded our elapsed time by a small amount. The difference lay in the constant motion from the disturbed ocean, the gray cloud cover, and the estrangement of the crew. For my part, I wanted to get back to Mountain View and decide the next chapter in my life.

I had started scheming on ways to repatriate a continuing supply of funds from the bank account. It seemed rather straightforward to start a consulting business with payments coming from a foreign account. I'd have to pay taxes on it, but what the hell? There was plenty of it. I'd have to research the question when I got home.

Candy remained in her cabin for most of the trip. She confessed a mild case of mal de mer, despite her motion sickness patch. Perhaps it was the feeling left behind after a buoyant outlook is replaced by disillusionment, just as the fringes of a tropical storm replaced balmy Caribbean weather.

We tied up at our home dock in the middle of the night. We quietly completed our mooring, and decided to leave cleanup for the next morning. Candy moved back into the condominium, Stephen left for his apartment, and I bunked in the boat; all the same as the night we'd departed.

I was first up and stirring about. I made coffee in the galley rather than risk disturbing Candy. Stephen had received my admonition to sleep late, so I didn't expect him before mid-morning. The weather in home port was fine and clear, with no effect from the turbulence to the east and north.

I started by gathering the trash in bags, then all of the bedding and towels for washing in the condo. Next I scrubbed the head and all the interior floors, cleaned the galley again, then found some wood treatment to restore the glow to the teak interior joinery. As I took a quick break for coffee, Candy stepped lightly onto the deck.

"Hi. Is anybody home?"

"I'm in here, Candy. Come on in. Coffee?"

"Yes, thanks." She joined me in the saloon. "Are you okay, Matt?"

"I slept a little weird, I guess. I think I still felt the motion, with some dreams thrown in. How about you?"

"I'll be okay, I guess. Our two little ocean voyages couldn't have been more different, could they?" Her blue eyes were large and luminous in the morning light reflected from the water. She was leaning toward me and looking directly into my eyes. "I promised myself, and I may have promised you, I wouldn't talk about this again. But I can't let us go back home without saying something to you, Matt. You mustn't think I regret coming with you. I'll always love you as a friend, just like before."

I took her hands for a moment. "Thank you, Candy. I've done nothing but berate myself for treating you the way I did, but I won't dwell on my apologies because you won't want to hear them. I love you and value you as my friend, also.

She squeezed my hands. "I'm glad I got away from the mundane life I lead in Mountain View. I'm grateful to you for bringing me with you."

"You've helped me more than you know. And I truly enjoyed being with you. I'm sorry for hurting you. I never meant to, but I lost control of myself when I should not have. Will you be okay, getting home? I mean, do you want to ride back with me, or take the plane back?"

"I'll take the plane back. My car's at the airport, and it's an easy flight." She patted my cheek. "Your treatment was pretty good, if I may say so. And maybe some day you'll tell me how I helped you."

She was the same Candy once again.

"Okay. Maybe Stephen will get you to the airport. I'm leaving this afternoon so I can be back Friday night. I feel like we've been gone longer than the calendar says."

"Well, that's all settled," she said. "What can I do to help with getting the boat back in shape?"

I assigned her a bottle of Windex and a roll of paper towels for all of the glass, as we did our best to go back to the way we were. I went outside to scrub the topsides from the flying bridge all the way down, using a deck brush, Joy detergent, and a hose.

Stephen arrived just as I was coiling the hose. He was apologetic when he saw our progress, but I told him he had done enough. Candy volunteered to wash the linens while Stephen and I went to refuel. I also bought a fine trolling rod for Jack, to leave with my thanks.

We left *Alicia Rose* serviced and spotless, a noble craft that had done well for us.

The drive back was grueling, but without incident. I pulled into my basement driveway in the darkness of Friday night. I was weary, but conscious of a quiet elation at having accomplished what I had started out to do.

I dragged my body and all of my belonging from the Explorer up the stairs to the main floor.

The eye was blinking on the answering machine and the computer voice informed me in halting cadence that I had eight messages.

Two were from John McMillen, asking me to please call about the house. Two were hang-ups. Both of my children had called.

David: "Hi, Dad. I think you're gone for a few days, but I wanted you to know all is well. I got my grades from the course and flunked everything. Nah! Actually, I hate to brag, but I aced 'em. What I wanted to discuss with you is what I might do during the break, if you approve. Some of my friends are planning on biking around Europe for a few weeks, camping or staying in hostels. What do you think? Give me a call when you can. They'll hold off until Monday. I won't go unless you think it's okay. Love ya, Dad. Bye!"

Cathy: The same greeting, "Hi, Dad. Just wanted to call and tell you I miss you. Everything is fine here. I worry about you there all by yourself. Do you get lonesome like I would? Hope not. Well, I hope we can talk soon. *Ciao!*"

Eileen: "Matt, this is Eileen. We'd like to have you come out for dinner or supper sometime this weekend if you can. We want to keep in touch. Call if you can. Bye."

Candy: "Matt, this is Candy. I got home just fine today. Thanks again, and keep in touch. Hope your drive back was good."

Her call had preceded my arrival by several hours. I'd call the kids tomorrow, but I didn't feel like doing much else except rest for the weekend.

After arising late on Saturday morning, I drove downtown to the post office and checked my box. There was a slip notifying me of a registered letter. The regular mail copy hadn't made it yet. I took it to the window and signed for the bank deposit receipt I had mailed to myself. The rest of the mail consisted of the usual wad of junk mail and a few bills.

I went straight to the bank and put the card from my wallet and the deposit slip in my safe deposit box. Now, no evidence existed except for the one still in the mail.

The bodies in the plane were on my mind again all the way back from the Keys, and I continued to debate with myself how to approach notifying the authorities. The only way I could see doing it was the anonymous approach, a phone call from a pay phone, with approximate location of the wreck. The problem was the act of letting someone know the caller, me, had been there.

I drove back home with my stomach crying for breakfast. When I had it ready, I seated myself at the kitchen table and started on it and a Knoxville paper I'd bought.

A scan of the front-page headlines produced the usual news, repeating the stories I had heard the day before on the car radio...until something caught my eye in the lower right quadrant:

WRECKAGE BELIEVED SIGHTED IN SMOKIES

An Ohio businessman reported seeing what he believed could be wreckage of a plane in the mountains on the North Carolina side of the state line. Timothy Estes, 46, of Lima, Ohio, landed for fuel at McGhee Tyson on his way back from south Florida Saturday evening. He spotted "something white," apparently far enough from settled areas to appear out of place. He said he made one circle over the spot, but could not be certain what the object was.

Edgar Baldwin, Squadron Commander of Civil Air Patrol headquarters in Knoxville, stated that a search began immediately. "By the time we got an aircraft over the site, however, darkness had fallen," he stated. "We didn't get the word until late in the day. We will resume early Saturday morning in the area indicated by Mr. Estes. If we see anything at all, ground search parties will be dispatched to the site."

Robert Jordan, an official of the FAA in Knoxville, confirmed they have no reports of missing planes in the area, but that they will monitor search efforts. Jordan said, "Unfortunately, it is not unusual for private pilots to fail filing a flight plan, making it difficult to start search efforts if they fail to reach their destination. Without the flight plan, we have to depend upon someone at their destination, or some other method, to notify us if they run into trouble. It's also possible the wreckage is from an old site, although a computer check of wreckage sites does not list anything in the location indicated by Mr. Estes."

Well, there it was. No problem now about notifying authorities. I felt guilty about letting them lie out there so long. But, what the hell, they were dead. At least I would not have to focus attention upon myself. It would be interesting to see how the news people handled the story when they were found. Also, I wondered who would show up to claim the bodies, if indeed anyone did. Knowing what had been there, I figured something would happen.

I called David in Paris, and caught up on his news.

"I was waiting for your call, Dad. I knew you'd come through for me. How was your trip? Any action on the business front?"

"It's all okay, Dave. It went just fine. Congratulations on your test results. Good, huh?"

"Just what I wanted. It's easy when you like the subject. What do you think of my plans for a trip?"

"Go for it. You've earned it. Will there be any way to track you down, in case something comes up?"

"Thanks, Dad. I knew I could count on you. Yeah, we thought of that. We don't want to have an itinerary, but one of the guys has a cell phone we'll take along. If anyone needs us, all they have to do is give us a buzz. You got a pencil?"

I took down the number, we chatted a bit more, then he brought up another subject. "Dad, I'm sorry I couldn't be with you for Thanksgiving. We didn't get time off, and I thought you were traveling..."

"I was. Don't be concerned about it. I was with a couple of friends, so it was okay. I just want you and Cathy to keep your careers moving. We can catch up later."

"Well, the reason I brought it up, I may want your indulgence to do it to you again. Cathy mentioned my visiting with her for Christmas, but she was afraid to ask, because we don't want you to be alone..." His voice trailed off, wanting me to comment.

"I'm going to call her in a few moments. Don't hesitate for a moment. She's excited about what she's doing, and I'm sure she wants Big Brother's stamp of approval. Maybe I can get away and we can all be in Milan for the holidays."

"That would be great! Let us know. And Dad...take care. I'll talk to you soon."

I had doubts about Christmas, but it would make him feel better about seeing his sister.

Cathy was full of her usual exuberance and excitement, coupled with concern for her only parent. I reassured her about Dave's coming for Christmas, mentioning an outside chance I might return. We chatted about her classes and her successes, and promised to talk again in a week.

Eileen answered my return of her call.

"We'd love to have you come out, Matt. Right now, I don't know what to plan, though. Did you hear anything about a plane down in the mountains?"

"Yeah, I saw a little blurb in the paper."

"Well, you know both states work together on searches in the mountains, and Woody and his horses are always in the middle of it. They alerted him last night, then this morning they called and said they wanted him to help. A bunch of them took off, and I don't know when they'll be back. We'll just have to wait and see. Excuse me. I've been running on and failed to be polite. How are you? And Cathy and Dave? Have you heard from them?"

Well, not only was the cat out of the bag, but a close friend of mine was directly involved. All I could do was wait and see. I had no idea when local news was on the tube on Saturdays, but I turned it to Channel 8 with the sound muted, to see what would turn up.

I went about my household chores, cleaning and putting things away. A news report came on at noon. The lead story was a short report about the downed plane. They'd had a reporter on the search, but no film yet; just a little paste-on logo of a plane wreck. The well-groomed anchor began her coverage:

Searchers this morning found the wreckage of a small twin-engine plane in the mountains, with the bodies of two victims inside. Authorities are puzzled by the fact they have no record of the lost plane and the missing persons, although the crash apparently happened some months ago. FAA and North Carolina authorities are cooperating in the search for the victims' families and the owner of the plane. We are told identification was found with the bodies. However, the names will not be released pending notification of next of kin. The origin of the plane is also being withheld.

The bodies are being transported to North Carolina's forensic laboratory in Raleigh for autopsies, in order to fix cause of death.

The crash site is reported to be deep into the National Park boundaries, at the headwaters of Big Creek. All persons are being asked to stay away from the area until the Federal Aviation Agency investigation is complete and the wreckage is removed.

Film and coverage will continue with this evening's newscast.

The Governor's office today announced he will ask for consideration
of an income tax....

Back to mute again. I would certainly make myself available for further
news coverage. Of course *I* know why the missing persons were not reported,
but how will the "next of kin" explain it? And what will they do when they
find out?

I managed to keep the television off and perform routine chores while I
waited for the local news at six.

Sure enough, it was the lead story. The earnest, polished, and lacquered
blonde looked me in the eyes and began:

North Carolina and Tennessee rescue personnel reached a downed
plane in the mountains this morning and removed bodies of the two
victims. A spokesman for the sheriff's office said the crash is some
months old. Here is Ken Smith with a report from the scene earlier
today:

Film began, showing a young male reporter with microphone in hand,
standing on the steep slope with part of the fuselage showing behind him.
Two other men were carrying a black body bag through the camera's field of
view as he spoke. The bag appeared light in weight and only partially filled;
no surprise to me.

The reporter, being from a Knoxville station, had sought out a Tennessee
citizen for his interview, none other than a certain little guy with a bald head
and a gap between his front teeth. He spoke into the microphone, then thrust
it into Woody's face.

"Deputy Hendrix, can you tell us what caused this plane to crash?"

"Well, if you take a close look, you'll notice it ain't got any wings on it.
They're layin' back down the hillside a piece. Other'n that I'd better not guess.
Who knows? I reckon the FAA will try to figure it out. A lotta' planes fly into
the mountains in bad weather, thinkin' they're still over the flat land."

"And why are they saying it crashed some time ago?"

"Well, if you seen the bodies, you'd be pretty certain they didn't die
yesstiddy, unless they was on a real severe diet."

"Why wasn't someone looking for them? I understand the FAA had no
report of this plane being missing."

Woody's eyes narrowed. "Well, one of two things, I'd reckon. Either
nobody knew they was missin', or nobody wanted 'em found."

The reporter had run out of questions, or knew a longer spot would be cut to fit. He pulled the mike away from Woody and turned toward the camera. "This is Ken Smith, reporting from a valley deep in the Smoky Mountains."

The anchor returned to the screen. "Thank you Ken for that report." Then she repeated the points that had been disclosed in the noon report, and moved on to other news stories.

Trust Woody to cut to the chase. His country-boy speech was even more in evidence on the screen, but I knew what lay beneath it. By the time he got back to Mountain View, he would have worked out several possible explanations, with most near the truth, unless I missed my guess.

The phone rang. It was Eileen.

"Hey, Matt. Woody's home, and he says it's all right to see if you can come to Sunday dinner tomorrow. Can you make it? We go to early church, so it would be a good time."

I couldn't very well refuse, and it would be interesting to see what Woody had to say. "Sure, Eileen, I'd love to."

"Good! You want to come out about eleven? I'm making fried chicken and mashed potatoes and gravy. You can pretend to be the Parson over after church."

"Don't ask me to carry the charade farther than eating a lot of chicken."

It was time to face Woody without giving up the turmoil inside my mind.

17.
REVELATIONS

There were only a dozen assorted vehicles scattered around the place as I drove in on Sunday. I carried a basket of flowers up the walk to the front porch, and Woody opened the door before I knocked.

"Hey, Matthew! Come in. Man, look at them flowers. They sure are purty. I'd better hide 'em, though. Eileen'll get jealous if she knows you've taken a shine to me like that."

"Yeah, sure, sweetie."

Eileen had the kitchen in wondrous aroma as she bustled about preparing our noon meal.

"You're sure I don't have to preach? I could if I had to, for what I smell cooking."

"No, dear, we'll let you off for now." She brushed a wisp of hair from her forehead and came to give me a hug and a kiss.

"It's good to see you, Matt." She leaned back and looked at me. "Hey, you look good. Not as tense as last time."

"I take that as a compliment. You look wonderful, as usual. Is Woody behaving himself?"

"Most of the time."

"Dear, look what Matthew brought us. I thought first they was for me, but then I remembered how you two carry on in front of me."

"Thanks, Matt. They're great." She scooped the flowers out of Woody's hand and cleared a space for them in the center of the table.

In short order, we were seated at the table passing dishes of wondrous food. I wasted no time crunching the crispy outside of a chicken wing.

"Woody, I saw you on TV last night."

He flashed his signature grin, with a sheepish look on his face. "You seen that, did you? I did pretty good, don't you think?"

"Yes, you did. I've heard Dan Rather may hang it up one day soon, and you might have a chance. Or you could get assigned to the National Transportation Safety Board. Your analysis of why the plane went down was super. Sometimes they spend months trying to figure it out."

He grinned again. "Ya liked that, didja? What are you gonna do when they ask stupid questions. Did you notice he didn't even blink when I said them things?"

"Yes, I liked it. I couldn't help laughing out loud. Especially the part about the wings."

"Well, he did ask one good question," said Eileen. "Why *would* an airplane go down and nobody be looking for it?"

"I think your husband summed it up pretty well. It's hard to imagine no one knew these people, so it looks like it could be the other reason."

"But why?"

"It's pretty easy to guess, Dear. I reckon we should wait and see, but just among us, I imagine it was drugs," said Woody.

"Why?" I asked.

"Well, I've been thinkin' all kind of things. Mostly what you said, Matt. Anybody with a plane like that knows somebody, usually. They found ID on them, you know. They couldn't announce it, but they was out of Jacksonville, Florida, which could be a port of entry for drugs. My guess is, they was makin' a delivery and was on their way back, 'cause there was nothin' in the plane except a little travel kit or two. They're gonna' make some calls and try to find out who answers at the address on the ID's. I'll know more later, for sure. North Carolina has the case but they'll tell us."

I said, "It is a little mysterious, I guess. I'm sure it'll clear up as soon as they track down where they came from."

"You was up that way awhile back, wasn't you, Matt? Seems I recall you said something about Walnut Bottoms. You know, when you borrowed Daisy and that little...?" Woody couldn't come up with a polite word to finish the sentence.

I began to feel uncomfortable. "I was at Walnut Bottoms. Was it near there?"

"On up past it. You know another funny thing?"

I waited for his pause to end.

"I rode Daisy up there on the search. And the funniest thing—we was ridin' up to this fork of Big Creek, way up near the mountain face where it comes from, and she almost jumped out from under me once."

"What was it?"

"I don't have a clue. She just spooked, and shied sideways like she was rememberin' some bad dream." Woody went back to his plate, as though deep in thought.

The bear, of course. I knew better than to react. "That's strange. She was really good for me. Something must have scared her."

We moved on to dessert and talk of other things. I told them all I knew about David and Cathy. I dodged questions about my absence from Mountain

View. Woody had little to say about his work, only that it was "about the same." Eileen's new job was keeping her busy but hadn't borne much fruit as yet. I reassured her getting the network out took the time, then things should start happening. She agreed, with some hesitation.

"She's always been her own hardest boss to work for," said Woody.

We said goodbye and I drove back home. I really wanted to know the rest of the inside story as it unfolded, but would have to be careful about asking too much of Woody. The papers would probably carry more details if there were any.

The next day, I waited until near noon in deference to the time zones, then called Jack Regis in California to thank him for the use of the boat. He insisted on details of the expedition, so I gave him the fishing-trip version, and threw in a couple of gambling comments. I spoke not a word about a former business acquaintance.

A week went by, then another. I read, I pursued the headhunters without result, and got the house in the best shape I could. John and his clients had slowed in their interest, with only a couple of desultory showings. The Christmas holidays approached. I made no plans to go anywhere.

Despite those slips of paper with the large numbers, I wanted to return to a normal life. At least I tried to convince myself I did. As I ran my morning run each day, I thought about how it would be to go to the office, to meet clients, to install equipment in some plant in another part of the world.

Frequently I wondered if there would ever be someone who loved me… someone who would look forward to my coming home. Someone I could love in return. Someone I could cherish as I had cherished Caroline. Someone I imagined, at least, I protected from harm.

One day, all of those thoughts were erased and my mind torn in another direction. I saw it first in the newspaper:

DOWNED PLANE OCCUPANTS IDENTIFIED

Occupants of the downed plane discovered in the Smokies late last month have been identified. The pilot's name was Bernardo Hernandez and the passenger was identified as John L. Capricio. A spokesperson for the CID in North Carolina stated that the long delay in releasing the information stemmed from difficulty in reaching anyone with information about the deceased. Neither appeared to have lived at their respective addresses in recent months, and had not listed forwarding addresses.

North Carolina investigator Brian Carlson said with help from authorities in Jacksonville, Florida, the victims of the accident were traced through ownership records on the plane to an importing company called Exotica Imports, Inc., in Jacksonville. The office was closed, but phone messages left on the answering device eventually led to finding a relative of Capricio's. Authorities are still searching for the family of Hernandez.

The relative, Leonard Testa, who gave his residence as the Island of Bermuda, further confounded police by informing them Capricio had a ten-year-old son, who has disappeared. "What happened to Joey, is what I'd like to know," he was quoted as saying. "Did they search the crash site thoroughly, or not? We've got to know what happened to him. Joey used to go with him everywhere, since his mother died years ago." Testa went on to say he was shocked to hear of his cousin's death. "I would never have known, except by accident," he said. "It was just by chance I came to Florida to see him. As far as I know, he has no other family except Joey and me. We kept in touch, but not frequently. You know how it is when you live apart. I will really miss him."

I bet he will. He no doubt will miss his seven million other relatives just as much. Why am I cynical, I scolded myself. Maybe the guy really is his cousin. It just doesn't sound plausible, and "Joey" sounds like a creation to allow digging into things up here. The article continued:

Testa will be coming to North Carolina to claim the remains as soon as they can be released. "I want to give him a proper burial," Testa said. "I'm all he had in this world. While I'm up there, I want to organize a search for Joey. I just can't understand where he could be. It haunts me to think of the kid surviving the crash, only to be lost in the wilderness."

Bingo. Now "cousin" can come to the area and evoke all sorts of sympathy for his search. They must have had a great time deciding how to handle this. They had to debate whether the money was found or not. The police might have kept mum about it to see who would come searching. If the police had the money, then Testa might wind up a sacrifice for the Organization.

My bet would be they did some frantic behind-the-scenes investigating of their own to discover it was missing from the plane. They must have satisfied themselves it was worth the risk to proceed in the open. Now the obvious focus would be to find out who had it. I felt a visceral tug of fear for the first time.

I didn't see how they could find me. No one could possibly know. And they wouldn't have the resources to investigate thoroughly. I didn't doubt this Testa character would go to the site to see for himself. But what could he do beyond that? The evening news provided an answer to my question, and another visceral twinge.

Mr. Testa had interviews on all of the local area television stations in Asheville, North Carolina, and Knoxville. The interview in Knoxville took place in front of the Knox County Courthouse, giving it an air of official respectability. I got to put a face on the fear that had lingered in my mind. Testa was big everywhere. And he was ugly. His face was red and pocked and he had no visible neck. He did not have the muscular build of an athlete, but a large chest and big gut. It was the kind of body that pushed his arms outward so the palms faced forward with his hands splayed outward in space. His hair was black and brush cut, and he wore about four pounds of gold around his neck. I hate it when men wear necklaces. For this performance, he was otherwise well dressed, with a navy blazer and a crisp white shirt open at the neck. He would be hard for me to forget if I ever bumped into him, which I hoped never happened.

The punch line of his performance was the announcement he "would do anything to find poor Joey." He offered a cash reward of $25,000 for information that would help him in any way to find out what happened. The reward would not be limited to only one award, and the public "had to trust that he was an honest man, and had plenty of money to help him in his search."

"It's the least I can do for family," he concluded, with a mournful look.

I hadn't thought about this kind of ploy. Perhaps I didn't think enough about the whole situation. Still, I didn't see how anything could be connected to me.

Woody called in the evening.

"How ya doin', Matthew?" he began. "Didja' catch the news?"

"What about?"

"You know, the airplane people."

"Oh, yeah. You mean the big cousin who's looking for a lost kid? It's too bad isn't it? You were there. Did it look like someone could have survived and tried to make it out?"

"Well, I reckon anything is possible. The back seat was pretty much all in one piece. Them fellars in the front had had a hard time, though. They kinda' snuggled up too close to the instrument panel."

"It was strange how long it took to find someone who knew them."

"Yep, it was. Hey, the reason I called, can you get away for a little while tomorrow? I'm gonna be at the shooting range at around two, if you get a chance to come by. It's not as far as comin' out to the house."

"Sure, Woody, I'll be glad to. You know I don't have a lot going on that demands a schedule."

"Well, I didn't mean to remind you about that, but I'll see you tomorrow."

The shooting range was nestled in the small hills south of town. The parking lot in front of the square cinder block building was almost empty. I couldn't possibly know whether Woody's car was there, because he rarely drove the same one twice. I parked and walked the sidewalk to the locked front door. A sign said to ring the buzzer, although there was a magnetic card entry for those who had one. My summons brought a bulky, graying sergeant to the front door. He squinted through the glass at my civilian dress, then let me in.

"**Cain' I h'ep you SIR?**" He barked.

"I'm here to see Deputy Hendrix, Sergeant. My name is Matthew Cross. He told me he'd be here."

He did not acknowledge my statement, but stabbed a blunt finger at a register on a stand and said, "**Sign in here, please. Are you armed, Sir?**"

"No, Sergeant, I'm not."

He beckoned me to step through a metal detector to see if I told the truth. Apparently they wanted to know about anything capable of uncontrolled projectiles flying about. I followed him to a standup desk where he withdrew a pair of sound-deadening earmuffs.

"Sir," he bellowed, "**You must wear these at all times out on the firing range, and you must stand behind the yellow line at all times unless actually cleared to go to the firing line. And you can only do that if I say you can. I'll inform Deputy Hendrix you're here.**"

Too bad for him the headset rule hadn't come along sooner. I put them on and followed him through a pair of doors that formed a sound-attenuating air lock protecting the entry and office area from the firing line. He led me to one of several doors halfway down a hall, and opened it to disclose Woody, who was reeling a target along a clothesline arrangement back to his firing position. The target's heart was chewed out in a ragged pattern. There were no other holes visible in the silhouette.

Woody turned to me and grinned. "Hey, there, Matthew! I'm glad you was able to make it. I was gettin' a bit rusty, so I thought I'd tune up the shootin' eye a little." He was wearing his ear protection and yellow-lensed shooting glasses.

The sergeant saw I had passed inspection, so he retreated back to his duty.

"You wanted to see me about something, Woody?" I worried about Woody. He was too smart. I hoped it was anything except his thoughts on the downed plane, but the conversation last night led me to believe he wanted to discuss it.

"Yeah, nothin' important. I just wanted to try a few theories on you about the plane. It just bothers me a little and I wanted someone with more than half a brain to tell me if I'm nuts."

"Gee, Woody, don't get carried away with gushy compliments. And anytime you want me to testify you're nuts, just call on me."

"First let's finish up some shootin'. You want to give her a try?"

"Sure, if it's okay with the sergeant!" I yelled.

Woody got me in position with a fresh load of .38 Special wad-cutters in his four-inch, Smith&Wesson .357 Magnum. It was old-fashioned in this new era of Sigs, Glocks, and Berettas for police work, but it was a nice weapon.

I squeezed off the first round, with Woody at my side. He touched my arm and stopped me before I could continue, then he reeled the target toward us.

Woody laughed and pointed at my first bullet hole in the target silhouette man. I hadn't killed him, but he would never have children.

"Remind me to never get in a gunfight with you! Dead is one thing, but that hurts! Try to aim a little higher. That one might have stopped a' elephant, but you can't count on so small a target....Well, on *some* folks, it's small."

With his coaching, and more practice, I started getting better. I'd fired Expert with pistol in the Army many years ago, and it gradually came back to me—good breathing, both eyes open, squeeze on target until you're surprised when it goes off.

We moved into the lounge area, after Woody had cleared his weapon with the sergeant, swinging the cylinder open to show him the empty chambers.

"Can we beg a cup of coffee, Elmer?" he asked.

"They's a kitty in there to feed. Go right ahead."

We did as directed, Woody inserting a dollar bill into the slot hacked in the top of a Coffee Mate jar.

We seated ourselves on overstuffed chrome and plastic chairs. Woody slurped some coffee, made a face, and began.

"This thing just don't add up." He began to tick off points by unfolding fingers, one at a time, on his right hand.

"It don't make no sense *nobody* knew they was missin'.

"It don't make no sense the cops couldn't find anybody livin' where their addresses was.

"It don't make no sense nobody else worked for their company.

"I just don't believe this big galoot is really a cousin. And I don't believe they's a kid missin'..."

I held up my hand. "Wait. Why tell me all this? How about your buddies at the Department?"

"Aw, none of them's got any imagination. Maybe I've got too much."

"What's your theory, Sherlock?"

"Well, if you make one assumption, everything else clicks right into place." Woody made a face this time before he took another swallow of coffee.

I waited. Woody cleared his throat and turned to me.

"If something *really* valuable was in the plane, everything else makes sense."

"Why do you say that? Seems to me it could be like they say it is." I had to play dumb, now that I had acted that way for the past several weeks.

"Well, Matthew. Think about what I've just said. You're a logical guy. Let me lay it out for you like I think it mighta' happened. These two dead guys—well, they wasn't dead at the time—was deliverin' drugs somewheres, or bringin' the money back. They screw up and crash the plane.

"Well, the boss probably goes ape-shit when they don't come back. His first thought might be they double-crossed him and took off. It takes a crook to know one. He may consider the possibility that something went wrong, or maybe they was high-jacked by some other crooks. Anyway, think about how pissed he'd be."

He paused and started to take another drink of coffee, looked at the cup, grimaced, and set it back down. I waited for him to continue.

"Don'cha see? That's why no alarm went up when they didn't come back. That's why nobody came forward for awhile when they was found. They had to scope out what to do about it, not knowin' whether we found anything in the plane. And that's why King Kong is lookin' for this missin' imaginary kid. He puts out $25,000 chunks of bait, just in case anybody seen anything, and he's got the sheriff's department helpin' him look for clues."

"Well, Woody, that's some story. It could be right out of television or the movies. Are you sure it isn't?"

"Come on, Matthew! You've got to agree this makes sense. There's only a coupla' things I ain't exactly figgered out."

"What's that?"

"It's who found it, and what they did with it. And, of course, what "it" is."

"Well, assuming your theory is correct, how could anyone possibly find it, if it was as deep in the mountains as you say?"

"Just luck, stumbling across it. Probably bad luck, I'd say. *If* it happened, I hope the poor bastard is a long way from here if they figger out who he is."

I didn't like the way this conversation was going. In my gut, I knew Woody was right. Still, how could anyone possibly know about me? If the conversation was bad, however, it could get worse.

"Matthew, if you was to find something like that, what would you do?"

I hoped the question was hypothetical. "Well, I guess I'd call you, since you're the law around here."

"Don't be funny. I mean, what would you *really* do? Supposin' you find a really big wad of cash, or a bag of diamonds. Would you turn it in, or would you keep it?" He didn't wait for my answer. "It's just something to think about..."

I decided it was best not to comment. Woody rose from his chair and poured the nearly full cup of coffee in the sink. Then he turned to look directly at me, his expression growing serious.

"If anybody was to do something like that, he could be in a heap of trouble. I'd hope he'd turn to his friends for help."

Woody had an intensity in his gray eyes and a look of concern that told me what I didn't want to know. He suspected I had something to do with this. It must have been the fool donkey I borrowed.

"One would hope so," I mumbled. "Look, if you really believe all this, why don't you investigate this 'cousin?' Maybe you can smoke him out."

And maybe if you smoke him out, he'll go back where he came from.

He gripped my hand. "Oh, I intend to. I got to get permission, but I'd like to know more about this company they say owned the plane. See if it really did exist."

"Well, be careful, Woody. If what you think turns out to be true, these are bad people. Give my best to Eileen."

"I will, Matthew. Thanks for comin' out to listen to me. You be careful."

We walked out to the parking lot, then he turned to me with one last question. "You gotta' gun?"

"Yeah, why do you ask?"

"Just wondered. Be careful."

18.
PRESSURE

I was shaken by the conversation with Woody. He was more clever than most, but others might figure it out in time, thanks to me. I thought about the people besides Woody and Eileen who knew something about my recent activities. My neighbors knew I had kept some unusual hours. Israel wondered what I was up to. There was the cop at the truck stop. Candy. Rudi knew everything, but he was out of reach...I hoped. And worst of all, Carol Fenton.

God! I'd left a trail like an elephant crashing through a bamboo thicket.

Should I give up and go on the run right now? No, it was too obvious. Surely there would be time, and perhaps nothing would come of Testa's search. If Woody found enough suspicious evidence about our large friend, maybe the heat would drive him off and I could do nothing. Or it could drive him underground, or bring others into town that would be invisible to me. No scenario I came up with made me feel much better.

What about my children?

That question loomed largest of all, if these creeps got into the situation far enough to learn about them. Thank God they were in Europe. It offered some measure of delay and complication. I would let them have me if necessary to prevent harm to my children. But would that be the end of it? My mind was racing and an edge of panic began to creep into my thoughts.

Remain calm. Think about the options. If worse came to worst, I would have to get in touch with Dave and tell him to leave no trail in his travel about Europe. I would call Georgio and request his protection for Cathy. And as for me? I could give myself up to authorities and spend a long time in jail, or I could flee...if *they* found out about me.

It amazed me how blasé about the situation I had been. It was unlike me to be so careless. But then I'd never before been confronted with the sight of seven million dollars in cash. And I had allowed myself to sink into self-pity, beginning to think the world owed me a break. It was a dangerous combination—greed and self-pity.

Now I had to come up with a plan. It would be best if I could change identities and go on the run. But where to? Also, I hadn't the slightest idea how to obtain false papers in a location such as Mountain View. Perhaps in Knoxville...but how?

The problem with dropping out of sight still left a big question unsolved. Would my children be safe? They had lives to live and careers planned, and a fugitive father was the last thing they needed. Of course I didn't think about all these things when I should have. Perhaps I didn't think at all.

The more I worried about it, the less clear the strategy became. I couldn't even give the money back. If I gave it back to them, they'd kill me to set an example, or just because it would seem the proper thing to do.

Perhaps I could cut a deal with the FBI, or whoever did these things, to obtain freedom and witness protection in exchange for the money. The rub was I didn't really know anything that would help them. I just had the money. And that approach still didn't solve the problem of the kids.

These thoughts chased themselves in circles in my mind the rest of the afternoon and into the night, precluding sleep until late into the morning hours. When I awoke in the morning, I went running to clear my mind. The dawn was bright and clear, a contrast to the turmoil inside my head.

By the time I returned to the basement drive, I had made one small decision. Whatever else I decided, I must have an escape bag always with me, ready to go at all times.

After breakfast, I began assembling a pile on the bed in a spare room. It gave me activity instead of worry. The pile began to grow as the morning progressed: first a collection of simple clothing, underwear, and socks. I added a travel kit, a first-aid kit, and basic drugstore medications. I went through my business card file and selected key contacts around the world from my business days, putting them in a vinyl folder. I added my pocket-sized Daytimer and my travel documents folder with my passport in the pocket.

Since I'm often about town wearing running shoes, I put in a good pair of leather casual shoes. Running shoes seemed appropriate in my current frame of mind. I would put the Beretta on top of the stack. I got out the remainder of the original hundred-grand bag of cash, then I reconsidered. No point in an open admission of guilt. I decided to make a run to the safe-deposit box.

I got the money out of the bonus room storage and removed two thousand dollars. The rest I tucked into a fanny-pack and headed for the bank. First I changed the travel money into fifties—unrelated in denomination and series from the found money. Then I placed the rest in the safe deposit box. I got out the pouch containing the few pieces of Caroline's jewelry I had saved, touching each piece and remembering where it had come from, remembering each occasion. One heavy gold chain she often wore was square in cross section, with intricate multi-layered links. It had come from the *Pontevecchio* in Florence, the "Old Bridge" spared during World War II. We had walked the city for days in the golden light of Tuscany, basking in the reflected beauty of the ancient city. The necklace had an antique look that always took us back there.

I snapped my mind back to the present. I can't go back now. I have said goodbye forever to those times. The future must be faced. It will lead to new memories, or perhaps none at all. I copied the Nassau account number on a sticky note, closed the box, and gave it back to the teller. Later, I copied the number into my DayTimer, disguising it as a fake telephone number.

When I got back home, I put the cash in the travel folder and continued assembling my gear. My Gore-Tex rain suit went into the pile. I added three paperback books. What had I forgotten?

I carefully folded everything, and found it fit nicely in a small black leather athletic bag the company had given me for some anniversary. The bag now represented my entire retirement plan from them, so it was appropriate to keep it with me.

From now on I would treat this bag like the so-called nuclear "football" that followed the president.

The weather had turned disagreeable, gray and rainy, hovering just above freezing. I spent the afternoon in front of the fireplace, pretending to read, but thinking instead about what revelations might lie ahead.

I put Sarah Brightman on the CD player and allowed her wondrous voice to transport me away from my troubles. "Nella Fantasia" washed over me, stroking the chords of my soul as always. However, magic though it was, it would work for only a little while. Visions of Testa and trouble kept intruding.

The next stage began with the six o'clock news. Coverage of Mr. Testa's trip into the mountains was the basis for the third story, following a fire in a college administration building, and the state legislature fighting over the income tax proposal.

Brave newsmen had followed Mr. Testa's bulky rain-suit clad figure through the brush to capture his first sight of the downed plane.

He repeated his now familiar lament about his sorrow over the death of his cousin and his concern for the lost little Joey. He made it a point to chum the waters again with the $25,000 bait.

North Carolina deputies with dogs were in the background, with the intention of looking for signs of Joey. Good luck.

Just before the camera panned away from Testa, I caught sight of a face in the background that was familiar to me. The face of the man was ruddy and full, and he had a red beard. Where had I seen him?

The same earnest young reporter faced the camera for his closing. "This is Ken Smith, reporting from the mountains of North Carolina."

Well, there it was. More publicity to make more people think about what they had seen in the mountains in the last few months.

The doorbell rang just before ten o'clock. I flipped on the porch light to disclose Carol Fenton standing there in her black trench coat. She was close to the last on my list of people I'd like to see at my door, probably running right next to Leonard Testa, who claimed undisputed last place. I had the sinking feeling Mr. Testa *was* there in spirit. Well, no point in needlessly antagonizing her by keeping her locked out. I opened the door.

She struck a nonchalant pose with hand on hip. "Well, if it isn't Mr. Cross, home at last."

"Mrs. Fenton, how nice to see you. What brings you out on a night like this? You have a late night showing?"

"There might be something showing, but not houses. If you will open the door and stand aside, we can talk about it." She stepped forward and I let her into the foyer.

She began removing her coat, and I hung it for her on a hall tree, where it could drip on the slate entry. She was wearing a royal blue cashmere sweater, with a soft plaid wool skirt to mid-calf.

"Just what is it you wish to discuss?"

"Don't get in a hurry. Our last conversation was not as pleasant as I would like. Let's go in by the fire, and start over. A scotch on ice would go well with this weather, don't you think?" She seated herself before the fire, in one of the twin leather chairs.

I went to the bar, dipped ice out of the icemaker into two cut crystal glasses, and poured double shots of Famous Grouse. I'd save the single malt for myself. I handed her a glass and waited for her to speak. My approach would be to let her say what she wanted, then get rid of her as painlessly as possible...for me.

"My husband is out of town, so I thought it would be good to visit old acquaintances, tie up some loose ends."

My response was a complete silence, to see where she was going with this.

"Do you enjoy going up into the mountains?"

"On occasion, yes. Often the pressure of other commitments prevents it, however."

"Have you been following the news lately about the mountains?"

Well, at least she was getting to the point. "What news? I don't recall anything in particular."

"Oh, you don't?" She attempted an expression of mocking amusement. I could not tell how sure of herself she felt.

Then she continued, with her mouth set in a thin line. "I can see you're going to play innocent, when you know exactly what I'm talking about. I'm about to make a little extra money, and thought you should be the first to know."

"Why me? You seem to have the mistaken impression I'm interested in your private life. We hardly know each other."

"Oh, but we're about to become better acquainted. With a few spoken words, I stand to make twenty-five grand. A nice little sum...about like selling a four hundred thousand dollar house at full commission. Nice...but still...not all that much. If the information I have to give is worth that much, then it's probably worth a lot more, don't you think?"

"I'm sorry, but I haven't the foggiest idea what you're talking about."

She arched her eyebrows, and leaned back in the chair. "Oh, re-e-a-l-l-y?"

We were at an impasse. I could wait as long as necessary for her to explain. Silence is a good negotiating tool. I emphasized my outward unconcern by getting up and fixing the fire. If I smoked a pipe, I could have scraped, filled, tamped, and puffed to further the illusion of relaxed nonchalance. Inside, my nerves were jumping.

She waited also, no stranger to negotiating.

"You say you sold a house?"

"God damn it! Don't play dumb with me! I'm talking about the goddam airplane! I'm talking about that ugly Italian creep with the reward!"

"Well, why didn't you just come out and say so. I'm not very good at riddles. You needn't be upset. But I still don't understand what this has to do with me."

She clinched her teeth and spoke in slow sentences. "I'm talking about someone who likes to ride in the mountains at night, pulling a pack animal. I thought then something strange was going on, and now that there's a reward, I'm sure of it. So, I'll explain it for you in more specific terms. Twenty-five thousand isn't enough."

"I'm sorry, Mrs. Fenton, but it sounds like you're trying to blackmail me for something I know nothing about."

"Maybe you're finally catching on."

"Perhaps I'd better show you out."

"I'm going to let you think about it. Let it soak in a little bit. Call me before tomorrow night at this time or I go to Big Ugly and tell him what I know."

I rose. "It's time for you to go."

"You're freaking hopeless!" She jumped to her feet and threw the crystal glass into the fireplace with a loud crash. She almost ran over me on the way to the front door.

I tried to help her with her coat, but she snatched it out of my hand and got into it after about three tries, the collar folded under on one side. She yanked open the front door and charged into the darkness, slamming the door behind her.

"Goodnight, Mrs. Fenton," I said softly.

I knew she was trouble from the beginning. I tried to pretend she would go away. Now I knew she would not. I also knew admitting anything to anyone would be fatal. If I bought her off, it would confirm my guilt to someone I couldn't trust.

My options were running out. I went back to the family room and poured another drink. I sat staring into the fire. It was time to do what I could to protect my children, then take some measures to protect myself. I wondered how long it would take for them to come after me.

Would they follow me, investigate me, be subtle or overt? I had to think this thing through, and quickly. I didn't want to scurry hopelessly about like a squirrel caught in the middle of the highway. Tomorrow I would call Georgio and give him some story and ask him to keep an eye on Cathy. The time had come. I would also try to reach David, wherever he might be. Coming up with a plausible excuse might prove difficult.

I banked the fire, put the screen in front of it, and went to bed. There proved to be little sleep in store for me.

The rain continued into the morning. It drizzled and dripped, with occasional gusts of cold wind. I made myself go running despite a dull ache in my head, and a body that protested against cranking up the respiratory system.

I would like to talk to Woody to see if any progress had been made in his investigation, but I decided to wait until evening. Surely I would have that much time. The best use of the morning would be to try to reach David, then wait until after lunch to call Georgio. He usually got home about seven, or one o'clock here.

I tried to picture where David might be. Winter wasn't the best of times to be touring Europe except in the south...or in the ski areas, if skiing was the objective. I would bet on Spain, the French Riviera, or Italy.

Nothing happened the first time I tried the phone number. It rang several times, than an undecipherable operator announcement came on.

I waited another hour, then tried again. This time, I got an answer. *"Pronto?"*

They must be in Italy. *"Boun giorno. Jean-Francois?"* This is Matthew Cross, David's father. Is he with you?"

"Oh, *oui, oui, Monsieur* C. He is right here. I put him on."

"Dad! Is everything okay?"

"Sure, David. I wanted to get in touch with you before Christmas, just to say a few words. I'll talk to you again when you reach Milan. I don't want to run up a big bill on this cell phone. Where are you?"

"We're in Assisi, working our way north. We decided to go as far south as we could, to get away from the damp winter weather. It's been great. We're staying in hostels, and living simply, the best way to see a country."

"It sounds good, David. But don't worry about your expenses. I'm doing some consulting now, and the money is good, so charge what you need to. That's also part of the problem. I don't want to go into detail, so just accept what I say. One of the deals turned out to be not what I expected, and it's causing a bit of trouble. Don't be alarmed, but take measures to protect yourself. In other words, go out of your way to keep your address and whereabouts known only to people you trust. I have talked with Georgio about watching over Cathy, and will speak with him again tonight."

"Dad? This sounds serious. Are you going to be okay? Have they threatened you? Have you gone to the police? I don't understand..."

"Please, David. I'll be okay. And maybe I'm over-reacting. I just want to make sure you two are safe. Now, we'd better sign off. Have a good time, and be safe."

"Okay, if you're sure you're all right, Dad. Be careful. I look forward to hearing from you in Milan." I could hear the puzzlement in his voice. When the connection was broken, I felt another wave of deep regret.

Parents should be the wise ones, making the best decisions always for the welfare of their children. I had violated that responsibility in a big way. If something did happen to me, what would become of them and their plans? I'd better do something for the short run, at least.

I went back to the bank and got nine thousand out of the safe deposit box. Then I asked to see the branch manager in her office.

"Betty, I have a little problem I need to address. My children are both in Europe—"

"Yes, I know. How are they? And what can I do to help?"

"I had saved back some cash for a rainy day, and want to put it in an account to take care of their credit card bills. My schedule may be a bit unpredictable, and I want to make sure the bills are paid on time. Their tuition is paid. This will be for incidentals. They both charge to the Visa we have through the bank here."

"Sure, no problem. We can just put it in your regular account and you can sign an authorization for this particular credit card, or any other bills you wish."

She took the stack of cash to one of the tellers without question, and we set up the paperwork. For some reason, everyone in town thought I was honest. While I was at it, I set up the house payment and the power, telephone, and water bills. It meant more chasing about town, but it was worth it. One small step out of the way. I convinced myself it was because I might have to run. I avoided thinking of other reasons for my absence.

Georgio was there when I telephoned. He traveled less these days, and also tried to keep a more regular schedule now that he was turning the reins of the business over to their son. Elizabetta called to him, and I could hear his footsteps coming down the marble hall.

"Matt-yew, my friend. I am happy to hear from you. How are you?"

"Well, Georgio, to tell the truth, things could be better. I'm really okay, but I wanted to talk to you if you have a few moments."

"Of course. Of course. Anytime you wish."

"Do you recall the conversation we had when I was there? About a business deal that might not work as I hoped?"

A pause, then a hesitant, "Yes..."

"It's not working out very well, and the people are not the kind of people I ever wanted to become involved with. Unfortunately, it may be too late to distance myself from them. To come directly to the point, I'm a little afraid of them..."

"Can you not go to your police? Surely there must be something..."

"I don't have any justification yet. And there may be nothing to my concerns. I just want to make sure Cathy is safe from anything that could come her way. Also, David..."

"Yes, yes, I understand. And I will see to their safety, you can be assured."

"Georgio? If it involves hiring some security for the short term, could you let me know what the charges could be? I will gladly send the correct amount. That's the problem with this deal, the money. I can now afford to hire whomever you recommend."

"Matt-yew, I respect what you say, and I will let you know. If you trust my judgment, I will take care of it and let you settle later. Okay?"

"Thank you, Georgio, from the bottom of my heart. *Mille grazie.*"

"*Prego*, my friend. May God watch over you."

I knew Georgio could be trusted, but I hated asking him.

19.
BETRAYAL

Despite my discomfort, talking to Georgio gave some measure of relief. Now I needed to figure out some way to disappear without a trace—in a manner of my own choosing. How could I make a connection with people who forged papers? It wasn't something you could look up in the yellow pages, or check the "Services" section of the want ads. I'd be willing to bet Woody knew who the shadier characters were, or could find out. Talking to him about it was out of the question.

Who could possibly know someone who could make a connection for me? I'm frequently seeing something on television, or reading in the paper about some dunce trying to hire a hit, only to find he's been set up by the police. On the other hand, it seems those who have been in prison for any length of time, even if they are now perfectly straight, know of people who do things. The only problem is, I don't know anyone like that.

Cab drivers haul people all over, and perhaps hear things. What about pawn brokers? I'm sure most of them are perfectly legitimate and would resent my fleeting thoughts in that direction. However, they are in a position to hear from the wrong people. The police certainly go after them enough. Could I find one in a seedy part of town that might do something for me? How would he know I wasn't setting him up?

Within a half-hour, I found myself in a section of Knoxville unfamiliar to me, though I knew it existed. It was a street of small shops, all with barred windows. The signs were garish and hand-painted, announcing the various specialties—Checks Cashed, Second Time Around Clothing, Tattoos and Piercing. There were small grocery shops, a locksmith, cleaners, and finally what I sought: Eddie's Pawn Shop, "Guns, New and Used."

I found a parking spot around the corner and went back to the shop, my knees shaking. I had the premonition I was about to make a fool of myself. I opened the door and walked into the shop, a bell jangled, and the proprietor got up from a stool behind a glassed case full of guns. He had been reading the paper. He was a tall, slender black man, with a fringe of gray hair, and a matching mustache.

"Hi, how're you doin'?" he said. "Let me know if there's anything you need help with."

"Thanks, I will." I walked around the shop, looking briefly at the array of guitars and other musical instruments, the jewelry, and items people felt they could part with. No other customers were there, which meant I'd better get on with my business.

I approached him, took a deep breath, and began. "There is something I need. I don't know anyone who can help me. You see, I'm looking for someone with special skills; skill that can't be advertised..."

He leaned over the counter and stared at me over his half-glasses. "I'm in the money-lending business. As I think you can see, this is a pawnshop. People bring me things, I loan them money. If they don't come back, I sell the things if I can. Is that what you had in mind? You got something to pawn?"

"No, no. It's not that. You see, I may be in trouble with the wrong people, and I need papers to get out of the country. Do you know anyone—"

"Why the **HELL** should I know anyone? Because I live in a poor neighborhood? Because I'm black? You turn around and get your white ass out of my store before I call the police!"

"Look, I'm sorry. I didn't mean any harm. I just thought maybe people in trouble might come here—"

"I'm not gonna' tell you again. Get the hell out of here!" He started around the counter, but I had gotten the message. I left.

That went even worse than I imagined. It was really stupid of me, and after the fact I could see how offensive it was.

I wasted no time getting the Explorer cranked and heading back home. That was enough for today on that particular mission. I'd give it some thought and see if some other brilliant plan would emerge. Surely I could come up with something better than that.

I waited until I was sure Woody should be home and through with his evening meal before I telephoned.

"Hi, Matt. You doin' okay?"

"Yeah, I was still thinking about the theories you had about the airplane deal, and wondered how you were coming...whether anyone believed you yet."

"Well, I can't say they're all thrilled about it yet, but at least they're lookin' into it. You know, I mostly do other stuff and check in now and then."

"Have they found anything?"

"Matt, I hate to say this, you bein' my best friend and all, but I ain't supposed to—"

"I'm sorry Woody, I wasn't thinking. I was just curious."

"I can say this much. That importin' business seemed to be what it was. They weren't doin' much lately, but they was in the business of bringin' in statues and carvings, pottery, and crap like that from South America...somewheres down in there."

"Hmm. Interesting. I don't suppose there's been anything on the kid, since you don't believe he exists."

"Naw. They won't find nothin', I perdict."

"You and Eileen doing okay?" He replied that they were, and we chatted a bit before hanging up. No news from that quarter.

I sat musing about my abortive day. The telephone rang about nine o'clock in the evening. It was Carol Fenton.

"Have you come to your senses?"

"I hope they have never left me. Are you still talking in riddles?"

"No riddles. Either you work with me, or I go to this Testa guy. Which is it going to be?"

"I'm telling you, I don't know what you're getting at."

"Okay. That's it. Don't say I didn't warn you." She cut the connection.

I was awakened from a deep sleep by the ringing telephone. My mind tried to fit it into a dream, then gave up and let awareness arrive.

When I picked it up, I heard a brusque, unfamiliar voice. "Who's speakin'?" it demanded.

I looked at the digital clock. It registered three-thirty-six. "Who were you calling?" I countered.

"This is Detective Stone, of the Knoxville Police Department, and I need you to identify yourself. It will save me the trouble of looking up your number."

"I'm Matthew Cross. What's going on?"

"Never mind that for now. It's just a couple of routine questions about a missing person. Where do you live?"

"I'm in Mountain View. Hey, can't you tell me what this is about? What missing person? Is anyone hurt? Why did you call me?"

"We'd just like to talk to you, if you're willing. How about coming in to the station, Mr. Cross?"

"Now?"

"Now would be fine. Do you want me to send a patrolman for you?"

"No, that won't be necessary. Just give me the directions, and time to get dressed."

I wrote down the address. "Thank you, Mr. Cross. We'll see you in about an hour?"

"I'll be there." I knew I'd better be, but I hadn't a clue what to expect when I got there. The mess about the plane was the only thing I could think of. Could the missing person be the "nephew"? And had Carol Fenton put them onto me?

I struggled with the question of whether to call Woody. Or should I call a lawyer? What did he mean, "save me the trouble of looking it up?" Since he didn't know who would answer, he didn't have my name, just my telephone number. But where did he get it?

At that ungodly hour, I was able to park right in front of the station. I'd made a cup of instant coffee, but felt hollow and strange inside, and my nerves were on edge. I felt as guilty as anyone would, summoned to appear at police headquarters in the early morning darkness. I felt inclined to rush in and confess, and plead for mercy.

I walked up to the counter in front and asked the desk sergeant for Detective Stone. He logged in my full name, address, and phone number, then walked me through a metal detector and back to the department.

Detective Walter Stone was waiting for me behind a small desk stacked high with folders and paperwork. It was in an open area, along with rows of other desks.

He was about my height and age, but growing fat around the middle. His hair was nearly gone except for a rust-colored fringe, his scalp covered with large freckles. He rose and shook hands, giving me a painful little smile. "Thanks for coming in, Mr. Cross. Let's move in to an office where we can talk."

He led me to a glass-walled cube, removed some papers from a chair for me, then closed the door and sat behind the desk. He took his time, steepling his blunt fingers, peering at me with green eyes. I waited.

"Well, Mr. Cross, I'll get right to the point. Do you know a Mrs. Carol Fenton?"

"Yes...sort of. She's a realtor in Mountain View. We've spoken a few times, but I can't say I really know her well. Has something happened to her?" Where was he going with this?

He ignored my question. "Have you spoken with her recently?"

"Yeah, she called last night, as a matter of fact. I think it was last night."

"What was the nature of her call, if you don't mind?"

"She kept pestering me to list the house with her. I had it listed with another realtor. Can't you tell me what this is about? Has something happened to her?"

"We're just checkin' out a report from a kid who works in a 7-Eleven over on John Sevier Highway. He seen this woman standing by a pay phone, got a fancy car, been sittin' in it for a little while. Then these two guys come and take her away in a mini-van. Didn't exactly look like she wanted to go. The kid dithers awhile, finally calls us. When we go over there, not much we can find out by lookin' at the car, but we reverse the license plate and find out who she is. Then I got this bright idea, learned it on Tee Vee. I picked up her cell phone, layin' there in the seat, and hit the re-dial button. Guess who answers?"

"That's strange. I hope she's okay. Did you talk to her husband? Maybe he knows something."

"Hey, maybe you'd make a good detective. We actually thought of that too. He thought she was just goin' out for a minute, to make sure a house she'd shown was locked up."

He sat at the desk and looked at me. I waited for him to continue, but my mind was racing. What *had* she been up to? Was her call to me my "last chance" before she went after her reward? That had a different ring to it, when I said it to myself. Going *to* her reward, perhaps?

Finally Detective Stone spoke. "You got it figgered out? Let's go over what we got here. Woman lies to her husband in Mountain View; drives to Knoxville late at night, maybe to meet somebody. Always the businesswoman, calls to ask for your listing again. Then she disappears with two guys in a van, leaving her fancy car unlocked. Is that about it?"

"All I know is the part about calling me for the listing."

"Can anyone else account for where you were after her call, and before I called you?"

"No. I live alone, and I was at home. I went to bed, and that's where I was when you called."

He sat and stared at me for several moments. "Well, I guess that's about it for now. If we have other questions we'll be in touch. You're plannin' to stay in town, I hope?"

"No, I hadn't planned on it. My kids are in Italy, and I was thinking of spending Christmas with them."

"Check with us before you go."

"Why?"

"We may want to talk to you. We don't know where this is going. Somehow it doesn't ring true. If we find out she was just out for a good time, then you can do whatever you want."

I made it back to the car as light was beginning in the eastern sky. This was a mess. I had a horrible feeling Carol was trying to be cute with them on the terms of the reward, just as she had pressured me. She probably had arranged the meet, then called me for my last chance. They had been smart enough to demand contact by pay phone. Those records would show where she had called, since the police knew which phone she had used. But I would bet it called another pay phone or some public place.

I had my escape bag and I thought about heading straight for the airport. I'd give it a little more time, long enough to go home and pack a proper suitcase and check out some flights. First, I'd have some breakfast on the way home.

I stopped at Woody's favorite truck stop, out on the highway near Mountain View. The same waitress as last time, Woody's recommendation, served me at the counter. God! It seemed years ago...a different place in time. Back when I was just *beginning* to lose my sanity.

She brought my breakfast with the same efficiency, the same tired smile. I ate my eggs and bacon and drank my coffee. I wondered where Carol Fenton was. Should I tell someone the truth about all this, and perhaps give her a chance at being rescued? There was not much doubt she had gotten in trouble. I rationalized that it was her fault, and that if she was in trouble, it was now too late to help her. On the other hand, maybe the kid was wrong. Maybe she went willingly. But the detective was right; it was strange to leave a car unlocked.

How easy it became to rationalize or make excuses, when life and reputation were at stake. I had to face the fact cowardice played a part in my continuing to hope for this mess to clear up on its own. Woody would know what to do but I hated the thought of lowering his regard for me. And I couldn't stand Eileen being disappointed in me.

I paid the check, leaving a generous tip like last time. Then I threaded the Explorer through the gasping, clattering diesels and onto the highway.

I knew something was wrong the moment the basement garage door started to rise. There was a set of storage shelves at the back end of the garage, and several metal cabinets standing along the walls. As the door came up, it exposed a scene of devastation. Every object was separated, overturned, ripped apart, and scattered. It horrified me to think about the rest of the house, and at the same time I wondered if they were still there. I'd been gone for perhaps three hours; long enough if they'd been waiting for me to leave, or had arrived by coincidence right after I left.

I called Woody on my cell phone. There was no answer. He and Eileen were both at work somewhere.

If I brought the police into this on top of my early morning summons to Knoxville, it didn't look good. It would increase their interest in Carol's telephone call to me the night before.

Woody sometimes went to his car auction on Wednesday mornings to start working on the next day's big sale. I tried that number, and waited while they looked for him. As I sat in the lower driveway, I wondered if my house was being taken apart upstairs. Probably not. The sound of the garage door opener would have sent them on their way, or they would be waiting to ambush me.

"This is Woody."

"Woody, it's Matt. I have big trouble here. I'm sitting in my basement driveway. I just got home. Somebody's been here and taken the place apart. I don't know if they're gone."

"Have you called the police? They need to come over before you go inside."

"Well, no...there's a complication. I had to go talk to the Knoxville police early this morning. Look, it's hard to explain. Maybe you're right, I shouldn't bother you..."

"I didn't say that. I can't come officially, but we're friends. We can stumble on this by accident. *Then* we can call the police, if we have to. I'm on my way."

The phone clicked. It would take about fifteen minutes at the most. I got the Beretta out of my escape bag and checked the load. I had carried this little weapon around for years in various circumstances, as a security totem. Would something ever happen that would cause me to use it?

Woody rolled up to the curb in an old blue sixties Cadillac, with huge trunk and fins. Woody looked undersized as he clambered out the huge door, · which swung wide with a screech. Any sense of incongruity disappeared as Woody approached me. He had on his game face, an intensity I had not seen before. His eyes were narrowed, his mouth set, the muscles of his body tense.

"Step inside," he said, in a near whisper, nodding toward the open garage door. "Now tell me what this is about, if you can. I'll give you a free shot off the record. I'm only part-time, but I took an oath just like everybody else."

I decided the wisest thing on my part would be to tell only part of the truth. I spoke in his ear in a hoarse whisper. "I think you know who Carol Fenton is?" He nodded. "She's been calling, and she even came by the house a couple of times. She's all excited about the airplane crash in the mountains and the twenty-five thousand reward. She and her husband were riding up in the mountains when I went up there with your horses. She's decided I have something to do with it, and hinted at what sounded like a shakedown to me. I told her to get lost, and apparently she did."

"What do you mean?"

"She called me last night to 'give me one more chance,' which didn't change my mind, of course. In the wee hours of this morning a police detective called, because my number was on her cell phone re-dial. They found her car unlocked and abandoned. They summoned me in to talk. That's where I was when this took place."

He looked at me with piercing eyes. "Matthew, I'm not gonna' ask if you are involved, but you *are* in trouble, there ain't no doubt about it. Jesus H. Christ, look at this mess! Let's see if they's anybody here, then we got to talk about gettin' you the hell out of here."

Woody reached across his body and brought out the Smith from beneath his jacket. "Stay right behind me," he commanded. I slipped the safety off on my little automatic, and did as he said. My hands were trembling, my knees shaking.

Woody walked forward in a crouch, in absolute silence. I could see him in a different decade, advancing into combat. We went from room to room, first in the basement. The downstairs recreation room was like the garage, with everything overturned. Cushions of all the chairs and sofa were slit open and the television was smashed. The laundry room had the contents of the cabinets dumped on the floor, soap powder like snowfall.

We moved quickly, disturbing nothing, then crept up the staircase, Woody and his shadow. I could hear my own rasping breath.

He calmly listened at the door when he came to the head of the stairs. Then he nodded at me and burst through, low to the carpet and rolling to his left. Nothing happened. I entered after him into the family room, which lay to the right of the stairs. All was silent, but all was destroyed. I could not know how many were involved, but it was difficult to see how they could have done it in the three hours I'd been gone. The upholstered furniture was all eviscerated, the foam ripped apart. Pictures were torn from their frames, glass shattered. Books were strewn on the floor with their spines broken. Holes had been punched in the wall behind the books, presumably to look for hidden compartments where there were none.

Woody listened again, then crept down the hallway in the direction of the bedrooms and den. I followed as before. Every room had been methodically and mercilessly dismantled. All of the kitchen cabinets' contents had been emptied on the floor. Nothing larger than the size of a cigar box could have escaped detection.

I dreaded each room. The living room was the worst, the room where Caroline had displayed her creative talents. The sofa and chairs were ripped apart and inverted on the floor. The one object that broke my composure was the portrait of Caroline. It had been slashed with a knife, the canvas hanging in triangular shreds. The deliberate destruction of my most cherished symbol was a vicious statement directly to me. I sat on the carpet and wept at my careless stupidity and frustration.

Woody put his hand on my shoulder and whispered in my ear. "I'll check the attic. You wait right here." He patted my shoulder and slipped away.

When Woody returned, I had regained my composure, and with it the resolve never to succumb to such weakness again. Now that I knew the rules of the game—there were none—I was better prepared to face what lay ahead.

He came back in a few moments, holstering his weapon reversed on his left hip. He sat on the carpet facing me. "They ain't here, and I guess they didn't get what they was after, 'cause they kept rippin' things apart through the whole house."

"That's because there wasn't anything here to get."

"Matthew, I'm really, really sorry for this. I know it's awful for you. What we got to do now is get you out of here. Now, go pack a bag and come with me to the house. We need to call the police and get them in here to investigate this, and find out who done it."

"Woody, I'm not calling the police and I'm not coming to your house. There isn't any doubt the Fenton woman has fingered me, and I'll be worse than the plague for anyone who is near me. And the police will connect this to last night. No, I'll pack a bag and go somewhere, but not to your place."

"You can't just go away, Matthew. How will you live?"

"I don't know. But I'm going to walk away from this for now. I'll find a small motel someplace and hide a couple of days while I sort out where I'm going. Then maybe I'll ask you to call the police about this so we aren't tampering with evidence. I'll have to get a cleaning service to come in and put it back in reasonable shape."

What about your children?"

"I think they're okay for the time being. I haven't thought ahead of that. Maybe I hope the people who did this will get caught because of the Fenton thing, or this break-in. Maybe I hope you'll find out something in Florida. I don't know."

"Well, you decide. But you'd better get crackin'."

"One thing you might help me with, if you have any idea how, is where I can find false paperwork—I.D. and passport."

"That's illegal as hell."

"I know it. Murder is illegal, too. And that's what happens to me if they find me."

"You got a point. I'll ask around."

I rescued a small suitcase and went back to my bedroom. I pulled together some necessities out of the tangle of clothes piled about. I went to the den to get my desk calendar. It included the addresses of all my personal friends, separate from the business file I had in the escape bag. It was nowhere to be found. I rummaged through the litter scattered everywhere, but it was gone.

20.
CHASE

The motel was a scruffy frame structure in the little town of Owensville, about halfway between Mountain View and Knoxville. It was on a highway once important, but now a backwater since the Interstate system. Its route was lined with abandoned filling stations and other businesses except near the small towns with their full-time residents.

It was a good place to hide for a few days until I could make my decisions and arrangements. It was unsophisticated enough that I was able to pay a week's lodging in cash and sign in with a fake name and address. The room was clean but tired. It was equipped with a dial telephone and a small, flickering television.

I looked at my surroundings and congratulated myself on how far I had come. I started with a few personal problems and parlayed them into a life-threatening crisis that could destroy any future I had with my family and friends.

After I checked in I located Woody, still at his auction house, and told him where I was. If the police started looking for me for any reason, I told him, he should let me know and I'd turn myself in. I couldn't allow Woody to become an accessory. My objective was to hide from the persons who'd torn up my house. I reminded him about the need for a forgery expert, not the thing you normally ask of your friends. He already knew about my missing desktop directory. That added to my guilt and worry. The thought of these people harassing anyone close to me was more than I could bear.

I confined myself to the room for the next two days, pacing the floor, waiting for word from Woody about the chance for false papers. I determined that if I hadn't heard anything by the third day, then I would take my chances as myself and try for a change of identity in another country. The police had not been after me again, as I regularly checked my phone messages at home. One question I struggled with was whether to tell them I was leaving the country. Perhaps I could leave for Christmas in Italy, then not return. On the other hand, I did not want to leave any trail closer to my children.

Television news had gotten hold of the story about the missing realtor from Mountain View, but gave little detail. They had a sad interview with her husband Tom, with his plea for help in solving the case. The airplane crash and the missing nephew no longer appeared on the evening news.

I finally reached the conclusion I would fly to Mexico City and book other arrangements from there. I decided it would be best to avoid booking in advance—just head for the airport with cash in hand and go.

With all the time on my hands, I thought about my children. I missed them terribly, now that I felt so alone and unsettled. What if I could not see them for a long time? Or ever? I couldn't lay this whole thing out for them and destroy their plans. I decided I would write each a short note telling them how much they meant to me. It could never hurt, even if this whole mess miraculously disappeared. It would be hard to put my true feelings on paper, but I decided to try. I'd brought my fountain pen and notepaper:

My Dearest Cathy,

I am so proud of you.

It is easy for me to assume you know that, but I want to tell you so again. You are beautiful, you are smart, and you have a charm and sparkle that lights up the room wherever you are. I can say this without the prejudice of a parent, because other people have expressed the same opinion. It doesn't stop me from swelling with pride that you are my daughter. At the same time, I willingly concede that you must have gotten most of those qualities from your mother.

We could dwell on the temporary departure we all took when your mother died, but I believe in all my heart that it is in the past, and I'm going to leave it there.

If I have any regrets about the years when you were growing up, they would focus on how I was busy too much, gone too much, and perhaps a little too uptight about my responsibilities as a parent. I was so determined to do a good job that I probably kept the pressure a little too high. And you really didn't need it. From the beginning, you were always such a good girl that you never really needed much discipline beyond a look of disapproval.

I won't try to recall everything, but a couple of things stand out. Remember how you loved to play Hangman? Remember the time you washed one of my suits for me in the bathtub?

I don't yearn for the past to any great degree. But when I look at pictures of you when you were a baby, or a little girl, I would give anything to hold you and play with you again. To make up for all of the times I missed.

On the other hand, when I see the woman you have become, perhaps I wouldn't change anything. It is just selfishness on my part, wanting to recapture some of the lost years.

But be assured I love you beyond question. I recognize that without you and David, and the love of your mother, my life would have had little meaning. Regardless of where the future takes us, nothing will alter these facts.

*I'm sorry that circumstances keep us apart for this Christmas Season. There is
nothing I would rather do than be with you and David. Just remember, in all the past
and forever, I am grateful that you are my daughter.*

Love,
Dad

Well, it was the best I could do. Better to keep it short. I was tempted to
reminisce about the many scenes I had played in my head the last two days, but
I might just dilute the message.

My dear David,
I am so proud of you.
*I think you must know that, but I want to tell you how I feel in my own words, if
I can. You have grown into the kind of man I hoped you would be; strong and reliable,
intelligent and caring. I see qualities in you I would like to have myself. You are more
patient with others than I, not so quick to lose your temper. It doesn't mean you accept less
than the best; you are just more mature about it than I have been.*

*There are parts of your growing up I would like to do over again, with the hope of
doing a better job. I wish I'd had more time for you and more patience with you. I told
your sister the same thing. When I see pictures of the two of you when you were small, I
would love to be able to hold you and play with you more. But we can't go back.*

*I always tried to mold you into a person of integrity and it worked, although at
times I feel I over-did it. It was hard to discipline you for some of the things you did. I
remember a particular time when you were about six and you consumed an entire cherry
pie. Well, perhaps half of it. The rest was all over the kitchen. Remember how angry I
was? I really wasn't, but I had to pretend to be.*

*You really came of age, I think, during your mother's illness. You held the rest of
us together and I have always appreciated that more than I can say.*

*Be assured I love you beyond question. I recognize that without you and Cathy,
and the love of your mother, my life would not mean a great deal. There won't be any
statues of me in the square, but there will be you and Cathy and what you have made of
yourselves. Regardless of where the future takes us, nothing will alter these facts.*

*I'm sorry circumstances keep us apart for this Christmas Season. There is nothing
I would rather do than be with you and Cathy. Remember that in all the past, and
forever, I am grateful you are my son.*

Love,
Dad

I folded the letters and prepared them for mailing. As I was doing so, I
looked through the partially opened venetian blind. Someone was approaching

209

from the direction of the parking lot. Eileen. I had specifically instructed Woody to keep this from her.

She looked uncertainly at the door, then knocked softly. "Matt, it's me, Eileen. Can I come in?"

I opened the door for her. "Eileen, what are you doing here? You shouldn't have come." I stepped inside the room and she followed.

She rushed into my arms and I heard a catch in her voice as she spoke. "Matt, we're both so worried about you. Don't blame Woody. I made him tell me where you were, but I didn't tell him I was coming. I knew something was badly wrong. I've never seen him like he's been the last two days."

"Eileen, you both must stay far away from me. It's too dangerous—not only for you, but selfishly, for me. You can't come again."

"Matt, what is it? Have you really done something wrong?"

"Some people think I have, I'm afraid. I just have to get out of the way for awhile until some things clear up."

"I'm so worried. Woody wouldn't tell me anything specific, but he said you were going away. I was afraid we'd never see you again..."

Her voice dissolved into a tremulous whisper, and tears began to flow down her cheeks.

I held her again as she began to shake with sobs. "Hey, don't worry. I'll be okay. I'll keep in touch. You'll see. But you really must stay away from me. There's nothing you can do, anyway."

She wiped her eyes with her fingers and looked at me. "Matt, go to the police if there is trouble. Even if you're involved in something you shouldn't be. Nothing is worth risking your safety and your future with your children. Please listen to me. Please do it. You will, won't you?"

"I'll try to figure something out. Now you go home and keep yourself safe. I appreciate your concern, but I don't want you around. Okay?"

"God be with you," she whispered, and she left, shoulders slumped and head bowed.

I reached the decision by late afternoon to go to the bank the next morning and get more cash from my safe deposit box. In the afternoon, I'd drive my car home and park it, then have a taxi take me to Knoxville. From there I'd catch another cab to the airport. I was not as imaginative as Agent 007, but it would put a little kink or two in tracking me down.

To get me through the evening, I telephoned a Mom and Pop diner down the road and ordered a hamburger and fries to go. I picked up a six-pack of Bud at a quick-shop and brought my dinner back to my little room.

To while away the time, I watched an old John Wayne movie on AMC, trying to keep from thinking about my situation. Woody hadn't called, which meant he had not found an answer to my identity crisis. At ten, I switched over to the local news and watched with half a mind as they went through the usual stuff about local politics, businesses failing or succeeding, and so forth. When they got to coverage of traffic accidents and other mishaps, they stunned me with a phrase that brought all of my attention into focus.

...A Hanson Creek resident was badly beaten this afternoon by unknown assailants. The man, identified as Israel Buchanan, was able to make his way to the home of a neighbor, who drove him to the hospital in Mountain View. Authorities have declined to speculate on the motive for the beating or the possible identity of the suspects...

I jumped from my chair and grabbed my Daytimer. My God, what would I do now? I'd have to do something to stop this, but first I had to find out about Israel. With shaking hands, I dialed the number of his neighbor, Fred.

"Yellllllll-o!"

Thank God he was home. "Fred, this is Matt Cross. I just heard on the news about Israel. How is he?"

"He's been knocked around a bit, Mr. Cross, but I think he's gonna' be okay. He's a tough old bird, you know. I been with him 'til I jest now got home."

"He's in Memorial in Mountain View?"

"Yep. He didn't even want to go there, but I made him do it. He may have a busted rib or two. He was hurtin' pretty bad when he drawed a breath, which ya' know we all gotta' do—"

"Thanks for taking care of him, Fred. I'm going to see him. Goodbye."

What had I done? Remembering the game I played with Cathy, I had visions of my personal game of *Hangman*. I felt a gallows looming over me, and I could see my segmented body beginning to take shape, dangling from the noose. The worst part, the unforgivable part, was the potential impact on those who trusted me.

In less than a half-hour, I pulled into the parking lot of the hospital. The lot was nearly empty, since visiting hours were over. The building was old, but in good repair. It was red brick, about six stories high, and sat on one of the higher hills in town. It was staffed with compassionate people for the most part, but lacked the reputation of the big, modern facilities in Knoxville. Generally, people went to Knoxville by choice if they had anything serious to contend with. In cases of emergency they'd get a ride in Lifestar, the med-evac helicopter.

As I got out of the car, I realized I'd forgotten my escape bag, which should have been on the seat beside me. Well, no problem. I probably wouldn't be long. I walked up the sidewalk in the faint light from the poles in the parking lot.

Inside, I presented myself at the reception desk, which was presided over by a formidable woman in a pink medical jacket. She had frizzled gray hair, and large plastic-framed glasses with thick lenses. She looked up without speaking.

"I'm here to see Israel Buchanan, please."

"Visiting hours are over."

"Yes, I know, but I just now heard on the news he was here. Please, I just need to look in on him for a moment."

"Come back tomorrow."

"I'm sorry, but that's the problem. I'm traveling out of the country tomorrow, and really must see him."

"Are you family?"

"He has no family. We've been very close for years, and I must see if there's anything I can do for him before I go."

"What's your name?"

"Matthew Cross."

"Any relation to Caroline Cross?"

"She was my wife."

I saw her shoulders relax, the bureaucratic veneer collapse.

"He's on the third floor in room 324. Try not to stay too long." Her tired features softened.

"Thank you. I really appreciate the chance to see him."

I did not like hospitals. There was the unmistakable smell, the combined scents of people, medicines, cleaning solutions, and worse. And like so many who have had tragedies in their lives, I associated them with misery and death. Unfair, to be sure, but it added to the guilt and dread weighing me down as I ascended the elevator to face what I had done. The hall on Three was deserted as I exited. The lighter staff at this hour were occupied elsewhere.

I tiptoed down the hall until I found his room. Taking a deep breath, I stepped inside. It was a double room with a curtain half-pulled between the beds. The other occupant was turned away, only a white tuft of hair visible on the pillow as he lay breathing deeply in sleep.

Israel also appeared to be sleeping, lying on his back with the head of the bed elevated. In the dim illumination of the nightlight, his weather-beaten countenance contrasted sharply with the clean white sheets. His eye sockets were blackened and there was a large bruise on his cheekbone. A bandage covered the other side of his face.

As I stood looking at him, wondering what to do, he sensed my presence. His eyes opened, and I waited for him to speak.

"Matthew? Are you doing okay?" He spoke in a near whisper. His hand stirred from where it rested on the sheet as he reached to greet me. I was touched by his concern for me under his own circumstances.

"Israel, I'm fine. I'm really worried about you. I didn't know about this until a few moments ago when I saw something on the news. What happened?" I took his hand and moved closer so we could speak quietly, and sat in a chair next to the bed with my face close to his.

He continued with difficulty. "I don't know what it was all about. These two men drove up the lane in a van, looked like they was lost. I went out to see what I could do to help. One had black hair, the other red, and both of 'em was big. They acted kinda' strange from the start. The blackhead says something like, 'You're Israel Buchanan?' I says, 'yes, I am, what can I do for you?' That kinda' thing. Then he says, 'You're a friend of Matthew Cross, aincha?'"

He paused for breath, and winced as he shifted his position. I dreaded hearing what was to come next.

"They moved up close to me, and this same one says, 'Your friend is giving us some problems, so we thought we ought to return the favor.' That's all they said. They grabbed at me and I tried to get away. But they got me. I got in a lick or two, but I wound up on the ground, and they kicked me a few times 'til I give up and just curled up and wrapped my hands around my head. Then they laughed and took off. I managed to make it to Fred's."

"Oh, Israel, I can't tell you how sorry I am for this. I'm mixed up with some bad people and I've got to do something about it. I may try to leave the country and make sure they follow. I don't know. I had no idea something like this would happen to you."

"I know. Don't worry about it none. I'll be okay. I've had worse things happen. You just look after yourself, you hear?"

"Thanks, Israel. I'll try to get it straightened out. Do you need anything?"

"No. Fred's lookin' after the place. And Matthew?" He paused. I waited for him to continue. "I didn't mention they used your name, and I won't. Not to anybody."

"Thank you Israel. If it's okay, though, I want to call Woody and tell him about this. We'll see what he can do to help."

I reluctantly bid him goodbye. I'd get back to the motel as soon as possible and lay this out for Woody. I know they found my notation on the desk calendar. Israel's birthday came the following week and I'd made a big note and highlighted it so I wouldn't forget.

It was chilly outside, and a wind had sprung up. A three-quarter moon had risen while I was inside. It shone through the black branches of the woods behind the hospital grounds. With the combined moonlight and the dim light of the parking lot lamps, the walkway was etched in dark shadows that moved with the wind. I supposed the hospital had a security staff, but I saw no one about as I made my way to the lot.

There were even fewer cars in the lot than when I came in. There was a van parked a couple of spaces over from my Explorer. I hadn't noticed it when I parked. My back was turned to it as I inserted my key in the driver's side door. Just as I lifted the handle, I heard a slight scraping sound on the pavement. I turned to see two large, dark shadows rushing toward me from either side. I whirled and ducked away from the car just as they were upon me. The momentum of their charge was spent in colliding with each other. It gave me the chance to tear away and sprint toward the nearby woods. With the layout of the lot, they were between me and the sanctuary of the hospital. Also, it would not have done to take a parking lot brawl into the halls where people had their own problems.

I had a ten-yard head start to break for the woods fifty yards away. A cable strung between posts ringed the lot, and I cleared it in full stride. I heard grunting and the scuffling of footsteps behind me of someone in full pursuit. They must have had a good idea of the layout of the place, as I heard an engine cough to life. Residential streets encircled the patch of woods on the lower side. The one chasing me was to keep up the pursuit until I came out the other side, into the hands of his accomplice.

The woods were dark, the scant moonlight contributing nothing but confusing shadows. Limbs of the brush tore at my face and clothing and it was difficult to keep my footing in the rocks and roots. My pursuer was not so fortunate. I heard him crash to the ground in a headlong slide, cursing and thrashing through the undergrowth as he rose to his feet. I ran a zigzag path, trying not to tip my hand on a direction. With the second guy out there somewhere in their van, it seemed my best bet would be to circle back to the lot. I'd dropped my keys in the initial scuffle and I hoped I could find them, if only I could get back to the car. He anticipated my thoughts, however, and continued to maneuver uphill between the lot and me.

I literally stumbled onto a different tactic. I ran straight downhill, crashing through the brush with my pursuer following twenty yards behind. Rounding a tree in the darkness, I slid into a gully that crossed my path. Crouching silently, quieting my heavy breathing, I groped along it to my right, back uphill. My stalker had stopped also, listening. Each time he would move, I would move also, trying to guess at the quiet intervals. I knew he was confused because he seemed to be thrashing about in circles, trying to flush me out. Meanwhile, I gradually drew farther away, closer and closer to the parking lot.

Their beating of Israel was designed to flush me out of hiding. I didn't figure it out until too late, not even when Israel described the encounter to me. Now I was in trouble, and only a bit of luck would help me get away from them.

I continued creeping slowly through the tangle of vines and undergrowth, my face brushing the dried leaves and occasional bare dirt and gravel of the wash. Soon I neared the cable. I could see my Explorer standing alone in the lot. There were still no signs of life about. The walkways and paved areas were clear. My best chance would be to sprint to the car and hope my keys were still under the driver's door, on the pavement. I'd have only seconds. If I couldn't find them, then I'd take a chance and race for the hospital entrance. I wondered if they would use guns. It would seem obvious they'd want to keep me alive, but I didn't like the odds against their making a mistake.

The brush man was still below me on the hillside, perhaps thirty yards away. I assumed the other guy was waiting on the road below. The time had come. I crept to the cable, rose, and sprinted for the Explorer. As I slid to a stop, I dived to the ground and felt for my key ring. I heard my pursuer running across the parking lot behind me, but at the same time saw another pair of feet in front of the car. I had miscalculated. There were three of them.

I sprang to my feet to flee, but the dark figure of the third man came around the Explorer with a gun in his hand. He leveled it and fired at point-blank range. I felt a sharp sting in my chest. I turned to run, but the other pursuer was upon me, pinning my arms to my sides. I struggled to break free, but a sensation of numbness swept over me, and I plunged into darkness.

21.
LOSERS

The common act of sleeping and the transition into consciousness is a little odd. My sleep is often entertained or tortured by dreams. With the drug, it was different—no dreaming, just a total void. I've wondered if it is the same with death. Who can know? The events that induced my unconscious state could have caused death, and nothing would be different except that I would not wake up at all.

From the black depths, a tiny flicker of awareness began, but confusion and trauma obscured it. My first sensations were waves of crawling flesh, as though my drugged brain began sending out random impulses along every branching nerve. Beginning at my feet, and up my legs, my muscles would involuntarily contract and relax at random. The waves moved up my body, tensing and relaxing my skeletal muscles in a shuddering reflex, repeated again and again. It was a thoroughly disagreeable sensation. I wanted to be awake and free from it, but couldn't summon the energy. Gradually my other senses began to function. I heard low moans, then realized they were coming from me. I tried to move my tongue to lick my lips, but my mouth was stuffed full of something unyielding.

I became aware of background noise, loud but muffled music and a distinct whine of machinery running nearby. And there was motion. In addition to the convulsions, my body seemed to be moving with subtle changes in momentum and centrifugal force. With considerable effort, I forced my eyes open. At first I could see nothing, then I became aware of dim light. I was in some kind of compartment. I tried to rise, but could not. Then panic overcame me and I struggled against my bonds. I was lying on my left side with my arms bound behind me. My ankles were also held tightly together. I could not straighten my legs, although my feet were not touching the compartment. As I pushed, I felt a tug at my wrists. I was trussed up like a chicken ready for beheading. The comparison gave me little consolation.

Due to the effects of the drug, at first I could not remember who I was or what had happened. Then images of the parking lot and crawling through the undergrowth in darkness began to form, and it all came back with a rush. I was a prisoner, and I was in the trunk of a car speeding down a highway. It was a large trunk with a flat floor.

My face was jammed against the carpeting. My cheek was in a pool of saliva that had drooled from the stuff in my mouth. I tried again to move, but could do little more than lift my head slightly. My left arm was numb and my muscles were beginning to protest, as I checked for freedom of movement. My leg muscles wanted to cramp, but I could do little about it except try to relax. My mind was still fogged by the effects of the drug in the dart they had used to bring me down. Still, I was able to appreciate the desperate situation I was in.

They must be taking me to some place where interrogation can be conducted. They seem convinced they have the right person, after what they did to my house...and now that they captured me without killing me. I had Carol Fenton to thank for this. I wondered where she was now. Was she with them, or had she been discarded after serving her usefulness? I knew only one way to stay alive. *Don't tell them anything!* Would it be possible? I didn't know what I could endure. I did know I would be killed if I ever admitted what I had done, or ever told them what happened to the money. That must be the mantra I repeated to myself, whatever happened to me: *Talk and you will die.*

I remembered another principle taught by the Army on escape and evasion. Attempt to escape as soon as possible after capture. The longer you wait, the lower the odds of success. That principle is based on military situations, when confusion and disorganization may rule after an engagement. Still, my physical strength was as good as it would get and my captors might not be as organized away from their base of operations.

What could be possible in my circumstance? I began to experiment with movement. My fingers were free to move. I twisted my wrists against the tape that confined them, trying to reach any seam or lap in the tape with a fingernail. I could not. I tried to turn over. Gradually, I was able to squirm away from the rear of the trunk, then roll over on my face, and thence to the other side. It was a minor triumph, giving my body a rest and me a new perspective. This maneuver also put my hands near the trunk latch, and I searched out some rough edges on the sheet metal surrounding it.

By straining every muscle, I was able to make contact with the rear of the compartment. Thanks to metal stamping, the parts had raised burrs that I put to good use. I could feel the tape start to divide, though I had to rest every few seconds and I was wet with sweat. They'd left my jacket on when they tossed me in the trunk. The road noise continued, as did their taste in country music. Talk about somebody done somebody wrong.

Eventually, I got one hand free and ripped the tape from my mouth, then removed a wadded handkerchief. Removing the rest of the tape from my hands and feet was relatively easy. I moved slowly so the motion could not be detected up front. Except for being locked in the trunk of a car, I was free. I began exploring by feel in the darkness of the compartment, trying to find an inside release for the latch. I could find nothing except the gas cap release. The car would have to be stopped anyway, before I could get out. I'd just have to wait for them to open it, and hope the element of surprise would allow me to get away. It would have to occur either at their destination, or it would probably be in some remote place with no one nearby to help. I had no idea how long I'd been unconscious, therefore no idea where we were. I could guess our eventual destination would be at their headquarters. Perhaps Florida? If they'd wanted to process me in Knoxville, we wouldn't be traveling down this highway.

We continued for a considerable time, the tires singing and country music stars doing what they do. I gathered the debris from my bonds and pushed it into the corner of the trunk. Whenever they opened the trunk, I'd be ready to leap. For now, I tried to relax and rest.

After what seemed hours, I could feel a reduction in speed, then a change in direction I took to be an exit. Soon we stopped, probably at a light. Then a right turn, and more turns and stops until I lost track of direction. Earlier I heard other traffic sounds, but as time went on we traveled slowly and I heard no other cars. The road became bumpy, with the large car swaying over an uneven surface. I could hear a muffled conversation, seemingly one-sided, perhaps a cell phone in use. At last we came to a stop. I got into my position, sick with fear and tension. The engine died, and there was silence. The car rocked as they got out, two doors slamming almost in unison.

I heard what I took to be sounds of urinating beside the car, then a voice. "Hey, Lenny, do you think we should check on Asshole back there?"

"Yeah, make sure he ain't croaked, or somethin'. The Boss wouldn't be too happy if we screwed this up."

"I be with you there. The Man's a mean little bastard. Why'ncha pop the trunk and I'll take a look."

"Wait'll I shake this thing. I'd better come with you. You can't be too careful."

There was a pause, then the loud clunk of the electric trunk lock disengaging. As it started upward, I gathered my feet under me and leaped through the opening. I tripped on the back rim of the trunk, and went sprawling at the feet of Mr. Testa, of television fame.

"Jesus Christ!" were his only words. The other guy was behind him. My brief glimpse revealed a muscular black man who looked more capable of speed than Testa. I scrambled to my feet and ran up a dirt lane in the moonlit darkness. We were in a rural area, in a small patch of second-growth pine forest. Undergrowth lined both sides. I considered darting into the darkness of the dense foliage, but decided to try for more separation first. The brush could have proven impenetrable.

I ran at a full sprint, with them gasping and pounding behind me. I couldn't keep this up for any length of time. As I rounded a bend in the lane, I saw headlights approaching. I raised both arms and waved to get the attention of the driver as I closed the short distance. The driver had to see I was in trouble, and I hoped for help. If only I could get in the vehicle and get the door locked before they got to me.

I reached the passenger side of the van and opened the door, just getting inside and locking it before they slammed the side of the van with their hands. I turned to the driver to explain, to beg him to get in reverse and get out of there. He was smiling and holding a gun in his hand.

"Hi, Mr. Cross. Want another shot a' dope?" He said, in a high-pitched voice. I remembered who he was. Most recently, a glimpse of him had appeared on the television coverage of Mr. Testa in the mountains. Before that, I had met him on the trail down from the mountains. Somehow, this semi-vagrant had latched onto news of the reward or a chance to act as guide in the mountains for Testa. For me, this was the end of very short-lived freedom.

"No, it won't be necessary." I raised my hands. He grinned with pleasure and triggered the automatic door lock. Testa opened the door.

"Want me to give him a shot?" Red Beard asked eagerly.

"No, Donny, not yet." He grabbed me with a huge hand and yanked me out of the van, where I sprawled again on the ground. "Maurice, put handcuffs on him this time. Enough of that tape crap."

Maurice stepped forward and jerked me to my feet with one hand grasping the front of my jacket. Maurice was shorter than I, but must have outweighed me by fifty pounds, all of it muscle. He twisted my arms behind me, and I felt the cuffs ratchet into place. Testa stepped behind me and grabbed my cuffed hands.

"Before you go back for your nap, Asshole, Maurice will conduct a little counseling session. Go ahead, Maurice. Show the man what a heavy bag feels like, when you're working out."

A smile gleamed in the moonlight. He went into a boxer's stance, and hit me with a combination to the rib cage before I could flinch. The left to my ribs sent an explosion of pain through my body. The hammer-blow of his right hand paralyzed my breathing. I doubled over, my mouth open, pleading with my system to breathe again. When I thought it would never come, finally I filled with a rasping breath. Just as I straightened, he repeated the same two punches. Testa let me fall to my knees and go through the pain of getting my breathing started again. Maurice chuckled.

"That's okay for now, Maurice. Let's get him back in the car and on our way. We want to save some for the boss."

The two of them dragged me to the car, followed by the third one, Donny. They lifted me into the open trunk and trussed me up as before, except this time my hands were both cuffed and taped. They found the wadded handkerchief and stuffed it back in my mouth.

"Okay, if you try to get cute again, Maurice will beat the hell out of you. And he won't leave your face so pretty next time. Donny, you can put him back to sleep."

I felt the prick of a needle in my buttocks, and a numbing wave crept through my system, providing an overlay to my feeling of helplessness. Again I sank into oblivion.

When I awoke, I had none of the same symptoms as before—the crawling flesh and muscular spasms. The sense of bewilderment was the same. At first, I could not focus my mind and I couldn't remember the recent past. My hands were not bound, but I could see nothing but blackness around me. I felt of my face to see if something covered my eyes. There was nothing. I moved my hand before my eyes, but it wasn't there. Was I completely blind? Where was I?

I lay on a hard, cold surface. When I moved, pain shot through my chest. Then I began to remember: the car trunk, the short escape, the beating. I managed to sit and painfully turn about. A faint line of light showed at floor level, a few feet from where I sat. Maybe light filtering under a door seal. I crawled toward it and felt the surface of a steel door. Using it for support, I rose. With the effects of the drugs and the intensity of the darkness, I wavered with feelings of vertigo, catching myself by grasping the doorframe.

I shivered violently in the cold, and my skin felt clammy. I realized I was completely nude. Even my watch was missing. I began to feel my way along the wall, soon reaching a corner. The walls were of painted concrete block, judging by their texture. I completed the exploration quickly. The room was small, perhaps eight by ten feet, and contained a steel toilet, a lavatory, and a bunk suspended from the wall. There were no interruptions in the surfaces of the walls except for the door. The door had a rectangular slot about halfway up, but it was blocked on the outside. It would be a pass-through for food, if I became so fortunate, or a slot to extend the hands for cuffs. I had seen the ritual performed on television. I could not reach the ceiling, even standing on the bunk, and I was afraid to leap in the darkness.

I drank from my cupped hand held under the faucet. The hot side produced no flow, so there was no chance to warm my hands. The bunk had a thin, cloth covered mattress over flat steel bands. I was able to wrap the mattress partially around me by lying where the bunk joined the wall. Still feeling the effects of the drug, I drifted off to sleep.

A contingent of intergalactic travelers had arrived to recruit team members to help them with an important project. The leader of the expedition was a handsome, blond man who was worshipped by his followers, a group of men and women of normal human appearance, except for one. This creature, always at the side of the leader, was large and hairy, a Chewbacca type without the personality. The creature was said to dine only on long-dead flesh, so the space travelers were constantly on the lookout for mammoths frozen in the ice cap, or mummies to be reconstituted.

The objective of the expedition was to travel to all points in space and collect specimens of higher life forms—human beings or their equivalent—for study and experimentation. From the study, they were to attempt combining the best features of all into a super race of inhabitants. I was made to understand all of this without verbal explanation. The group merely smiled at us in a friendly and comforting way. I was convinced it was a noble cause, and agreed to join the expedition, along with others who joined us for the journey.

We entered their spacecraft through a polished metal venturi—a cylindrical metal tube with a flared circular opening. Rather than allowing us to transport ourselves by walking, the tube varied its dimensions in waves, a peristaltic motion that swallowed us into the interior of the craft. Once inside, I looked around me at those of us who had joined the expedition. We were all of different races and human types. With a wave of terror, I realized we were the ones being collected for the experiment...

I awoke with a start, bewildered again by my surroundings. The noise that awakened me was a hammering on the door of the cell. A sudden shaft of light appeared at the opening in the door, and a voice shouted.

"Hey! Wake up in there! Come and stick your hands through the hole for the cuffs."

I hesitated. My real fears were worse than the dream. The time had come for me to face the most desperate trial of my life. I determined to do so with as much dignity as I could muster, despite having no clothes and feeling cold and ill from the ordeal of my capture. I would deny everything, even to the end. At the same time, I would try to control my anger and remain calm. And I would not let my nakedness humiliate me, as it was intended. I would pretend I was better dressed than my adversaries.

"Hey, get over here! Don't make us come in after you." They banged on the door again.

Reluctantly, I went to the door and thrust my hands through the slot. I felt cuffs being placed on my wrists.

"That's better. Now stand well back while I open the door."

I did as directed. A key rasped in the lock and the door swung open, blinding me with light from the hallway. I recognized the silhouette of Maurice. When my eyes adjusted, I saw Donny in the hall with a riot shotgun at port arms.

Maurice flipped a light switch outside the door, illuminating my cell in dim light. "Donny, come over here and cover him while I change his cuffs."

He reached gingerly with a key and unlocked my left wrist. "Now turn around. That's it. Now follow behind me, and don't try anything. Donny, you bring up the rear."

I did as I was told. I hoped we were going someplace warmer. I was freezing cold, and my bare skin was gooseflesh. We exited into a hallway. Donny looked me up and down and smirked. I followed Maurice past two other doorways similar to mine, then through another door and up a concrete staircase. Donny poked me in the rear with the barrel of the shotgun as we ascended the steps, giggling softly to himself each time. I ignored him and tried not to flinch.

Maurice opened the door and preceded me into a room at the top. I gathered myself into my best posture and made my entrance. We were in a vast recreation room, from its appearance. It would have been a pleasant room under other circumstances. It was painted in warm, bright colors, and contained groupings of furniture suited to a variety of activities. One area contained an expensive array of workout equipment. Another had two pool tables and a couple of game tables. A kitchenette filled one corner. None of these held any interest for me in those opening seconds. My focus was on a combination office and sitting area—A large desk and computer setup, and an arrangement of couches and chairs.

A man was seated at the desk in a high-backed chair, facing away from us. Standing nearby was a Hispanic man dressed in a khaki-colored poplin uniform, holding an Uzi machine gun. Testa was seated on one of the couches. He and the guard glanced up at me, with obvious amusement. I, in turn, was pleased to see Testa's face was slathered with calamine lotion.

We stood in silence while the man at the desk clicked away at the computer keyboard. I used the time to look further at my surroundings. The long wall of the room was all glass and opened onto a terrace paved in Spanish tile. Some of the windows were covered with bamboo shades, but I could see a large body of water a few hundred yards away, down a slope from the house. There was a lap pool just outside, and a larger pool and terrace at a lower level toward the shoreline. This entire vista was enclosed on both sides by high concrete walls, stuccoed in white and topped with razor wire. Palms swayed in the offshore breeze. From the shadows, I guessed late afternoon. If the connection to the wrecked plane wasn't a phony, we could be in Jacksonville. I looked wistfully at the sunlight and the sparkling blue water. In the distance, a sailboat was reaching in the stiff breeze, her bow wave visible. Someone out of my vision dived into the lap pool, and started swimming laps, but my attention was drawn back inside.

The man jabbed a final key and swiveled in our direction. He was not what

I expected. Though he was seated, it was apparent he was slight in stature. I judged him to be around fifty, with tangled sandy hair, gone to gray. His complexion was ruddy, with a network of veins showing on his cheeks and nose. He was dressed in white linen slacks, a French blue dress shirt, and soft Italian loafers. He removed half glasses and looked at me with pale blue eyes.

"So here is the infamous Mr. Cross. He doesn't look so impressive that you should have had so much trouble." He glanced at Testa, who reddened and looked at his feet.

"You are an annoyance, Mr. Cross. You have something that belongs to me. I don't like annoyances. Before we are finished with you, you will tell us all about it." He waved a hand in a dismissive gesture. "But I don't want to hear it now. The boys will want a little exercise first, to keep their interest up. And don't think you can hold out and not talk. None of your predecessors have been able to."

"I demand to be released. I have nothing that belongs to you, and I'd like an explanation for the behavior of these apes. You and they will pay for this."

He smiled, as though enjoying himself. "You *demand!*" Standing there as you are, you *demand?*" He laughed, and was joined by the others. "We know, on good authority, you took a pack animal to the scene of the plane crash. We have a second witness who placed you in the vicinity. Yes, you know exactly what we are after. But don't be in any hurry to tell us. It's a trifling amount for a person in my position. But I won't be trifled with. We will start with a mild lesson, to give you something to think about."

"I assume you're going on the word of that real estate woman. She did come to me with some kind of crazy story. Too much television, too little excitement in her life. What have you done with her?"

He looked at Testa, who exchanged glances with Maurice and Donny. They all laughed again. I doubted Carol Fenton would ever be seen again.

He stood. "Let's get on with it. I have work to do. When I get back, I want him crying and pleading to tell me what he did with it. I want him to yearn for my return, and count the hours until he can see me again." He paused to savor his speech, then snapped his fingers and continued. "Get the bitch in here. It'll be good for her to see this."

I was sick with dread of what was to come. At the same time, I thought Carol might be alive after all. The guard went outside through a sliding door, while I waited, my knees trembling.

In a few moments, a woman entered the room. She was dressed in a white terry robe, her feet bare, and she was toweling her hair. It wasn't Carol. She would not look in my direction, but cast her eyes downward at the carpeting.

The man at the desk looked pleased with himself. "Gabriella, this is the man who found your dear husband. Perhaps you'd like to express your thanks."

She looked up, startled, and glanced briefly in my direction. "He has been *found?*"

"Oh, I guess we forgot to tell you. Yes, this man found his body in the mountains and just left it there."

"He's *dead?* Oh...!" She put her hand to her mouth and started to turn and flee. He grabbed her arm, jerking her back. She dropped to her knees and held her face in her hands, her body shaking with her sobs. It was a disgusting demonstration of cruelty for pleasure.

"Oh, come now. He didn't mean that much to you. Now you can begin a new life." He smiled at his audience, pleased with himself. She remained on the floor, slumped over in defeat.

"Let the demonstration begin. Manuel, you provide the cover. Maurice, are you ready? Lenny?" He reached down and jerked the woman to her feet. "You get to watch this, my dear. If you do not, then you will be asked to participate."

She composed herself and wiped her eyes with the sleeve of her robe. She looked directly at me for the first time. Her eyes were filled with tears, but I could see strength in her expression, a determination to get through whatever we faced. There was pain also, as though she was trying somehow to express compassion for my predicament.

Testa grasped my cuffed hands as before. Maurice swaggered forward, pulling on leather gloves. I decided I had little to lose. As he stepped in front of me, I aimed a quick kick at his groin. I drove the arch of my bare foot into his testicles with all the force I could muster, then wrenched free from Testa. It would have been at least a 40-yard punt.

Maurice howled in pain and doubled over, protecting himself with both hands. I leaped past him and drove myself toward their leader. He shrieked in terror and tried to run, but the furniture hemmed him in. I drove my head into his chest and the two of us smashed an end table to the floor, with him on the bottom. The woman managed to step out of the way.

After their initial surprise, the other four men converged on me and dragged me away. The man on the floor managed to get to his feet, disheveled and shaking with rage. Panting and spitting, he pointed at me and shouted, "I want you to beat the hell out of that son-of-a-bitch! Don't kill him. Just make him wish you would!" Then an afterthought, "Get over on the tile, not the carpet."

There could have been no positive end to it, with my hands cuffed behind me. Maurice savored the opportunity to return my kick, and he pummeled me with his fists to my face and body. I slipped as many punches as I could, but

Donny joined him, using a baton to find every part of my body. In the end, I was barely conscious, lying on the floor for the last of their kicks and blows. My nose was streaming blood, and cuts on my head were leaking blood into my eyes.

They dragged me below and left me on the floor of my cell. After they left, I crawled to the bunk and wrapped the thin mattress around me as before. At last I could give in and slip into an unconscious state, willing the pain away as best I could.

I awoke from a combination of sleep and unconsciousness. The letdown after a large infusion of adrenaline had provided a sedative effect to help me rest. Though still in utter darkness, I began a damage assessment. My body was a mantle of pain I felt from every nerve ending. As gently as I could manage, I traced the exterior damage, starting with numerous knots on my scalp, some of which were still oozing blood. One eye felt as though it was nearly shut, and my lips were swollen and split. Two upper teeth were loose, but still in place. My nose felt like it was broken. The rest of my body ached from the blows to the long bones and the punches to my rib cage. I was swollen between the legs to a size that felt like a grapefruit. I was a mess.

At the same time, I took a small measure of satisfaction from my few seconds of retaliation, the odds being as they were. I enjoyed the cowardice of their chief, now that I could reflect on it. I had survived the first round alive, but dreaded subsequent repetitions. Was this a "mild lesson" as their chief had termed it? What other measures would appear next time? When would they come for me again? I supposed the waiting and uncertainty were all part of the pressure. Would a time come when I would rather be dead? Would that be the time I told them all about the money and let them get it over with?

He said something about being away. That should mean their numbers would be reduced for some period of time. Only one foot-soldier was present for our session. It would be a good guess to assume there were others about—perhaps a gatekeeper and outside guards. At least they would have shift arrangements. There would be housekeeping or kitchen help, judging from the size of the facility, but I would expect them to be more neutral in the equation.

What about the woman? He indicated she was the wife of one of the unfortunates in the plane. My guess would be the passenger, probably sent along to oversee the business interests. The pilot had a Hispanic name, if I recall, and the passenger more North American—no, Italian. But English-sounding given names, I think. Yes, he was probably staff. Where did she fit in now? She was treated miserably in the drama of the afternoon. Why would she stay all this time, if it was how she was normally treated? Obviously, she didn't know her husband's fate until then. Was she staying until she knew, or was she being held against her will also? She seemed to look at me with some compassion.

I had to find a way to tip the odds in my favor, and it had to be soon. I wondered when I would be summoned again, and who would be present. My tactic this time would be to suffer as little damage as possible, and find out as much as I could for the next time, if there was to be another time. If she happened to be there, I would try to get a better reading on her body language and expression. She was an interesting looking woman, perhaps more exotic than beautiful, but now was not the time to consider anything but how she could help me escape.

I rose stiffly from my bunk, my body protesting with pain. I shuffled slowly to the lavatory to quench my thirst. When I turned on the tap, nothing came out. The hot side was still dry. Now I would have thirst to worry about in addition to receiving no food since my capture. Because of circumstances, hunger had not tortured me. But I recognized weakness was overtaking me, with no energy to bounce back from the low feeling after the adrenaline had departed. The cold temperature of the air-conditioned room was also rapidly draining any reserves.

There was still a pool of water at the bottom of the toilet bowl, but no tank, since it was the industrial type. I thought about drinking the water, but decided against it. If any contamination remained, my resistance would be low. Gastrointestinal upset would be devastating in my present state.

To give myself something productive to do, I crept slowly around the room again, running my fingertips over every surface I could reach. I could find nothing to give me encouragement. Any means of escape had to come from outside the cell.

Time dragged on. Without the benefit of light or sensory stimulation of any kind, measuring the passage of time was impossible. I was dozing again in a half-stupor, when banging on the door came again. I got a sick feeling in the pit of my stomach. It was Maurice again who had come for me.

"Get over here to the door. Time for class." He chuckled in his bass voice.

I thrust my hands through the door for my handcuffs, then retreated again while the door was opened. Maurice appeared as before, but a different guard was waiting in the hall, this time armed with an Uzi rather than the shotgun used by Donny. They probably didn't trust Donny with anything but a shotgun. Maurice circled warily around me and re-cuffed my hands behind me.

I was surprised when he spoke, almost in a whisper. "Hey, man, it's a job, you know. I haf'ta do what I'm told. It's what I do."

We trudged up the concrete stairs again. The guard behind me remained stoic, performing his duties, nothing more. He was large, also Hispanic, but with the appearance of Native American blood.

When we entered the bright room again, Donny and another guard were waiting near the workout equipment. It was the same guard as the first time, a man I thought of as Little Guard. He was tense, on the balls of his feet ready to react to any move I might make. He stayed at least ten feet away, and held his machine gun at ready.

The sun outside was in a different location. This time it appeared to be late morning, with foreshortened shadows pointing toward the house. I had survived a long night. I wondered what today held for me, then noticed two devices in Donny's hands. One was an ugly black plastic device with a head like a stag beetle, the other a baton about two feet long with electrodes on the end. He giggled and waved them in front of me. This morning's session was to include a stun gun and a cattle prod. Neither would be fatal. I would have to take it, and look for my opportunity to change the odds somehow.

Maurice was the holder this time. "Okay, let's give him a little lesson in electric. Man, is he gonna be ready to talk when the boss gets back! That's when we get our big bonus."

Donny advanced with a look of anticipation. Little Guard smiled eagerly, while Big Guard looked at his feet. I tried to twist away but Donny got me on the hip with the cattle prod, causing me to jump from the shock. He giggled and repeated the process. Maurice and I did an improbable waltz together while he held me in an iron grip. I took the punishment without giving them the satisfaction of crying out.

Once I was able to create enough movement at the right time, and Donny's probe got Maurice on the arm.

"Ow! Goddammit!" he shouted. "You dumb sonofabitch! Watch what you're doin'! Here, gimme that thing."

He grabbed the prod out of Donny's hand and yanked my arms around. "Here, you take him."

He flashed a big smile and deliberately prodded Donny's large buttocks before he could jump out of the way. Donny yelped from the shock and Maurice laughed loudly. "There, Dickhead, how do you like it?"

I appreciated their lack of attention to their original task, as I danced about with a different partner. Maurice was concentrating more on Donny than on me. Finally, Donny let go of me and hit Maurice on the shoulder with the stun gun. Maurice dropped the prod, and his body went slack, his mouth sagging open. He swayed on his feet and stared stupidly into space, then collapsed to the floor.

Before I could move to take advantage of this lapse, Small Guard shoved his weapon in my chest. Large Guard raised his gun for the first time, concern showing in his eyes.

Donny quickly turned on me and pressed the stun gun to my hip. The jolt of high voltage electricity caused my body to collapse and I hit the floor. My mind went blank. I had no will to move and I could not focus on where I was or what was happening. For several seconds, I lay there at Donny's feet and tried to get my mind working again. Out of the fog, I was aware Donny was suddenly removed, and Maurice stood over me.

From a great distance, I heard him say, "Take this prick back down and lock him up. We'll see him again later."

The two guards came and dragged me to my feet. I felt weak and barely able to walk. Before we left, I caught a glimpse of someone peering through a gap in the blinds at the far corner of the room.

Back in my cell again, I wrapped myself in the thin mattress and sank into a troubled sleep.

Something woke me up. I heard a light tapping at the door. It was not the same as before. My tormentors always banged hard on the door, making noise that would startle me out of my sleep. The light tap-tap-tap was repeated. I crept to the door, and spoke in a whisper, sensing something was different. *"What is it?"*

A strong whisper replied in an accented, feminine voice, *"Are you there? Can you hear me?"*

I put my face next to the slot and whispered back, "Yes. Who is it?"

The slot was opened from the outside, making it easier to hear. *"I am the one you saw upstairs. My name is Gabriella. I have something for you, and I must tell you we have only one chance. We act, or we will both be lost. Do you know about guns?"*

"Some, yes. What do you have?"

"Here, take this." I could feel something being passed through the slot. It was a pistol wrapped in a small towel. She spoke rapidly. *"It is a Walther PPK, .380 caliber, with silencer. There are six rounds in the magazine and one in the chamber. The safety is on. It is a thumb safety on the upper right side. Push up to fire. The pistol is double action, so all you have to do for the first one is to pull the trigger. Do not pull the slide or you will waste one. You need not cock the hammer. After that, it is semi-automatic. Do you understand?"*

"Yes, but what happens next? Do you have a plan?"

"No. We will have to find a way to get out of here. When they come for you again, you have no choice but to use this. Can you do it?"

I thought about the alternatives, and there were none. I could not know whether anyone in the outside world was searching for me, or if there was any likelihood of success. *"Yes, I can do it. But where will you be? And how many of them are there?"*

"Now is the best time, while he and Testa are away. In addition to Maurice and the Hillbilly, there are three guards. One is always on the gate, another one roaming. One is off duty right now, and is not in the building, as far as I know. There is a cook and a housekeeper inside, and a gardener outside, but they will all stay out of the way. I will be armed and I will wait upstairs. If you are successful, then we will get out of here together. If not, I must go alone, because they will know who gave you the gun. Now I must go."

"What time is it?"

·   *"It is just after noon. They had a big fight and now they are resting. I would guess they shall come for you again this afternoon. Good luck."*

"Thank you. I'll owe you my life. Watch out for yourself."

With that, she was gone. I had renewed hope, but anxiety over the coming confrontation. This would be my only chance, and I had to do whatever became necessary. It meant using the gun. Could I do it when the time came? There wasn't an option I could see. Either I would be dead, or I would be free again with a chance to escape my prison.

Time dragged slowly by. My breathing was slow and measured as I listened for sounds from the outside. I sat on my bunk with the mattress covering me as well as possible, holding the precious pistol in my hands. All details of it were familiar to me from exploring it with my sense of touch in the darkness.

My plan was simple. I would lay it on the floor in front of me while I let them handcuff me. In that way, they would have no warning before the door was open. I would back into the darkness with the gun held in both hands, then wait for the silhouette to appear.

I waited for hours, the tension mounting, before the usual loud banging startled me. "Hey, Asshole, get over here. Time for more fun." It was Maurice again.

With my whole body shaking, I knelt before the door, laid the gun on the towel in front of me, and thrust my hands through the slot. With the handcuffs in place, the gun in my hands, I backed away.

The key turned in the lock, and the door swung open.

22.

WEEPERS

The crack of light widened into a wedge that brightened the room. I held the gun between my knees with both hands, the muzzle downward, safety off. When the door swung wide, Maurice was silhouetted against the light, Small Guard behind him in the hallway. Without hesitation, I raised the gun and fired three quick shots. Two hit him in the chest and the third in the forehead. The silenced pistol made a loud thumping sound I had never heard before. It sounded like a sudden loud release of compressed air. I either heard, or imagined hearing, the last bullet strike him in the head as he fell. He crashed to the floor, exposing the guard behind him. Small Guard was frozen with a look of surprise, then recovered and started to bring the machine gun to bear. Before he could move, and before I could think about what I was doing, I shot him twice in the chest.

Both lay on the floor, their bodies thrashing in convulsions of death. Red blood pooled in the light of the hallway and glistened black in the subdued light of the cell where Maurice lay. I had never before looked someone in the eye and killed him. I did it without thought or hesitation. There was no time; and the scene continued the surreal world I had inhabited since that moonlit night in Mountain View. The future would provide time to analyze what I had done, if there was to be a future.

I waited a few seconds until he stopped moving, then began a frantic two-handed search of Maurice's pockets for the key. After struggling with his bulk and the disagreeable nature of it, I remembered what he was about to do. The key was lying under one of his large hands, released when his body went slack. I maneuvered it into the keyholes and was at last free to leave the cell.

The guard was lying on the machine gun, so I rolled him over. His eyes were open and staring, and a sigh gurgled from his lifeless form as it flopped over.

I wiped the blood from the grip using the guard's shirt, checked the chamber to ensure the Uzi was ready to fire, then released the clip. It contained a full load. I latched it back, then ascended the concrete stairs, the machine gun balanced in my left hand, and the pistol ready in my right. Two silenced rounds were still available in the little pistol, which I would use first if possible.

If anything went beyond that, the Uzi would be making a lot of noise. The selector was on full automatic.

I didn't know what to expect when I entered the room. The woman had promised to be waiting, but I could not be sure. Would Donny be there? Would others have returned? Had they heard the muffled shots below?

I could not delay. My captors and I were expected to return to their recreation room for more games. This time, the nature of the contest would be different. I took a deep breath at the top of the stairs and prepared to burst through the door. The movies always have the combatant in such a situation doing an acrobatic roll, with guns blazing. No such thing would work for me. I would try to stay low, but would have to stand my ground and make the most of it. My life could end in the next moments, or I could have a chance to go free.

I turned the knob, shoved the door open, and leaped into the room. Donny was half lying across the end of a couch. A guard I had not seen before was seated in a chair near the exercise equipment with a machine gun across his lap. In a frozen instant, we looked at each other. My mind saw it as a photograph, exposed by a flash of light.

They both sprang into motion, the guard bringing his gun up and Donny rising to run away. I was ready with the pistol and fired both shots into the guard, who collapsed. Before I could bring the Uzi up to a firing position, Donny was through the grouping of furniture, and had started around a standing screen. He stopped suddenly, threw his hands in the air, and began backing up.

"Please don't shoot," he whined. "Please, please. I'm not one of them."

He backed up several steps and got down on his knees. The woman stepped from behind the screen, with a black automatic pistol held before her in both hands.

"Shut up and get down on the floor," She said. "Get flat on your stomach and put your hands behind you."

He did as he was told, but began sobbing and continued his supplication. "Please let me go. I'll help you escape. I don't want to be here when they come back..."

"I told you to shut up! Not one more word!" Then she glanced at me, "What shall we do with him? Shall I shoot him?"

"Please!" he screamed.

"Quiet!"

I didn't know if she meant what she said. I made a suggestion. "Let's lock him up downstairs."

"Good idea. You lead the way and I will follow." She prodded Donny with the toe of her shoe. "Get up and do not try anything. I would welcome the chance to get rid of you."

We began our odd procession through the door and down the stairs, a naked, battered man, a sobbing red-bearded hulk, and a woman with a gun. When we got to the bottom of the stairs, Donny reacted to the sight of the guard on the floor, with the growing pool of blood.

He wailed again, *"Please, ple—!"*

This time she said nothing, but whacked him on the back of the head with the flat of the pistol barrel. I tried the first door and found a cell just like the one used for my confinement. A key was conveniently stuck in the door on the outside. We pushed Donny in and locked the door.

We stopped and faced each other. I was trembling with fatigue and tension, and suddenly felt my nakedness. I put my hands down to cover myself, still holding the Uzi.

She noticed the gesture. "I have clothing for you upstairs. Shall we take care of that, then decide what to do about the man on the gate? He is the only one we have to worry about now."

"Is it the large man? He seemed better than the rest."

"Yes, he is. His name is Alvaro. He does not seem comfortable in his role."

"Would he come to the house if you call him?"

"Yes, I think so."

"Then it's settled. I'll get handcuffs." I went back my cell to get them, gingerly stepping around the bodies and the pools of congealing blood.

When we were back in the recreation room, she went behind the screen and brought out two small duffels.

"See if these clothes will fit you. They were my husband's. And there is water, also."

My mind flashed to the corpse disintegrating in the mountains. Her husband, whose clothes I was to wear. I drank, quickly draining a plastic bottle.

Without thinking of the incongruity, I stepped behind the screen to dress. The polo shirt and khakis fit well, except the leg length was a little short. The athletic shoes fit. She had provided a pair of deck shoes, another change of clothes, spare underwear, a windbreaker, and a kit I assumed to be toiletries.

Except for my hunger, my bruises, my painful body, and the desperate acts I had committed, I felt better.

The tension was still showing in her face when I rejoined her.

"Are you ready?" She asked.

"Yes. How shall we do this? I prefer not to harm him."

"I, also. I will call him on the intercom. He should come through that door over there. If you wait behind it, we should be able to disarm him."

I took my position and she pressed a button on the desk. *"¡Alvaro, hay problema con el prisionero! ¡Necesitamos tu ayuda! ¡Venga pronto a la casa!"*

233

She stepped away from the desk and nodded to me, holding up two fingers. "Two minutes." She mouthed the words.

She stood in the middle of the room with the pistol held behind her. She looked a defiant warrior, standing erect, dressed in black slacks and a teal-colored cotton sweater. A black headband held back her cloud of auburn hair.

On cue, Alvaro burst through the door and skidded to a stop when he saw her. *"Señora?"*

She spoke in English this time. "Alvaro, you must drop your gun and surrender. It is okay. You will not be harmed."

She brought out the pistol and leveled it at him. At the same time, I stepped up behind him and touched him with the gun barrel. He flinched, then did as he was told, placing the gun at his feet. For the first time, he saw the body of the other guard and he trembled with fear.

We handcuffed him to the largest piece of exercise equipment, leaving bottles of water for him. I covered the body with two large towels so he wouldn't have to look at it. He sat with head bowed as we walked away.

"When are they coming back? Do you know?"

"Not with any certainty. Tomorrow, I think."

"What will we do about the domestic help and the gardener?"

She thought for a moment. "Perhaps we can pretend to kidnap them and have them drive us somewhere. They will understand. I want to give them cover."

"Will they call someone? The police or their employer?"

"Neither. They would not dare involve the police, and there is little chance they know how to reach McFarlane. No, they will either go home or back here to see Alvaro. I doubt even he knows what to do. It would surprise me if they planned for this contingency. It is not the first time I have been underestimated."

"Do you have money?"

"Yes, plenty of it."

"Any extra .380 ammunition?"

"Oh, I forgot." She went to the desk and extracted a box, along with a spare magazine.

Indecision over the next step troubled me. "Let's borrow the maid's car if she has one, then leave it somewhere for her. Then we'll improvise. That way we don't have to get them involved."

She looked at me without expression. "I will get her keys and explain to her." She turned and left.

The old Ford Escort was parked in a carport reserved for garden equipment and hired help. The gardener was there, focusing all of his attention on maintenance of a lawnmower, pretending we weren't there. I had my first chance to see the house from the outside. It was a three story Spanish structure, white stucco with tan tile roof and wrought iron balconies. The landscaping showed evidence of money and a full time gardener, but all was enclosed behind the fortress-like white wall.

The woman—I had trouble thinking of her any other way—drove the car. When we got to the gate, down a curving driveway of brick pavers, I went into the little booth and pushed a button to open the heavy gate. When she drove through, I pressed the "close" button and sprinted to the car.

She had extracted a promise from the maid that Alvaro would not be released for two hours. In exchange, we would leave the car in a Wal-Mart parking lot a few miles away.

"I assume you know your way around?"

"Not very well. I have not been outside the walls since the plane disappeared."

"You haven't?"

"No. I have been a prisoner. You see, they did not know what had happened. Naturally, at first they suspected the double-cross. I was a hostage." She lowered her voice, as though speaking only to herself. "But I was not of so much value."

We were driving up a beautiful, broad boulevard with a center median planted with trees. Extravagant homes bordered both sides. Most were protected by walls and gates much like our place of imprisonment.

Soon the boulevard gave way to another street less luxurious, then an intersection with a busy commercial four-lane. We turned toward the north, if my sense of direction was working.

She glanced in my direction. "Do you have any ideas?"

"Obviously, I will attract a lot of attention with the way I look. So will you of course, for different reasons. I must get some recuperation soon."

She remained silent while I thought for a moment. "I don't want to go to the police until we think things through. I just killed three men, you know, and there is more than that. Do you have any place to go where you will be safe? Is there anyone who can help you? I don't want to hamper your chance to escape—"

"I cannot think of any safe place for me." She turned to me again. "Besides, I want to get even first. Will you help me?"

"In any way I can. Without you, I'd still be there. How do we do it?"

"I have information, but no plan. We will have to think of a way."

"We need a place to hide for a few days where we don't have to come in contact with the public. I think perhaps we should steal a boat."

"Steal a *boat*? Would that not be risky? Have we not done enough already?"

"I should have said 'borrow' a boat. I'll make sure it's returned. It seems to me a better way to hide than on land. Most people who own boats don't use them much after they have them for a while. We could take the chance. I can easily spot a neglected boat in a marina."

She said nothing for a moment. "For how long? What comes after? That is what we must decide."

"I don't know yet. For now, we have to find some transportation and a place to rest. I'm about to collapse. I'm sorry." I was truly getting close. My body protested in every fiber. Without food since the hamburger in Owensville, I was running out of fuel.

"No, no, I am sorry. I was not thinking about what you have been through. We have to get you some rest. We are getting close to where I promised to leave the car."

What to do? I didn't want to risk taxis. It was getting to be late afternoon. Rush hour traffic was building. "How much money do you have? Enough to buy a car?"

"I do not know. Many thousands. I got it out of the safe."

"Then we can find a car lot and buy a car. A small lot with old cars would be best."

We passed a strip mall anchored by the destination Wal-Mart. We continued, and she soon found what we were looking for. Banners on ropes were strung across a seedy lot containing not a car under ten years old. Prices and slogans were painted crudely on the windshields, all of the numbers ending with three nines.

When we pulled in front of the small trailer office, a caricature used car salesman stepped out. He had thinning, greasy hair combed over his scalp from a part just above his ear. Two front teeth were missing.

I got out of the car.

"Hi, neighbor. You look like a man who knows what he wants," he greeted me. His eyes darted in Gabriella's direction. Then he looked back at me and did a classic double take. "Jesus Christ, what happened to you?'

"I asked too many questions of the wrong people."

His hanging jaw snapped shut, making clicking noises wherever teeth matched up.

"Can I interest you in a fine automobile?"

"Probably not, but I might take a look at some of yours."

We settled on an old Buick Skylark, priced at $999. I offered him $750, with the stipulation that we completed no title application and he would leave a dealer tag in place. I told him he could have the car back and sell it again if he could find it after a week had passed. If he tried to find it sooner, then he would be in trouble. He looked at me, then peered at Gabriella again in the other car. He pocketed the cash, gave me a bill of sale, and we were on our way.

We dropped off the other car and I gave her one set of keys for the Buick. The next thing I knew, she was shaking me awake in front of a low budget motel. I roused myself to look around. She had done well. It was U-shaped and well back from the street.

She held up a key. "We will both stay in the same room. It is supposed to have two beds, but I will stand watch while you sleep. I went through a drive-in and got some food."

I was soon shaved, showered, fed, and asleep. My image in the mirror had been a shock to me. Both eyes were black, with the lid of one still swollen and drooping. The bruises on my face and limbs were turning spectacular colors of green and purple. I gently washed crusts of blood from my hair.

My guardian angel stood watch over me when I crawled gratefully into the sagging bed. I had come to think of her in those terms. She had rescued me from almost certain death and now protected me while I slept. Through it all she was without emotion, eyes sad, voice without expression. Her face was constantly set in a mask of concern, lines of worry between her eyes.

When I awoke from my deep slumber, I heard faint noises of traffic, and light was filtering past the drawn blinds. I arose quietly and saw Gabriella sound asleep on the other bed. She was lying on her back, with the Uzi cradled loosely in her arms. Her face, in repose, was relaxed at last. Her mouth was parted slightly and I could hear her soft snoring, like the purring of a cat. As I watched, her eyelids trembled in the depths of sleep and a slight smile played across her mouth. It transformed her appearance. For the first time, I realized she was beautiful. She had high cheekbones and full, soft lips. Her nose was slender, with a little bump at the bridge that gave it character. Her skin was smooth and golden. In profile, she would be perfect for a Roman coin, exotic and mysterious. During the action of yesterday afternoon she had moved with the grace of an athlete. Her height was average, her body trim, but with soft curves in all the right places.

I sat on the bed and watched her sleep. Where did she come from, and where were we going? We were linked for the time being in a partnership born of desperation. I was determined to do what I could to set right the things I had done, and to help her in any way I could. When she awoke, we would have to make a plan. And I wanted to learn all I could about her and how she came to be in the house that became my prison.

A flicker of the old expression of worry came back to her features, and her breathing pattern changed. Her dreams must have been mixed, with only a momentary departure to a happier time. I decided to let her sleep as long as she could. Who could guess when the opportunity would come again?

Maybe it was unfair to her for me to sit there and watch her in the vulnerability of sleep. At the same time I found it fascinating, much like watching the innocence of a sleeping child. This view of her presented such a contrast to the grim determination I had seen yesterday. Now, if one could ignore the machine gun in her arms, she could be any lovely woman taking a nap. On the sleeping exterior, mostly calm, but within her awakened mind, I knew there was something else entirely. I felt humbled she had decided to trust me.

· My reverie and her sleep were suddenly interrupted by the maid tapping on the door and announcing herself. "Housekeepin'."

Gabriella bolted upright into a sitting position, looking bewildered. I arose and walked closer to the door, speaking through it. "We're still here. Be out in a little while." I heard the maid shuffle on.

"I am so sorry. I was supposed to stay awake," Gabriella said. She looked down at her hands.

"It was my fault for not taking my turn. But no harm done. We both got some rest."

"But soldiers who go to sleep on guard duty are shot."

"You're given a full pardon and restored to active duty. Sorry you had to be awakened so suddenly. How do you feel?"

"I feel better, I think, after the shakes go away. Thank you."

Her worried features relaxed a slight bit.

"While you were sleeping on guard duty, I sat here and thought through a few things. Let me go over them with you and see what you think."

We spent the next half-hour discussing my plan, modifying with her suggestions until we were satisfied.

"There is one other thing I'd like to discuss and I hope you won't take offence."

"What is that?" She said.

"Well, it's the way you look." Her eyes widened. "I know you can't help it, but anyone seeing you will remember you." I felt tongue-tied. "I don't mean to sound patronizing, and I realize you must know this already, but you are striking in appearance. Traveling incognito will need some adjustment, or some sort of disguise—"

"And you do *not*?" She said indignantly. "What shall I do? Baggy overalls and pigtails? Black out a front tooth? Perhaps stuff a pillow in the front of my clothes?"

I couldn't help my amusement. "I don't think even that would do it. But please, all I ask is for you to think about it, okay?"

"Okay, okay." Then she looked directly at me. "You have disguised yourself as an accident victim, right?"

We looked at each other with an undeclared truce.

We made some lists, then I tore the yellow pages out of the phone book in a couple of places, and the little map out of the middle. I hate people who do that. We needed to do some serious shopping, and find a marina with lots of boats to choose from. I figured to get just about everything from a big Wal-Mart—one with a grocery. Gabriella had never been in one, further proof of some difference in the cultures we came from.

When we talked about groceries for the list, she asked what we should get.

"As simple as possible. Whatever we get, keep in mind the stove will probably have two alcohol burners and no oven. There are lots of pre-prepared rice dishes, noodle dishes, and so forth. I should know. I eat a lot of them."

She gave me a steady look again. "I, on the other hand, am accustomed to an excellent cook who serves me fine food three times each day."

Was she joking? I didn't try to explain Hamburger Helper. "That's another thing you can expect to change rather suddenly."

We gathered all of our purchases, including a small instant camera and the current Jacksonville paper to pin down the date. We needed pictures of me in all my glory. A stop at a liquor store provided wine and beer to supplement our cases of bottled water. I was becoming nervous about pursuit and wanted to get out of circulation as soon as possible. Clerks and shoppers glanced in my direction, then tried to avoid looking at me. Consulting my crude map and the yellow pages, I tracked down a sign company that advertised computerized instant signage.

When we parked in front, I asked, "What do you want to name our boat?"

"Is it important? It is usually a female, is it not?"

"Doesn't matter. Female is good. Short is better—easier to apply."

I could see something going through her mind. "Would 'Sabrina' be okay?"

Wondering where the name came from, I told her it would be fine.

I waited for the name to be computerized, then plotted and cut on the large cutting table. Gabriella went to a beauty salon at the end of the strip mall and used their facilities to change into her Wal-Mart fashions. She came back to the car wearing loose-fitting jeans and a large sweatshirt, carrying a baseball cap and sunglasses.

She looked like a beautiful woman wearing loose-fitting jeans and a sweatshirt.

"Try the cap and glasses."

She did. They made her look like a beautiful woman wearing loose-fitting jeans and a sweatshirt, who had just put on a baseball cap and glasses.

"What if you put your hair up inside the cap? Will that work?"

She gave me a dark look, and gave it a try. It would have to do.

Jacksonville had waterfront everywhere, being intertwined with the St. Johns River and its tributaries. All this water gave the impression it was on the Atlantic Ocean, but my map showed it several miles inland. I counted more than a dozen marinas in the general area, scattered from the downtown area all the way to the beaches and barrier islands, and south to St. Augustine. One of the most notable islands was Amelia, to the north, providing cover for the Intracoastal Waterway and blocking the exit of the Nassau River.

It made sense to me to find one away from downtown and closer to the ocean. Studying our city map, we decided to try the Lone Star Marina, out past Fort Caroline. I navigated while Gabriella drove, dressed in her new traveling clothes. We had repacked all of our purchases as best we could into purchased duffels, ready to board.

Getting away from the glitter of downtown seemed to work. The marina was large and remote, filled mostly with sailboats. It did not appear busy. We parked in a gravel lot overlooking the slips, and I studied the boats with my new binoculars. I could not afford to be wandering aimlessly about. I needed to pick a target or two and go directly there like I knew what I was doing. I settled on a general area that had two or three possibilities close together, and no other activity around that particular finger of slips.

I stepped out of the car in my own casual costume—khakis, sweatshirt, canvas cap, and sunglasses. I carried a small bag for cover, and to hold my tools.

"Good luck," she said.

The docks were connected to the parking area with three walkways. The office and shop were at the far end of the lot, and a trailer launch ramp was adjacent. The shop area had a large fenced lot with a few boats on cradles scattered randomly about. A travel lift straddled a slip near the shop, and yard laborers were preparing to hoist a sailboat that already had its mast removed.

I strolled to the nearest walkway. There was a gate, but it was not locked. A sign warned all not to trespass unless they were boat owners or invited guests. Well, I intended to own a boat in a few moments. As I approached the main section of the dock, I met a real owner, his toolbox in hand, headed toward the lot. I greeted him cordially and he replied in the same manner. It was a clear, cool day, with a nice breeze coming in from the direction of the ocean. The music of halyards slapping masts, water lapping at hulls, and docks creaking broke the stillness of the late morning.

Many of the boats I passed showed signs of little use—spider webs, gull droppings, weathered teak. Others shone with owner pride and attention. Their topsides were clean, the teak oiled, and dock line tails done up in Flemish coils. Of the three boats I targeted, I picked the one with the most neglect, reasoning that it was least used. It was a Hunter of several years age, about thirty-five feet in length, and had a solar panel on top I considered a bonus. It would be more likely to have the battery topped out. The gull crap and spider webs were all intact. Perhaps I could return the boat in a little better shape.

I glanced about quickly to see that I was alone, then stepped boldly aboard. The spring steel pry bar I had purchased made short work of the lock. One quick motion, and the screws gave way in the upper hatch board. I quickly pushed the sliding hatch back and lifted out the three boards, carrying them down the short ladder into the saloon. I went directly to the nav station immediately on the starboard side and lifted the hinged top. Sure enough, an extra set of keys were there, attached to a small vinyl foam float. I found the correct key, and removed the dangling padlock from the hatch. Now, as long as the hatch board was out of sight, it appeared my entry was legitimate.

A search through the papers revealed my other objective, the registration with the name of the owner: Frederick C. Dalton, 13242 Palmetto Drive, Jacksonville. I stuck it in my pocket for future reference, then set about opening hatches to air out the interior. It smelled of stale diesel fuel and mustiness.

I had a feeling of triumph as I walked back to the car. Things were beginning to fall into place. I snagged a cart from the main dock and took it with me to haul our gear. Gabriella got out as I approached, and silently started to unload the car. I was unsure whether she thought this scheme would work, but I hoped to convince her as time went by. I had chosen a slow form of transportation for the escape, but one I thought so unlikely it could be safe.

We made the first trip with no problems. I helped her aboard, then passed the groceries, clothing, and supplies to the cockpit to be carried below. Just as I turned to go for the last load, I saw a young man approaching. He was definitely coming to intercept me.

"Good morning!" I called out.

"Morning," he replied. He didn't look particularly happy. "You're not the owner of that boat, are you?"

"No, no. I wish I were. Fred loaned it to me to take my girl for a sail. Said if I cleaned it up a bit, we'd be square." I reached out my hand. "Josh Davis is the name."

He took my hand, looking slightly startled at my appearance. "Did Fred tell you he owes us money?"

"No-o."

"Well, he does. The boss said to watch for him to come out, and not let him get away without settling up."

"How bad is it? Fred's been on an overseas assignment, and I guess he forgot to take care of it."

"It's several hundred dollars, I think. It's all just dock fees, and stuff."

"Tell you what I'll do. I'll pay it, and get it back from Fred, if you'll give me a receipt. Okay? While I get another load, maybe you can get the exact amount."

Relieved, I got the last load and locked the car, leaving my set of keys under the driver's seat. He met me on the way back, receipt book in hand, with a bill for seven hundred twenty-five dollars. I peeled off the cash from the thick wad Gabriella had given me, and we were free to go.

As he turned away, he said, "Let me know if you need anything getting started."

I reported the transaction to Gabriella. She looked concerned, then relieved. "Thank goodness."

"Yes. The boat's name is "Cash Flow," but perhaps there wasn't enough of it."

We worked together for a half-hour, stowing everything. One of the keys fit a dock box, and I got a few cleaning supplies out of it for later. The first action was to get out of here and find a place to hide for the night. I checked the oil in the Yanmar diesel, then with fingers crossed, turned on the ignition and pressed the starter. It ground over slowly, then came to life, thumping softly at low rpm. I checked out the stern for a stream of cooling water, then set the throttle at fast idle to let it warm up.

Gabriella joined me in the cockpit. This was another turning point, a step taken that could have significant impact on whether we made good our escape and survived. I asked her if she was ready.

"Yes. I am ready for whatever comes."

I took her hand in mine for a quick handshake, and we cast off the dock lines.

We motored the several miles of broad waterway until we reached the open ocean. I showed Gabriella how to hold the bow into the wind while I hoisted the main, then we fell off a few points toward the north and unfurled the Genoa jib. She held steady on the helm while I trimmed the sheets. The wind was just behind the beam. We heeled nicely and accelerated to better than six knots. With pleasure, I pulled the kill knob on the diesel. All that remained was the hissing sound of the water past the hull and the burbling of the wake.

It was an exhilarating feeling of true freedom, no matter how insecure the future might be. I studied her face as she gazed at the retreating shoreline. Then she caught my eye for a lingering moment, and favored me with a little smile.

23.

GABRIELLA

I'd forgotten how great it is to sail a big boat in a stiff breeze. The wheel felt alive in my hands. The bow methodically rose, then fell into each trough, sending up a light spray that drifted back into the cockpit. Gabriella seemed content to relax on a cockpit cushion, gazing into the distance, alone with her thoughts. I couldn't keep from smiling to myself.

I handed her a folded map. "I'm going to sail up the east side of Amelia and Cumberland islands. The weather's good, and the wind will be steadier outside."

She studied the map and nodded.

With the approach of late afternoon, however, we dipped back inside through St. Andrew Sound and into the mouth of the Satilla River. I located a cove a couple of miles inland, sheltered by mangrove trees.

"I'm going to need your help, Gabriella." I said. "I'll get us to a good spot for you to drop the anchor off the bow, then I'll back into the trees to tie up the stern."

I showed her how, and she dropped it with a splash, letting out chain and rode, until I had the stern tied off to a large mangrove root. We eased away from the trees to a comfortable margin as dusk was falling over the broad river. We were secure for the night.

Being with someone I didn't really know in the close quarters of the boat was uncomfortable at first. As we'd sailed northward, I had sorted it out with her. She insisted I take the larger bed in the stern, with her in the V-berth in the bow. We decided to alternate on four hour watches through the night, at least until our nerves settled. We would alternate days on meal preparation. She warned me cooking was not her strong suit. I bravely promised to eat anything she cooked.

I fixed spaghetti for the first meal using prepared sauce from a jar. I opened a bottle of Merlo and sliced some French bread. She was mostly silent, deep in thought, and I gave her that option without pressing her. I was eager to learn how she came to be there and what her background was, but it would have to wait. The few times she did speak, her speech was pleasing to my ear, soft and musical in cadence. She retained the slightest of accents, with a faint little trailing "a" on some of the words. I had not heard her use the contractions, slang, or clichés that crept into my own communication.

There was bedding aboard, laundered, but tucked away in lockers on the boat, slightly musty, but clean. She made up the beds while I cooked, so all was in order as we finished our first meal, two almost-strangers keeping house together.

Afterward, we sat in the cockpit drinking our coffee. A chill was in the air, making us grateful for our borrowed jackets.

She broke the comfortable silence. "I would like the first watch, if I may. I do not know if I will be able to sleep. I am a night person anyway, and the circumstances...well, I must get used to them."

"Sure, that'll be fine. You see, I'm a morning person, so we're complementary. It usually works out that way. That's the way it was with my wife and me— opposites in sleeping habits."

"You have a wife? A family?"

"I had a wife. She died nearly three years ago."

"I am so sorry," she said quickly.

"I have a son and a daughter. He's doing some post-graduate studies in Paris and she's in design school in Milan."

"*Milano!* Oh, how I would like to return to Italy, perhaps to start my life over. I now have so many regrets." She looked into the distance.

"And I'm sorry about your husband and the way you found out about him. I should have handled everything about that differently, also. I'm afraid I've created a lot of problems."

"You could have done nothing for him. He was already the victim of the accident when you found him."

"I tried to rationalize it the same way, but it doesn't make me feel any better."

"If you look at it a different way," she continued, "if you had not been involved, I do not know if I could have escaped. I know nothing about the actual accident because they did not tell me. And you do not know, of course, what happened in Jacksonville when the plane was lost."

"I can imagine it must have created a great deal of turmoil."

"Oh, yes," she said.

"If you wish, I'll tell you everything from the beginning. I'm not proud of myself for what I've done. Perhaps it will help to tell you all of it."

"I will be happy to hear what you have to say," she replied.

"They say confession is good for the soul. At least you will know, then you can help me decide how we should bring it to a conclusion."

I began my narrative, and she listened with only an occasional comment to ask a question or signify she understood. To set the stage, perhaps to justify my errors in judgement, I went all the way back to the collapse of the company. Then I told her about the fateful discovery and the twisted path that followed.

I talked far into the night. A full moon rose, sending a shimmering golden path across the water and lighting her features as she listened. I could see the pain on her face when I spoke of the wreckage in the forest. Her eyes grew wide when I described what I found inside and how I felt standing there in the cold rain looking at my discovery. She listened with interest through all of the sequence of hiding the money, and of the involvement of Carol Fenton.

"Knowing them as I do, I fear they have killed her," she said quietly.

Arriving at the present, I concluded. "I don't know what made me do what I did. It was not something I thought was part of my nature. What I'll do now, if given the opportunity, is give it to a good cause—every last dollar—and rid myself of it as one would exorcise a demon."

She put her hand lightly on my arm. "I am sorry for what you have been through, within your own mind and at the hands of those people."

"Thanks for listening without condemning me."

"You must put it behind you, as you suggest, and become the kind of person you were before. Only then can you be happy with yourself."

"Thanks. Now, I think it's time for one of us to rest." I glanced at the green glow of my new Timex. "Are you sure you want to stay awake first?"

"Of course. I am not sleepy this time and I promise to stay awake. Shall I wake you at four o'clock?"

"If you last that long. Don't hesitate to wake me sooner if anything concerns you, okay?"

"I will. And goodnight...I am sorry, I never found out your given name."

"Matthew. Please call me Matt."

"I shall. If we did not have to face the trials of tomorrow, or worry about the past, I would find it very pleasant being here. It is so peaceful and the night is so comforting. Good night...Matt."

"Good night, Gabriella."

She woke me on schedule, with fresh coffee brewed and a steaming insulated mug placed in my hand. I put on a foul weather jacket and climbed out in the cockpit, placing hatch boards in place to keep the damp out of the saloon. The topsides were wet with dew, and the moon still lit the river, now from the west. I took up the position she had vacated, a nest of cushions using the deckhouse for a backrest. We'd found a small cloth tarp for covering. The Uzi was there, under the tarp. It seemed unnecessary in this quiet setting and I hoped that proved to be the case.

A cabin cruiser motored downstream a few hundred yards away. No lights were showing except the required navigation lights. It moved at a languid pace, spreading Vs of wake. In a few moments the ripples reached our position, and we gently rose and fell.

Gabriella was a mystery to me. How did she get mixed up with that operation? Where did she get the knowledge she seemed to possess about weapons? She spoke of getting even. What did she mean by that? The coming day would be her turn to tell her story.

I sat with my thoughts until the coming sunrise began to brighten the sky, bringing the horizon to light with hues of gold and pink. Sea birds rose to begin the day's hunting. River traffic had picked up slightly, with an occasional fishing boat, motoring sailboat, or cruiser. I decided to let Gabriella awaken on her own. My intentions were to make the name change and clean up the boat before we departed. My thoughts were centered on Savannah, or even Charleston, if necessary. We needed a city of reasonable size if our plan was to work.

It was after nine o'clock before she appeared, her eyes still clouded with sleep. "You did not wake me for my watch," she said.

"It didn't seem necessary. I need to work on the boat, but didn't want to disturb you."

"You are kind. How does the shower work on this boat? Does it have a hot water heater?"

"I'll start the engine. It has a heat exchanger that warms the water. Just give it a few moments. I want it running anyway, because I want to use an electric pump for cleaning."

We worked for the next couple of hours. She straightened the inside, and I scrubbed the deck from stem to stern, removing oxidized gelcoat and grime with Soft Scrub and a stiff brush. Fred had installed a pressure pump for using a hose, which helped.

Gabriella brought me coffee, fruit, and cheese for breakfast. She looked fresh from her shower, her hair wet like the first time I saw her. While we ate together in the cockpit, I caught myself staring. Her eyes were remarkable, the color of the sea behind her—not quite green, not quite blue. Her demeanor was still distant and troubled. Like me, she probably wondered where we were going with our escape.

I tackled the name change by removing the old painted name with Easy Off oven cleaner and a razor blade scraper. I had to hang over the stern for part of it, then lower the stern ladder for the rest. The new name was all fastened to a paper tape for alignment. It was a simple matter to remove the backing and smooth each letter in place.

I called to Gabriella, who came into the cockpit. "Are you ready to go?"

She nodded.

I raised my cup of coffee. "I christen this fair vessel 'Sabrina.' May fair winds and tides keep her safe from harm, and always carry her safely to her port."

Without a word, she turned quickly and went below. I followed to the hatch. "Is anything wrong?"

I could barely hear her reply. "No, no. Everything is all right."

I left her alone and made preparations to depart. The sun was well up, with some clouds sliding in from the west. Weather reports on the VHF indicated nothing expected until well into the next day. By the time I had the sail cover stowed and all lines prepared, Gabriella returned and asked what she could do to help. We started the engine, recovered the anchor, and got underway.

With the favorable weather, I decided to go outside the protection of the islands again. We sailed out of St. Andrew Sound and headed north-northeast around well-populated Jekyll Island. We sailed at a leisurely pace, and I spent the time teaching Gabriella all about handling the boat and the sails. She soon felt comfortable enough for me to go below and sleep.

I awoke and returned the favor with St. Simons Island abeam. With gathering clouds in the west and an urge to find an early mooring, I tacked back toward the Intracoastal, heading inside the southern tip of Sapelo Island. The wind was unfavorable as I entered the narrower channel, so I reluctantly furled the sails and started the diesel, hoping it wouldn't wake her.

Gabriella joined me on deck, stifling a yawn. "Is everything okay?"

"Sure, fine. I decided to come inside the islands and look for a place to tie up for the evening. Also, I thought it would be nice to find a place to eat in one of these small towns. The way you spoke about your cooking..."

We found a small restaurant on the water near Pine Harbor. We tied up at a weathered dock and had a "fish camp" type meal of hushpuppies and fried fish, washed down with beer. This was off-season, so the restaurant was sparsely occupied, mostly locals, it appeared. Gabriella attracted some notice, even though she wore her costume. I tried to keep my face averted or in the shadows as much as possible. I drew a curious glance or two.

Nearby, we found transient mooring floats in a small harbor and elected to spend the night there, since there were not many other boats about.

As dusk fell, we took a bottle of wine to the cockpit and bundled in our borrowed foul weather jackets. Clouds were gathering more densely in the west, promising a change in the weather. It was time for Gabriella to tell her story.

"Shall I start with the evidence I have gathered?"

"I'd prefer to hear first about you. How did you become involved with such people? It doesn't seem to fit the person I've seen for the last few days."

"Thank you. It was not what I wanted and it became even worse as time went by."

"Was it your husband?"

"It is easy to blame someone else, but in this case, I must. I gave in because, in a way, I had stopped caring what happened to me. I will go all the way back to the beginning...

"I was born in Italy, in a small village near Parma. Our family name is Zucci. My papa had a brother in the United States, who urged him to come to America, so we did, when I was six years old. My mama was never very well and he hoped to find a way to take better care of her, he said." She accented the second syllable when she spoke of her parents.

She paused and sipped her wine, staring into the night.

"We settled in Queens, and he became a New York City policeman. He loved his work and I was very proud of him in his uniform. He was gone so much it was a problem, and my mama and I were alone together most of the time. She loved me, and I her, but she was sickly most of the time, and she never adapted to our new country, never learned to speak English. She died when I was twelve and it was very hard. Papa did all he could, but it was quite lonely for me during that time."

"I'm sorry. It must be difficult, starting over in a new country."

"Yes. But things began to change when I was old enough to go to high school. I worked hard, and became more of an American. Boys began to notice me, and I found that doing well in school made one more popular with almost everyone. I plunged into all of the activities I could—drama, music, school politics. In a word, I left the old ways behind and began to appreciate myself a little more, rather than feeling like the ugly duckling."

"It is hard to imagine you would ever have negative thoughts about yourself, when I see you now."

"Thank you, but it is true. I mention it now so perhaps you will understand some of my fears and feelings of insecurity that remain. I won a scholarship to New York University, where I studied criminology and computer science, a dual major. Because of my papa, whom I admired, I wanted to do some work in the same field, but not exactly as a policewoman."

"It must be from your father that you learned about guns."

"That is true. For learning about criminals, I had my classes, then the lessons of life. It was in one of my classes that I met my future husband. He was of an Italian background also. He was handsome and clever, I thought, and I felt very fortunate to be chosen by him. His name was Gianluigi Capricio when he was christened, but before he entered school, his father officially changed it to John Lewis, 'to make him more of an American.'"

"Were you married right away?"

"No. John went to law school at Columbia University, and I graduated and went to work for the City. We were married after he graduated and passed the bar. My specialty was in setting up computer systems and teaching the precincts how to use the data available to track down criminals and solve crimes. John specialized in criminal law, and after graduation connected with a large firm with a reputation for representing some of the most unsavory of characters. I think perhaps you can see where this is heading."

I refilled our glasses. "I think I can. The wrong kind of connections made, temptations in the wrong direction?"

"Unfortunately, yes. He changed. At first, he saw himself as a defender of the downtrodden. Then he started admiring the things they got away with. He started thinking of acquiring wealth, no matter how it came about."

"You spoke of giving up, not caring..."

She sipped from her glass of wine, and watched gusts of wind make cat's paw ripples across the mirrored water in the inlet. Several silent moments went by. She turned to look at me, and I could see the shine of tears in her eyes. Her voice was soft and low.

"This is the part that is so difficult for me to talk about. After we had been married for several years, and before things changed, I had given up hope...then I became pregnant. I was filled with joy. Despite preparing for a career, my goal in life was to be a mother, with lots of children. I wanted to live a simple life in a small town, in a Victorian house, and take care of my family. It was just a dream, but now one small part of it would come true."

She paused again, and looked out over the water.

I waited for her to continue. "You had a child?"

"A beautiful daughter. She was born with dark hair, and as she grew up, it stayed dark, with auburn highlights. Her eyes were the color of mine, a sort of blue-green. I loved her with all of my being..." She stifled a sob, and wiped her eyes with her fingertips. I gave her a handkerchief.

"And she's gone?"

She nodded. I waited. She sat very still, and would not look at me.

I didn't know what to do. I moved to her side of the cockpit and sat beside her, putting my arm around her shoulders. She did not respond, maintaining a rigid grip on herself.

"She died?"

Gabriella nodded again. Then she spoke in a whisper. "She was...only... six."

"Gabriella, I am so sorry. Please, if it hurts too much—"

"No, I must continue. A speeding car ran over her...right in front..." She clenched her fists, and closed her eyes.

"We don't have to talk about it now."

"Yes, we must. It is important for you to understand why I happened to be there. Remember how I felt about myself when I was a girl. I believed I was on the outside of society, looking in at others who seemed to be leading the more glamorous and romantic life I wanted for myself. I saw the movie, "Sabrina," the original with Audrey Hepburn. I went to it again and again, spending my allowance to become *her* in the movie. So of course when my daughter was born, she was named Sabrina."

I nodded, encouraging her to continue.

"After she was gone, I could not bring myself to care again what we did, or where we went. It caused big problems between my husband and me. He blamed me, because I was with her. Then after months had gone by, he chastised me for not 'getting over it,' as he said. I was angry with him for not caring enough."

"Is that what drove him in the wrong direction?"

"No, I do not think so. It was already happening. When he proposed moving to Jacksonville, to work for the 'organization' full time, I went along with it. I could not bear to stay in New York."

"I think I can understand that."

"By then my father had passed away, so I had no one to worry about except my elderly uncle. He was taking care of himself. We moved to an apartment and I set about keeping house, trying to forget. I began to take long walks and wear myself out with exercise so I could sleep. I pretended I was okay, that I was happy again. But I did not like the way my husband kept moving farther and farther away from the values I had, and what I thought he had. Everything was over between us, before he went away."

"The time of the plane crash?"

"Yes. It was a trip to Detroit, I found out later. They came for me early the next morning, to tell me something had gone wrong. I was afraid. When I got to the house where you were imprisoned, MacFarlane was in a rage. He called me all kinds of vile names I have never heard before. I was stunned. Through all of the incoherent raging, I finally gathered my husband and the pilot of the plane did not show up as scheduled. MacFarlane was convinced they had double-crossed him and escaped with something of great value. I did not learn until much later what it was."

"Did you think MacFarlane was right?"

"Because of the way things had been, I thought he could be. I believed John would do something like that if the stakes were high enough. And I did not think leaving me behind would matter to him."

"And they kept you there?"

"They never allowed me to leave from that day forward."

"I don't know what to say. Though it seems terribly inadequate, I'm so sorry about your daughter. It's a loss no one else can comprehend, I'm sure."

"Thank you, Matthew." She took my hand and squeezed it. "I feel better now that you know this much. There is more, but I feel very tired. Can we continue another time? I will take the first watch again."

"Of course. But I don't think we need to stand watch. I can't think of any way we'd be found here. We can talk another time. Thanks for confiding in me."

I closed the main hatch, pinning it from the inside, and we retired to our respective ends of the boat. I lay in the darkness and thought about Gabriella. During the escape, she moved with grace and confidence. Yet tonight she revealed a different person altogether, the lack of confidence as a young girl, the disappointments that caused her to give up hope. Since we'd been together, she kept a wall around her feelings, depressed but determined.

Rain started to patter against the deck overhead, then gradually increased to a steady buzz. Water ran into the cockpit over my head and gurgled out of the scuppers. It was a wonderful soothing sound, and I soon fell fast asleep.

Something woke me—movement? Sound? Rain still whispered on the deck above. The boat rocked slightly. Was it a gust of wind? Then I heard the slightest of sounds and I felt the foam mattress move. I held my breath, wondering how to react. Then she spoke softly to me, "Are you awake?"

"Yes."

"I could not sleep, and I feel very much alone. May I come back here with you?"

"Of course." I shifted to one side of the bed and she lay next to me. She had brought her pillow with her and plumped it down next to mine. She wore an oversized tee shirt and warm-up pants.

"Now I will feel more secure. Maybe sleep will come. Sorry to disturb you. Goodnight." She covered herself with her blanket.

"Goodnight, Gabriella."

I could tell by the sound of her breathing she was soon asleep. Not so for me. I lay awake listening to the rain, thinking about the unknown future. I had not yet heard all of her story, and what she meant by "getting even." I thought about the complexity of her character. On one hand, she was strong and determined; on the other, her vulnerability was much in evidence. I was touched by her need for whatever security I could provide. These thoughts chased themselves in circles around my mind, then merged with the white noise of the rain, and sleep came again.

Consciousness came to me in the morning with an urge to sneeze. Her hair was fully in my face, a strand toying with my nose. I was lying on my left side and she was spooned against me, her back against my chest, her head on my arm. My right arm lay across her slender waist, tucking her close to me in a natural reflex. She was purring softly in deep sleep. I crinkled my nose and turned my head to avoid the sneeze. Then I realized that my right hand was tucked in a place it shouldn't be. What was I to do? If I moved it, she might wake up and think I had been fondling her breasts while she slept. Then what would she think of me? There weren't a lot of options: she'd wake up sooner or later. Reluctantly, I extricated my errant hand with the stealth of a stalking leopard. She changed the pattern of her breathing, but didn't stir.

In normal circumstances, when I wake in the morning, I want to get up and moving. That morning I made an exception. My left arm was numb and my muscles ached to change position, but I forced myself to lie still. I thought of the old coyote-ugly joke, but I couldn't imagine anything farther from the point of that story.

I don't know how we got into that position. We started with a discreet space between us, but somehow our souls and subconscious minds pulled us closer together. It was an altogether pleasant feeling, warm and secure, with the pattering of rain overhead.

Finally she moved, and with a little snort, was awake. She realized where she was and quickly moved away, sitting up and wrapping her blanket around her like a cloak.

She lowered her eyes and said softly, "I am so sorry if I crowded you."

"It wasn't altogether unpleasant for me."

She looked embarrassed. "I was really deep in sleep."

"That you were."

"I trust you slept well?" she said in a stronger voice, regaining her more formal speech.

I chose to respond in kind. "Yes, Madame, thank you. Shall I crank up the diesel engine to warm your bath?"

She actually smiled. "Yes, that would be nice." She wore no makeup and her hair was tousled from sleep, but the smile was dazzling.

Getting out of the tight quarters I bumped my head, trying to maintain some dignity in my underwear. I don't know why I worried. The first few times she saw me, I was completely nude.

An hour later, we were underway, fed and coffeed. She joined me in the cockpit, wearing the foulies that no doubt belonged to Mrs. Fred. A cold rain was still falling and there was no appreciable breeze, so we motored northward up the Intracoastal, the diesel chuckling us along at five knots. I sat on a cushion behind the wheel, and Gabriella sat in the corner of the cockpit, next to me.

Her face was framed by the yellow hood, pulled snug with elastic cord, and her nose was pink from the chill damp. She resumed her narrative from the night before.

"I have computerized records that contain great detail about McFarlane's so-called business. I believe that in the right hands, it will destroy him and many others. That is what I mean by 'getting even'."

"How did you do it without getting caught?"

"They never took me seriously, because I am a woman, I suppose. I was just 'Johnny's woman' to them. It is how he liked it, also. It is ironic they never knew what I was trained to do. I would steal a number here and there—that is the way I got the safe combination—and I would work on the computer system when no one was watching."

"Wasn't it dangerous?"

She shrugged. "I downloaded file after file. I will show you the CDs. And McFarlane computerized *everything*, putting it all in code. It was a fetish with him. He did everything—names, dates, shipments, origin—everything."

"And the code? Do you have it?"

She looked at me with a gleam in her eyes. "Of course. It was difficult, but I had plenty of time. It is the kind of thing I do. I can read it like a novel."

"So what is he? Head of mob? What?"

"I would describe him as more of a consultant. He was particularly good at several things, bringing in advanced business techniques and applying them to the drug trade. Some of the larger organizations have carved out territories and left others to do the same in their own areas. He sold his services to several of them in different regions. He would do sophisticated market analyses, just like a business, and advise on whether performance was meeting expectations, and how to correct it if it was not."

I made a slight course correction to stay in line with buoys marking the channel. "A consultant in crime. That's a new one to me."

"It is what he is. One of his most powerful influences lay in predicting the activities of the DEA—where and when they would strike next, and where to bring in goods with the least risk. He liked to lead them to believe it was all in computer analysis, but the truth is he had a 'mole' on the inside, highly placed."

"Wow! *That* should be of interest!"

She smiled grimly. "Yes, I think it will. But it will require us to be very careful whom we select to receive this information. It sounds incredibly foolish to record everything as he did, but it was arrogance, another form of stupidity."

We met a nice modern trawler-type cabin cruiser, headed south. Through the rain streaked cabin window, the man at the inside steering station waved a greeting.

We continued in silence for a time, then Gabriella turned to me with concern in her eyes. "I must explain something to you, and I don't know how to begin."

"However you wish. I'll try to understand."

She watched a pelican make a successful power dive on a top-swimming fish, then sighed and began. "When I came to the back of the boat last night, I feared you would misunderstand."

"No. It's okay."

"I feel so alone and afraid. That is what it was all about. I wanted the comfort of someone close by I could trust, and I do trust you. You are strong, and it comforts me to be near you. It seems for years now, I have had no one to rely on. If only things could be different...If I were...If I..."

She swallowed and gazed at the passing shore of St. Catherine's Island. I waited in silence for several minutes. "I understand, Gabriella, believe me. For the moment, we have only each other. I trust you completely and I owe you my life. No matter what happens, I'll be here for you. There'll be a happier time, believe me."

She turned to me. "I wish I could believe I would be happy again...but I will never be."

"You must believe that you will be. It's what keeps us going."

She shook her head. "No. Now I exist only to do what must be done.... We are taught revenge is a bad thing, that we must forgive wrongs inflicted upon us. But I am not such a good person. I want vengeance. I do not like myself like this, but it is how I am."

"Don't give yourself a hard time over it. Most people would feel the same way."

"There is more I have not told you. When the plane did not return, McFarlane screamed at everyone and threatened us. He cursed people over the phone and hired investigators. You see, it was not just the money, it was his precious reputation, since he was responsible for the shipment. Eventually, he turned his attention back to me."

I didn't want to hear what would come next.

She looked down at the deck beneath her feet. "Now I will never be worth anything to anyone. I will never feel clean..."

She looked back up at me, and her face dissolved in misery. "I should have let them kill me. I should have killed myself, but I didn't do it...He said he would give me to the 'boys' if I did not go along with him...I willed my mind to go to a place far away...I wanted to stay alive."

She held her face in her hands. I spun the wheel to move toward the mainland. It was time to stop, to provide whatever comfort I could.

There was a small island covered with scruffy vegetation to our port side. The tide was out, so with safe water under the keel now, I knew we wouldn't get stuck. I used the chart and the depth sounder, and found a sheltered anchorage. She was still sitting, her face in her hands, when I completed securing the boat and killing the engine.

I lifted her gently to her feet and helped her below. She was silent and trembling, drained with the effort of sharing her pain. I got us out of the foul weather gear, found blankets, and seated us on the U-shaped settee, with her facing me, cradled to my chest. I wrapped the blankets around us, secure against the cold and damp.

She started crying softly at first, then increased in emotion until her sobs were shaking us. I simply held her and stroked her hair, and waited until it subsided. Finally she stirred, dried her eyes with her sleeve, and looked at me, inches apart.

"Thank you for listening to me," she whispered. "It has been so difficult, keeping everything inside. I have felt so worthless, so unclean."

"It helps me understand why you seem so sad."

"Now I have burdened you with everything."

"I'm glad you can."

"I never thought I would trust anyone enough again to speak of such things, but I feel so much better now."

"Gabriella, it isn't your fault. Don't blame yourself for what happened to you. It doesn't change the way anyone would feel about you. Believe me. I have great admiration for the way you never gave up, and you found a way to save yourself—and me."

"It is such a relief for me. Now I am not alone." She sat more upright, and actually hugged me in a tight embrace.

"Comrades forever?" I asked, to lighten the moment.

"Comrades forever." She said.

24.

SAVANNAH

The rain had ceased by morning, but the weather was still gray and cool. We threaded our way under diesel power up the Intracoastal, through the islands that made up the Savannah River delta. We secured the boat along the wharf a few blocks downstream from the historic district. It was nearing noontime and we calculated with some difficulty that it was the first day of the workweek.

The disclosure of the day before brought a dramatic change in Gabriella. To be sure, she was still focused on the trials that were to come, but it was as though a great weight had been lifted from her. Her worry lines had relaxed and she smiled more easily. She had taken the first step to recovery, and the change was visible.

We'd slept together again, with the discreet distance separating us. At the same time, we benefited from the closeness as though we had a long and loving relationship. Whether this could continue, and where it would lead, I could not guess. I believed resolving our issues with the past would determine everything about the future.

We went over our action list together.

"The first thing I have to do is call Woody. He deserves to know I'm alive...at least for the present. But I won't tell him where we are. Are you sure you don't want to talk to anyone?"

"I am sure. It would only confuse my Uncle Vito. As far as he knows, everything is normal."

"Okay. Next we have to find a lawyer, the toughest we can get."

"Why must we do that?"

"I'd feel better if we had somebody to deal with the FBI in our behalf. I think these things have a way of getting out of control."

She nodded. "You are probably right. I hate to take the chance to leave the boat, but I suppose we must."

"We'll just have to take a chance. I guess they've put out some underworld version of an All Points Bulletin, but I don't see how it can be too complete. I think we can stay in the background, and it's best if we avoid being seen together."

I went ashore first and walked several blocks to the tourist area on the waterfront. Her 9-millimeter Glock pistol was tucked in my waistband. I purchased telephone cards and found a telephone booth standing alone in a cobbled parking area at the end of the street. I knew Woody was often home on Mondays and it was near lunchtime, so I might be lucky enough to catch him.

After several rings, he picked up with a sleepy, "Hello?"

"Were you asleep?"

"Who *is* this? *Matthew?*"

"The very same."

"Praise the Lord! You're alive! What happened to you?"

"It's a long and complicated story, but for now, I was kidnapped and taken away—"

"Where are you now? Are you safe?"

"Yes, I think so. We managed to escape—"

"We?"

"Yes. Someone else was also being held, and she—"

"She?"

"Yes, Woody, 'she.' Please, I'll tell you everything when I can. For now, we have to find a good criminal lawyer and make some arrangements. I can't talk long and I can't risk talking about where I am. I wanted you to know I'm okay, and I'll be in touch as soon as I can."

"Matt, I'm overjoyed to hear you're alive. We was frantic when you disappeared. I can tell Eileen, can't I? I mean it's been terrible for her. The Fenton woman isn't with you, is she?"

"No, I'm sorry, Woody. I doubt we'll see her again. Yes, tell Eileen, but please keep this between you two until I call again."

"We will. Let me know if I can help with anything. And praise the Lord!"

I reported back to Gabriella. I had already told her all about Woody and Eileen.

"I would enjoy meeting your friends, Matthew, if all of this can be put behind us."

"It will be. Now, we've got to find a lawyer."

I'd been thinking all the way about how to determine someone suitable for what we needed to do. I didn't want anyone to know where we were, even if they could to be trusted. The less information we put out there, the smaller the risk. And we couldn't just start calling law firms. I thought of going through newspaper archives looking for landmark cases, but that would take too long.

This time I found a phone in the lobby of a Marriott nearby, first calling Information, then the number.

"Marker and Hamilton," a voice answered.

"This is Matthew Cross. May I speak with Scott Lindsey, please?"

A pause, then, "Matt, how are you? How's the family?"

He didn't even know about Caroline. It had been that long since we had worked together. "Couldn't be better. I have a favor to ask of you."

"It's good to hear from you. Let's hear it. Got another contract pending?"

"I'm afraid not, at the moment. This isn't that positive. But I have some dear friends in trouble and I need to find the best criminal lawyer I can get to handle the case. You know how hard it is for a stranger in town to decide where to begin."

"Where is it? Here in Atlanta?"

"No, they're in Savannah. I know this is completely outside your normal focus, but I thought you might be able to network, or have sources that could give a recommendation."

"Well, sure. Can you tell me anything about the case? That might help."

"I don't have all of the details, but they aren't actually charged with anything. They just need someone tough enough to negotiate with a couple of federal agencies, protect their rights, and so forth."

"I'll make some calls. Are you in your office?"

"No, I'm traveling. I'll have to call you back. How long should I wait?"

"I'm in the middle of something right now, but I should know something by the end of the day. Okay? Why don't you try me about five."

"Thanks, Scott. I really appreciate it."

I walked back to the boat with three hours to kill. Gabriella was waiting in the saloon, the hatch locked from the inside.

"How did it go?" She asked.

"I have to call back in three hours. Are you getting stir-crazy, while I've been running errands?"

"Quite so, yes. It plays on the nerves, mostly."

"Why don't we risk a little shopping? If this works like we intend, we may need to appear in more businesslike surroundings."

She smiled. "You mean I would not have to wear baggy sweat shirts? Great idea. I might see if I can get a walk-in beauty appointment. My hair is a mess."

Her hair was full and naturally curly. It cascaded in shining auburn waves, the color of polished mahogany. "I think it looks great, but you're the boss. I want to keep you in sight, but perhaps we won't walk together. Do you have the little pistol?"

"I do. Let us hit the streets. You can give me directions."

I trailed behind her as she walked up the street and turned left toward the heart of the shopping district. She was in semi-costume, wearing the loose jeans and the foul weather jacket. She was successful with the salon, and I strolled on by to find a store for my purchases. Next I loitered in a coffee shop until she came out. She looked both ways, no doubt wondering where I was, then went shopping herself. She was wearing a scarf instead of the baseball cap.

Less than an hour, and a couple of shops later, she headed back toward the boat, packages in hand. I let her see me lurking in a storefront on the other side of the street, then followed her back to the boat. There weren't many people about, since it was far from tourist season. The stores were decorated for Christmas, but it was hard to think of holidays at times like these. My children were out of touch, and I had to dissipate some dark clouds before I could think any normal thoughts.

· "Well, did you have a good time?" I asked, as I descended the steps. She was still wearing the scarf.

"Yes, believe it or not, I did. For a little time, I felt almost normal."

"Maybe you'll look too good. If you do, I promise not to be critical. We'll soon know what kind of protection we can expect, and then we can allow you to be as beautiful as you really are."

She looked embarrassed. "I am sorry I snapped at you that day. And you should not say such things to me."

"Hey, I know what my eyes see."

"I do, too. Now that you are mostly one color, you are not so bad yourself. Maybe I will insist that you wear bib overalls and a straw hat...to see if people will think you are Farmer Cross."

"I can have an enlargement made for you of the pictures we took, so you can remember all the shades of purple and green."

I left for my appointed phone call. Scott had given me his direct extension.

"Lindsey here."

"Scott, it's me, Matt."

"Thought it might be. I have good news, I think. Check out a Walker Travis, and see what you think, okay? And it's not Walker-comma-Travis. Walker is the first name. You can drop Richard Hamilton's name."

"I got it. Thanks. I'll let you know how it comes out. I really appreciate it."

I hung up and dialed the number for Travis Rensselar and Wilkins from the yellow pages. A receptionist was still on duty. I told her what I needed, urging her to mention Richard Hamilton, the FBI, and the DEA. After placing me on hold for a long ten minutes, she came back and said I could come in at 10:00 Tuesday morning.

When I returned to the boat, I was in for a surprise. I tapped on the hatch and heard her unlatch it from the inside. When I descended the ladder, Gabriella was standing in the middle of the teak and holly sole of the saloon.

She was wearing high heels and hose, a black suit with skirt to mid-calf, and a teal silk blouse. The scarf was gone, revealing sleek, razor cut hair, sculpted to a taper at the nape of the neck. She was wearing makeup for the first time since we had been together—perfect lip-gloss, facial makeup, and whatever it is women do to their eyes.

I stopped, mouth hanging open, staring at her.

"Will this be okay, do you think?" I couldn't tell if it was a serious question, or if she was fooling with me. I decided she was innocent.

"Yes, I'm sure that will be fine, Gabriella." Inside, I felt increasing concern. How was I to continue like this, trying to maintain my composure, denying the feelings for her that were developing? Worst of all, she continued to share the bed in the after compartment. Knowing how fragile she was after the treatment she had received, I was determined to keep our relationship on a platonic, supportive level—as long as I was able.

"We have an appointment tomorrow morning at ten. You look perfect for a legal conference. And I won't insist on a blacked-out tooth or a pillow stomach."

That dazzling smile flashed again. Her new haircut made her eyes even larger and more luminous, and displayed the line of her neck. I would have to stop thinking such thoughts.

"I wish we could go out for dinner, but I'm still afraid to risk it."

"It is okay," she said. "It is still your day to cook, is it not?"

"Yes, I'm sure it must be. And you'd better change before you start scrubbing pots and pans."

A taxi delivered us to the address of the law firm. It was in a large stone mansion centered in a plot fenced with wrought iron and stone. The grounds were landscaped with azaleas and dogwoods. It must be spectacular in the early spring.

The receptionist was seated behind a mahogany counter. She was small and trim, in her fifties, by my best guess. She looked at Gabriella with admiration and asked us to be seated. After a few moments, another woman appeared and led us to the back of the mansion. She could have been a classmate of the receptionist. At least they had experience in the front office.

The man seated at the enormous wooden desk glanced at us, then rose, removing his half-glasses, and walked around the desk. He extended his hand to Gabriella and smiled. "I'm honored to meet you, ma'm. I'm Walker Travis."

She took his hand. "I'm Gabriella Capricio. This is Matthew Cross."

He shook my hand. "Mr. Cross. I'm pleased to meet you, sir."

He glanced at his secretary. "Thank you Miz' Maddy. Can you see about some coffee for us please?" Then to Gabriella. "Or perhaps something else?"

"No, coffee is fine."

He led the way to a grouping of green leather furniture in the corner of the office and indicated we should sit on the couch. He took a chair diagonally across a glass-topped coffee table.

He was wearing a navy suit of worsted wool, white shirt, and silk bow tie. His full head of wavy hair had gone white, contrasting with a ruddy complexion. He was tall, perhaps an inch or two over six feet, and tending toward overweight. His eyes were bright blue under bushy brows. He exuded the air of confidence I had hoped to find.

He positioned a long yellow pad on his knee, placed the half-moon glasses on his nose, and took out a Cartier fountain pen. With a smile he began. "Now, how can I help you-all? Surely you two aren't in any kind of trouble?"

We glanced at each other and Gabriella gestured to me to begin. "Yes, I think you'll agree that we are. It's a complicated story, but I'll try to hit the headlines first, so you can decide if it is something we can work through. I assume our discussion is privileged?"

He nodded, "Absolutely."

"We have both been held captive in Jacksonville by some people in the drug business. She has been there for months and I only a matter of days. She helped me escape. In the process, I shot three of their guards. She has a tremendous amount of evidence that would help the DEA, but there is also a ringer there. Some of the evidence will point to someone inside their organization. Hence the mention of the FBI. Now, we'll have to back up and tell you how we got involved. Does this sound far-fetched? I assure you it's all true."

"My goodness! I've heard a great deal in my career, but that's some opening statement. Nothing really surprises me though, I can assure you. How did you get here?"

"We borrowed a sailboat and came up the Intracoastal. We have to see about getting it back to where it belongs."

He smiled. "That's a novel getaway vehicle. Probably would be the last thing they'd think of. One of the first considerations, I'd think, is the safety of you two. Some of these organizations are pretty far-reaching."

"That's what we thought also. With your advice, of course, we thought the sooner we can get protection by the FBI, the better off we are."

He pursed his lips, thinking. "Let's hear the rest, then we'll make a decision together. What I see here is the potential for a trade. But let's continue."

"I think Mrs. Capricio should tell you her story first. Gabriella?"

She told her story in an unemotional manner, a condensed and less personal version of what she had told me. Travis asked few questions, merely nodded and made scribbled notes on his pad.

At one point he asked, "Did you have any duties with the so-called business?"

"Absolutely not. I spent very little time there until they detained me. It was a place my husband worked. That was all, in the beginning."

"And were you harmed?"

It was still a problem for her to talk about. She looked down at her hands, tightly clasped in her lap.

"It's okay," he said.

She spoke almost in a whisper. "Yes. In retaliation for what he thought my husband had done, I was...assaulted."

There was a momentary silence while Travis absorbed the meaning. "I see. Do you also wish to bring charges on that basis?"

"No. I want to see them go where they belong. I will testify as necessary, and help in any way I can. I can decipher all of the codes."

"And the information you have is all in the form of computer records?"

"All except for two things. I have McFarlane's appointment calendar from last year, in his own handwriting. He had this year's with him. And I kept a personal log of everything I could learn."

"I think I have a good understanding. Thank you, Miz Capricio." Travis said. He turned to me, pen poised over a fresh sheet in his yellow pad. "Mr. Cross?"

I had been thinking of all the options I could employ, whether to tell the whole truth, or try to avoid part of it until I could fix it. In the end, I concluded I would lay it all out and get out of it the best way I could.

"I made one big error in judgement, and the rest all followed from there. At first it was indecision, then it got away from me. Now I want to do everything possible to set it straight and get it behind me."

"That's the way it usually works; a stone is dislodged and it becomes a landslide. We'll see what we can do."

"It all began for me with a walk in the mountains. I'd lost my job, including retirement, and I had some thinking to do..."

25.
QUESTIONS

It was past noon by the time I finished. Again, Travis took notes, saying very little. I concluded by saying, "I want to correct one of the mistakes before we go any farther. I want to get rid of all the money they considered theirs. Then I'll be able to truthfully say I have nothing. If you can't legally participate in that, then I can get it done myself. It will go to a good cause, one no one could claim benefits any individual." I told him what I had in mind.

"I can't advise you to hide evidence or commit perjury. If you can figure a way around it on your own, then that's up to you. If you need any assistance with setting up bank transfers and checking state regulations on such dealings, I can steer you to someone who can help you." He wrote a name on a corner of yellow paper. "Maddy can set up a contact for you this afternoon.

"Now," he continued. "Here's what I see as something we will have to contend with. They may want to split the two of you into separate issues. All should go smoothly with Miz Capricio—"

"I will not do it!" She said. "It is a package deal. Whatever happens to one of us happens to both of us."

"Gabriella, I can't let you do that, if it means problems for you," I protested.

"Yes you can. I will trade my information and testimony to benefit us both, or not at all."

Travis watched the interplay between us. "And you've only met each other a matter of days ago?"

"Yes," she said. "But in ways it has been a lifetime. Before, we were as good as dead. Now we are alive."

Travis nodded.

"And I have been thinking ahead," she continued. "I must be the one to testify in court if need be, to change my name, to go into a witness protection program."

She turned to me. "You must stay in the background. You must think of your children. If you become the focus of a court trial, it could affect them and their careers. I have no one. As much as we can arrange it, you must fade into the background."

"That's very generous of you, but—"

"No buts. Think about it. It is how it must be."

I decided not to argue the point now. We could do that later, after we knew more about the future.

"Be that as it may," Travis said, "it appears Miz Capricio has all assets—the evidence—and no liabilities. You, Mr. Cross, on the other hand could be tainted with some suspicion because of that woman's disappearance, the fact *they* thought you did something, and lastly, your admission you shot three men, regardless of the circumstance."

"I understand," I said.

"Miz Capricio, I believe you can tell your story to the FBI exactly as you told it to me. The only sticky issue I see is the question I have already raised. They will want you to hand them the evidence and wait to be called as a witness. You, on the other hand," he said, turning to me again, "should do the same, except for an obvious issue which I will leave to your discretion. It has no bearing on interstate kidnapping and torture, crimes committed against you."

He looked over his glasses at us.

"I am interested in assisting you with this case. My billing rate is four twenty-five an hour, if you can handle that. Looking ahead, through all the rounds of testimony and so forth, we can start with a retainer of fifteen thousand, then go from there. Is that agreeable? If we don't use it, you get it back, of course. I need to step out a moment, so perhaps you can discuss it between you."

After he left, I asked Gabriella for her thoughts and whether we had the cash.

"I am for it. And I lifted fifty thousand, so that should keep us going for awhile."

"Good. Then it's settled."

Travis had lunch brought in, and we talked a bit more about our coming testimony. He gave me the name of a banker in town and had his secretary call for an appointment for me the next morning at ten. He would try for a meeting with the FBI at two o'clock in his office. He advised Gabriella to see that the evidence was in a safe place. We would have to take care of that.

The taxi stood by while Gabriella secured her package from the boat, then took us to the bus station across town. Again he waited until she came back with key in hand. We had him drop us near the Marriott. I called Woody at his auction house. I thought I remembered the number I needed, but I would confirm it if I could. It took a few moments for them to find him.

"Hi, Woody. It's me again."

"Hi, Buddy. How are you and 'she' doing?"

"Good. Hey, I need to know what happened to my stuff I had in the motel room. Do you have it?"

"Right now, it's locked up in the evidence room down at the department. You see, they still think you're missin', which you still are, I reckon, since we don't know where you are."

"Can you get to it without attracting attention? I need a telephone number out of my little Daytimer. I need the number for Percy Smith. If you can get it, then I'll call you back tonight."

"Percy Smith? Who the hell is that?"

"Just somebody I need to call."

"Whatever you say. Yeah, I can get it. And Matthew? When they got done with your house, I had it cleaned up and fixed back as best I could. I also left your answering machine on and collected calls for you now and again as I'd run by there. When do you want all that? Your kids have called, you know. They're worried. I called 'em, said you'd get back to them, just so's they wouldn't worry."

"Thanks, Woody. If you don't mind, could you let the kids know I'm okay? The rest can wait awhile. I'll square things as soon as I can."

"Sure thing."

I was able to handle the transaction with the referenced lawyer by telephone. I represented a wealthy donor who wished to remain anonymous. I gave him the information on the targeted account. He promised to check the local regulations and work out a transfer path by the time of my appointment the following morning. He also agreed to attend, to assist in the details of the transfer. I called Travis's assistant, Maddy, and confirmed our two o'clock the following day.

We spent the night just as before, inches apart in the darkness of the aft quarters. Since that first time, we had maintained that distance. Being together seemed to provide the feeling of security she needed to sleep peacefully in the circumstances of our mission.

For me, on that night, I lay awake far into the early morning hours. It could be the last time we would find ourselves like that. After we told our stories the following day, we could be separated by the problems I faced. Or we could both be held—me until my problems were resolved; her for the sake of protecting a key witness. I was deeply touched by her unselfish desire to protect my children and me.

I listened to her sleep, and fought against my restlessness. The small distance that separated us might well have been a yawning canyon. I could not encroach upon that space, endangering the trust she had placed in me. For now, the problems to resolve and the trauma she had faced stood squarely in the way.

Still, with each passing moment, I wanted to hold her close to me and tell her how much I cared for her. I wanted to confirm the spiritual bond I was almost certain she shared after today's discussions. I would speak to her of it at the first opportunity after the day to come.

We arrived at the bank building by taxi five minutes ahead of schedule. I saw a man standing inside the door, portfolio in hand, looking like a visitor. He was portly, with small hands and feet, and bald head. He appeared to be about five-seven, less than Gabriella's height in her heels.

"Mr. Preston?" I asked.

He smiled. "Yes. Mr. Cross?"

"Yes. And this is Mrs. Capricio."

"How do you do?" She said. Then to me, "I will remain out here in the waiting area. Okay?"

We talked to a receptionist and were ushered back to a large glass office, with a gold shingle that read "G. W. Lee, President" on the opened door. G. W. himself rose from his desk and we all exchanged the usual meaningless pleasantries before being seated.

G.W. was a nice-looking man in his late forties, about my height, with dark hair. He was a sharp dresser, wearing a well-tailored suit and expensive tie. His shirt was one of those custom-made jobs with French cuffs, a striped body, and contrasting white collar and cuffs.

"I understand you wish to transfer some funds, Mr. Cross."

"Yes, I'm acting on behalf of an organization that is making an anonymous charitable gift. Mr. Preston has been working on the details of the transfer. I understand from our phone conversation this morning that everything is in order. Right, Mr. Preston?"

"It is. Naturally, they wished to give public credit to the benefactor and they were eager to know the amount of the gift, but I explained the conditions were not negotiable. They readily agreed. The receiving financial institution has set up a temporary receiving account as a vehicle to protect the account number of the charity. Yes, I think we're all set."

It was as simple as that. The transfer was done in a matter of moments by computer. It flew electronically from "Percy Smith's" modified telephone number I'd gotten from Woody, to the temporary account number and thence to the destination.

We entered the law offices of Travis Rensselar and Wilkins with trepidation. Bringing closure to our situation was something that we desired, but lack of control over the future was frightening. Gabriella reached for my hand as we were ushered back to the conference room across from Travis's office. Her hand was uncharacteristically cold and clammy.

"*Good luck,*" she whispered.

"*You, too,*" I replied. We released each other's hands as we entered.

Travis was standing at the side of the room by a table that held a coffee service and canned drinks in a bowl of ice. With him were two men in the uniform of the FBI—dark suits, white shirts, conservative ties, short haircuts. He introduced us, beginning with Gabriella. The senior of the two was in his fifties, with thinning gray hair. He was about my height and weight, but with a lean, lined face dominated by a hooked nose. His greeting was cordial, particularly to Gabriella, who seemed to inspire warmth from others. His name was Paul Miller.

The other was much younger, an athletic man with the build of a tight end. He had close-cropped receding dark hair, and would probably have gone with the modern style of shaving his head if the FBI allowed that sort of thing. His name was Wayne Hill.

We seated ourselves at the conference table, Travis at the head, the agents on one side, the two of us on the other side facing them.

Agent Miller began. "Mr. Travis has given us a general idea of the nature of your situation. I propose we treat your testimony, if we may call it that, informally. We will not be cross-examining you, but will be asking questions. I would like to record it for transcription later, if that's agreeable. There are a couple of other points to bring up at this time. I know you have some concerns about information you may have about the DEA. Because of the nature of this case, I simply must have one of their agents present, or we'll have all kinds of accusations of conflict between agencies. Okay?"

Gabriella answered. "It will be okay with me, as long as you can handle the situation that one of their people may be involved."

"Good enough. Whatever comes out, I can assure you, the FBI will take care of it…and you. The other point is—when we get to the point of telling about your escape, we will want to interview you separately—"

"Is this agreeable?" Travis looked at us.

"As long as it is just that, and nothing more." Gabriella interrupted. "Is it okay with you, Matthew?"

"Sure. It happened as it happened."

"Fine," Miller continued. "It's just standard procedure. Individual testimony combined later sometimes gives the event greater depth, and tells us more about what happened. Each of you played individual rolls part of the time and we'd like to get it from the individual perspective."

And see if our stories match, I thought.

There was a pause while the DEA agent was summoned from an office where he was waiting.

He was in the same uniform as the FBI. He was a husky five-eleven, and had flat-topped blond hair. He shook hands around and introduced himself to us as James Neilson, out of the Atlanta office.

Miller took charge of the proceedings, starting the tape recorder and speaking into it with his name, and the names of the other two agents.

"Mrs. Capricio, please begin with your full name and address."

"Gabriella Zucci Capricio, of Whispering Pines Apartments, Number 24A, Riverside Drive, Jacksonville, Florida, although I have not been there for six months. I do not know what the status is."

Gabriella began with her story, much the same version as the one she had told Travis. In both cases she left out most of the personal information she had shared with me, providing only a narrative of events. She outlined the criminal dealings of MacFarlane and the download of information in her possession. At that point, Miller asked her if she had the computer disks and desk calendar with her.

"No," she replied. "It is safe. We will discuss later how the information is to be exchanged."

Throughout her discussion, Miller provided any prompting and asked all of the questions. Hill sat stoically, hands clasped in front of him, his eyes on Gabriella. At one point, she became uncomfortable with his silent staring. She stopped, stared back at him, sweeping her hands apart. "What?" she said, looking down at herself. "What is it? Is something out of place?"

He promptly looked away, and kept his eyes elsewhere. When she completed a description of her captivity, Miller interrupted with another question.

"And when did you first see Mr. Cross, or hear of his involvement?"

"There was a fragment or two of telephone conversation by MacFarlane. I realized later it must have been about him. I did not see him until one day they called me in from the pool, and there was a naked man in handcuffs. They began—"

"Let's stop at this point," said Miller, holding up his hand. "Mr. Cross, will you excuse yourself?"

I rose to leave, but Gabriella said, "Let me repeat my understanding that when I am finished with the intervening discussion bringing us to where we are today, then Mr. Cross and I will be together for all discussions about our future course of action."

"I'm not sure we should follow that course," said Miller.

Travis began to rise from his chair. "Then the meeting is over. Those were the conditions set forth in our first telephone conversation. This man and woman are here to assist as witnesses. Good day, gentlemen."

"Hold on, hold on," said Miller, raising his hand. "I guess we can agree to talking with the two of you together."

"Those are the conditions," replied Travis. "We have agreed to these specific individual discussions only as a matter of good faith."

All settled back into their chairs, slightly red-faced, and Gabriella began again as I exited.

I spent the next hour sitting in the corner of Travis's spacious office, drinking coffee and absently thumbing through magazines. It was nearing five o'clock when I was summoned back into the conference room. Gabriella looked tired, but confident.

As I seated myself, the tape recorder had been turned off. "Before we begin, have we reached a stage where we can talk logistics a bit? We need to make safe living arrangements, and I need to have the boat returned to its marina. Have you heard enough to agree at least temporary protection is in order?"

"Yes," Miller said. "Agent Hill left the room during Mrs. Capricio's narrative and made reservations at a hotel. We have booked you in under assumed names, and will provide protection there until we decide the next step."

"Good. Also, this might be a good time before she leaves the room to give you a gun used during the escape. It was the only one we fired. Also I have pictures of myself taken the next day."

Gabriella opened her purse, and all three men tensed as though they were in the main street of Dodge. She calmly ignored them, ejecting the loaded magazine, and jacking the slide back. The .380 round flipped out of the chamber onto the table, landing in front of Agent Neilson. She handed the Walther butt-first to Hill, across the table. Then she took the silencer out and rolled it across to him.

Miller was obviously flustered he hadn't thought to ask us about weapons. He cleared his throat. "Is that all you have?"

"No," I replied. "We have a Glock and an Uzi on the boat. We thought we'd use that one for protection to get us here. I'm sure you'll want to check the other ones out. No telling what they've been used for. Now, what about the boat?"

"We can hire someone to take it back, or get the Coast Guard to deliver it," said Neilson.

"Well, it needs to be cleaned up. And I'd like to buy a sail cover and a cover for the pedestal and wheel. His canvas is pretty grim, and it's the least I can do. Oh, and we have to have the proper name painted back on it."

"We'll see about a little shopping trip tomorrow," Neilson said with a trace of sarcasm. "Whoever takes it back can get the marina to clean it up, and see about the name thing."

They had sandwiches brought in and we continued late into the evening on my part of the testimony. I told them briefly of my business background, then skipped straight to the strange behavior of Carol Fenton after the news about some plane crash made the local news.

"What did you do to arouse Mrs. Fenton's suspicions?"

"Nothing except enjoy the mountains, as far as I was concerned. Of course I was in an area not far from the crash, I found out later. But it's a popular hiking and trail riding area. If my understanding is correct, something like six months elapsed from the time of the crash until it was located."

"Again, why did Mrs. Fenton pick you?"

"You'll have to ask her, if we ever see her again. Mrs. Fenton and her husband were in the same place I was, as were hundreds of others throughout the summer. If I had to guess, I'd say she was prone to jumping to conclusions."

There was pause while Miller stared at his notes. Hill stared straight ahead, highlighting the differences between his interest in Gabriella and me. Neilson fidgeted in his chair and loosened his tie.

I told them about the break-in of my house, and my consuming fear for my life, particularly after Carol Fenton's disappearance.

"Why didn't you go to the police?" said Miller.

"I did. They woke me the night Fenton disappeared, and I also called a deputy, who happens to be a friend of mine, about the house—"

"That would be Mr. Hendrix?"

"Yes." I was thrown off balance. They'd been doing some homework since Travis called them yesterday.

We ground on into the evening. They asked question after question during the telling of my torture at the hands of my captors. I described the scene in the lower level when I gained my freedom, then repeated it in minute detail.

"Why didn't you just hold the gun on them and force them to release you?" asked Miller.

"It didn't occur to me at the time and doesn't sound like a good plan now, when I look back on the conditions. There were two of them, with others upstairs. One of them had a machine gun. They were fit; I was in handcuffs, naked, weak, and beaten. No, I think I made the right choice."

"But three men are dead, according to you."

"It was the line of business they had chosen, correct?"

We returned to the narrative, and the details of our escape to Savannah. Again there were questions.

"Why didn't you go straight to the police? Why all of this delay, this recreational cruise in a stolen boat?"

"It's really quite simple. We didn't know whom to trust, I was weak and battered; we had to think through the best way to convey her information without winding up victims of retaliation. That's still the primary concern, incidentally. I'm concerned for her safety."

Travis saw a pause in the proceedings. "I believe everyone has had enough for this evening. Is it agreeable to resume tomorrow at nine?"

All wearily assented. I wanted to see how Gabriella had fared during her forced exile from the meeting. She turned out to be okay when she returned. She whispered to me that she was eager to hear how my session went.

Agents Miller and Hill drove us to the boat, where we retrieved our belongings and gave them the other two weapons. They had checked us into the Savannah DeSoto Hilton, where we entered through a side door without going to the front desk. When we got our keys, Gabriella asked whether ours were connecting rooms. Finding out they weren't, she sent Hill to the desk demanding this oversight be corrected, while we waited in the corner of the lobby.

When he looked at her, then back at me, she asserted herself again. "Look, make of it what you will, but we have been looking after each other for the past several days and it is going to continue that way. Now that we have been disarmed we must depend on you also, so try to be alert."

The door at last closed behind me, and I gazed longingly at the king-sized bed. At the same instant, Mrs. Jones knocked gently on the connecting door of Mr. Smith's room. I went to open it, and there she stood, just looking at me. I could tell how weary she was, but I could also see she shared my feelings of relief.

"Hello, Mr. Smith," she said.

"Hello, Mrs. Jones," said I.

With that, she set about propping open both doors. "Can we trust them?" she said.

"I don't know. I assume we must. Miller assured me they have electronic monitors in the halls, and additional agents we haven't met guarding the elevators and stairways."

I knew the time had come. "Gabriella, I have to talk to you. The circumstances are all wrong, but it can't be helped."

"Yes, what is it?"

"Well, about the testimony, of course, but it's more than that..." I felt myself searching for words. "Is now okay, or do you want to rest? I'm sure you're tired."

She stared at me. "Now, of course," she replied.

I led her to the couch in the corner of my room, and we sat turned toward one another. I took her hands in mine. Her eyes were wide. Lines of worry creased her brow.

"This is difficult, because I don't know what to expect. I feel I should be kneeling before you—"

"What?"

"I have to say what's on my mind. Gabriella, we've been together for such a short time in terms of days, but I feel so close to you—"

She jumped to her feet and backed toward the door to her room. "I do not want to hear this."

I followed her and took her hands in mine again. "Please listen to me, Gabriella."

Tears started to flow down her face, and she tried to pull away again. "No, no, I will not listen. You are going to tell me goodbye—"

"No, no, no. Don't you know about kneeling?"

"Kneeling?"

"Yes, I said I should be kneeling." I dropped to one knee and looked up at her. "Haven't you seen what has been happening to me? What I want to say to you is just the opposite of goodbye."

She stared down at me. "What are you saying?"

I rose. "I'm saying I can't bear the thought of *ever* telling you goodbye. I don't want to be apart from you, now or ever. I want you close to me for the rest of my life."

She just looked at me and began to cry. I took a deep breath. "I have so little to offer in return, so much uncertainty, but I had to tell you while I could...and you don't have to say anything if you don't want to..."

I was afraid for a moment I had made a mistake. She leaped into my arms, putting her cheek against mine. It was no mistake. We kissed each other hungrily, teeth clashing, lips searching. My face was wet with her tears...and mine.

"Oh Matthew, how I have longed for you to want me." Her words tumbled out. "But I was so afraid you would want to go on with your life...you were preparing to leave me behind. I am the one that has so little to offer."

"Sh-h-h. That's not true. I'll love you forever, no matter what."

"I do not know if I...I don't know if I can...be what I should be for you. What you deserve to have..."

"For me you're the most desirable woman on earth just as you are; just as we are right now. I'll wait for you as long as it takes. The important thing is for you to be with me always."

"I want you forever, also. I thought my life was over when I was imprisoned by those people. And when...it happened."

"Believe me, I thought all was lost, too."

She spoke in a whisper. "When I saw you for the first time, and how you stood up to them, I knew we had to escape together. Will you be happy with me?"

"Of course, Angel. I already am."

"Angel?"

"Since that first day, when you helped me escape and watched over me while I slept, I've thought of you as my guardian angel."

She smiled, "Me? An angel?"

"Yes, you. The Angel Gabriel is an angel of good tidings. Instead of blowing a horn, you watched over me with an Uzi. You're my Angel Gabriella. My Angel."

The future arrived quickly. On that night, the demons of the past were exorcised as we held each other in our newly declared love and commitment. After a tentative beginning, she was able to leave her damaged feelings behind, awakening a passion that transported us to a private paradise.

26.

JACKSONVILLE

I awoke to the pleasant sensation of kisses on my neck, my cheek, and my ear. When I opened my eyes, I was greeted by her beautiful smile. A little dimple formed on one side when she smiled and her soft upper lip inverted slightly over her perfect white teeth.

"You are a worker of miracles," she said softly. "But we are going to keep it a secret from the rest of the world."

"You don't want me to be famous?"

"Not in that way." She touched my lips with her index finger. "You have taken me to a place I have never been before."

The smile disappeared as she continued. "Someone wonderful had to believe in me before I could believe in myself." She wiped a tear from the corner of her eye, then smiled again.

I caressed her face. "And I never thought I could feel this way, my Angel. I'd take what they did to me all over again if it meant I could have you. I want to marry you as soon as we can."

"I, too, my love."

We ordered room service sent to Mrs. Jones's room for breakfast. It would take forty-five minutes for it to arrive, so we made good use of the time.

Eating our breakfast together, seated on her bed, was a most pleasant experience. The world was right side up again, so there was much to talk about. For a time, however, every thought had to be prefixed with an "if," or a "when," or a "perhaps."

We gathered at the appointed hour in the law firm conference room. Travis went to a flip chart and began writing bullet points.

"Let's see if we can agree on an agenda of sorts. These are my thoughts. Please contribute as you see fit."

He had written:

- GC's evidence
- Protection program for GC, MC
- MC charges? Next step?
- Venue, further testimony?
- Take care of boat, etc.

"It looks okay to me," said Miller. "Anyone else?"

"I want to get to this alleged involvement of the DEA. I assume it will be in point one," said Neilson.

Travis turned to Gabriella. "Would you like to begin?"

"All of you recall from yesterday my description of MacFarlane's business, as he called it. I have CDs of all his activity for the past several months— nearly a year. It names names, has dates of shipments with quantity and type, collection of payments, and so forth. It is all in code, but I can write macros which will convert it to clear text."

"What kind of code?"

"A rather simple one, actually, but it looked complicated to begin with. It is a simple substitution of alpha and numeric characters for each other, with the match-up changed on a fairly frequent basis."

"You spoke of certain market areas. Do you recall which ones?"

"I may not remember all of them, but they include parts of Detroit, St. Louis, Louisville, Miami, and Chicago, to name a few. The most sensitive information, I believe, is a contact in high places within the DEA who supplied information to—"

"This is bullshit!" Neilson exploded. "Who would believe this crap? We're just pissin' into the wind here!"

Gabriella glanced calmly in his direction. "I love it when a man can express himself with such eloquence. Perhaps I will be able to give you a small sample. What is today?"

Travis glanced at his gold Rolex. "Wednesday, the fifteenth."

"Good. There is still time to use the example I had hoped for." She consulted her notes. "Unless they have changed their minds since I got the information, this Friday the DEA and Coast Guard plan a joint operation."

"Nonsense!" said Neilson.

Gabriella ignored him and continued. "They have heard of a shipment coming in and plan to encircle Fort Myers on Friday night. It has been planned for some time. Of course, they will be disappointed. Please check it out. It has not been published in the newspapers, you understand."

Agent Neilson smirked and got up from his chair, reaching for his cell phone as he headed for the hall door.

"Mr. Neilson," said Travis. "I know you must realize how sensitive this is, if we assume there *is* a problem in the DEA."

"Sure, sure, don't worry about it," said Neilson as he exited.

We waited in relative silence, chatting about the weather and the approaching holidays. Hill doodled on a yellow pad, making geometric designs, carefully coloring in alternate squares and triangles. He stayed in the lines really well.

The door opened slowly and Neilson slunk silently back into the room, taking his seat. He looked directly at Gabriella. "Ma'm, I owe you an apology. I was rude to you."

Gabriella replied softly. "I understand. I know it was hard to accept."

Miller moved on. "When do we receive this information? Now would be a good time, so we can begin acting on it."

Travis replied. "Let's talk about point two."

Miller countered. "We can subpoena the information, you know."

"What information?" Said Travis.

"We have her on record concerning 'what information;' however there is no point in quibbling about it. If it is what she says it is, then we can understand the need for protection. We'd just like to authenticate it and get going."

"I have drafted a simple agreement which allows you to void it if the information proves to be false. Ms. Capricio is not asking for continued payments, or anything of that nature. Just interim protection, all documents for a name change, and one relocation. Only the basics."

He glanced at me. "And the same for Mr. Cross. He has told you of what he did in self-defense to enable escape for both of them. He would expect to be exonerated either by the district attorney's office or a grand jury hearing this whole affair. If he is charged, so be it. He would then stand trial. In any case, whenever he is free to go, he needs the same kind of protection. We discussed this in detail during my first meeting with them."

Miller thought for a moment. "It's not that we aren't grateful for the chance at this kind of information. Let me have your documents and I'll get on the horn to my district supervisor."

Neilson added his comments. "Well, let's get with it. Time's wasting. I believe them. Let me know what I can do to support the request. It's not unreasonable."

Travis rose. "Let's take a recess for about an hour while you see if you can secure approval. Shall we meet back here..." he glanced at his watch. "At ten-thirty?"

"Mr. Travis, may we have a word with you? It'll take only a moment," I said.

"Of course. Come to my office."

When we were seated, he looked at us. "Is everything going to suit you?"

"Yes, but there is something else you should know." I looked at Gabriella, who smiled back at me. "Gabriella and I have decided we belong together... permanently. Does it create any complications in our discussions?"

Travis smiled. "I don't know when you decided this, but I knew it when you first came to see me."

"Why didn't you tell us? It would have made things easier for me," I said.

He laughed. "You two are a perfect combination, and I knew it immediately. Let me be the first to congratulate you. You're a very lucky man, Matthew." He used my given name for the first time.

"I certainly am."

Travis smiled again at Gabriella. "I don't see a problem. It will make for some interesting application forms if they come through with witness protection."

"We did not think of that," Gabriella said. "But it will not stop us. Perhaps we will not need to create as many fictitious names."

We waited in the reception area until Maddy summoned us. Miller smiled, the first one we'd seen, and gave us a thumbs-up sign when we returned to the conference room. "We have it all worked out. A team is assembling while we speak, to investigate the house at the address you gave us. We're also making arrangements to transfer to Jacksonville to proceed, based upon what is discovered. The Florida Attorney General's office will be involved with the drug distribution system, and the local prosecutor will be involved in anything to do with Mr. Cross. By the way, I also have document packets for changes in identity on the way to our safe house in Jacksonville."

"When will we leave for Jacksonville?" I asked.

"As soon as we get a chance to see what the data looks like. Mid-afternoon, I'd guess," said Miller.

"I have the Coast Guard standing by to provide a couple of sailors to take the boat back," said Neilson.

The documents were signed, and Gabriella went with Miller and Hill to get the disks and calendar. It was hard to let her out of my sight.

Neilson and I went "shopping" as he called it. I found a yacht supply and picked up what I needed. I inspected the boat once more, making sure everything was in order. I made a sketch of the lettering for the original boat name and made a list of work to be done before they left it at the slip. I marked up a chart to show where to return it, and attached Gabriella's car keys, in case the heap was still there.

When we returned, I was relieved to see Gabriella in the conference room, setting up a laptop computer. It was linked to a device to project onto a pull-down screen. She looked at me and smiled.

After all were seated, I asked permission to make a couple of phone calls at some time before departure. "I just want to check on my house and my children with a friend in Mountain View. You may be in the same room if you like—it's nothing personal."

"Sure," said Miller. "At the first break. As a matter of protocol, perhaps Agent Hill can accompany you."

Gabriella began her masterful presentation by asking Neilson to pick a disk from the stack. She inserted it into the floppy drive and called it up on the screen. It was in a spreadsheet format, and appeared to be total garbage.

"I can tell from what I see that this is from mid-summer. This disk—" she held one aloft—"contains the translation codes." She saved the first file to the hard drive and popped in the second disk.

"Here we see the Rosetta Stone, or perhaps the Rosetta Disk." She moved the cursor and highlighted the numbers for July 15 to August 15. Then she split the screen into two windows, showing both the data and the code.

"We can read the text letter by letter like this." She picked one line and pointed to one character at a time, spelling out the details of a shipment that had come into Jacksonville on a freighter, the contents cocaine hidden in a cargo of bananas. The record showed where it came from in Columbia and where it went in St. Louis, and the value. She translated the name of the organization and the receiving agent.

"Wow," said Neilson. "Is it all like this?"

"The records are all about like this one. Another disk contains all of the information on movements of the Coast Guard and the DEA. To your organization, it will be the most sensitive."

"Let's get it over with," he sighed.

She picked a numbered disk from the stack and replaced the first file. Another spreadsheet flashed onto the screen. "I am used to the dates, so I will move to the file for the same period, just to keep the same code in play.

"Here you see a triple line of data for each encounter in the columns— when MacFarlane predicted a strike might take place based on his own study, when 'REM' said it would, and when and if it really did."

She looked again at Neilson. "I am sorry, but R.E.M. are the initials of the contact in the Miami office of the DEA."

Miller interrupted, looking at Neilson. "Because of the nature of this accusation, I believe this must go to the Director of the FBI, and let him work with the top level of the DEA. If you go up your chain of command, no telling what will happen."

"I don't like another agency snoopin' in our business."

"In this case, it's our business. We invited you in as an observer and coordinator. We can't allow this person to be spooked by getting the word from inside."

They stared at each other in silence, until the force of Miller's apparent seniority and determination appeared to win. However, I could not see an obvious way for him to control what Neilson did, short of placing him under arrest. I worried about the leak that might already have occurred because of his call about the raid.

They were soon satisfied with Gabriella's demonstration. Decoding all of the data could wait until Jacksonville. I went into a spare office, with Hill sitting in the corner, to call Woody. I would rather have been alone, but I decided to prevent arousing any suspicion about my motives.

I found Woody at the auction again, preparing for Thursday's afternoon and evening car sale.

"Matthew! Ya still doin' okay? How's 'she'?"

I barely managed a syllable before he continued.

"You ain't gonna' believe what happened! I just about lost our Eileen! They called from the bank and told her this anonymous person chunked millions into her fund-raisin' account. She dang near fainted. She just couldn't believe it. Now she don't know what to do with herself, she's so far beyond what they was expectin' to get—"

"Give her my congratulations. That's really good. I'll talk to her next time I get a chance. I need to change the subject. Have you talked to my kids?"

"Yeah, sorry I got carried away on that thing. But it was just...well, never mind. Yeah, they're both fine but worried about you. They can't understand, just like I can't, what's going on with you. But I played the part well and they're okay until you get a chance to talk to them if you do it soon."

"Good. Thanks, Woody. Any other messages I need to know about?"

"That real estate fella' left a message for you to call him. I wrote down his number."

"Is the house in good enough shape to show?"

"Yeah, we boxed up everything that was broken, and got rid of a couple of things we knew was beyond repair. We also had a' upholstery guy sew up a few things."

"Thanks again. I owe you a lot." He gave me McMillen's number.

Hill yawned and looked at his watch.

"Oh, and your Eye-talian friend called. Georgie? Is that his name? Said it was urgent. I got the number here for him, been carrying this stuff around in my shirt pocket in case you called. It's a long 'un." He slowly read me all of the international digits.

"Mr. Hill, I have to make one more call. I'll try to keep it short." He nodded, without comment.

It would be the dinner hour in Milan. I dialed the number.

"Pronto?"

"Elizabetta, it's Matthew Cross. I hope I'm not interrupting your dinner."

"Oh, it is fine. We are so glad to hear from you. I am sorry Cathy is not here right now. She so wanted to talk with you. You know your son is expected in a few days. Is there a chance you can come for Christmas?"

"It doesn't look as though I can. I'm terribly busy right now. Is Georgio there? He left a call for me."

"*Sì.* Yes. I will get him."

After a pause, Georgio spoke a warm greeting. Then, "I know you are busy, so I will get right to the reason for my call. I hope you have not already found a position, because I have something I would like for you to do. I have bought a plastics company in Torino. I think you may know them, because I think you did the installation of some of the equipment. Remember the time your dear Caroline stayed there with you?"

"I remember them. They're a good company."

"*Sì*, yes. You remember they make blown film, extruded film and foil laminations, injection molding, and so forth. Many high quality products. Anyway, I want you to run it. My son runs the other businesses and I want to slow down, enjoy life. It will be perfect for you, and you for the company. What do you say?"

"Without a doubt, I'd be honored and delighted. But before we go forward, I have to talk with you about what I've been involved in."

"I am not sure I understand, but we will talk again. Soon, I hope? The current manager wishes to retire, but will keep it going for a short time."

"Yes, we'll talk very soon."

We hurtled southward on I-95 in two government-issue Crown Victorias. Gabriella and I rode with Miller in the lead vehicle with Hill and Neilson following. Miller's cell phone chirped. He flipped it open and pulled out the little antenna.

He listened, grunted a reply, then relayed the information to us. The raid on the mansion in Jacksonville had managed to net only one fish. "The man Testa was there. MacFarlane was gone and Testa had no idea where he was. There were servants, but no guards. The rooms you described as cells are now storage rooms and a wine cellar. Everything is freshly painted. I have a feeling tying them to your kidnapping and you to the escape may be difficult, unless we get someone to talk."

"What chance do they have for MacFarlane?"

"We have a pretty elaborate net out. We'll see."

Their safe house in Jacksonville was in a condominium complex, the type that is about half rental, half purchased units. With residents coming and going, I suppose it would provide some anonymity. Hill had the good sense to park down the street. Two identical Crown Vics would be a dead giveaway. One was bad enough.

We carried our meager luggage to the second floor entrance. Miller knocked on the door to H24. After a pause, another agent introduced as Charles Keith opened the door. He led us into the living room where we met his partner, Eddie Valasco. The two of them would be our protectors, alternating on guard duty twenty-four hours a day when we were there.

Jacksonville police in plain clothes assisted on the street as backup, and would check in from time to time. I felt some relief about the security, but still concerned about Gabriella. We were in a game with high stakes, and there was still a niggling worry about the DEA connection.

The agents ordered in pizza for the four of us. One of the Jacksonville cops intercepted it and brought it up, taking a slice of pizza in payment. It was late when we finished, so we went to our assigned rooms. The condominium was all on one floor, but was on the second story. Gabriella got the master bedroom and I had the one across the hall, both at the back of the condo, away from the front entrance. The agents would alternately use the third one, which was up the hall.

I went across to check out her room. It had a balcony along one side, reached through a sliding glass door. "I don't like this," I told her. "Maybe you'd better come to my room. It has a sheer wall outside."

She made a cute face. "This sounds like a trick to lure me into your bed. Well, I planned to surprise you and be with you anyway. So it is your place rather than mine."

"Angel, you may think me paranoid, but let's keep our plans to ourselves. You should make everything indicate you're staying there alone. In fact, we'll put pillows in the bed to look like you're sleeping there."

I awoke in the darkness with a gentle hand over my mouth and whispered words in my ear.

"Matt, I hear something. I heard a door creak."

I listened intently, holding my breath, but could hear nothing. As a precaution, I crept out of bed and moved to my door, Gabriella behind me. Still nothing. Did she imagine something? Was it part of a dream? Could it have been one of the agents walking down the hall?

We had no weapons, no way to defend ourselves. I slowly opened my door and looked into the hallway. Dim light from the living room spilled a soft yellow glow on the walls. Gabriella remained behind while I tiptoed softly to the front of the condominium.

Valasco was sound asleep on the couch, his mouth open. I shook his shoulder, but could not rouse him. I shook him again, vigorously, and slapped his face. He was unconscious or dead; I didn't stop to find out. A chill went down my spine. I sprang down the hall, shouting an alarm and hammering on the bedroom door as I went, trying to awaken Keith.

As I approached my bedroom, I heard a muffled cry and the sound of a scuffle. I hurled myself through the door in the semi-darkness. A dark figure was crouched over a struggling Gabriella. I dived into him, butting my head into his ribcage and knocking him loose from his grip. We rolled in a tight embrace, struggling for leverage. I didn't know if he had a weapon, but intended to give him no chance to use one.

I could hear Gabriella gasping for breath, but she ran to the light switch, flipping it on. The man was wearing a stocking mask and black clothing. He was smaller than I, but strong and wiry. He managed to roll on top, clutching at my throat. I saw the shining wire of a garrote in his other hand. The stocking gave me no purchase on his face but I countered him by grabbing his throat and raising my knee to lever him off me.

At that moment, out of the corner of my vision, Gabriella appeared with a brass lamp in hand. She took a mighty swing and brained him with it. He went limp and rolled off, unconscious on the floor.

I leaped to my feet and held her shoulders. "Are you alright?"

She touched her throat and spoke in a rasping voice. "Yes, I think so, but my throat hurts. I am shaking all over. Thank God you came when you did!"

She dropped the lamp as I held her in my arms. "I shouldn't have left you, even for an instant! Thank God he didn't get the wire around your neck. Let's get this creep tied up."

I yanked the cord from the lamp and tied his hands behind his back, then sacrificed another lamp cord to tie his feet. I found a roll of tape in the medicine cabinet and taped over the wire. Then we went to check on Velasco and Keith. Both were alive but unconscious, with no signs of a struggle.

I tried the telephones, but the lines were dead. Velasco's cell phone had been crushed on the kitchen tile. I searched through Keith's belongings while he slept peacefully on the bed, and found one that worked. Dialing 911, I pondered the best method to summon help.

When I got an answer, I began, "We have an emergency which involves the FBI, and I need for you to contact them."

"Sir, what is your name and location? The location isn't coming up on my screen."

"It's a cell phone. Please listen to me. My name is Matthew Cross. Call the FBI and tell them to contact Agent Miller. Tell them my name. Have them come immediately. We have an emergency."

"Sir, I can't—"

"You can and you must! Please do it, or get me your supervisor! Now!"

There was a pause. "This is Sergeant Irving. What's the problem?"

"The problem is, Sergeant, I'm being protected by the FBI in a secret operation, and my protectors are all unconscious. I need you to scramble some help, but I can't tell you where I am. Please call the FBI and get in touch with—"

"I got it on the screen. Will do. Are you in immediate danger?"

"I don't think so. Just hurry."

It was nearly a half-hour before I heard a knock at the door. Through the peephole, I recognized Agent Hill. He had another bulky man with him. I opened the door, and both burst in, guns drawn. I held up my hand. "It's all under control, but you'll want the guy back in the bedroom."

The other agent spoke into a tiny radio. "Send the doc up here."

They advanced to the back, guns at ready, to where Gabriella stood over the now-conscious intruder, the lamp in her hand. She'd taken the shade off and the bulb out, so it looked like a mace of centuries ago. The agent with Hill cuffed the prisoner and jerked the stocking mask off. The captive had close-cropped black hair and swarthy, pock-marked skin. He stared at Gabriella with hatred in his eyes.

She returned his stare with a smile, and patted the lamp against her palm. I knew it took some effort, because I had felt the trembling in her body earlier, and I had looked at the bruises on her throat.

Miller arrived by the time the doctor had managed to revive both of the other agents. After their confusion cleared, they were able to tell us "one of the Jacksonville police," they thought, had brought them coffee. After that, they remembered nothing.

"Did you check his badge?" Miller demanded.

They both hung their heads in silence.

"How could you be so careless!" Shouted Miller. Then, remembering the rest of us were present, he said more calmly. "We'll discuss this later."

We were in the darkness of early morning hours. As soon as the agents were sent away and others took their place, I got Miller's attention. "We need to talk. Let's go to one of the back bedrooms."

He and Gabriella followed me.

I could barely contain my anger. "We've had enough. What do we do with our 'safe houses,' advertise them in the paper? She's risked enough. You have her evidence, now she's got to go into hiding."

"Now, wait. Let's not be hasty. It was a stupid mistake, and believe me, there will be consequences—"

"She could have paid the ultimate consequence. We just can't risk any more mistakes. Apparently there's no security in this operation."

"Let us have another chance. And why don't we hear what she has to say."

She took my hand. "Matthew, I understand. But I started this and I want to finish it. Will you allow me to?"

I understood the urgency in her voice and I knew her determination. "Only if we can get what we need. This whole setup is just too loose, too dangerous."

"What do you need?" Miller asked.

"First, we need to find a hiding place on our own—no advertised schedule. Next, we need a couple of agents to go with us, with no contact back to prying ears. I don't know whom to trust. We need our own weapons. A table lamp isn't enough, in case everything breaks down. And last, if she goes anywhere in public, she must wear a protective vest and be physically shielded by several agents."

Miller didn't hesitate. "We can do everything you requested. The only sticking point I see is communication with our agents. If I can ask you to trust me, I will personally guarantee I will be the only one who knows where you are. But someone must; surely you can see the practicality of that?"

"I guess. My main problem is with the DEA, at least one of their people. Apparently he knew all about this safe house."

"We should have thought of that. It's been used before in joint operations. All of our past history is tainted."

I checked us into a Residence Inn on the west side of the city, our two agents waiting discreetly in the parking lot to join us later. Hill was back with us, along with a veteran agent named Jim Fox, who was senior to Hill and obviously in charge. Fox was about my age, and exuded a feeling of quiet confidence.

Gabriella and I, weary from our ordeal, went to sleep in the comfort of each other's arms.

When our alarm awakened us at noon, it was time to go to work. A computer and copies of the disks had been brought for Gabriella and she set about decoding all of the information.

I ordered some lunch for the four of us, then killed some time until three. I wanted to give Georgio a chance to finish his dinner.

The bedroom offered me the privacy I needed for my discussion with him. Fortunately, he stayed home most weeknights. This time he answered the phone himself and we exchanged a few pleasantries before I told him why he might wish to reconsider his offer to me.

I described the discovery and the indecision, the temptation that caused me to sideline my moral character. When I told him of the escape, I omitted the shooting of the three captors, a continuing cowardice on my part to gamble on his judgement of me. I rationalized that what I did to escape had little bearing on future business management. Being tempted by large sums of money was another matter.

Georgio listened patiently through it until all had been told. "So you have given all of the money to a charity to minister to those who are damaged by this drug business?"

"Nearly all. There is still a fragment of it to return as soon as I can get to a safe deposit box. I can assure that the full amount will be returned."

"It seems to me you have done a service."

"But don't you see? I can't even convince myself that my motives were honorable."

"Does it matter, Matthew? It doesn't to me. Who can truthfully know what they would do in the same circumstance? I believe you are an honorable person. I have known you too long to think otherwise. I still want you to manage my business in Torino. Will you do it?"

"There is nothing in this world I would rather do. Georgio, thank you for being a true friend. I'll spend the rest of my career justifying your faith in me."

"You are most welcome. Is all settled. I look forward to having you here."

"There's one other little complication, which I must ask you to help me with. I haven't talked to Cathy or David about this yet. During my capture and escape, I met a wonderful woman. I am in love with her and want us to be married—"

"You say 'complication?' Such a good surprise!"

"She's not the complication. But she's provided information and testimony that will shake the drug distribution system to its foundation. Because of that, she has to go into witness protection with a new name. Therefore, I'll have one also. The manager you hire will have exactly my qualifications, but a different name, and he will want to avoid unnecessary publicity."

"I understand fully. And congratulations! My congratulations to this woman also. She must be very brave and very special."

"She is. And she was born in Italy, by the way."

"Well, that explains everything, I think."

"Georgio, I don't want my children to know I was in danger. I'll tell them I was tied up in a business deal and couldn't get in touch with them. Okay?"

"Of course. And Cathy just came in while we were speaking. Would you like to speak with her?"

"Oh yes. And give my regards to Elizabetta."

"Dad! I've been so worried! Are you alright?"

"Yes, Sweetheart. I'm sorry I was out of touch for so long. I really wanted to call you, but I just couldn't. I want so much to know how you are, and how your studies are going. Is everything okay?"

"Sure, Dad. And I loved the letter you wrote to me. It made me cry. But it almost sounded like a farewell, so it scared me."

"I'm sorry if it scared you. I'd just been thinking about how important you are to me."

"Thanks, Dad. We're all looking forward to Christmas. And David's coming in tomorrow. Is there any way you can get here?"

"No, I'm sorry Kiddo. Just a little more to finish up here. And I have some news for you, which I hope will be good. I'd rather we could discuss it in person, but it can't wait for then. Are you sitting down?"

"Yes. Come on, Dad, don't keep me in suspense!"

"I've met someone I hope to marry. I realize this is sudden for you, but I just couldn't talk to you before—"

"You're kidding me!"

"Is it so hard to believe?"

"Well, it's kinda unexpected."

"When you meet her, you'll understand why."

"You really are serious?"

"I guarantee it. She's beautiful, but more important, she's very nice and intelligent. She is also very brave. She has exposed a large drug network to federal authorities, so she has to go into hiding. Therefore, I'll be doing the same."

"Dad, Dad—this sounds like a spy novel. My head is spinning. In the first place, if you like her, it's good enough for me. I can't wait to see her. What's her name?"

"She is widowed. Right now, her name is Gabriella Capricio…maiden name Zucci. But she will change it, of course."

"Yeah. Once when she marries you, and again when she goes into hiding? Won't it be a complicated life?"

"I don't think so. The main thing is to get the next few days over with. That's what keeps us away from you through the holidays. After that, I promise we'll be together soon. You can tell David for me when he arrives, and I'll call again as soon as I can."

"Gosh, this is something. I can't wait to see what David thinks. It'll blow him away."

"Probably, but I'm sure you can handle it. And there's one other issue. Since I'll be leaving Mountain View, I have an offer on the house, and plan to accept it. I don't want you to feel homeless, but you know I can't remain there. We can do whatever you like when your schooling is finished. Wherever we wind up, it will be your home as long as you want, and Eileen wants you to consider their place home—"

"We'll be fine, Dad. I'll explain to David, too. You have enough to worry about for now. We'll make it work."

Gabriella was working away on her laptop computer in the sitting area when I came downstairs. I got her to take a break and go into the kitchenette, where I brought her up to date on my conversations. She was thrilled at my prospects for employment and a chance to escape to a way of life we both yearned for.

Jim Fox reported Miller planned to come over and give us the latest information on the investigation. When Miller arrived in late evening, he came in carrying a couple of Kevlar vests, along with his briefcase. Gabriella had finished her translations by then. She gave him copies on disks, along with the laptop.

"Thank you very much," he said. "It's rare to have a witness who can also do the work of the department. I'm glad we didn't have to get a lot of other people involved. We'll get this printed out and ready for depositions."

"You are welcome. It was faster this way, and I will be ready for them when the time comes."

Fox had also joined us, and the four of us sat in the living area while Hill rested in one of the bedrooms. Miller addressed all of us.

"You'll be happy to hear we captured both MacFarlane and his informant trying to escape together."

"Really!"

"Yep, REM turned out to be Richard Marks, Deputy Chief of the Miami office. Testa tipped us to the name of a flying service MacFarlane had used before in Miami. We had it staked out, and sure enough, these two showed up about eight this morning to fly out of the country. They are both in custody."

"That's a relief," I replied. "What happens next?"

"I believe the plan is to bring both of them here and bring formal charges, based on your evidence and on Testa's testimony." He nodded at Gabriella. "Testa has turned State's evidence. He hates MacFarlane with a passion. MacFarlane liked calling him a 'dumb wop', and made him look bad in front of the others every chance he got. He claims MacFarlane cheated him out of his 'commissions' if they turned out to be too large."

"Honor among thieves," I said.

"Right. Testa had built his own protection package in a safe deposit box, just in case he needed it. He'll get Accessory to Murder, in addition to drug trafficking, but MacFarlane goes up for Murder One. Testa has him on tape identifying himself and mentioning 'Fenton,' then giving the orders to have your friend Maurice 'break her neck, then get rid of her body.' He also told us what they did with it, but you don't want to know. From what you tell us, Maurice won't have to stand trial for his part in it."

"I'm sure. What has he said about that part?"

"Testa confirms he was gone when you made your escape, and did not return directly with MacFarlane. When he came back a couple of days later, the rooms were changed and MacFarlane wasn't there. That's about when we came in and captured him. He says he knows nothing about Maurice, Donny, the 'small guard,' as you called him, or the others."

He paused and reached into his briefcase. "I have something else for the two of you. Here are two sets of papers to fill out. You'll need birth certificates, passports, and so forth, and you will have to pick out names you want to live with for the future. If all of this goes forward, you'll be given an address for your friends to send mail addressed to your present names. It works like personnel overseas in combat zones. They will have no idea where you are or what your new names are, but mail will be sent to you efficiently, and vice versa."

"I thought it was more complex than that."

"There are different levels. We think this will suffice in your case, since the ones directly involved will be under our control."

"I need to inform you of something," I said. "We plan to marry as soon as we can. Is there a way we can arrange it, while you're building the case and transporting your prisoners? We'd like for it to be in Tennessee. It may be the only chance for us to see my friends for a long time. Safety would be the only concern."

"Congratulations!" Miller extended his hand. Fox followed suit.

"I think we can arrange it," Miller continued. "We'd have to keep a low profile, but we could use a department plane and accompany you with our agents. Yes, I think it could be done."

"Oh, thank you!" exclaimed Gabriella, and went around the table to kiss him on the cheek. Miller looked uncomfortable, but smiled.

"I still have bank accounts here," Gabriella said to me. Then to Miller, "perhaps sometime I can go there to get my papers out of the safe deposit box. And I must obtain a death certificate for my husband. They kept the fact he was dead from me, as you know."

In the evening, we sat together on the bed filling out our papers. We talked about our future names, and Gabriella had fun with it. She giggled at nonsensical suggestions, such as "Lisa Carr" and "Peter Abbott." She paused for a moment, her eyes sparkling. "As I recall, you proposed to someone named Mrs. Jones, who had the room next to yours. Is it possible for me to take her place?"

Then she became more serious, realizing how difficult and strange it would be. "When you live with one name for so long, it is part of you. It is hard to think of yourself as someone else. I think it shall be difficult."

She seemed satisfied with the choice I finally arrived at, but couldn't settle on a first name for herself.

I gave her my suggestion.

"Is that possible?" She asked.

"I see no reason why not. We'll be married as we are, so you can be Mrs. Cross for a little while. Or you can hyphenate, I suppose."

"I do not want to hyphenate. I want to be Mrs. Cross."

27.
CONVERGENCE

Eileen's living room was aglow with candles and Christmas colors. Banks of poinsettias graced the room and a beautiful native pine stood in one corner, ablaze with tiny white lights. She had strung a decorated garland of holly boughs along the fireplace mantle, and stockings hung there for herself and Woody, and Gabriella and me.

My priceless Christmas gift stood beside me in a cream-colored wool dress. On her left was the Matron of Honor, who was also our hostess, wearing a soft red dress. On my right was my best friend, beaming with his gap-toothed smile, and dressed in his finest dark suit. We stood before the minister of their church, who had agreed to perform this ceremony under unusual circumstances. Unusual because of the haste with which it had been arranged and because of the two large men stationed in strategic locations, standing guard over us.

The minister rose to the occasion with a warm but dignified service. He delivered a touching homily about the way the trials of this world can be left behind when man and woman find true love, and unite their trust in God.

When the ceremony was over and I had enthusiastically kissed the new Mrs. Cross, we went directly into the family room and kitchen area to mingle with our guests. They were few in number because of our need for continued secrecy until the troubles in our lives could be drawn to a conclusion. Israel Buchanan was there, as were Mary and Ralph, and Mother Millicent. Our only out-of-town guest besides the FBI agents was Gabriella's uncle Vito, flown in from New York. Uncle Vito was in his eighties, small and white haired. It was a poignant reunion for Gabriella when Woody drove him in from the airport on the previous evening. He was her only connection to family, and she had not seen him since leaving the City.

During the reception I was able to talk with each of the guests individually. A continuous cluster developed around Gabriella since all were meeting her for the first time. They were fascinated by her, as I knew I had been from the first time I saw her. Some of them had enjoyed teasing me about being smitten so suddenly, but soon found out for themselves how it could be.

In the beginning, Gabriella was bashful at this attention, but quickly warmed to their sincerity and their apparent regard for me.

Millicent was awestruck at the first moment they met, then quickly recovered and spoke her mind. "You are so beautiful, my dear," she said softly, almost to herself. Then in a firmer voice, "And Matthew is a good man. I'm not sure even he deserves a woman so lovely, however."

To show the last was spoken in fun, she poked me in the rib with a gloved finger. A couple of times during the afternoon, she had secretly caught my eye and winked, shaking her little fist with the thumb up-thrust.

Now she stood looking up at me, dressed in a trim black suit, a white silk blouse, and the scarf from Fendi. "I am so happy you have found someone, Matthew. She's such a wonderful girl. I only regret you have sold your place and won't be nearby. You will promise to visit?"

"If I possibly can."

"I don't understand all of this trouble about the witness thing, but Mary said Mrs. Cross has done a very brave deed and it is the only way."

"It's the only thing we can do. And you slipped up on me with that 'Mrs. Cross.' We'll visit when we can, and I want you to write to us with some of those letters you're famous for."

Ralph and Mary expressed similar sentiments, Ralph mostly nodding agreement as Mary did most of the talking. "The town won't be the same without you, Matthew. It's going to be tough breaking in some new neighbors. Won't be too long, though, 'til I know all their private business," she added. "You know me."

"I'll miss the both of you. And you'd better keep an eye on Millicent. She's spending a lot of time with Uncle Vito."

It was difficult to say goodbye to Israel. Our relationship went back to a happier time, but was clouded by the pain I had caused when I last saw him.

We embraced each other. "Israel, I'm so sorry for what happened because of me. If I could undo it all, I would."

"I wouldn't let you change it. You know some good comes from all things, and this is the best example I've seen. I don't claim to know all about this situation, but you wouldn't have found that wonderful girl without it, would you?"

"I guess I wouldn't have."

"See. There you are."

"Israel, you might like to know the black-haired man is in prison, and the authorities will find the red-headed one, unless he's dead. They used what they did to you to flush me out. I can't get into the details, but it's all over now."

"Good," he said with a twinkle in his eye. "I'm glad to help out when I can."

Soon the time came to say farewell to my hosts. "Eileen, there's no way I can adequately thank you for all you've done. Taking care of this wedding for me, all these years of support and friendship, all of the things you did to help me through the hard times with Caroline..."

"Matthew, I love you and your family, and anything I might have done is nothing compared to what I've gotten in return. Friends like you come along only rarely in life. And Caroline was like a sister to me."

I nodded. "She loved you very much. And I still think of her often, but I've finally been able to put the past behind, I think. She'll always be part of me."

"She will be, but I believe she'd be happy you have found someone. You've been alone long enough. You weren't complete, but now you are. And I love Gabriella already. It's a shame we can't see you more. And I guess you can't even tell us where you will be."

"Not for some time at least. We'll not lose touch, I can assure you."

Woody gave me a warm embrace. "Matthew, some time you're gonna' have to tell me the details of what happened to you during this past few weeks. You're a changed man, that's for sure. It's like you've seen the elephant, as we used to say in the service. An innocent man comes into the combat zone, and after the first firefight, you can see it in him. But I understand you can't talk about it."

"Maybe some day, Woody. It's a complicated story. I know I'd never have made it through without you."

"Aw, it was nothin'. Say, I still wonder who this unknown person was that chunked all the money into Eileen's account. Happened while you was gone. Strangest thing. I've thought about how that would look if it was all in cash. Man, there'd be a pile of it, wouldn't there? Why, a man 'ud need a pack horse...or a donkey...to carry it all."

There was no need for rice when we made our departure, as snow pellets were driving down out of the gray sky outside. We left in the rental Lincoln, not the average honeymoon couple, with two FBI agents occupying the front seat as we drove out of the circular drive.

Fox and Hill met us at the airport flying service hanger when we landed in Jacksonville. I didn't want anyone else to know where we were staying. Our fellow honeymooners handed us off and went on their way, wishing us well.

Fox relayed the information that we both had appointments at nine the next morning. Mine was with the District Attorney, with the FBI sitting in, for a deposition on the escape. Gabriella would meet in the United States Courthouse also, but with the State Attorney General. She would have DEA and FBI in attendance. Both depositions would be videotaped, Fox said. Some way to spend our first full day of marriage.

We slept fitfully that night, keeping each other awake with our tossing and turning. Gabriella faced a grilling performance, not because of wrongdoing on her part, but because she was so important to building a strong case. Later, she knew she would have to face questioning by defense lawyers and perhaps a grand jury.

I, on the other hand, would have to convince the District Attorney's office my actions were in self-defense. Without doubt, they would also call Gabriella. It all added up to several lengthy sessions. Our real honeymoon lay beyond our reach for the foreseeable future.

At the appointed time, I helped her into her protective vest, adjusting the Velcro straps.

"My jacket does not fit very well over this thing. And I think it is going to be hot."

"I know, Angel, but please don't be tempted to take it off. At least wear it if you go outside the room where you're testifying. I don't trust even the hallways, and particularly not the streets and sidewalks. It does match your black suit."

She smiled and promised to wear it, then kissed me goodbye. We were going in separate cars because the timing would be uncertain. Fox and Miller would be with her all day; Hill and Jacksonville police with me. Walker Travis had arrived in town and would be with Gabriella. He'd be on call in case I needed him.

An Assistant District Attorney took charge of the meeting when we were all seated. She sat me in the middle of the conference table, across from a video camera on a tripod. My image was displayed on a television screen much like the setup in discount stores designed to catch the fancy of the geeks walking by. Her name was Anne Keeler. She was blonde, slender, and businesslike, with sharp features normally set in a worried expression.

"Mr. Cross, you realize you may have an attorney present if you like?"

"Yes. However, I'll just be explaining what happened. If any controversy develops, I reserve the right to stop proceedings and call for help. The lawyer representing me is in the building assisting Mrs. Cross." There was that name again which pleased me so much.

Hill and a Jacksonville police detective listened as I went through the entire escape sequence, after I was kidnapped and beaten. They kept silent about questions they might have about the kidnapping itself until I had finished the basic narrative, then Keeler handled the questions.

"Mr. Cross, why did they kidnap you in the first place? Why you?"

"I'm sure you have my statement made to the FBI. I think Mrs. Fenton used too much imagination in her attempt to claim the reward being offered. Like I said at the time, it was just coincidence she saw me in the mountains.

It was in a place I have gone repeatedly over the years, as thousands of·others do."

"What was it they suspected you of taking?"

"They never came right out and said what it was. They used expressions like, 'something that belongs to us,' that sort of thing. My best guess would be money or drugs, knowing who they were. I was suspicious from the beginning about the story of the kid lost in the wilderness."

"I see. Let's move on to another subject. We have found no bodies, and no evidence anything like you describe even took place there. What do you have to say about that?"

"You haven't looked closely enough. But then, maybe it's in my best interest if you don't. You'll have Mrs. Cross's testimony, and I think you should find traces of blood upstairs, at least, if you fume the recreation room, or use that special light, whatever it is. One guard spilled some there." It surprised me every time I thought of Gabriella as Mrs. Cross. "And you have the pictures of me the day after I escaped, holding a front page...although of course they don't prove how I came to look like that."

Keeler turned to the detective. "Did you use a Luma-Lite in the rec room?"

"No, ma'm we didn't. The place had been cleaned and painted—"

"Yes, but had the rec room been re-carpeted?"

He hesitated. "I don't know. I'll get right on it." He left the room.

Keeler steepled her hands, and looked down at her notes. "Mr. Cross, what it boils down to is this. We have no bodies, so we have no reason to charge you at this time with anything." She relaxed her expression into what might pass for a smile. "My instincts are to believe it happened as you describe. I think you'd be cleared anyway. We already knew these people involved. We do want to keep our investigation going. If anything turns up that we need you for later, we may have to call on you again."

"I'm happy to help. And thank you. You've lifted a great weight. It wasn't a pleasant thing, but I'm sure neither Gabriella or I would be alive if we had done nothing."

Back at our hotel suite, I paced the floor and waited for Gabriella to return. Hill watched television, but I couldn't sit still. Miller had called around seven to tell us they were bringing in sandwiches and would continue while everyone was assembled. He assured me Gabriella was fine, and they'd have her home by ten. Ten o'clock was only minutes away and I had looked at my watch a thousand times before I heard her key in the lock.

Hill silently rose to his feet and stepped to one side of the door, but it was Gabriella who stepped into the room, followed by Fox. I rushed to greet her and held her in my arms, her bulky body confirming she had kept her promise with the vest.

"Are you worn out?"

"Absolutely. But everything is going well. They think we can finish tomorrow."

"I hope so. Tomorrow is Christmas Eve. Surely they won't let it go into Christmas Day, will they?" I turned to Fox.

"I don't think so." He smiled. "Even the legal system celebrates Christmas."

I gave her a hot bath and cradled her in my arms until she slept. Our current routine was not a good way to spend the early days of our life together, but being together made it bearable. We agreed we'd persevere until it was done, then begin afresh. I was beginning to get cabin fever, staying in the hotel all of the time. Since we couldn't risk being alone, I'm sure some roster discussions occurred about who our babysitters would be for Christmas Eve.

Voluntarily or otherwise, Fox invited us to dinner and said he would bring his wife with us. He knew of a quiet restaurant and felt the security would allow it. We would celebrate together the closing of Gabriella's first round of depositions with the state.

The next morning, plans were made for me to come downtown in the afternoon with Hill, and join Fox and Gabriella when they left the courthouse. Hill and the rest would go home, and we'd be under the care of Fox. I was still allowed to carry my own weapon when needed as a backup.

I strapped Gabriella in her vest again, then kissed her goodbye. She left for work with her escort and I stayed behind. The day dragged slowly. I couldn't go running, and I could tell I needed exercise. I read a detective novel, but couldn't concentrate. Hill and I watched Fox News Live until I could repeat the news stories in unison with the anchors on the third time around.

We had lunch out of the refrigerator, then I decided to see if I could catch David in his early evening in Milan.

Betta answered the telephone. She was in the midst of preparing a Christmas feast for the evening meal. She gave me her congratulations before calling David.

"Dad! Congratulations. And Merry Christmas. When do we get to meet our new mother?"

"Thanks, Dave. And Merry Christmas to you, too. I'm sorry to spring a change like this on you without discussing it first, but life was too complicated to do otherwise."

"That's okay, Dad. It really was a surprise, though. Last time I talked to you, I think you had the 'mental mopes' about the future. Now, I think things will change. How will you celebrate Christmas?"

"You're correct, but we still have to get the complications out of the way. Gabriella's continuing her deposition as we speak. They think they'll be done today, then we plan to go out to dinner at a nice place. Other than that, we couldn't risk shopping or anything. We'll make up for lost time as soon as this is finished."

"How long before you're free? Cathy says you have to go into witness protection. Will I have to call you something besides 'Dad'?"

"You might switch to 'Uncle' so they won't know it's me. Seriously, we don't know how long. And I think we can work around the other issues to keep in touch."

"I'll be serious, too, Dad. Thanks for the letter. It meant a lot to me."

I talked to Cathy and Georgio in turn, exchanging good wishes for the holidays, before ringing off and returning to my vigil with the clock. Three more hours dragged slowly by until the telephone rang.

"Darling, it is me. They tell me we can wrap things up in about an hour. They will have their car brought to the curb out front at six. You can do the same thing."

"We'll be there. I can't wait to see you, my love."

"You too. I love you Sweetheart."

It was a clear day, but dusk was beginning to soften the light as we drove downtown. Traffic was heavier than usual, and I began to fret silently about getting there on time. All of the last-minute Christmas shoppers were out. People with plans for parties, family gatherings, and dinner were beginning to stir, clogging intersections and filling the streets.

Agent Hill drove aggressively but skillfully. I heard him sigh to himself more than once as he missed a light or was cut off from a faster-moving lane. I knew he would be glad to be released from his assignment for the evening.

We finally drove up North Clay and turned onto Monroe, the one-way street in front of the courthouse. It was five past the hour, and cars lined up along the street to pick up the people streaming out of the courthouse. I began to look for Gabriella. As we approached, looking for a clear spot at the curb, I spotted her coming down the steps surrounded by four men who kept a moving circle around her. As they descended, the ring continuously shifted and I saw her face searching the street for our arrival. At last she saw us in our conspicuously anonymous car and she smiled and waved.

At that instant, she was suddenly thrust backward through the small phalanx. My heart stopped as I heard the sharp report of a gunshot and I saw her sprawl to the steps behind her.

There was instant pandemonium in the scene before us. I started to hurl myself out of the car, but Hill floored the accelerator and charged forward in the right lane.

"Stop the car!" I shouted. "Let me out!

"No! They'll take care of her! We don't know what the hell is going on, and my job's to protect you!" He leaned on the horn, dodging traffic, and scattering the people running in all directions on the sidewalks and street.

"Stop the damn car! I'm getting out!"

Well down the block, he was cornered by traffic at the stoplight on Hogan. I clawed the door open and ran back up the street. She was gone. A large black car went hurtling around the corner, the wrong way down North Julia, a confusion of movement inside. They hadn't waited for emergency vehicles.

I stood there in desperation, not knowing what to do. The sidewalk was now deserted, and sirens wailed in the distance, gradually becoming louder. I cursed myself for staying behind. My Angel, I should have come with you and sat outside your door. I've failed to protect you when you needed me most.

Hill had managed to find a place at the curb and now came running toward me. When he drew near, he grabbed my arm and tugged me back toward the car. "Don't stand out here in plain sight. They could still be there."

"What can we do now? Where will they take her?"

"I'm trying to get someone on the phone, but they haven't answered yet," he said, as we hurried through the gathering darkness. "There must have been a sniper in the parking garage. I just don't know yet."

We couldn't go anywhere until we knew where to go, so we sat in the car with the engine running. Jacksonville squad cars converged from all directions, uniforms spilling out and running into and around the parking garage on the corner of Julia and Monroe.

Hill finally got an answer on his cell phone. I listened while he grunted unintelligible responses.

I grabbed his arm. *"How is she? Ask them how she is!"*

He snapped the phone shut and turned to me. "I'm sorry. It doesn't look good. They're headed straight for the emergency room at Columbia Memorial. She's unconscious. They're doing what they can. I'm sorry."

His words were an icy dagger in my heart. He pressed the accelerator to the floor and made a skidding turn onto Hogan. Behind us, flashing lights from the cluster of patrol cars created a surreal atmosphere, painting the scene in blue stroboscopic light. Hill barely stopped in time to avoid running over a uniformed cop in the middle of the street. Hill rolled down the window and flashed his ID. The cop waved us forward and we accelerated into the unknown.

...God shall wipe all tears from their eyes and there shall be no more death, neither sorrow nor crying. Neither shall there be any more pain; for the former things are passed away.
Oh how glorious is that kingdom: wherein all the saints do rejoice with Christ! They are clothed with white robes and follow the Lamb whithersoever He goeth...

We stood around the open grave under a canopy to shield us from the bright sunlight. The clear, unseasonably warm day was an odd counterpoint to the somber mood of the small gathering. Woody and Eileen flew down to be with me for the graveside services. Other than the two of them, all the rest had some connection to the case. Travis was there. The maid, cook, and gardener from the house had somehow heard about the shooting and they stood apart in a small cluster, grim expressions on their faces. I think they appreciated Gabriella's kindness to them while she was a prisoner.

Miller had assisted with the arrangements. In the absence of any connection Gabriella had with the community, the police department chaplain conducted the service.

"...I am the resurrection and the life," saith the Lord; "he who believeth in me, though he die, yet shall he live, and whosoever liveth and believeth in me shall never die..."

The remaining mourners made the gathering seem more official than personal—The FBI agents involved, Neilson from the DEA, and someone from the Attorney General's office I had not met. A half-dozen Jacksonville police in dress blues represented that department and had served as pallbearers, giving the service a military atmosphere.

The minister intoned the final words before the casket would be lowered into the grave by the apparatus upon which it rested.

In sure and certain hope of the resurrection of eternal life through our Lord Jesus Christ, we commend to almighty God our sister Gabriella, and we commit her body to the ground; earth to earth, ashes to ashes, dust to dust. The Lord bless her and keep her. The Lord make his face shine on her and be gracious to her. The Lord look upon her with favor and give her peace. Amen.

A ragged response of "amens" answered, then the funeral attendants removed the sprays of flowers and placed them on wire stands. One of them pressed a concealed foot pedal, and the casket slowly sank into the depths of the grave.

Someone handed me a nickel-plated shovel and I stepped forward to do my duty, sending a symbolic handful of earth on top. The funeral home people would have to lower the top of the vault in place before they filled it in. I'd leave the rest to them. Woody and Eileen led me away, one on either side, to the waiting limousine. The bright sun was hot on my dark suit with the protective vest underneath.

I looked in all directions around the cemetery, but no one was in sight. I wondered if eyes were following me. I'd have to condition myself against paranoia. They hadn't caught the sniper, and I assumed our enemies were still out there, perhaps transferring their attention to me.

On the way back to the funeral home to hand me off to my regular keepers, Eileen patted my hand and asked me a question we had avoided before. "What will you do now, Matt? Will you come back to Mountain View? I know you've sold your house. Why don't you come and stay with us until you get your feet on the ground?"

"Eileen, I can't do that, but thank you for offering. It may be years before I would feel safe leading a normal life. No, I'll do what they ask of me here, then I'm going into the witness program as we originally planned. That way, maybe I can start a new life and I won't be endangering the ones I care about. They tell me it works very well keeping in touch with old friends, so it won't be all bad."

"Matt, I'm so sorry," she said again, starting to weep. "She was such a wonderful woman, and it's so tragic..."

"I can't believe it," Woody added. "One day everything's so happy, and just days later it's completely the other way around. I guess there are things in this life we just ain't—aren't supposed to understand."

"It's something I can't explain," I said, holding the hands of these two people so dear to me.

I spent the next few days after they left clearing up a few things before leaving Jacksonville, always in the hands of my protectors. The Attorney General's assistant questioned me for a half day to confirm the sequence of events after Gabriella and I first saw each other. The paperwork came through for my new life. There was my passport with my picture and a different name. I had credit cards, driver's license, membership in a health club I'd never use, and other bits of flotsam for my wallet.

The coroner's office issued numerous copies of her death certificate, but I needed few of them. She left Jacksonville almost without a trace. After the plane went down, she no longer occupied her apartment. Later, when the wreckage was discovered, her captors had removed all of her belongings from the apartment and disposed of them without telling her. Again, all traces of her stay in captivity had been removed after we escaped. All I found in Jacksonville were three bank accounts and a safe deposit box.

I had to get help from the FBI and my new friends at the prosecutor's office to clear the bureaucracy surrounding the death of her husband. They smoothed things through probate to allow Gabriella's estate to inherit the joint property, which consisted only of their joint bank accounts and the safe deposit box.

I was surprised to find she had accumulated a substantial sum of money in her own name, probably from her father's pension. I had that and the other accounts closed and totaled into a certified check, paid to "bearer." Not very secure, but I didn't want to leave a trail to my new name. The bank box was of interest to the FBI. In it we found documents and mini-tapes stashed by John Capricio, a case he was building for protection and blackmail.

It also contained several pieces of jewelry, her birth certificate, which was of no importance now, and a sheaf of stock certificates. After starting the paperwork through the system to change the ownership, I was through.

On the morning of my departure, skies were low and gray. A light rain was falling. Miller and Hill, my original contacts, escorted me to the airport for my flight to New York. On the way, we allowed time for a visit to the cemetery. Hill remained in the car while Miller shadowed me to the new grave. We both carried umbrellas as we walked through the wet grass and threaded our way through the tombstones. I glanced at these final chapters in other people's lives as I made my way to close a chapter of my own.

Now for the second time in my life, I stood staring at a red granite stone engraved with the name of my wife. The wet surface highlighted the carved letters. "Gabriella Zucci Cross," it read, "Beloved Wife of Matthew Cross." Then it gave the dates of her birth and death, and St. Andrea Bagni, the little village where she was born. Below that, I'd had them engrave in script the one simple word, *"Angel."*

I placed the bouquet of yellow roses on the new sod and walked away in the quickening rain, never to return.

EPILOGUE

Portofino is a sapphire jewel in the *Riviera di Levante* on Italy's west coast. For centuries it has been a tourist destination greatly desired. The first time I saw it, I could understand why. It has a perfect little harbor sheltered from the sea by a rugged promontory of land. I have walked all along the gravel path that skirts the cliffs, where a lighthouse sits on the point, both beckoning sailors into the harbor and warning them of the dangerous rocks below.

A picture-perfect village nestles around the harbor, with quaint inns, hotels, shops, and restaurants. I have spent many pleasant hours on the quayside, sitting under a striped awning, gazing out over the water, enjoying a meal to be found only in Italy. Fishing boats ride at their moorings, and rowing skiffs are dragged up onto the shingle beach above high tide.

Steep mountain slopes enclose Portofino on all sides, save the opening to the sea. In the lower reaches the slopes are covered with villas; above, olive and eucalyptus trees. To me, it is one of the most beautiful spots on earth.

At the head of the village, the mountain slopes meet in a fold that provides a natural channel for a foot trail. The trail begins where the streets end and ascends the mountain ridge that fronts the ocean. It travels along the crest for a time, then descends into a tiny village on the Ligurian Sea. The trail is the only way into the village from Portofino. The trail and the sea, of course.

On the way to the top, the ascent is so steep at times that steps have been carved into the face. At other times, the trail passes through glades and small meadows. Sparsely scattered cottages lie along the way wherever the terrain allows. Traveling along the track, you will walk past their vineyards and gardens, porches and small lawns.

The greatest reward on the journey is to reach the summit, clear the last height, and suddenly face the expanse of the open sea. You will feel the steady force of the onshore wind in your face, and witness the grandeur of the surging waves far below.

My name is Thomas Clark. My companion and I now stand at that spot, in that grand moment. We are beneath the tall pines that grow at the summit, adding their fragrance to the scent of the sea. We hold each other and she gazes at me with eyes the color of the sea—not quite green, not quite blue. There is joy in them, the same joy she must see in mine. She is my beautiful wife, Sabrina, named for a movie role once played, and a little girl lost.

Roger Meadows is the author of *HANGMAN, A Deadly Game*, a suspense novel about the boundaries of personal honesty, and what happens when they are violated.

After college and a tour as an Army aviator, he began a career in industry, completing graduate school along the way. He conducted business throughout the world, dealing with many cultures. He has written dozens of essays and short stories, and edited the works of other writers. He has participated in writers' groups in Knoxville, Spartanburg, Greenville, and Hilton Head.

Mr. Meadows enjoys reading, sailing, kayaking, travel, and wooden boat building. He and his wife live in the Upstate of South Carolina. They have three adult children and two grandchildren. He welcomes your comments to him at RDM730@aol.com.